A TRANSCONTINENTAL AFFAIR

OTHER BOOKS BY JODI DAYNARD

The Midwife's Revolt

Our Own Country

A More Perfect Union

A TRANSCONTINENTAL AFFAIR

JODI DAYNARD

LAKE UNION
PUBLISHING

Published by Lake Union Publishing, Seattle

www.apub.com

Amazon, the Amazon logo, and Lake Union Publishing are trademarks of Amazon.com, Inc., or its affiliates.

ISBN-13: 9781542004091
ISBN-10: 1542004098

Cover design by Kathleen Lynch, Black Kat Design

Printed in the United States of America

A
TRANSCONTINENTAL
AFFAIR

Monday, May 23, 1870, 8:30 a.m.

MISS HARRIET EAMES HAD MEANT TO LEAVE home half an hour earlier, but she had become embroiled in an argument with her father. What began as a restrained request on her father's part had now devolved into a shouting match.

"You will change your dress!"

"I *won't!*"

The pair stood at the top of the carved mahogany staircase in their townhome on Beacon Hill, having left their estate in Easton the previous day. Fortunately, an unspoken agreement among the residents of the exclusive address held that no one ever saw or heard anything, although certain complacent rats residing in the walls had heard the ruckus and scurried off.

Harriet wore her new "reform" dress, one of two such outfits that her mother had allowed her to purchase in exchange for agreeing to buy two new gowns. The dress was not actually a dress but rather a heavy bell-sleeve tunic that came to Hattie's thigh, beneath which ballooned a pair of baggy trousers à la Turque.

Congressman Eames's handsome face dripped perspiration, though the morning was quite cool. He was an imposing, large-waisted man with two affable chins and a normally pliable manner.

"Why must I look like everyone else anyway?" Hattie blurted.

"Why, why, why. Always why!" Mr. Eames exclaimed, slamming his fist on the railing.

Hattie always had to know the "why" of everything. Not merely why the sky was blue but why steel was stronger than iron and why some currents flowed east when others flowed west.

"Because it's ugly as sin!"

Before Hattie and Mr. Eames left Easton the previous day, Mrs. Eames had expressed her desire for Harriet to wear either the lavender or the hyacinth gown, because both set off her dark coloring to excellent advantage. Either would have been perfectly fine by the esteemed congressman. He was saddened to see his attractive daughter wearing something that made her look like one of those foreign wrestlers of indeterminate sex.

She was an exotic-looking girl with rich brown hair; discerning, almond-shaped brown eyes; and olive skin. Mr. Eames had often wondered whether his forebears hadn't somehow gotten mixed up with the local gypsies. Though not tall, Hattie's body was well proportioned, strong from hours of playing outdoors with her brothers. She was voluptuous, like her mother, and would have been downright plump were she not such an athletic girl. Like him, she had a hearty appetite. A simple gown would have allowed her natural beauty to shine. But no. Here she stood in all her absurdity. Recently, such dresses began to appear on young, rebellious Suffragists much, Mr. Eames thought, like rust blight upon healthy ears of corn. Most alarming to Mr. Eames, however, was that, rather than growing out of her youthful rebellion, his daughter seemed to be growing into it.

Mr. Eames launched back into the argument. "Why must you be so stubborn? Surely you see how this'll mortify me before all my esteemed associates. Why, even the governor will be aboard." Mr. Eames referred to the excursion they were both about to take aboard the Pullman Hotel Express, bound for San Francisco. It had been arranged by the Boston

Board of Trade, of which he was a member. For, in addition to being a congressman, he owned a successful shovel manufactory.

"Ooh, the governor!" Hattie waved her fingers in the air, taunting her father with mock fright. Outside, Clarkson, the coachman, had been waiting for more than an hour. At eight, he was supposed to have brought them to the Boston and Albany railroad depot. It was now past eight thirty. His horses, bored, shifted from one foot to another on the cobblestone street. Clarkson sighed a plume of smoke into the cold morning air and gave up waiting. He tucked his chin down into his chest, let the reins go slack, and fell asleep.

Mr. Eames made one last effort to persuade his daughter to wear a different outfit. He whispered harshly, "Well, if you care nothing for my friends or me, at least have some consideration for your fiancé, Mr. Durand!"

At the mention of Mr. Durand's name, Hattie's furious expression eased.

"Oh, Leland," she said. Back in March, when Harriet had agreed to marry him, Mr. Durand sent Hattie a carte de visite. The portrait showed a serious young man with clear, light eyes and a thick head of dark, wavy hair. Clearly, he had tried but not entirely succeeded in taming it with pomade, as a large cowlick stuck up in the back, which made her giggle. She liked that. For there was nothing more tedious than a vainglorious man. The gift pleased her a great deal, and she had replied by sending one of her own.

"Yes, Leland!" Mr. Eames cried. "What on earth will he think of you?"

"I hope he'll respect me for who I am, Papa," Hattie replied, her voice uncharacteristically soft. "Not all the young men these days are as old-fashioned as you."

"Old-fashioned? Is that what you think? Why, we employ servants I sheltered when they fled the South as contraband! In Congress, I'm a known and esteemed liberal. And as for you—why, I have even let you steal your brother Robert's tobacco and my silver flask filled with my best bourbon! And not a word from me. Not a word!"

"You knew?" Hattie said, surprised.

"Of course I knew—though no doubt you think so little of me as to believe I am ignorant of the goings-on in my own home. But I said nothing. I *deny* you nothing."

"Except a college education."

"Don't start on that, Harriet."

The subject of Hattie's education was another sore one. Mr. Eames had always known about his daughter's intellectual predilections. After he bought the townhome, he sent her to Mr. Emerson's School for Girls. But when she turned sixteen, she announced that she wanted to go to Harvard like her brothers. "I've already worked my way through half of their math books."

"Women don't go to Harvard."

"Well, some woman will have to be the first."

"It won't be *my* daughter! Not over my dead body!"

Now, secretly, Mr. Eames worried that the man he had procured for her, Leland Durand, would find Hattie unacceptable even by California standards. He sighed loudly, and his shoulders sagged in a gesture of defeat.

"Oh, Papa," Hattie said. She reached out and touched him on the arm. The truth was, she was far fonder of him than their current shouting match would suggest. Suddenly, Mr. Eames looked at his watch and cried, "Oh, but what are we about? We'll miss the train for sure. Clarkson! Clarkson!" Mr. Eames shouted for his coachman, who made no reply, being both outdoors and fast asleep. "Golding?" he tried again, calling for his valet before remembering that Monday was Golding's day off.

Hattie's father grumbled a curse and raced down the steps, where he bent to lift one of their trunks himself just as the front door opened, nearly pushing him over.

Standing in the hallway, out of breath, was his younger son, Thomas.

"Sir." Thomas bowed. Then he wiped his brow, having traveled in great haste since before dawn.

"Hattie, come on!" Mr. Eames called up to his daughter.

Hattie descended the stairs.

"Oh, hi, sis." Tom leaned over and kissed his sister on the cheek. A mass of damp sandy hair fell onto his forehead.

Mr. Eames asked, "What is it, son? We're just out the door."

"It's Mama. She's ill."

Hattie snorted. "God, Tom, you scared me. I thought by your mournful look that someone had died!"

Mr. Eames sent her a stern warning glance, but Hattie couldn't help how she felt. Her mother, Katherine Eames, had taken to bed at the beginning of the Civil War and never left it. First, it was fear for her sons. Then it was "headaches." Miraculously, she always seemed to rally for company, and Hattie suspected that she enjoyed *playing* a congressman's wife far more than being one.

"Oh," she said, responding to her father's disapproving look, "you know Mama is always complaining of some illness or other."

"Yes, but Hattie," Tom objected, "she's got a high fever. Her throat is inflamed, and the doctor fears it's diphtheria."

Hattie paused, suddenly doubting her judgment. She felt a stab of pity in her breast for her mother and knew herself to be uncharitable. But lately she had been uncharitable toward everyone.

"If it's an infectious fever, Hattie, you can't possibly return to Easton," the congressman said, "though I must."

Hattie looked questioningly at both men. Already, her mind began to appreciate the possible advantages of this turn of events.

"I'm to go *alone*, then?" A small smile crept to one corner of her mouth.

"I'm afraid so, my love. I'll catch up as soon as I can." Then he added, "Try to stay out of trouble."

Here, Mr. Eames reached into his waistcoat pocket and removed a solid-gold watch, which he handed to his daughter.

"But—"

"No, I insist. They say the time changes can be maddening. I don't want them leaving you behind anywhere because you've lost track of the time."

"I would never lose track of time," she said defiantly. "That sounds like something you would do, *Tom*."

"Hattie," Tom objected.

"Well, but I'm sure you don't know that we lose one minute for every fifteen miles of longitude we travel. Chicago, being about a thousand miles west, would therefore be one hour earlier."

Tom slapped his head, and Mr. Eames grumbled a grudging assent. Then, suddenly, he blurted, "But wait—what could I be thinking? I can't let you go alone."

Hattie began to object when Mr. Eames placed a finger beneath his nose and said, "There's a Mr. Hunnewell on the train, from West Needham. Good man. Has a big estate called Wellesley. Knows his flora and fauna and all that. An Indian expert too."

"Great," Hattie said. "He'll know precisely which tribe it is when they attack us."

Her father scowled but went on. "He has a daughter too, about your age. I believe he is bringing her along. I'll write him at once."

"Write?" she said incredulously. "Papa, there's *no time*! I can tell him myself."

"No, no. That doesn't feel proper."

"Missing the train won't feel proper either."

"Oh, go, go—I'll send him a telegram."

"Father—" She stomped her foot in protest, and the floor vibrated beneath her heavy new travel boots.

"I *will*." Mr. Eames drew himself up, letting his daughter know that the conversation was over.

Mr. Eames then reached into his trouser pocket and grabbed a thick leather billfold, from which he removed his own ticket.

"Just in case of the worst, and I don't catch you before you arrive in Sacramento—"

Hattie's eyes widened. "What's all that?"

"Your ticket and your dowry. Five hundred dollars." Then, espying a tiny envelope tucked behind the greenbacks, he added wistfully, "And the bill of fare." Back in March, when Mr. Eames had received the invitation to join the Boston Board of Trade's excursion to the Pacific, it had included the train's bill of fare. Though printed on a tiny card, it promised a world of pleasure: veal cutlets and porterhouse steak for breakfast; stuffed chicken and baked jacksnipe for lunch; and all manner of relishes and desserts. So much for that.

Mr. Eames concluded, "Keep these upon your person. The train'll be brimming with thieves." He smiled wanly at his own joke, since they both knew the train would be filled with Boston's most prominent businessmen. "Now run, girl—or you shan't make it!"

Impulsively, Hattie hugged her father goodbye before stepping outside. Her brother called to her, "Hey, ripping outfit, by the way!" She grinned, her dark, almond-shaped eyes glancing back exultantly at her father. Then she placed his billfold in her trouser pocket and slammed the front door with such force that the sound woke the coachman at last.

2

IT WAS A COLD SPRING MORNING, THE kind of morning New Englanders knew to still be winter. Others, either more credulous or more optimistic, mistook the tender, freshly unfurled leaves and the bright flashes of yellow forsythia for signs that coats were no longer necessary. And so they froze almost solid as they came out to cheer on the Pullman Hotel Express before it headed off to San Francisco, California.

The eight-car train stood slick and huffing on the old Coliseum grounds on Dartmouth Street, its newly lacquered chocolate-brown surface so shiny that some ladies adjusted their bonnets in it. Nailed onto the exterior of each car were proud placards in gold lettering: THE PALMYRA, THE MARQUETTE, and even SMOKING CAR NO. 70. The train's two engines had been stoked since dawn, and their exteriors were now hot enough to vaporize a wayward finger.

Above the windows of the hotel cars, long letter boards proclaimed, PULLMAN PACIFIC CAR CO. One could not mistake the manufacturer of these cars even from a distance. That, of course, was the point.

Off to one side, in their neat blue uniforms, a row of soldiers stood at attention. On the other side, a loud brass band played "My Country, 'Tis of Thee," and dozens of dignitaries greeted one another with hearty handshakes. These were neither Mayflower aristocrats nor elderly revolutionary heroes but the new elite whom some sneeringly referred to as "magnates of money." Some were politicians, like Mr. Price, who also served as president of the Boston Board of Trade. Others were merchants or bankers. Many of the men had ties to the railroad, and many had already made fortunes by it, although no one understood precisely how.

There were rumors, though, and one man, Charles Francis Adams, descendant of the incorruptible John Adams, had the temerity to suggest that it was graft, plain and simple. He stated in no uncertain terms that the railroad executives were paying themselves out of the government railroad subsidies. For the contracting company they had hired to do the work was none other than themselves.

George Pullman, celebrated railroad car manufacturer, stood among the crowd, pride making him seem taller than his five-six frame. He would ride upon the cars he had built until Chicago. Then there was Captain Robert Forbes, sea captain and China merchant; Alvah Crocker, state senator and president of the Fitchburg Railroad; and more than 130 other souls, among them fifty women and a dozen children.

In this sea of black-clad men and their families stood Louisa Finch. She wore a lavender-and-white-striped gown with huge hoops that were no longer entirely in fashion. But she wore it well, standing half a head taller than most of the men. With her long neck, wavy blonde curls, saintly pallor, and large, limpid green eyes, anyone looking at her might have thought that Botticelli's newborn Venus had come to life at a railway depot.

Miss Finch suddenly bent down, and one white-gloved hand picked up a wool cape draped over her valise. She put it across her shoulders with a shiver. "It's so cold. Mother Nature has fooled us again."

Her father, Reverend Finch, glanced at her but didn't reply. He was a sour-faced man with thinning black hair, pale lips, and a narrow band of beard that just managed to conceal a weak chin. He finally nodded, clapped his gloved hands together, and blew on them. His breath made light puffs of smoke in the air.

Louisa thought the men of the Boston Board of Trade looked quite fine in their imported wool suits and hats. Indeed, in the bright morning air, they looked very like the train they readied to board: polished, broad, and far more stalwart than mobile. Louisa glanced down, suddenly reminded of her own right foot, encased in a heavy black boot. Nineteen years earlier, she was born a clubfoot. And she still was a clubfoot, despite years of suffering many a newfangled torture device, all of which only made her limp more pronounced.

Reverend Finch looked at his watch and grumbled, "They're late."

"Only by a few minutes, Papa. It must be a trial to work one's way through this crowd."

"Well, they should have taken that into consideration and set out earlier."

Reverend Finch prided himself on both his foresightedness and his celerity, though in truth he was neither very perceptive nor very swift. He failed to foresee the invasion of Alexandria, Virginia, in '61 by Union troops, and by the time he decided to leave that city in '64, fighting had broken out around Washington, and they had to flee for their lives.

Since moving to Boston, father and daughter had lived in genteel poverty, Mr. Finch working as a substitute pastor at a church in Roxbury; recently, Louisa began taking in laundry. She also taught painting at a girls' school, but the work paid poorly—when it paid at all. The owner, she recently learned, hovered on the edge of bankruptcy.

When the reverend got wind through a parishioner that the Ridgewoods of Cambridge were seeking a governess for their excursion to California, he offered up his daughter. Her chief virtue, he said, was that she was "unlikely to be swept precipitately into marriage." The Ridgewoods agreed to take her with them. "We'll see how she fares," said Mr. Ridgewood to Reverend Finch when they met in Cambridge to seal the deal.

Louisa was right there the entire time, but neither her father nor Mr. Ridgewood gave any indication that she actually existed. Mr. Ridgewood was exceptionally handsome: he was very tall with black hair, full lips, and a statesmanlike bearing. She thought, *Surely such a handsome man must be of a benevolent nature.*

Now Louisa felt the lateness of the Ridgewoods to be a bad omen somehow. She was raised by superstitious slaves and believed in omens and portents. Not merely believed but *felt*, as one sometimes feels an approaching storm.

But she replied merely, "Don't wait on my account, Papa, if you're eager to depart. They'll arrive soon, I'm sure."

Reverend Finch shot his daughter a malignant glance, as if she were trying to trick him somehow.

"And leave you in this madding crowd? Why, I doubt you could recognize Mr. Ridgewood, nor do you know his family."

"No, but they shall know *me*." She smiled and raised her petticoats just high enough to expose her stiff leather boot. But even this self-deprecatory remark made the reverend avert his eyes and retract his aquiline nose with distaste.

"Is that the first thing you would have them notice about you, child?"

"No, Father, but it is certainly what they will notice."

"So be it," said Reverend Finch, needing to have the last word.

Suddenly, the music ceased, and a pair of trumpets sent two wild, curling flourishes into the air. The restless crowd fell silent.

Mr. Price mounted the platform. He was a tall, dignified man with a neatly trimmed black beard, well-known to many in the crowd. Mr. Price had been the mayor of Boston and was now a state senator. He was also known to be a major stockholder of the Union Pacific Railroad. Though well past forty, there was something of the truant schoolboy about him. His smirk suggested a practiced glibness.

"Welcome, friends. Welcome on this historic occasion!"

Loud cheers erupted. Mr. Price held up a bottle of murky green water.

"Behold." He waited, and the crowd accommodated him with hearty laughter.

"Behold this bottle of Atlantic Ocean water! Upon our arrival in San Francisco, we shall have the very great pleasure of emptying it into the Pacific Ocean, as a symbol of this unprecedented moment in our history. Make no mistake about our lofty aims: we go to unite America, our vast and great country!"

The crowd let out a roar of applause. But Mr. Price sheepishly waved them down. "Not just yet, friends. Not just yet." He then proceeded to thank his fellow executives and to extoll the imminent moral and financial triumphs of their excursion, having made the amateur's mistake of leading with his best material.

But Mr. Price's long-windedness was fortunate for Harriet Eames, who would almost certainly have missed the train had he been less effusive in his remarks.

3

BY THE TIME HATTIE ARRIVED AT THE depot at five minutes past nine, the speeches were over and the dignitaries had all boarded. Hattie's mouth opened in awe at the sight of the train, which appeared to shimmer before her eyes like the conjuration of a mythical being. She descended too enthusiastically from her carriage, and the bottom hem of her trousers snagged on the edge of the steps, nearly tossing her headfirst to the ground.

"Oh!" she cried, landing awkwardly, hand on bonnet and legs splayed in the air.

Several ladies standing nearby tittered.

"Will you look at those trousers!" one said.

"Yes, but only imagine if she hadn't worn them!"

Hattie grunted and endeavored to right herself.

A porter in a neat blue jacket came flying out to help her. The porter's movements were agile, his dark face smooth, his eyes bright. He could have been thirty or fifty, impossible to tell. His voice was unexpectedly musical when he asked, "Do you have a ticket, miss?"

"Just a minute. Yes—here." Hattie found the ticket in her father's billfold. "I'm afraid my father, Mr. Eames, couldn't make it."

The porter squinted farsightedly at her ticket. "I'm very sorry. Do you have someone to accompany you?"

"He's on the train," Harriet replied.

"Very good. You're in the Arlington car." Then he corrected himself. "That is, your seat is in that car."

Hattie smiled. "I imagine that my seat and I shall be one and the same for quite some time."

After assessing that she mocked herself and not him, the porter smiled back, though still avoiding her eyes.

"The car's there, to the right, miss. It's best to get in the correct car now, for once the train moves, it's not safe to walk between the cars." Then, suddenly realizing that he might have overstepped his position, pronouncing upon something best left to their imperious conductor, Mr. Straight, he looked down at his feet.

"Well, thank you for letting me know . . . ?" Hattie's inflection indicated that she wished to know the porter's name.

"Alfred, miss," he said, his eyes widening. "Alfred Macalister."

"Well, thanks, Alfred."

He bowed stiffly. "You're most welcome, Miss Eames."

Hattie glanced warily at him. "How did you know my name?"

"You said your father was Mr. Eames, miss."

"Oh yes, of course." Hattie was about to say one more thing when Alfred, apparently feeling he had enjoyed quite enough interaction with her for his own safety, turned and fled.

Another porter soon approached her, swept up her trunk, and, quickly tipping his cap, heaved it off to the baggage car. Hattie gathered her other bags and looked at the train: it went on and on, eight nearly identical brown cars plus the engines and tender.

The cars were wider and taller than any ever fabricated before. When Mr. Pullman made his first model, President Lincoln commissioned one of them for himself but then found it too "fancy" to ride in while so many soldiers were suffering and dying. Its first use was to bring the president's body back to its final resting place in Springfield, Illinois.

Hattie knew the story, but the actual sight before her eyes gave her goose bumps.

Hattie found the Arlington car and boarded it. Within, the aisle was crowded with excursionists. They looked down at their tickets and then back up at the numbers on the walls as they endeavored to find their seats.

Hattie had been on a train several times before but only for short distances. Her first ride was eight years earlier, when she and her family had gone to condole with an aunt in Newburyport whose son had been killed in the Shenandoah. It had been the spring of '62, and she recalled wearing a new tarlatan dress that was too tight around the collar. She kept pulling at it, and her mother kept discreetly swatting at her hand. Her brothers wore starched broadcloth jackets and Highland caps. Hattie recalled being revolted by that train and its human smells, its floors sticky with spit. But she had been galvanized by the train itself: its massive wheels, shiny brass trim, steam-spouting chimney, and bright-red cowcatcher. She had never seen anything so powerful or complex, and her first thought was, *I should like to know how to make one!*

The interior of the Pullman Hotel Express was even more magnificent than its exterior. Here were no crying children or dirty trunks, no shabby oak seats or coarse baggage men. Here, money and luxury were everywhere: in the paneled walnut marquetry and etched French mirrors, in the plush velvet upholstery and Brussels carpets, and in the brass spittoons placed thoughtfully beside each bank of chairs.

Above Hattie's head, bulging walls loomed like giant eggs. With a turn of the key, these would fold down to reveal sleeping berths. And plush brocade curtains, now tied back between the windows, would fan out for privacy.

Hattie finally found her seat beside a large buxom woman and, across from her, a scowling adolescent boy. Occupying the fourth seat in their group, the place where her father would have sat, was an enormous potted plant.

17

"Oh, hello!" The woman nodded. "I'm Mrs. Lovelace. Marie Lovelace. And this is my son, David."

The woman spoke with a well-to-do British accent and seemed of the very amicable variety of foreign traveler.

Hattie introduced herself. Then she said, pointing to the plant, "And who's this? Miss Begonia?"

"Miss Begonia? Oh, ha-ha! Excellent!"

Hattie wondered why Mrs. Lovelace was aboard this train when she did not appear to have a husband. But she asked instead, "Why is it you've brought along this enormous plant, Mrs. Lovelace?"

"Shh!" Mrs. Lovelace put a finger to her lips and looked about for the conductor. "I don't want them to take it. For it shall surely die kept in the frigid baggage car for six days. It was my husband's favorite plant. He was an importer of the most lovely Axminster carpets. He was supposed to be on this train with me. We all thought he was recovering so nicely, but then he took a turn for the worse just two weeks ago. Its flowers gave him great cheer as he lay dying. Of course, it's not flowering just now . . . Been shook up, poor thing. I suppose we all have."

David rolled his eyes as if to make light of his mother's grief. But Hattie was moved by the story. "How come you chose to continue on the journey, Mrs. Lovelace?"

"No money, you see." She proffered her open palms. "Not a penny. Unfortunate investments. We are going to my husband's brother in San Francisco to throw ourselves upon his mercy. Personally, I'd rather have gone to New York. That was the plan. But as the great poet said, 'the best-laid schemes of mice and men often go awry.'"

Hattie didn't know what to say. She glanced back at the plant. "Well," she said, "we could always place a hat upon it and hope they don't notice."

Mrs. Lovelace glanced at Hattie, unsure of her meaning. Then she laughed easily and repeated, "Oh, put a hat upon it! Yes, yes indeed!"

Hattie, becoming aware of a certain physical discomfort, reached beneath her tunic and undid the button at the waist of her trousers with an audible sigh. Then she pressed her face to the glass and peered outside just as the train began to move. As it pulled slowly away from the station, she could hear the roar of the crowd applauding and crying, "Huzzah! Huzzah!" Then the train sent off a series of harmonic whistles and began to move, the band continuing to play its patriotic song.

The train soon picked up speed, but many excursionists remained standing in the aisles, greeting old acquaintances or meeting new ones. A cacophony of helpful if high-pitched comments flew about the Arlington car: "Oh, but Miss Peabody, I think you are over here!" Or "No, dear, we're on this side!" Others wished to appear blasé as they silently bent to examine the newfangled gas lamps or air vents.

Hattie muttered, "They should sit down."

Mrs. Lovelace smiled. "I imagine they're all vastly thrilled and excited, though some pretend not to be."

"Well, they won't be thrilled when they're thrown across the car at thirty miles per hour."

"Certainly not!" Mrs. Lovelace tittered.

One minute later, a poorly laid section of tracks suddenly sent everyone flying with shrieks of "Spare me, Lord!" and "We're going to die!"

As soon as they were able to release their hold upon their neighbors' arms, the excursionists scurried to their seats, where many assumed an air of total absorption in the views.

They traveled without incident for nearly an hour, and Hattie gradually noticed a pattern of behavior emerge: an excursionist would exclaim, "Oh, look!" and point to sights that, unless one was already staring in that direction, were gone by the time one turned one's head. She was tricked twice but then no more. Never again would she allow her head to swivel in baseless curiosity!

In any case, Hattie found nothing of great interest beyond the windows, except for the constant *chukka-chukka, chukka-chukka* sound as the Arlington's two eight-wheel trucks ran over the rails.

She doubted that any of the men or women on this train had ever moved through space at thirty miles per hour. But even Hattie, who understood the principles of locomotion, was amazed by the trick such speed played upon her senses: the fields, farms, and stands of trees all streaked by as if *they* moved, not the train.

She felt a twinge in her lower back and shifted in her seat. She had not yet removed her oiled silk bonnet or heavy duster, now besmirched by her fall from the coach. She stood up and removed both, which relieved her greatly. She disliked clothing in general, especially when in an overly warm place, and wished she could strip down naked, a thought that made her smile.

The excursionists slowly began to move about once more, stopping to chat with those they knew. Hattie rose to get a better look at them: though of a higher class than those passengers she'd ridden with eight years earlier, their behavior was much the same. They coughed, sneezed, and spoke too loudly; the men spat into the brass spittoons. Why could men not manage to swallow their own spit?

It wasn't often that she suffered such crowds of people, riding a private coach between her Beacon Hill townhome and their Easton estate, and she'd forgotten how much she disliked them. Crowds possessed all the negative aspects of humanity, she thought—greed, self-concern, thoughtlessness, and incoherence—while lacking its redeeming qualities, such as rationality or restraint.

Hattie did notice one handsome young woman about her own age, sitting quietly and knitting two rows away, on the other side of the aisle. She had dark-auburn hair, an oval face, and thick eyebrows. She was impeccably dressed in a pale-blue gown with a darker-blue velvet trim. Her skirts fell in multiple layers of ruffles and flounces, with a lace overskirt pulled up at the sides to reveal the blue underskirt. She was obliged to sit forward in her seat due to a fashionably high bustle. The effect was quite charming, but Hattie wondered whether the poor girl could breathe.

The girl was about to turn away when, as if feeling Hattie's eyes upon her, she looked up to reveal a pair of amused hazel eyes and an endearing gap-toothed smile.

Hattie smiled back at her. Was this an intelligent human being, one with whom she could converse? And would it be asking too much of God to let this be Miss Hunnewell?

Hattie sat back down and proceeded to remove the thick boots her mother had insisted she buy. She disliked shoes, though she saw their necessity. She disliked stockings almost as much, as they made her leg hairs hurt. She would have liked to remove them but didn't dare.

Just then the conductor came around to take tickets. Mr. Straight could easily have played the part of a conductor upon the stage, with his blue cap, full gray beard, and rotund belly. Well past sixty years of age, he carried a clipboard in the crook of one elbow, and as he moved through the car, he checked off each excursionist on a diagram.

"Ticket, miss?"

Hattie handed him her ticket. He looked at it, then glanced back at Hattie with a frown.

"Is Congressman Eames aboard?"

"I'm afraid not. He was detained."

"We left him behind?" The conductor glanced behind him, as if ready to turn the train around.

"Oh, I mean, detained for a day or two. Mama got sick."

"I see. A shame, a shame." But clearly Mr. Straight was relieved that it was her mother's illness and not his neglect to blame for Mr. Eames's absence.

"Who accompanies you, then?"

"Mr. Hunnewell and his daughter," Hattie replied.

"Excellent," Mr. Straight said. He was about to move on when his eyes lit upon Mrs. Lovelace's enormous begonia. His brows knit, and he opened his mouth to speak when Hattie rose and tapped him on the shoulder. The knitting girl stopped knitting and looked up curiously.

"Just one more thing, sir."

"Yes, Miss Eames?"

"I was wondering: Do you think it would be possible for me to ride in the caboose? I've long wished to do so. Not at this very moment, of course, but . . ."

The conductor seemed to consider Hattie's words. Then he bellowed, "Tickets! Tickets!"

"I guess not, then," said the knitter with a wry smile.

Hattie grinned. "Oh, I know the rules," she whispered behind one hand. "I only asked him so that he'd forget about Mrs. Lovelace's plant."

Mrs. Lovelace, overwhelmed, smiled warmly at Hattie. "Why, aren't you a darling!" she said, then removed a ladies' magazine from her bag. Hattie was just about to open the issue of *Scientific American* she had brought with her when she heard a ruckus up ahead.

"But we specifically requested a stateroom! Why have we been put in *here*? It is entirely unacceptable."

"I'm sorry, ma'am," Mr. Straight was saying to a stylishly dressed young woman with neatly curled dark hair and nearly black eyes. She wore a fine French frock, but the elegant effect was spoiled by a long, narrow face blotchy with rage.

Two children stood by the woman's side. These were a boy and a girl, both of similar height and age, perhaps eight or nine. The girl was pretty and quite blonde, with bright-blue eyes. She was dressed in a crisp ruffled pinafore and white stockings. The boy, dark-haired and dark-eyed like his mother, wore expensive British wool short pants and braces. He narrowed his eyes at Mr. Straight and set his teeth into a grim, defiant frown.

The conductor added, "There are only seven such rooms available."

"I know. But why is it the Peabodys got one and the Forbeses but not us? Not the *Ridgewoods*? I'm certain my husband specifically asked for one."

"Yeah, we want a stateroom!" the boy echoed his mother.

"I'll see what we can do, ma'am. Though, mind you, the room won't be in this car."

"I am indifferent," she replied coolly.

Hattie snickered. "Oh, yes. Very indifferent."

Mr. Straight bowed deferentially. "In the meantime, kindly take these seats just here. It's not safe to remain standing."

"And *I* will meantime inform Mr. Ridgewood," declared the woman. "Oh, there you are!" she cried, suddenly espying Mr. Ridgewood himself emerging from the men's lavatory.

"What is all this, Vivian?" Mr. Ridgewood scowled.

"Why . . ."

She proceeded to explain, but instead of sharing her outrage, Mr. Ridgewood said, "This hardly merits a *scene*, Vivian." And pulling the conductor aside, he whispered something to him, to which the conductor nodded his agreement. Hattie heard some of the women in the car titter among themselves.

"Oh, but he's so *very* handsome!" one woman said to her companion.

"I wonder why he married *her*," replied the other.

"*Do* you?" insinuated the first, at which they both giggled.

"Ugh," Hattie grunted. "What disgusting behavior." She disliked this young, proud mother, but she disliked the gossipers even more. And Mr. Ridgewood, embarrassing his wife in front of everyone, was worst of all.

Hattie sat back into her seat. Then she removed her father's pocket watch from her trouser pocket: it was ten o'clock. At the head of the car, Alfred was sitting on a campstool, polishing a boot. A line of boots stood at his feet, patiently awaiting their turn.

She closed her eyes, and a twinge of conscience pricked her like a sudden head pain as she recalled her parting scene with her father.

Hattie knew she could be stubborn. It was not unreasonable for her father to request that she wear a gown. But the more he had insisted, the more Hattie had pushed back. It was a mere dress, yet Hattie felt as if she had been fighting for her survival somehow.

From thoughts of her father, Hattie's conscience then assaulted her with other memories, of people and places she might never see again: her brothers, Robert and Tom, both good-natured boys, if not very bookish. Growing up, they had been her best—her only—friends.

Robert was with them by the grace of God, having nearly been killed in the war when a cannonball passed within an inch of him before it removed the head of a friend beside him. He achieved the rank of captain and, after the war, was awarded a medal for bravery. Now Robert was a partner in her father's shovel business. She had not had a chance to say a proper goodbye to him, as he'd been off visiting his fiancée in Newport when Hattie left Easton for the city.

Hattie gazed up at the egg she would crack open to sleep in and was instantly overcome with nostalgia for her Easton home. Her father had purchased it six years earlier, with money whose sudden appearance in their lives she had attributed to the great need for shovels during the war.

Built during the Georgian era, the home contained six bedrooms and half a dozen broad, efficient fireplaces. Her own room faced a rose garden and a small pond that was surrounded by cattails and stocked with fish. Beyond the pond, a lush stand of firs continued all the way to Boston Road. She and her brothers often played games in those woods, of catch and Hide and Fox. Sometimes they raced each other up the fine old beech trees that had been planted along the eastern edge of the property.

Hattie thought wistfully too of her comfortable bed, covered in a white embroidered counterpane, with a matching mirror and wardrobe.

Upon her dressing table sat a sterling brush, a comb, and a lace-trimmed toilet glass that would have been the envy of girls everywhere. But Hattie rarely used them, not being someone who thought to brush her hair every day, and they only gathered dust over the years. But she missed them to the point of tears now.

"Ladies and gentlemen!" The clarion cry startled Hattie from her reveries. It was Alfred. He stood at the head of the car and announced, "At Springfield, lunch will be served! You may remain in your seats. Tables will be brought to you. Men who wish to dine in the St. Cloud or the St. Charles cars may head there now. Ladies who wish to do so, please descend once the train has come to a full stop." Then he smiled, his teeth as white as his jacket.

Mrs. Lovelace set down her magazine and exclaimed, "Oh my goodness! Lunch! Imagine that!"

Hattie, who had wondered how they would fit 130 people in two commissary cars, was impressed. It would be no small feat to convert the sleeper cars each day to dining cars and then back to sleeper cars.

The train slowed, and Mrs. Lovelace rose. "Well, come along, David! I for one would like to dine in a proper commissary car." David rolled his eyes and followed her, displeased to have to go with the ladies.

Hattie wanted to dine in one of the commissary cars as well, mainly because she could not imagine sitting in one spot for an entire week. She rose. Immediately, she smelled broiled steak wafting in her direction and recalled that she hadn't eaten breakfast thanks to the argument with her father. Now she was ravenous.

Suddenly, everything that had come before—her revulsion at the crowd, the argument, the wistful regret, and the tender nostalgia—all vanished, and Hattie thought most cheerfully, *Oh, but I would kill for a cup of coffee and a porterhouse steak!*

4

STANDING ON THE PLATFORM AT THE END of the Arlington car, Hattie considered that perhaps it had been unwise to choose to leap between the cars while they were still moving. The link and pin coupler allowed for far too great a gap. Every few moments, the space yawned wide enough to swallow a person whole.

But she had no wish to arrive in the St. Cloud only to discover that all the seats were taken; from what she could glean, the choice to dine in the commissary cars was a popular one. As she jumped, she caught a view of the landscape on either side of her, and a blast of live sparks from the smokestack nearly lit her loosely pinned hair on fire. Long wisps had already come undone from where she had very hastily pinned it atop her head. She looked up to see the Revere car's elegant roofline, which, though stylish, did little to block the winds or cinders. Her feet were freezing; too late, she realized that she had forgotten her boots and stood in her stocking feet, now black with dirt.

Hattie passed through the Revere car and into the Palmyra saloon car, which was filled with men. They sat on the leather banquettes between the windows or reclined in ornately fringed chairs placed with artful insouciance. One of the men suddenly stood up as if waking from a dream. "Oh, but we're in Springfield already!" he exclaimed. Hattie recognized the man as Massachusetts governor William Claflin. "It seems I'm to make a speech."

Governor Claflin had an enormous forehead and a clean-shaven cleft chin. When he saw Hattie, he narrowed his eyes and frowned, then paused, as if trying to place her.

Hattie curtsied. She had met the governor several times at various soirees, both during the war, as an abolitionist friend of her father, and more recently. She could tell that he struggled to recall where he knew her from, which gave her an idea.

"Hello, Governor." She curtsied again.

"Forgive me." He blushed. "And you are?"

"Constance Cook. We meet again."

"Of course, of course! Miss Cook!" He bowed uncomfortably. "But I must recall what I mean to say." He laughed self-deprecatingly and descended the train, joining Mr. Price and a throng of well-wishers.

Hattie caught sight of them through a window: Mr. Price grinned, and his arms were wide open, as if he might take flight, powered by sheer optimism.

The next car, the Marquette, was identical to the Palmyra save that the latter contained a well-stocked library of literary classics unlikely to tempt any of these business-minded men. In the Marquette, Hattie was obliged to stop, for a bottleneck of excursionists now entirely blocked the entrance to the St. Cloud car.

Hattie wondered at the sagacity of placing the commissary cars at the end of the train rather than in the middle, where one could enter from both sides. The human block soon eased, though, and she found herself in a splendidly appointed car lit with etched-glass gas lamps. The car was divided into two parts, with a kitchen in the center. The kitchen looked neat and compact, containing an icebox beneath the floor, a special range, a steam boiler that Hattie guessed communicated by means of pipes to a carving table, and a pump for ice water. On either side of the kitchen stood four tables, impeccably outfitted with bright-white linen tablecloths, crystal goblets, vases of flowers, and gleaming new Union Pacific Railroad china.

Hattie could not fathom how the cooks managed to roast beef and potatoes for 130 people in two such kitchens. Then she recalled that the Revere and the Arlington cars had kitchens as well, though perhaps not so well outfitted. The St. Cloud's kitchen was a mere thirty inches wide and was manned by four Negro chefs, all in spanking-white buttoned jackets with white aprons. They swayed slightly against one another as they cooked, their identical towels swaying from their apron strings. It occurred to Hattie that Mr. Pullman sought to have the staff look so uniform in appearance that one might take them for part of the machinery.

Hattie had only moments to choose a table before all the seats were taken. When the man in front of her suddenly took a seat, Hattie's white-stockinged feet were revealed to all, and a few ladies tittered. Hattie shrugged and sat down beside David and the voluminous Mrs. Lovelace, who had already begun to jiggle the portable table to make room for her enormous bosom. Suddenly, she heaved it so forcefully that Hattie, having survived the gaps between cars, feared she would now be cut in half by Mrs. Lovelace.

"My, but this seat is cramped!" the older woman exclaimed.

"I should think it is," Hattie replied.

David smirked. Then Mrs. Lovelace belatedly caught the joke. "Oh! 'I should think it is'! Excellent!"

Speeches over, the train began to move again just as their waiter arrived with a plate of kippers and a basket of fresh bread. This was soon followed by a platter of fruits and vegetables with a sour cream dip. Hattie dug in without another word, but Mrs. Lovelace was inspired to comment on her every bite.

"What perfect little kumquats!" she said. Then, a few moments later, "Why, these beans are as fresh as my garden ones!"

Lunch arrived. Everyone in the car murmured their delight at the excellent quality of the fare. As she ate, Hattie gazed out the window. The landscape was hilly and dotted with farmsteads. The sun had reached its apex, and the train, ascending, appeared to head directly toward it.

The waiters cleared the dishes and prepared to serve coffee and dessert. Hattie was just dreaming longingly of the cherry pie when the train suddenly accelerated so quickly that her heart began to pound. The journal boxes, where the car's axles joined their large round bearings, would overheat if they continued at such a speed.

"This train is going too fast," she finally said aloud.

Several excursionists anxiously looked about them to see who had spoken.

"Oh, but I'm certain the men know what they're doing, dear," said Mrs. Lovelace. "Why, do you know, Mr. Pullman himself is on this train!"

Hattie nodded. She was a great admirer of Mr. George Pullman. He had begun life as a humble carpenter and designed the greatest railroad cars the world had ever seen. But no one was infallible, and she knew for a fact, having recently read an article about them in the *Railroad Gazette*, that the train's journal boxes left much to be desired.

"Yes, Mrs. Lovelace. But at this rate, the boxes shall overheat."

Mrs. Lovelace shrugged. "It's in God's hands, I suppose."

Hattie frowned. "I certainly hope not, for I doubt He knows much about the proper lubrication of journal bearings."

"Oh!" Mrs. Lovelace appeared horrified at Hattie's blasphemy. But young Master David found Hattie amusing enough to bestow upon them all a disaffected smirk.

No one came to take their orders, nor was a single porter in sight. Suddenly, Hattie smelled burning oil. Five minutes later, just before two, the entire train slowed to a stop.

Hattie looked out the window. They were in the middle of a field, surrounded by hilly farmland and patches of uncleared forest.

Mrs. Lovelace looked about bewilderedly and exclaimed, "Why, what has happened?"

"The journal boxes have overheated."

"But what is that terrible smell?" she asked.

"Burned oil."

Mrs. Lovelace clutched her throat as if she might be sick. At once, the men poured out of the cars to see if they could be of assistance. One man cried, "Where in hell are we?"

Another replied, "We just passed Stockbridge."

The porters scurried about shutting the windows against the stench and flying cinders. Then the women began to fan themselves even as they wilted like parched houseplants. With the windows closed, the cars heated rapidly. The engines were still quite hot.

Hattie had just risen from her seat to descend the St. Cloud when the twins she had seen previously leapfrogged down the aisle and careened into her. Both seemed determined to sully their new outfits. Their mother looked faint with heat. "Lou-*eeza*! Lou-*eeza*!" she cried. "Mind them, will you, for goodness' sake!"

A very tall, willowy girl in a lavender-and-white-striped gown with stiff hooped skirts limped after the children, her lips pursed tight in determination. She glanced at Hattie long enough for Hattie to see the fine creases in her pale cheeks and her moss-green eyes. Hattie flattened herself against a bank of seats to let the girl through.

The girl caught the culprits by the shoulders just as they were about to leapfrog down the steps into a cloud of steam. Then she turned back and glanced at Hattie, who smiled in sympathy.

In the field, the porters produced tables and tablecloths, bottles of cider and water, and coffee but no offers of dessert or spirits. Hattie was disappointed; she had planned to order a glass of champagne with her cherry pie.

Soon Mrs. Lovelace appeared, struggling to carry her large plant after David refused to remove it from the killing heat within the car. She released it with a sigh and then dropped herself down beside it. They watched in silence as some excursionists wandered aimlessly about like lost spirits, crunching through the matted wheat stalks. Others looked impatiently at their watches.

One older gentleman, whom Hattie recalled had been sitting beside the pretty knitter, now darted madly about the edges of the field. "But I believe there are new species here!" he cried to no one in particular. He then ran back into the train and soon reemerged with a small notebook and a comically large magnifying glass.

"Precisely whom we lacked," Hattie muttered to Mrs. Lovelace.

"Who's that, dear?"

"Charles Darwin."

Mrs. Lovelace hesitated, glancing up as she tried to place the name. Hattie turned back to gaze at the Pullman cars; then she rose, determined to examine the journal boxes for herself. The brakeman had already pried up their lids and was racing back and forth to scrape out the smoldering waste. He then splashed water from a pail into them, which created a great belching of smoke, and with his bare hands he proceeded to shove a slimy substance—matted hay, perhaps—into the boxes.

"Careful there—it's hot!" he cautioned Hattie as she peered into one of the boxes.

"I know it's hot." She frowned. Seeing the boxes' construction clearly from her crouching position, Hattie wondered: How could they expect to race along at nearly sixty miles per hour with such bearings? Disgusted, she stood up and cast about for the celebrated Mr. Pullman. *He must be somewhere,* she thought, but she didn't know what he looked like. So Hattie put her fingers together as her brothers had taught her and produced a deafening whistle.

"Mr. Pullman!" she cried. "Mr. George Pullman wanted by the St. Cloud car!"

No one answered, but the excursionists in the field stared at the girl in the reform dress as if she were a lunatic escaped from an asylum.

5

AS THEY WAITED FOR THE JOURNAL BOXES to cool, Hattie noticed a young man with bright-red hair wearing a bold red cravat and a dusty black suit. He had been among the first to hop down off the train, and he carried a foldable easel, the better to draw a picture for the *Trans-Continental*, the train's special newspaper. The circular they had received back in March had boasted that there would be a newspaper and printing press on board.

The bell clanged, and the porters hauled all the folding tables and chairs back inside the train. When the conductor finally cried, "All aboard!" the "artist" put down his pencil with a sigh.

"But I've only just begun!" he moaned. Hattie thought she heard traces of an Irish brogue.

The willowy girl with the limp was herding her two charges onto the train when the little boy stopped in his tracks and cried, "But *why* must we? Mama did not say so."

"Well, your mother isn't here, but she would say so if she *were*."

At that moment, the artist, sight obscured by his easel, nearly ran the girl over. She let out a cry of fright, which the children took as their signal to run. The artist looked in horror at his victim and cried, "I'm so sorry!"

The girl replied with a shy smile, "Oh, I'm all right." Then she looked off anxiously toward where the children had disappeared.

Sensing an opportunity, the artist continued, "But what a fool I am, to have painted the train and not this celestial vision before me."

Hattie rolled her eyes, but Louisa blushed and curtsied. Then she called, "Children! We're leaving!"

The children finally came running as the artist said, "Allow me," taking Louisa by one arm to mount the steps into the Revere car. If he noticed her foot, he gave no indication of it.

With all aboard and the conductor making a last check that they had left no one behind, the Pullman Hotel Express finally moved on, though far more slowly than before. The excursionists settled in to read their tourist guides or to play cards. Some dozed. Hattie pulled the latest edition of *Scientific American* from her bag and read until she, too, fell asleep.

Sometime later, she was awaked by a commotion. The train had come to a stop, and an enormous crowd stood upon the platform, clapping and shouting "Huzzah!" She heard the bizarre operatic peal of an Italian aria. They were in Rensselaer, New York.

The door to their car was flung open, and the singing ceased. But before anyone could descend, a boy entered and ran down the aisle tossing copies of magazines in every direction. Then, just as quickly, he leaped off the train and vanished into the teeming crowd.

Someone let out a scream of horror, and Mr. Price and Mr. Bliss soon came running into the car, searching for the culprit. Apparently, the boy had polluted their train with copies of the gruesome *Railway Accident Gazette*. This issue featured two fatal accidents, one involving a collapsed bridge, the other a snowy winter crash. Many dead and broken bodies.

"Where is he?" they cried. Mr. Bliss's square jaw was clamped and bulging on either side. The Boston Board of Trade's vice president was bald apart from a thin halo of white hair that encircled his skull. His face was plump and bright red, reminding Hattie of Friar Tuck from her childhood copy of *The Merry Adventures of Robin Hood*. Except that Mr. Bliss was far from jovial.

The knitting girl raised her hand as if she were in school. "A boy came on, but he descended at once."

"Blast him!" Mr. Bliss cursed.

Both men began to gather up the papers, politely demanding them from even those who, perversely, enjoyed reading about trains plunging into icy rivers from failing bridges or cars telescoping into one another through drifts of snow.

The knitter across the aisle set down her knitting and looked directly at Hattie. "I wonder what that boy hoped to gain?" she asked. Then she stood unsteadily and approached Hattie, curtsying. "I'm Julia, by the way. Julia Hunnewell."

"Oh, it's really you! Excellent luck!"

"What do you mean?" Miss Hunnewell looked warily at Hattie.

"Only that you and your father are meant to be my chaperones. Papa couldn't make it at the last minute. I must admit, I saw you earlier and hoped you and Julia Hunnewell were one and the same."

Julia grinned, relieved. She said, "I understand perfectly now. And the Mad Hatter you saw running about the wheat field with the magnifying glass—that was Papa."

Hattie laughed. "I noticed him. I'm Harriet Eames." Then she curtsied and said, "But—may I? The seat across from you is currently empty . . ."

"Of course," Julia replied.

Hattie stood up and moved to sit with Miss Hunnewell. Julia picked up her knitting—some shapeless green thing that might have been the arm of a man's sweater—and shoved it back in her workbag.

"I noticed you've been knitting," Hattie remarked.

Julia sighed. "An activity I don't enjoy nearly as much as I pretend. But it does prevent many otherwise inescapable conversations."

"A clever ruse," Hattie replied. "By the way, did we pass an opera house? I thought I heard the most exquisite voice, but it ceased abruptly when that boy entered."

"Oh, that was Mrs. Lovelace."

"Mrs. Lovelace? You mean—"

"Yes. Apparently, she's rather famous in Europe. But by her own account, she is too modest to share this information." Julia smirked.

"She's my seatmate, along with her rude son, David. They must have gone off to one of the saloon cars." Suddenly, Hattie slapped her forehead. "Oh!"

"What is it?" asked Julia, alarmed.

"Oh, sorry. It's nothing. I just realized a solution to a puzzle of sorts."

"A solution?" Julia was surprised and not a little alarmed by Hattie's abrupt shift in thought.

"Well," Hattie began, "when I crossed between the cars—"

"We ladies were warned not to do that."

Hattie caught Julia glancing at her reform dress.

"I know." She waved her hand with some impatience. "But when I did, I discovered a woeful pin holding the cars together, which at the time I believed could be much improved upon."

"And now you've got an idea?" Julia stifled a smile.

"Indeed, I do," Hattie said, needing little encouragement. "I just now envisioned a vestibule, something like an accordion upon a steel frame, wrapped in an elastic diaphragm. Such a vestibule would make passage between cars far safer. It will also have the added advantage of eliminating much of the cars' oscillation." Hattie paused, blushing uncharacteristically. She realized that she had not been among company other than her brothers and father in quite some time, and she hardly knew how to converse. "I like knowing how things work."

"And how is it that you've learned so much?"

Hattie considered the question. "I've been stealing my brothers' books for ages. They never had much use for them anyway. And Papa subscribes to all kinds of magazines . . ."

But Julia's thoughts had already taken a turn, and she asked, "Miss Eames?"

"Call me Hattie."

"Hattie. Would you join us for dinner? You'd be doing me a great favor."

"So I haven't frightened you away with talk about coupling pins and vestibules?"

Julia laughed. "Not in the least. I'd rather that than be forced to listen to another lecture about the flora of the Northeast. Papa is a dear, but if he starts up on that topic, I'll run screaming."

"That *will* be difficult," Hattie said. "Since there is nowhere to run."

Julia smiled, and Hattie was pleased. A girl with a sense of humor. Now that was most fortunate!

• • •

Dinner was served not long afterward, and, as promised, Hattie sat with Julia and her father. Fortunately, it seemed that the excursionists had chosen to return to those seats they'd taken at lunch. She had noticed this behavior among her own family, each of whom had his or her "seat" at the table, and in her fellow students at school, who never took kindly to having to change their desks. But it had not occurred to Hattie until now that human beings might actually have an instinctual drive to stake their claim.

Hattie introduced herself as "Mr. Eames's daughter," and the light of recognition came on in Mr. Hunnewell's eyes. Seeing him up close, Hattie concluded that he was an elegant, intellectual sort of man. He had long, thin legs and long, delicate fingers that he pressed together, a nervous habit. His light-brown hair was thinning, like the rest of him.

"Yes, I received a telegram about you back in Springfield. A shame he couldn't make it. Terrible shame. But we shall take excellent care of you," he added. "Shan't we, Julia?" Then he proceeded to disappear behind his newspaper. The thought that Mr. Hunnewell would be an ineffectual chaperone suddenly made Hattie quite hungry.

"I'm starved," she announced cheerfully.

It took her ages to choose between the oysters or lobster salad, the chicken with truffles or mutton chops. She finally settled on the oysters—broiled, not fried—mutton and potatoes, and the upside-down apple cake for dessert. How her poor father would have enjoyed this meal!

"Ooh, that cake does sound good," Julia remarked. "I must admit to being fond of sweets. If Papa weren't right here to stop me, I think I might just skip the meal and go straight to the cake!"

She laughed pleasingly, though Mr. Hunnewell commented from behind his paper, "That would be morally unsound, my dear."

At the mention of moral unsoundness, Hattie became aware of her flask of bourbon pressing against her hip. It was still tucked into one of her large trouser pockets. She would have loved to take a swig but didn't dare—not before her chaperone.

While they waited for their meals to arrive, Julia said, "Tell me about yourself. I have a feeling you're very interesting."

"Oh, somewhat, perhaps. Well, we live in Boston, on Beacon Hill, but we also have a house in Easton. Papa is a shovel manufacturer and congressman, as you might know. He was meant to be here, but my mother took ill at the last moment."

"I'm so sorry," Julia replied, reaching to touch Hattie on the wrist.

"No need." Hattie smirked. "She's never *truly* ill. Although this time she *was* running a fever," she added a little uncertainly.

"Not truly ill? Does she pretend to be so?" asked Julia, in some confusion.

"I think it's more that she believes herself to be ill."

"Oh." Julia was thoughtful. "My own dear mother died when I was nine. My siblings are all grown up and married. One lives in Hartford, the other in New York City. Papa and I live in Needham together. He hasn't yet succeeded in marrying me off . . ." She glanced toward her father, who had been so quiet that Hattie had forgotten about him. "I've let him know in no uncertain terms that I wish to marry for love."

"I'm right here, my dear," said Mr. Hunnewell from behind his paper.

Julia continued, with some fortitude, "What's more, I should like to be useful to my husband, not merely ornamental."

Here, Mr. Hunnewell finally removed the newspaper from his face and looked at Hattie from above a pair of spectacles. "But you must admit that my daughter is a very fine ornament."

"She is, indeed," Hattie replied, smiling at Julia, whom she had already decided she liked a great deal.

"Furthermore," Julia resumed, "I'm convinced that in these times of great promise and expansiveness, too many young men lose their way. The chance for quick fortunes makes them greedy. I should consider it a successful life were I to convince a man that his happiness is standing right before him, in love and family."

Hattie was appalled. "So you plan to hold an ambitious man down, tied to your apron strings?"

"No, indeed!" Julia objected. "Merely to . . . balance him, as it were. For I'm certain there is little happiness to be found in mere wealth."

Mr. Hunnewell interrupted. "I'm inclined to agree with my daughter. Life has not been the same for me since her mother died, though we have every creature comfort imaginable."

Hattie said nothing more. She was fairly certain that she herself would not be content merely to "balance" a man's ambitions. It would be like—like serving as a human column for a Greek temple.

Julia asked, "And how about you, Miss Eames? Do you have a beau?"

"Me? Oh, why yes, I do. In fact, I'm to be married in Sacramento."

"You're to be married?" Julia could not have looked more shocked.

Mr. Hunnewell now set his paper in his lap, in anticipation of the story. Their bald disbelief made her uncomfortable, and she said, leaning toward Julia, "It's a long story. I'll tell you later."

"Very well," said Julia, well bred enough not to insist. She changed the subject. "Did you know, Papa has a rhododendron garden that is the envy of horticulturists everywhere."

"Rhododendrons!" Hattie exclaimed, though secretly she believed them to be one of the ugliest shrubs on earth.

• • •

Their meals arrived at six forty-five, just as the sun descended upon the horizon, casting the western side of the train in a burnished orange light. In the commissary cars, the gaslights had come on even though there was no real need for them. Then everyone fell to eating, and the room was silent apart from the clinking of glasses, the ting of forks hitting plates, and the exclamations of several excursionists who concluded that dinner was as fine a meal as one could get at Delmonico's.

6

LOUISA FINCH HAD BEEN TRYING TO DRAW ever since the train had left Stockbridge, but now it was too late; she was obliged to descend the train and head to the St. Cloud car for dinner with Mrs. Ridgewood and the children. At first, the train's malfunction had given her a temporary reprieve from the care of the children, because Mrs. Ridgewood would not permit them to run amok in the strange field, surrounded by such ramshackle farms and shadowy woods. Who knew what savage beasts lurked there!

They said the journal boxes had overheated. Louisa knew little about the workings of this train and didn't wish to know. It was enough to feel its power, its ambition, and its astonishing locomotion. But her true interest lay almost solely in what she could perceive beyond the train's windows.

They had remained in the field long enough for her to capture the unlikely lavender sky by smudging two of her pastels together. Then, just as the harmonic whistle blew, signaling their imminent departure, the twins leaped from the train, defying their mother, and darted away toward the surrounding woods.

Louisa dropped her sketchbook and ran after them, as they knew she would. That was the game they played, after all: Torment the Governess.

Louisa's run was uneven and limping. She could get no real traction on her clubfoot despite its heavy boot, and after a few paces, the entire leg had nearly slipped from beneath her. She gave up her pursuit, breathing hard, her heart thumping wildly with fear for the children and for herself, that the Ridgewoods would revoke the offer of employment, and she would have to return to Boston to live with her father.

Outside the window, Louisa caught sight of several large warehouses and, beyond them off to the left, a massive river. She thought that must be the Hudson River. Over it spanned a wooden bridge. Their train would have to cross it, she believed. Louisa disliked bridges, and she turned away.

Sheila sat next to her with her knees drawn up and her thumb plugged into her mouth. Her mother and brother sat opposite, and Frank kept kicking his sister until Mrs. Ridgewood traded seats with him. She turned to her daughter and said, "You may put your legs back where they belong now, Sheila. And take your thumb from your mouth. You're not a baby."

Then Mrs. Ridgewood turned toward Louisa and asked, "What's that you sketch?"

"Oh, it's the field where we stopped. The hills beyond it, actually. The sky was a beautiful shade of lavender."

Dubious, Mrs. Ridgewood plunged her long nose farther down into the space between the sketchbook and Louisa's bosom, reminding Louisa of a hummingbird seeking nectar. The work was upside down, and Mrs. Ridgewood said, "Turn it around, please." Louisa turned her sketchbook.

"Now I see what you mean." Then Mrs. Ridgewood glanced suspiciously at the nanny. "It's the color of your dress. Yet *I* don't recall seeing such a lavender sky. Is that what you call artistic license? Anyway, come. The train has stopped, and we must descend if we're to get seats in the commissary."

Around thirty years of age, Mrs. Ridgewood was a pretty woman, apart from her hummingbird nose, with well-tended brown curls and uncurious eyes. Louisa thought that Mrs. Ridgewood had the face of a porcelain doll who had come to life long enough to be displeased by it before returning to doll-dom.

Louisa had been the children's nanny for approximately nine hours now, and already she knew it was a mistake—if one could call something absolutely necessary a mistake. She had never worked as a nanny before, but when her father first told her of the position, Louisa had imagined a happy family with sweet, rambunctious children. They would sit at meals together, and Louisa would feel much like an older sister in charge of the wayward siblings she never had.

But this family was nothing like Louisa had imagined. For one, the children were not in the least likable. With each other, their mother, and especially with her, they had been cruel, sly, and spiteful. In nine hours' time, they had grown from openly mocking Louisa to being willing to sit beside her, but that was all. She doubted they would ever grow to care for her or she them.

Mrs. Ridgewood, though constantly scolding, did nothing to enforce her commands, and for the most part, the children did whatever they wished. What's more, Louisa did not like how Mr. Ridgewood had demeaned his wife in front of the conductor and everyone else.

Descending the train behind Mrs. Ridgewood and a throng of other ladies, Louisa sighed. Perhaps it was all just a bad first impression, though Louisa's first impressions tended to be accurate. Once inside the St. Cloud car, she noticed the girl in the reform dress sitting diagonally across the aisle from her. She was chatting amiably with another young woman and her father. In brief pauses, the girl in the reform dress ate heartily and sipped her wine, something Louisa's father forbade in no uncertain terms. Louisa looked out her window, hoping to find relief in the beauty of nature. But the train, moving quite slowly as it crossed the river into Albany, soon passed a wooding station where a pair of workhorses toiled in endless circles cutting wood for fuel.

"Oh!" she exclaimed, feeling no mere pity but a kind of annihilating empathy. She could feel the horses' weariness as they went round and round, the unquenched thirst of their dry mouths and tongues frothing at the corners of their bits. She leaned her forehead against the window and opened her lips, searching for moisture.

Frank, who sat facing her, giggled because he thought she cried over how he kept secretly kicking her. But he had been kicking at her heavy leather boot, and Louisa felt only the horses' dry tongues beating against their brass bits.

7

Albany, New York, 7:10 p.m.

JUST AS THE EXCURSIONISTS WERE FINISHING THEIR main course, two well-dressed young gentlemen boarded the train and proceeded to surprise everyone by offering to sell them life insurance. The excursionists all had a hearty laugh, greatly relieved by the fact that the only thing truly threatening them was mundane greed.

Mr. Price and Mr. Bliss came hurrying through the commissary cars to dispatch the insurance men at once.

"So that was why they tried to scare the wits out of us with that *Accident Gazette*?" asked Julia as they sipped their coffee and waited for dessert to arrive.

"It seems so. How stupid. Don't they know that this train is different? It is unlikely to suffer any such catastrophe, though there shall be annoyances, such as those inferior journal bearings."

Suddenly, Julia looked questioningly at Hattie. "How is it you know so very much? About the train, I mean?"

Hattie's apple cake had just arrived, and she paused with obvious regret. "Genuine interest usually leads to knowledge. Don't you find that to be so?"

Julia shook her head. "I've seen such interest in men. But never, I confess, in a woman."

Hattie set her fork down and turned to Julia with a look of alarm. "I hope you don't believe that women are so congenitally deformed as to lack curiosity."

"Oh, I didn't mean that." Julia blushed.

"I *hope* I'm not a freak of nature," Hattie murmured, almost to herself, as she took up her fork and resumed eating the cake. The apples were caramelized, and the sugar was just slightly burned at the edges, the way she liked it.

Julia, intent upon making amends, replied, "Well, if you are, then I suppose Louisa May Alcott and Susan B. Anthony are too."

Hattie glanced at Julia with suspicion, but when she saw how entreating, how eager she was to soothe Hattie's wound, she softened. "Excellent company is always a consolation," she allowed.

• • •

When Hattie and Julia arrived back in the Arlington, they found excursionists crowding the aisles, waiting for the porters to remove the dining tables and make the beds. Many grumbled their dissatisfaction, but Hattie saw that the porters worked as quickly as possible; they were obliged to wait until all the passengers had finished eating, and many had lingered over their coffee, oblivious to the porters who stood by, silently tapping their feet.

Soon enough, however, their seats had been transformed into plush beds. The upper berths were suspended in midair by two straps attached to the ceiling, the beds covered in snow-white sheets and fluffy pillows. Brocade curtains waited for the sleepers to pull them closed before the nighttime scenario was complete.

But it was stiflingly hot, and now the aisle was crowded with excursionists waiting to use the WCs.

"Can you open the window below me, Alfred? The ashes have already entered, and I feel I shall melt."

He shook his head sadly. "No, miss. I have to shut all the windows and keep 'em shut."

"But no one is beneath me," Hattie insisted. "Only Miss Begonia." Mrs. Lovelace and David had the next berths over.

"Miss Begonia? You mean this plant? Well, this plant's got to go in the baggage car, miss."

"But Mrs. Lovelace shall be very upset. It was her husband's dying plant."

Alfred cocked his head.

"I mean, his dying wish. For her to take care of the plant," Hattie added.

Alfred appeared to consider the options. "Well, I've just *got* to move the plant. But somebody might steal it when I turn my back to make up that other berth over there." He pointed vaguely to the far end of the car. "And someone can open the window once I've gone. I won't know a thing 'bout it."

"Oh, thank you, Alfred!" Hattie would have kissed him if she didn't think he'd drop dead of shock.

That settled, the porter asked one last question. "Head or feet toward the engine, Miss Eames?"

"What's that?"

"Do you wish your head or your feet to be nearest the engine?"

"Oh, I see. Well, feet, I suppose," she said. When moving at thirty miles per hour, it was probably best to lead with the feet.

Hattie hopped upon the foot box he had provided, and at once, Alfred jumped to clean its carpet covering with a stiff brush.

"There's no need, Alfred—I've no shoes on, as you see."

"Yes, miss, there is!" Then, glancing about him, he took the liberty to say to her, "Things got to be a certain way. There'll be hell to pay if they ain't."

●　　●　　●

Pulling the curtains closed, Hattie wrestled her tunic over her head and replaced it with a night shift, leaving her trousers on. This solved the problem of where to safely hide her father's billfold for the night. What's more, she wished to be reasonably dressed in the event she needed to use the WC in the middle of the night.

By now, others had returned to their berths in the Arlington. Hattie peeked out from her curtains to determine who her bedfellows were: mainly, they were other women, daughters of the Boston Board of Trade members. But a few couples had bedded down as well. Hattie pulled her curtains shut only to discover they were not ample enough to cover both side gaps simultaneously. She needed to choose: Would she have Mr. Eastburn smelling her feet or Mrs. Lovelace watching her snore?

Hattie could not decide and so, leaving both sides slightly open, she lay down on her back with a sigh as the train sped onward to Niagara Falls. Her entire body rocked back and forth, though not displeasingly.

Suddenly, Hattie remembered about Mrs. Lovelace's plant. Where was that woman anyway? Probably off gambling. She descended her berth and tiptoed down the aisle. Sure enough, the plant was sitting squarely in the middle of the aisle at the front of the car, near the men's WC. She picked it up and brought it back to the berth beneath her. Then, finding the foot box, she carried it to her own berth and used it to hop up.

In half an hour, the gaslights on the ceilings lowered to a flicker, and the sconces in the walls shut off. The hot glass cooled. Soon, she could hear throat clearing and whispers and Mrs. Lovelace's soprano voice admonishing David, "But you must use it now, my love. For getting there in the dark shall be most unpleasant for all involved."

Several people began to snore. Tired as she was, Hattie tossed from one side to the other. She dozed, then woke with a start when someone shrieked, "Captain Forbes!" But it was only Mrs. Lovelace, who had discovered that the sea captain could see her near-naked figure in the cantered mirror framing her berth.

Hattie sat up with a sigh of annoyance, instantly bumping her head on the ceiling.

"Ow!" She grabbed her bag and, feeling to ensure that her father's billfold was still in her trouser pocket, slid to the edge of her berth. A sudden jolt sent her flying forward. Her feet landed on the floor, but her arms pushed through a shut curtain and braced themselves upon the chest of a sleeping man. He merely grunted and turned in his sleep, taking one of Hattie's hands with him.

"Oh!" She yanked her hand out of his and returned to her own berth. There, she donned a robe and clutched it to her breast, which did not cover her ample bosom as much as her father would have liked. She crept her way through the rocking aisles heading for the baggage car.

Hattie's feet were bare, and her loose, wavy hair hung heavily down her back. Jumping across the gap in the dark was a challenge, though she was becoming more adept at it.

When Hattie reached the smoking car, she paused to marvel at the ingenuity of its design. The car had been divided into four rooms: a hairdresser's salon, a smoking room containing several euchre tables, a comfortable lobby and wine room, and, finally, the printer's office, replete with black walnut cabinets and several desks.

Finally, Hattie entered the baggage car. It was very cold, and Hattie soon saw why: by means of a gibbous moon hovering in the center of the car's window, she could make out four large iceboxes and, most amazingly, a large vapor-compression refrigerator, something she had read about but never seen.

Trunks were piled neatly on top of one another, almost to the ceiling. But she found a lone one and sat down upon it. She removed the tobacco and rolling papers from her bag, rolled a cigarette, lit it, and inhaled. It tasted even more delicious for the fact that it was her first one that day. Then she removed her father's silver flask. The purloined bourbon was sweet as candy, but it infused her with a fiery flare of warmth. She sighed with satisfaction. It had been several years since she had discovered the miraculous power of drink to assuage both physical and spiritual discomfort. And tobacco calmed her restless spirit, forcing her to sit still for five minutes together.

Eventually, Hattie stubbed out her cigarette on the metal strap of the trunk. She gazed at the stars and the moon through the window and continued to sip from the flask. She felt a moment's unheralded regret, a sudden contrition for everything and nothing. Why had she fought with her father that morning? Why did she continue to push the limits of his tolerance? The reform dress was ugly; even she would admit that much. But she loved it nearly as much as she loved her father, maybe more so.

Then a jab of loneliness struck Hattie as she realized that this was not a holiday excursion, as it was for the others. This was a one-way ticket to somewhere and someone entirely unknown. A life unknown. She took a long sip of bourbon, then several more. She capped her flask and sighed again. *You chose this,* she reminded herself. Then Hattie slid to the floor, curled up with her back against the trunk, and fell asleep. She slept deeply, until a gentle tap upon her shoulder woke her with a start.

8

LOUISA HAD LONG SINCE FINISHED HER OWN dinner but was obliged to help the children eat theirs, even though they could hold their own forks. They made a sport of locking their jaws so none of the food could pass through. Then, when Louisa wasn't looking, they would steal a piece of meat with their fingers and chomp it down with great relish.

The porters were making up their beds for the night when they entered the Arlington car. Louisa and the others were obliged to crowd into the aisles while the remaining tables from dinner were removed, the windows closed, and the beds pulled down.

Mrs. Ridgewood, already upset at not having heard from the conductor about their stateroom, became nearly unhinged when she could not find her children in the crush of bodies. "Oh, Louisa, the children! Where are the children?"

Louisa could feel one of them poking her in the rear. She frowned and replied, "They're just here, ma'am."

Sheila and Frank popped out from behind Louisa and cried, "Boo!"

Mrs. Ridgewood put a hand over her heart and exclaimed, "You children shall be the death of me!"

They giggled and looked triumphantly at one another.

Mrs. Ridgewood continued, "But I am most distressed that we haven't been given a stateroom of our own. Apparently, we are *not* to be treated like the Peabodys or Danas, and I am to sleep in the public car with the children's nanny and Lord knows who else! Given our luck, we shall find ourselves beneath that British woman with the enormous plant, or the bizarre Miss Eames. Really, I don't see how her father could let her travel in that hideous outfit!"

"Who is that?" Louisa inquired. "I haven't met any Miss Eames."

"Congressman Eames's daughter. Surely he was meant to be with her; I don't know the details. But—remaining here is utterly impossible!"

Louisa had just begun to nod sympathetically when the conductor appeared, out of breath. He approached Mrs. Ridgewood.

"We've found a room for you in the Revere, Mrs. Ridgewood. If you would just take your things and follow me." Mr. Straight proceeded to help them all across the gap into the Revere car. Once inside, he led them to a stateroom in the car's far corner.

Mrs. Ridgewood entered, but the children remained in the aisle, beside Louisa's new berth.

Frank frowned. "We like it out here."

"Yeah," Sheila echoed. "We like it better. And look—the berth up above hers is empty."

"Come along children." Mrs. Ridgewood ignored their words and reached for her children's hands. But neither would take hers when proffered.

"We want to pretend we're stowaways," said Frank.

Louisa smirked. *Yes, what hardship it shall be for them, to sleep in a soft bed and eat creamed chicken with truffles!*

Mrs. Ridgewood said glacially, "Suit yourself. You may stay with the governess if you prefer."

At last, the sky grew dark, and the gas lamps were turned up, casting everyone in a benevolent yellow glow. After the children had finally settled in the berth above Louisa, having grown bored with their stowaway game after about ten minutes, the train fell silent except for the engine's chug, the wheels going *chukka-chukka, chukka-chukka* over the tracks, and the creak of the cars pulling and pushing against one another.

The gaslights lowered, and Louisa stared up at the berth above her. The polished marquetry glowed faintly in the dim light, and in it, she suddenly saw her father's grim face as he had looked at her at the depot. She recalled his stinting nod as she curtsied and turned her back on him to board the train.

"I shall write," she had offered.

Reverend Finch had nodded and pursed his lips more tightly. Louisa had not been able to tell if he was sad at her departure or at the thought that she would rejoice to be free of him.

It was not as if he ever physically constrained her. It was more his persistent attitude, old as her consciousness, that she would never be independent. This had less to do with her foot than some congenital weakness of her very spirit. Without him, she would wither and die. "The kitchen skills of a slave don't make for an independent woman," he often told her. "Only a husband of excellent means and stature can do that, and that is hardly likely to be *your* situation."

Now, staring up at the ceiling, Louisa sighed, thinking that in fact she had not broken free; she had merely changed cages.

Louisa finally slept. Toward morning, she dreamed of her childhood. First, it was spring of 1861. She was ten years old, and people were running toward the depot. Upon the platform of the Orange line, a dense crowd waited to board a train heading west. On King Street, carriages, wagons, carts, and rude drays were all packed mountain-high. Everyone was crying, and Louisa sobbed too as she saw her school friends leave the city. Who knew if or when they would ever return?

Then it was several months later. She looked up beyond the depot: Shuter's Hill was covered with the tents of the Ellsworth Avengers, an infantry brigade from New York. Their flags flew, and their bayonets were fixed and pointing to the sky, like a field of steel willows.

Now she could hear the firing of cannon even from a distance of twenty-five miles. A cart barreled down the street to the city hospital. In it was a boy who had been shot in his face. The ball had gone into his left cheek and passed through, carrying away his right eye. But he was breathing; his hand clenched and unclenched convulsively.

Louisa cried out, waking several of the excursionists but fortunately not the Ridgewood children. "Sorry, sorry! It's only a nightmare!" she whispered. She had had these dreams many times before, and they always ended with the image of the dying boy with the missing eye.

Louisa took a deep breath and let it out, relieved to learn that she was not in Alexandria and that the war was long over. The images in her dream were real, though. She knew they would always be real, and she thought that it was perhaps because of them that she bore a faint but perpetual sense of foreboding.

Louisa rose, made her way to the WC, glanced at a pocket watch that someone had left accidentally on a box stool—it was just after three—and returned to her berth. A thin, pale line emerged upon the horizon, and the train slowed. They were at Suspension Bridge, Niagara Falls. Several excursionists descended and stood on the bridge to gaze at the massive, deafening downward rush of water.

Louisa listened to the excited voices of those who chose to leave the train in the middle of the night to see the Falls. She was tempted to leave the train too but feared that the roar would overpower her. She did not trust herself with dramatic shocks to her system because of the nightmares.

Most of the excursionists, knowing that they would be visiting Niagara Falls at a more godly hour upon their return, chose to sleep through the stop. The few who had descended the train had now returned but were too excited to settle. They only half whispered when they shared, "Have you ever seen anything like it?"

"No, indeed."

"That alone was worth the price of a ticket."

"Thrilling."

"Absolutely cracking."

"But—the sound!"

"I've gone deaf!"

"I wish!" someone trying to sleep cried, and they piped down.

Louisa soon fell back asleep but woke again just as dawn appeared as a thin red line on the horizon. She decided to rise, not knowing when she could get an hour of peace again. She fetched her robe, wrapped herself against the chilly morning air, reached for her heavy leather boot, and laced it up. She walked toward the front of the Revere car and nearly turned back when she saw the gap yawn open between the cars. She stood on the platform for some time. The train was moving quite slowly. She heard its chugging, felt the night breeze, saw the darkness with its flashes of bursting sparks and clouds of smoke, and above her the thousands of twinkling stars—oh, what delicious freedom!

Emboldened, Louisa grasped the railing on the Revere platform, placed her left foot on the Arlington's platform, and quickly pulled the rest of herself in line with it. At the next gap, she gripped the railing and hoisted herself over it, but her heavy boot missed the platform, tipping her treacherously forward. Her heart kicked with fear, but she soon entered the baggage car without further incident.

It was very cold. A printing press tucked into the left-hand corner of the car confirmed the circular they had received in March, which boasted that a newspaper would be printed aboard the train. As her eyes adjusted to the scant light coming through the car's small square window, Louisa noticed that the car was piled to the ceiling with luggage. A row of iceboxes stood at one end, and she was just about to open one out of curiosity when she heard a sound.

Louisa crouched in fear. Another sound made her turn to find the reform-dress girl, the one who had come to lunch in her stocking feet, lying upon the floor in front of her between two rows of trunks.

The girl was sound asleep but grimaced as if she dreamed of some unhappy event. A small, hard leather case served as her pillow. Had Louisa not seen her previously and learned that she was the daughter of an eminent congressman, she might have thought her a stowaway.

Now the girl wore only trousers covered by a nightshirt and robe, and she smelled fearfully of tobacco and alcohol. Louisa shuddered to look at her, a revulsion that soon turned to pity and then to curiosity: through the robe and nightshirt, she saw the languorous curves of a strong, comely young woman. She placed a hand upon the girl's shoulder.

"Hello?" she whispered. "Hello!" Gently, she jiggled the girl's shoulder.

Hattie's glazed eyes opened.

"Thank God. You're alive."

"You're that nanny," Hattie murmured.

Louisa smiled. "Yes. But come, or you shall freeze to death!"

9

HATTIE WAS JUST AWAKE ENOUGH, IF NOT quite sober enough, to recognize the girl who stood over her as the beleaguered nanny. It was still quite dark, with only a glimmer on the horizon, as they made their way slowly back through the cars. Hattie had no idea where they were or what time it was.

The train had picked up speed, and crossing the gaps proved difficult. The air was cold, and neither girl had much to protect her from the live cinders or freezing breeze that pricked their skin.

They entered the Arlington car, and Hattie said, "I'm just here."

But Louisa replied, "Come," and kept going, her hand resuming its place upon Hattie's shoulder.

When they arrived in the Revere car, Louisa seemed pleasantly surprised to find the berth above her empty.

"This shall serve, I'm sure," Louisa said, her firm tone much like the one she used with the children.

Hattie just shrugged and, no box in sight, stood on Louisa's bed and hoisted herself into the berth, feeling its crisp linens in the palms of her hands. She felt the girl cover her with a blanket, and the last thing she saw before the curtains closed upon her was a sliver of dawn rising through the window.

•   •   •

Alfred woke Hattie several hours later, wishing to convert her berth. He had already converted most of the berths and brought in dining tables. People were having their breakfasts all around her.

Hattie reached confusedly for her clothing, only to recall that she had not slept in her own bed that night.

She glanced out the window and at the same time asked, "Excuse me, Alfred, but—where are we?"

"London is the next stop, Miss Eames."

"Canada?"

"I believe so, miss."

"Oh no. I missed Niagara Falls, then."

"You can see it on the return journey."

Hattie sighed. "I'm afraid I'm not returning. Well, anyway, my things—I left them in the other car, the—"

"Arlington? I expect they're right where you left them. I can fetch them for you."

"Oh, no. I can do it."

"Are you planning to remain here, then, Miss Eames?"

"I suppose so—if it's allowed."

"Don't you worry." He smiled. "I'll let Mr. Straight know."

Hattie was grateful for Alfred's help, given the confused state into which she had awakened. She thanked him and crept back to the Arlington car, ignoring the tittering diners and clutching her robe about her. Her things were, indeed, just where she had left them. She grabbed her bag and headed to the nearest lavatory to change.

When Hattie entered the St. Cloud car, all the other excursionists were happily dining, chatting, and sipping their tea or coffee from the shiny new railroad china.

She glanced about her to see if she could find the girl with the limp who had rescued her earlier that morning. But she didn't see her and assumed she must be dining with the Ridgewoods in another car.

Suddenly, she heard, "Miss Eames!" and saw Julia waving at her to sit with them. Just as she had sat down, a second porter appeared before her. He leaned over the table and asked, "Coffee or tea, miss?" In his crisp white jacket, he looked at first glance much like Alfred. On second glance, she realized: It *was* Alfred!

"Alfred, why—it's you!" she blurted.

Alfred nodded. "Yes, miss."

"But how did you get here so quickly?"

"Walked, miss."

Hattie laughed. "They've got you doing everything, don't they?"

"I suppose so, miss."

After Alfred had gone, Hattie turned her attention to Mr. Hunnewell and his daughter, who had nearly finished their breakfasts. Mr. Hunnewell set his paper down upon his bony knee and asked Hattie, "Remind me, Miss Eames, why your father is unable to be with us? I'm certain both you and he already told me."

"My mother took ill at the last moment. He didn't wish to leave her."

"Oh yes. Terrible. Terrible. Please send my best wishes for a speedy recovery."

"I will." Hattie nodded. She decided she did not entirely dislike Mr. Hunnewell. Though obviously wealthy and connected in some way to the Boston Board of Trade, Mr. Hunnewell seemed to care more for things of the mind than of the pocket. That, at least, was something.

Squaring off the table was the "artist," the young man with the red silk cravat and curly red hair. This close he, like Odysseus, looked older, more nearing thirty than twenty. His pale eyes had crow's feet, and the skin on his nose peeled, as if from a slight sunburn. He had the first edition of the *Trans-Continental* on his lap, which he soon offered to Hattie. "Care to read our paper, miss?"

"Oh yes, please."

He extended the paper to her. "Mr. Byrne, at your service." A jolt tipped him forward, and the paper slapped against Hattie's face.

"Oh, so sorry!" he cried, pulling back. Other excursionists shrieked as they clutched at their crystal goblets and coffee cups.

"That's all right." Hattie, unharmed, merely smirked. "I can always find a mirror and read the paper off my forehead."

Hattie's breakfast soon arrived, and she ate hungrily, occasionally glancing at the paper beside her. She had been taught that it was rude to read the paper at the table, although her father never seemed to take instruction from himself. *Few men do,* she thought. She could not help noticing the *Trans-Continental*'s front page, with its ornate typeface and true-to-life rendering of the train. At the top of the page, a banner read, Let every step be an advance. Below that, Niagara Falls, May 24, 1870.

Mr. Byrne said proudly, "I drew the train myself."

"The drawing is an excellent likeness. And I think it's marvelous that you print a paper right here on the train. Do you disseminate them beyond the train?"

"Indeed we do. We'll hand them out at all the important depots. Mayors, newspapermen, and the like can grab 'em up. Then, what with the telegraph, our news will spread to the four corners of the eart', like. At least we hope so."

"Amazing. But tell me, why do you say Niagara Falls, when we did not stop there?" Hattie pointed to the banner.

"But we did," he replied. "For twenty minutes anyway."

"You didn't print the paper there, however."

"How do you know dat?"

"Because I was asleep next to the printing press. Oh well. I suppose 'Niagara Falls' sounds far better than 'Rochester' or wherever you actually printed it."

"Indeed it does, Miss Eames," replied Mr. Byrne.

"Still, it's not quite accurate, is it?"

"Well—I do what I'm told," he murmured abashedly.

Hattie shrugged a concession. "That's certainly more than I do." She stood up, brushed the crumbs off her tunic, took her leave, and returned to the Revere car. There, she found a porter whom she did not know standing on a step stool, reaching up to polish one of the hanging gas lamps. And, just as he had the previous morning, Alfred was sitting on a campstool at the front of the car, beside the men's washroom, polishing a boot. Squarely facing the body of the car, he had one hand inserted into the boot and with the other seemed to be playing it like a violin. A line of boots stood at his feet, patiently awaiting their turn.

Hattie took out her father's pocket watch and saw that it was now ten o'clock Boston time and that the porters were made to seem identical not only in their uniforms but in their actions as well. They did the same tasks at the same time each day, as if they lived by the clock as precisely as the train itself did.

Hattie endeavored to meet Alfred's eyes so that she could roll hers in sympathy, but he assiduously avoided looking at her.

She settled in to her new window seat.

They were at London Station now, where flags flew and bells rang out in honor of the queen's birthday. Suddenly, Miss Finch appeared and sat herself down beside Hattie with a relieved sigh.

"You're still here." The young woman smiled briefly as she smoothed her windblown blonde hair. Hattie noticed a fetching dimple appear in the girl's pale cheek.

"I hope that's not a bad thing," said Hattie.

"Oh, no, I simply mean, I wished to meet you—properly."

Here, her fair skin flushed red, beginning with her long neck and spreading upward to the flaxen knot of hair above her collar.

"I'm Louisa Finch. My father sometimes calls me Lou."

"Harriet Eames. Hattie. Pleased to meet you."

They shook hands, and Hattie noticed that the fair skin at Louisa's collarbone was stained with fawn-colored freckles.

"Thanks for rescuing me last night. I'd have woken up with a crick in my neck for sure."

"I'm not convinced you *would* have woken up. It was freezing in there."

"Well, I hope I wasn't snoring. I do that sometimes."

Louisa pursed her lips. "Only slightly."

Hattie glanced at Louisa and then laughed. "Yes, *slightly*, I'm sure." Once again, she noticed the blush that crept upward upon the girl like a fever rising.

"Well." Hattie slapped the paper on her thighs. "I was just going to read the paper."

Louisa sighed. "I would like to finish my drawing, if the children would only give me a moment's peace."

"Take my window seat. Do. I've no need of it." Hattie stood up. "I'll provide at least one line of defense."

Louisa and Hattie exchanged places, each eyeing the other's costume. Louisa, staring at Hattie's reform dress, said, "That looks comfortable."

Hattie, looking at Louisa's tight bodice and voluminous ruffled skirts, said, "That doesn't. How can you possibly sit for hours on end without fainting?"

Louisa smiled. "I suppose I'm used to it." She then removed her sketchbook from a bag beneath her seat. For several minutes, the women pursued their separate activities in silence. Hattie read the *Trans-Continental*, her expression gradually darkening. Having been favorably impressed by Mr. Byrne's rendering of the train, she now thought his illustrations—of Mr. Price, Mr. Bliss, and Mr. Pullman— mere toadying caricatures.

Every few minutes, Louisa glanced up from her sketchbook to ascertain whether the Ridgewoods had returned from the commissary car.

After a while, Hattie looked up from the *Trans-Continental* and asked, "Did you know who was on this train with us? Would you care to know who?"

Louisa shrugged.

"Well," Hattie continued, "the Ridgewoods you know, of course. The Honorable Alexander Price, C. Alvah Crocker and wife, Thomas Dana, Miss M. E. Dana, Mrs. Thomas Dana the Second, Robert B. Forbes and wife, W. S. Houghton, H. O. Houghton and wife. The Peabodys—it's a veritable Noah's ark of Brahmins."

"You forgot one," Louisa said, not looking up.

"Who's that?"

"Yourself."

Hattie smirked. She could not deny it, but she was dismayed to be called out so quickly.

Louisa returned to her work, but after a few minutes, Hattie blurted, "Why, listen to this! 'A bass and tenor are wanted in the Revere car.'"

Louisa stopped drawing. "What about it?"

"Why, don't you find it a marvelous innovation that they may advertise in this way?"

Louisa considered Hattie's question. "Actually, I find it rather pretentious of them."

"Pretentious? How so?"

"Well, if a bass and tenor are wanted in the Revere car, the men could just give a holler. No need for a newspaper to advertise it."

Hattie conceded the point with a shrug. Pretending to return to the newspaper, she actually watched Louisa's progress from the corner of her eye. In Louisa's drawing, a fine woods emerged on a hillside, with an old cabin nestled at its base. A river wended through the property, and a boy with a pail gathered stones.

"Hey, you're rather good," she blurted. "Did we pass such a scene? I don't recall it. But then, I've been busy reading."

"No," Louisa said. "I'm afraid I've made an awful mishmash. Everything speeds by so quickly, I can only catch bits here and there, then put them all together."

"Yet you've united them quite pleasingly," Harriet admitted, noticing the girl's Southern cadences.

"Thank you." Louisa smiled, but already she had slipped back into her world by the river and the boy with his pail.

Hattie suffered the silence for five more minutes before she placed a hand on Louisa's forearm, startling her enough for her pen to slip.

"Oh, but you *must* listen to this!" she cried, not noticing how Louisa had stiffened with displeasure. "'In Boston, three men were killed when a brick wall collapsed. In La Crosse, Wisconsin, a fire on the steamer *War Eagle* burned immigrants on the lower deck. Many burned.' Oh, but *here* is what I wished to share: 'A newly married couple was burned to death in their stateroom.'" Hattie read the news almost gleefully.

Louisa turned to Hattie and asked pointedly, "Why do they share such horrible news with us?"

"To keep us informed about the outside world, of course. Why else?"

Louisa frowned. "Well, Miss Eames, if you know the *an*-sah to everything, why *both*-uh sharing anything with *me*?"

Hattie suspected that Louisa's drawl grew more pronounced when she was annoyed. She folded the paper and set it down in disgust. Did the girl have no critical faculties whatsoever? And another thing: Louisa *seemed* like one of those sweet, passive creatures the South was so fond of producing, yet how contrary she was in her own soft-spoken, Southern-drawling way!

Louisa, apparently, had not finished with Hattie. "Only imagine how superior these excursionists feel, in such handsome and secure lodgings. Yet they risk nothing themselves, *live* nothing themselves." Louisa's arm swept upward toward the paneled walls and ornate French mirrors.

Hattie shot back, "Would you *rath*-uh a fire consume us, Miss Finch, simply to prove that we do partake in real life?"

"I'd *rath-uh* people understand the *dain*-juhs of *arrogance*."

"By God, you sound like a Sunday sermon!"

Hattie rose, feeling for her tobacco pouch. "I'm having a smoke!" she announced. At that moment, Hattie saw Mrs. Ridgewood enter the car, dragging Frank and Sheila behind her. Hattie glanced at Louisa, who did not glance back at her but hastily shut her sketchbook and cried, *"J'arrive!"*

10

Tuesday, May 24, somewhere west of London, Ontario

AS HATTIE SMOKED HER CIGARETTE IN THE baggage car, she resolved not to return to the Revere. She couldn't talk to that Miss Finch, who, when not silent as a stone, willfully checked Hattie's every comment with one of her own. What's more, she didn't think it quite fair for a person to *seem* so soft and compliant and yet *be* so hardheaded!

Hattie stomped out the smoldering tip of her cigarette and passed into the smoking car, where she nearly careened into Mr. Byrne. Beside him was Mr. Steele, editor of the *Trans-Continental*. Both were standing in the aisle, in conversation. Bent over desks behind them, two assistants were hard at work.

Mr. Steele was a man of perhaps sixty, with a full head of gray hair and a serious air. Both men turned, surprised to see Miss Eames emerge from the baggage car in a cloud of smoke.

Mr. Byrne smiled, but Hattie noticed a mysterious antipathy in his eyes. "Oh, hallo," he addressed her in his singsong brogue. "Would you look at dat, Mr. Steele—we've got ourselves a stowaway. You'd better not let Mr. Straight catch you."

Mr. Steele peered down at Hattie under bushy eyebrows so black she wondered if he dyed them. "The congressman's daughter?"

"It is I—tomorrow's news, perhaps? 'Congressman's daughter found in baggage car. Interested parties may inquire within the pages of the *Trans-Continental*.'" She curtsied and hoped to make a quick getaway, but Mr. Byrne checked her with a hand on her arm.

"Say, wouldya be willin' ta tell me the name of that girl yer wit?"

"I'm not with any girl."

"Y'are. The one wit the limp."

"Oh, you mean Miss Finch? But I only just met her."

"No matter. Would you introduce me? She's a pretty lass."

Hattie was not insulted, though she might have been. "Why don't you introduce yourself?" Then she relented. "Oh, very well, Mr. Byrne."

He tipped an imaginary hat as she took her leave.

"Eedjit," she muttered once she was out upon the platform.

Back in the Arlington, Hattie's old seat had been taken by a gentleman reading the *Trans-Continental*. Rudely, he had piled all his hand luggage on the seat beside him, next to Mrs. Lovelace's begonia, nearly crushing it. She glared at him, but apparently the dagger look did not penetrate the *Trans-Continental*'s opaque paper.

Hattie nearly objected that it was not his seat but thought better of it, for he might just as well ask her whose seat *she* had occupied all that time. She made her way back to the Revere car. There, at the far end, Louisa was crouched in the aisle playing a card game with the children. If she noticed Hattie's return, she gave no indication of it.

Hattie sat down heavily and removed a book from her bag. This was *Crofutt's Trans-Continental Tourist's Guide*, which her father had meant for them to peruse together. She crossed her legs and began to read just as Frank tossed his cards down the aisle and shouted, "Unfair!"

"Is not!" Sheila cried, and then she too tossed her cards in the air.

"Children! That's *very* naughty of you," Miss Finch scolded. "Pick those up at once."

"We won't," they said in unison.

"Then I shall tell your mother." Louisa rose.

"Mama doesn't like it when you scold us," Sheila reminded Louisa slyly.

Hattie had heard enough. She stood up and approached them.

"Mind your nanny, children." She smiled like a wolf in Grandma's clothing.

"Or what?" Frank challenged, looking up at her.

Hattie bent down and whispered to him, "Or I'll have them grind you up and put you in a pie for lunch."

The twins stared at her, all shiny eyes and gaping mouths. Then Sheila, the braver of the two, stood with her hands on little hips and cried, "I'll tell Mama what you said!" Off she went in search of her mother. But she got only as far as the platform gap before she was forced to turn around.

"There's nothing there!" she cried tearfully.

"What do you mean?" Louisa frowned.

Hattie moved off to check for herself and returned, saying, "We've arrived in Windsor, and they've unhooked the cars. They're moving us onto a ferry to cross the river." She peered out the window to find cranes, barrels, lumber, and small wooden buildings on either side of them. The first four cars had already moved onto the steamboat, and Hattie wasn't sure how they meant to transport the final four cars.

Meanwhile, Sheila huddled next to Louisa, stuck her thumb in her mouth, and began to sniffle.

"You scared her half to death, I think," Louisa whispered to Hattie.

"Well, she'll behave now, anyway." At that moment, Hattie saw a new engine approach, and the engineer hopped out of the caboose to attach the engine to their car. Soon, they moved onto the same ferry as the other section, on a parallel set of tracks. In another few minutes, she could see Detroit and cried, "Oh, look!"

Louisa leaned over Hattie to look out the window too, astonished to find perhaps a thousand people waving from the wharf.

As they drew closer, the silently cheering crowds acquired sound that built into a deafening roar. Boys raced up and down the depot platform, shouting out their wares, eager to make easy money. Other boys sold newspapers or handed out advertising circulars.

"Worm candy! McKenzie's Dead Shot Worm Candy! Twenty-five cents!"

"Vestris's Bloom! Fifty cents!"

"Sugarplums! Luscious sugarplums!"

"Fifty cents? That's highway robbery," Louisa said.

"Railway robbery, you mean," replied Hattie.

Louisa rolled her eyes.

The excursionists began to descend amid a blizzard of handbills and vendors' cries. Taking her leave of Miss Finch, Hattie moved away from the train and walked down the platform to get a better look at the roundhouse of the Michigan Central Railroad, whose domed roof looked like it might have come off the Vatican in Rome. Much to Hattie's amazement, a pair of enormous doors opened and disgorged two gleaming new engines. Their fresh blue, red, and black paint gleamed in the sun, and they were covered in waving flags and crepe bunting. Giant portraits of Mr. Pullman adorned the tops of both, just above the headlights, much like portraits of Christ in Byzantine frescoes.

Louisa was not far behind Hattie when she mounted the tall steps and entered the smoking car. But the men were holding a meeting in there, which forced all the excursionists who had boarded to descend and reboard farther down the train.

Taking her seat at last, Hattie grumbled, "I don't see why the men always have to hog the smoking car."

Louisa, who had caught up to her, said, "Something strikes me, Miss Eames."

"What strikes you, Miss Finch?"

"Well, if you dislike this train so much, I wonder why you're *on* it?" Her voice was soft, even pleasing. "Goodness knows but it cost a princely sum. Or so they tell me."

"I don't dislike the *train*," Hattie parsed. "It's a masterful feat of engineering. It's the men I dislike—well, the *people*, really," she amended.

Miss Finch stifled a smile.

"As for why I'm on it, well, my father was supposed to join me but was detained, as my mother took ill at the last possible second."

"Oh."

Was that a wince of sympathy in the girl's green eyes? Hattie thought it was.

"It's nothing," Hattie said. "My mother is always 'ill.' But where are *your* parents?"

"Papa is back in Boston. Mama died when I was born."

Hattie was momentarily at a loss for words, having made such sport of insulting her own mother.

"It's all right," Louisa said. "You see, I don't remember her." She then whispered, "Papa says she is the reason for my affliction."

"What?"

"He says that my foot is retribution for her infidelity. She appears to have had a torrid affair with some rapscallion artist."

"So he chose to do nothing for your condition? I'm no expert, but I believe there are good treatments these days."

Louisa shook her head. "He didn't send me for treatment until several of his parishioners insisted upon it. And by then things were . . . more complicated."

Hattie was shocked, less by this news than by prim Miss Finch's willingness to share it.

"Your father sounds like a fool," she replied.

"Well." Louisa shrugged. "He's a reverend."

Hattie smiled but was unsure whether Louisa meant to make a joke. "*My* father hopes to meet me in Sacramento, where my husband awaits."

"You're *married?*" Louisa's astonishment was so extreme that she rose slightly from her seat.

Hattie replied, "Well, I'm *to* be married."

"You are? *You're* to be married?" More astonishment.

"Yes, I'm betrothed. Though clearly you find it impossible, Miss Finch. His name is Leland. Leland Durand, and he lives in Sacramento." Then Hattie added, masking hurt with pride, "He's the son of a successful grocer."

Louisa replied contritely, "I'm sorry. I didn't mean to offend you. Pardon me."

Then Louisa let out a gawp of strangled laughter, which turned into a great heaving laugh coupled with an occasional snort.

Hearing her, Hattie began to laugh as well.

Louisa finally mastered herself and wiped her eyes. She said, "My own papa has despaired of my ever marrying. So I must enjoy it vicariously, Miss Eames. Tell me, if you would, what's he like, this Leland Durand?"

"No idea," Hattie admitted, placing a hand on her chest to steady a sudden hiccup of anxiety. "We've never met. Oh, we've corresponded for ages. He's the worst writer; you cannot even imagine it." Then, suddenly recalling, she cried, "But wait. He sent me a picture!" Hattie reached beneath her seat and pulled out *Crofutt's Guide*. She fanned its pages until she came to a carte de visite tucked in the back like a bookmark. She held it up proudly by its edges, face to Louisa. "Isn't he fine-looking?"

Louisa caressed the carte with one long, delicate finger. "Very."

"Do you really think so?" Hattie asked, her shoulder pressed against Louisa as she nudged the carte closer.

"Yes. *Very* handsome." Louisa paused. "Should I tell you what else I see?"

Hattie drew back. "Are you a clairvoyant or a student of physiognomy?"

"Neither. But it is fair to say that my visual sense has become highly developed, perhaps to compensate for—well." She looked down at her black boot, then back at the photograph. Hattie nodded.

"Here." Louisa pointed. "See the forehead and the eyes, so open and unapologetic? That's ambition. He wishes to make something of himself. Always an excellent trait in a man, I should think. But the eyes are warm too." She pointed to one of Leland's eyes. "Yes. I believe he looks at *you*, Miss Eames. At least, the person he imagines you to be. For you said you've never met." Louisa handed the carte back to Hattie.

"That's true." But Hattie was eager for more, and she asked, proffering the carte again, "Is there anything else you see?"

"Do you really wish it?" Louisa glanced at Hattie dubiously.

"Yes, please."

"Well, all right." Louisa took up the picture. "Do you see his mouth? The slight smile at one corner?"

"Of course."

Miss Finch nodded. "That's sensuality. I feel he won't be prudish."

Hattie was all right with this, but Louisa continued, "He'll welcome the . . . more earthly pleasures . . . of the marriage bond."

"Earthly pleasures!" Hattie exclaimed with a shiver of horror. "Goodness! I'd forgotten all about that." She snatched the picture from Louisa and returned it to her *Crofutt's Guide*. Then she removed the bill of fare and fondled it absentmindedly.

"What is that little card you carry about?" Louisa asked. "A psalm? I noticed you looking intently at it yesterday."

"A psalm? Not exactly." She proffered it to Louisa. "It's the train's bill of fare. We received it with our tickets. Didn't you?"

"If Papa did, he didn't give it to me. What is it?"

"The breakfast and lunch menus. I so enjoy reading it. I never tire of imagining each and every item. Gamey jacksnipe, buttery Scotch buns, juicy pies—yum!"

"It gives you pleasure to imagine these things?" Louisa asked almost gravely.

"Of course it does."

"You have a large appetite, then?"

"I suppose so," Hattie said, blushing as if she'd shared something quite intimate.

"I haven't," the other girl affirmed. "Moving as little as I do, I become terribly indisposed if I overeat even slightly."

"What a shame," Hattie said. "For I do believe food to be one of mankind's greatest pleasures."

But their conversation came to an abrupt end when they heard the now-familiar cry: "Miss Finch!"

Mrs. Ridgewood had come down the aisle in search of Louisa.

"Oh goodness," Louisa whispered to Hattie. "She's in a snit."

"Please make the children presentable for lunch!"

Hattie shrugged sympathetically as Louisa rose.

"*Oui! J'arrive!*"

11

Tuesday, May 24, somewhere west of Detroit, midafternoon

HATTIE JOINED JULIA AND HER FATHER FOR lunch, after which she strolled off to the baggage car. Passing through the smoking car, she came across two large boxes of chewing tobacco set out upon a table, a gift from the mayor of Detroit. She peered longingly at the shiny hexagonal tins.

A dozen or so men sat enjoying their plugs, occasionally spitting into one of the shiny brass spittoons placed all about the car. One group played cards around a small table; another conversed about the politics of the day.

"If you ask me, the country's not ready for the Fourteenth Amendment. I don't care if we did fight a war over it."

"Ah, a progressive thinker, I see," quipped another man affably, not wishing to start a contentious discussion. Though it had been five years since the end of the war, a man needed to be careful about what he said to a stranger. Few men their age had made it through the war without the loss of a son or brother or nephew, and even the most high-minded among them secretly wondered whether the victory had come at too high a price.

Hattie suddenly grabbed a tin of tobacco, holding it up to indicate to all that she wasn't stealing it. She moved on through the hairdresser's and the editorial offices, where Mr. Steele, Mr. Byrne, and their assistants were working on the next edition of the *Trans-Continental*.

"Hello, Mr. Byrne. Hard at work, I see."

"Dat we are, Miss Eames. Dat we are."

"Well, if it's not too late, some news for the ladies would be greatly appreciated. You know how easily bored we are with business or current events. Maybe you could include an item on, say, the latest Parisian fashion?"

"Why, that's an idea, 'tis," Mr. Byrne agreed, missing the irony of Hattie's statement as she stood there in her ungainly reform dress.

Hattie took her leave, but Mr. Byrne called after her, "That's the wrong way, Miss Eames!" He shoved his thumb back toward the hotel cars.

"It's not the wrong way if you're a woman who wishes to smoke!"

Suddenly, Mr. Byrne assumed an authoritative air. "It won't do to light all the trunks on fire, miss. Smoking is not allowed in there."

"So call the sheriff, Mr. Byrne."

She curtsied and moved into the baggage car.

In the dim light, Hattie sat down upon a trunk and opened the tin of chewing tobacco. Though frigid and dark, the baggage car was fast becoming her favorite car. Here, one could think one's own thoughts in peace. One could stretch out and relax too without one's toenails scratching someone's face. She popped the plug into her mouth, bit down, and felt her teeth lock into it—much like, she imagined, a clay mold to make false teeth. For a moment, Hattie panicked that her jaws would be locked together forever, but the plug finally softened, and she was able to open her mouth wide enough to extract it with her fingers and hurl it out the window in disgust.

Hattie remained at the small square window atop the freight door, gazing unseeingly at the landscape. She began to wonder about her father and mother back home. Her mother was probably already on the mend. It had been only a day, but she missed her dogs and pony and the copper beech tree from which she liked to sit and look down upon the world and the chummy teasing between her brothers as they strolled beneath her, unaware of her presence above them.

That they all loved one another had never been in question. But the farther west the train moved, the more relieved Hattie began to feel, the more aware she was of how draining it had been always to disappoint people. Her father, though proud of her, was fond of saying that she had a "masculine energy." Her brothers alternately teased her, included her, or grew angry with her for "showing them up." Once, she had taken Robert's building blocks and made a bridge over the hall runner. She placed a little carriage upon the bridge and was very proud. But when Robert saw it, he flew into a jealous rage and knocked the bridge down. Her parents had sided with Robert. "You mustn't use your brother's toys without asking first, Harriet," her mother had said at dinner that night. "Why don't you play with your own toys? You have so many dolls."

"Dolls are not interesting," she said with a pout, arms crossed defensively. Mrs. Eames sent Mr. Eames an alarmed glance.

The girls at school were particularly cruel, perhaps because they did not believe Hattie had feelings to hurt. In her first week at Emerson's school, where her father had enrolled her, hoping that school would cure her of her exhausting curiosity, a classmate pulled up her blouse to see if she had breasts. Hattie ran home crying and refused to return for several days. But here, in the baggage car, alone with her excellent drink, she felt right and comfortable.

Hattie dusted off her tunic and trousers and made her way back to the Revere car, where she found Miss Finch gazing out at the late-afternoon landscape, her sketchbook resting on her lap. They were somewhere in Michigan, and there wasn't much to see besides endless fields of grain.

"Hello," Hattie said, "I didn't expect to find you here just now."

"No?" Louisa replied, a single dimple appearing on her fair cheek. "Well, the children are annoyed with me. They insist they'll never play with me again."

"Excellent news!" Hattie sat down. "What did you do to them?"

"Do? Nothing. A porter came through offering biscuits, and I didn't let them have one. It will ruin their appetites for dinner, and I told them so."

"Cruel, cruel governess!"

Louisa glanced warily at Hattie before satisfying herself that she was teasing her. Then she resumed her drawing while Hattie finished reading the copy of *Scientific American* she had begun earlier.

The afternoon wore away, and once more the sun began its decline in the sky, forcing the excursionists to close their window curtains against the too-bright light. Hattie and Louisa had been pursuing their own interests in companionable silence for more than an hour when suddenly Hattie grabbed her own throat with a grimace. "Miss Finch, shall I read to you the most disgusting thing you've ever heard?"

"No, thank you," Louisa replied politely.

"Oh, but I will anyway! For it will truly amaze you. This passage is from a British trade journal called *Morgan's*." Hattie sat up straighter. "Are you ready for it?"

"Most ready, Miss Eames." Louisa rolled her eyes, but Hattie didn't notice.

"Very well." Hattie cleared her throat and read aloud:

> An analytical chemist has extracted from a portion of Thames mud, taken from the river at Battersea, a pure white fat. At this stage it lacks both taste and smell. But, properly manipulated, it makes a very popular article of food. Whether traceable to the refuse of manufactories or ships or other sources, it is impossible to say—

Louisa placed a hand over her mouth, as if forestalling a typhoon of nausea. Just then a porter came through the car calling, "Dinner is shortly to be served! Ladies, please descend only after the train has come to a full stop!"

"I can't possibly eat now," she said.

Hattie's eyes were filled with bizarre delight when she cried, "I *know!*"

For dinner, Louisa was obliged to sit with the Ridgewoods, although Mr. Ridgewood took his meal with his associates in the St. Charles car. Hattie found herself sitting next to Mrs. Lovelace, her son, and Julia. After his meal, David asked to be excused and left the table, but Mrs. Lovelace and Julia lingered.

It was now nearly seven. The sun had begun to set, and the moon began to rise in a milky gray sky. They were passing through Jackson, Michigan, and a flatter or more treeless landscape Hattie had never beheld. As if sharing Hattie's sentiments, Mrs. Lovelace looked out the window and mourned, "Oh, but the moon is not nearly so nice here as it is in England!"

Hattie gave a squawk of laughter before she felt a swift poke under the table from Julia.

•   •   •

The train moved slowly after Jackson, and it was midnight when it finally reached Chicago. Several fractious excursionists exclaimed that the timing of their arrival might have been better planned. However, they were to stay at two of the city's finest hotels, at the invitation of the Chicago Board of Trade, which kept them from mutinying altogether.

Hattie for one was looking forward to taking a real bath and to stretching out in a full-length, ash-free bed. Against Louisa's advice, Mrs. Ridgewood had allowed her children several sugarplums after they had turned their twin button noses up at dinner, and they now caromed at full tilt down the aisles with scowls and flapping arms, pretending to be birds of prey.

Hattie felt a pang of pity for Louisa who, caring for those little pests all day, must have been ready to collapse.

At the depot, a sea of carriages stood waiting to carry the weary excursionists to their downy beds. Mr. and Mrs. Ridgewood and the twins queued up to take a coach heading to the Sherman House Hotel, while Hattie found herself in the queue heading to the Tremont.

Hattie glanced over at Louisa and saw that, indeed, she was practically falling down with exhaustion. She favored her good leg with a grimace of discomfort. Then Hattie heard Sheila whine, "But I'm tired! I want to be carried!" whereupon she jumped up on the listing nanny like a monkey upon a crooked tree.

"Get off Miss Finch at once, Sheila," said Mrs. Ridgewood.

"I won't."

But Mrs. Ridgewood made no attempt to enforce the action she desired and abandoned Sheila as she went to mount the carriage. Louisa endeavored to move toward the carriage with Sheila still clinging to her, when all at once Hattie lurched toward them and cried, "But oh, Miss Finch! Do remember your awful rash!"

12

Friday, May 20, Sacramento

LELAND DURAND WAS ALREADY HALF AN HOUR late to the family grocery store, and it would be well on to an hour before he finished the blasted letter to Miss Eames. By rights, he should have sent it out two days earlier, because he wanted it to reach her in Chicago. But then Leland had been even more stuck for words than he was now.

He had nearly sent a telegram but hemmed and hawed and finally pulled back from the idea, fearing a telegram would make him seem too eager. He didn't want Miss Eames to think him eager, anxious, or delighted by the thought of her, even though he was, at that moment, all of those things.

Leland would be twenty-five in June and had been ready to conquer the world for more than a year now. Tall, brown-haired, gray-eyed, and quick of movement, he reminded many in his town of a young Abe Lincoln, if perhaps less high-minded. One year before, just as the two railroads, the Union Pacific and the Central Pacific, raced to join tracks in Promontory, Utah, Leland received a vision. Not a spiritual vision, although it had all the awesome power and clarity of one: a chain of grocery stores running the length of the Transcontinental Railroad.

In the vision, Leland Durand saw that with the advent of the fast trains and refrigerator cars, he could sell California lemons and oranges in Boston and Nebraskan corn in California. Beef, beans, not to mention goods from the Orient, could be sold throughout the country to eager settlers in fast-growing rural areas. Things born in nature needn't stay where they were born.

Provisions of every variety would easily move from coast to coast too: apples, pears, chickens, clothing, cheese, pins, plums, grain, and even baked goods. And Leland Durand, only child of Ernest Marcus Durand—a hardworking but taciturn French immigrant—was just the man to build this empire.

In one corner of Leland's vision stood a beautiful woman. At first, her figure was shadowy. But then she too became perfectly clear: beautiful but not merely so. No, he wanted a helpmeet, someone who would work alongside him to build the dream. Someone, preferably, who could elevate his down-to-earth western industriousness with her own eastern social flare. In short, a girl who could comport herself with confidence and aplomb, whether in a grocery shop or a governor's mansion. And in this too, it felt to Leland as if his destiny were being overseen by a higher power. Harriet Eames, daughter of the illustrious congressman from Massachusetts, Woodrow Eames, had agreed to marry him.

At the very least, Leland reprimanded himself, he should be capable of writing his fiancée a warm and engaging letter. But whatever his many virtues, Leland was not a man of words. He could write either a warm sentence or an engaging sentence, but he could not write both a warm and an engaging sentence at the same time.

Leland had been taught to believe that there was something wrong with his mind. His schoolmasters had told his parents he was, in turns, either stupid, lazy, or illiterate. It was true; he never learned to read very well. The letters always had a way of mixing themselves up before his eyes. They were like the fruits and vegetables of his vision, never remaining in one place.

With his eyes closed, Leland saw the letters perfectly, but once he opened his eyes, the letters perversely jumped around, arranging themselves willy-nilly. The anxious boy needed to read each and every sentence half a dozen times before the least meaning became clear. Adding insult to injury, Leland's penmanship was nearly illegible, even to himself. He had failed penmanship twice in school. He seemed a hopeless case.

But Leland Durand refused to believe that he was quite as stupid as his masters had told him. For one, his energy was boundless. For another, there was nothing wrong with his comprehension, which he derived more from the faculty of imagination than from his eyes or ears.

But the letters! Oh, the letters.

Leland sat in the parlor of his family's comfortable home on Front Street, across from the wharf. The townhome, sandwiched between two commercial buildings, was both spacious and cozy, though the decor was far too old-world for Leland's taste. Dainty antimacassars adorned each chair, and doilies sat upon every table. Now, having pushed aside one of the doilies, Leland pored over his last draft, glancing enviously at the fine day without. His large, slender feet tapped impatiently against the carpet as he began his sixth and hopefully final draft. The others were crumpled at his feet.

Leland rose momentarily and then sat back down as if resetting a faulty mechanism within himself. Then, in a winner-take-all assault upon the page, he poured out several sentences at once. He read them over, frowned, and muttered, "Hell and damnation!"

"What's that you say, dear?" His mother had just floated into the room in her big skirts and invisible feet. Mrs. Durand was still a young-looking woman, not yet forty-five. Pretty too, with her dark-brown hair and bright-blue eyes. Her husband's financial success had given her an aristocratic air. In Sacramento, unlike in the East, wealth created aristocracy, not breeding or lineage. Mrs. Durand's lineage, like her husband's, traced back to parents who came west with the gold rush, although she herself had been born in America. They didn't find gold, but they did meet the Durand family, who had just begun a lucrative little business with what they had in hand: fertile soil. In her youth, Mrs. Durand had not been too highborn to help Ernest dig trenches and spread manure. Now, however, she sat in a very fine parlor in a very fine frock, looking to all the world as if the only purpose she served was a decorative one.

"Oh, nothing, Mom. Just trying to get a letter off to Miss Eames before I head to work. You know how it is."

His mother pursed her lips. For years, she had watched her sweet-natured, hardworking son struggle with his studies. He'd been teased by the other boys—never too harshly, fortunately, for Leland's sweetness, his eagerness to befriend even his tormentors, made it impossible for them to dislike him for very long.

"Well," she said brightly, "Miss Eames shall very soon meet you in the flesh, and writing her shall be entirely unnecessary."

"Oh yes," he said, cheered by this obvious thought. "You're right. Well, I'd better go if I'm to get to the post office before work."

"Goodbye, my love. How's steak for dinner? You must tell Papa to wrap it for Lisa." Lisa was their cook, a heavyset blonde woman of German origins. As a schoolboy, Leland had often watched her prepare their food. Her hands were large, and when she cleaved through meat, he was shocked to see that she had the strength of a man.

"Steak would be grand."

"But—" Mrs. Durand suddenly looked at her son with some vexation. "Have you even eaten breakfast?"

He was going to lie. It would have been far easier, he knew. But in the end, the guilt of lying always made him miserable. "No, but I'll get something at the store."

Without a word, his mother disappeared and returned moments later with a freshly made muffin. "Lisa made these just this morning. I'm shocked she didn't offer you one. I'll have to have a word with her."

"No, don't. Please," Leland pleaded. "She must have seen the state of things"—he pointed to the crumpled papers on the floor—"and decided not to disturb me. It's not her fault."

"Very well. Here."

"Thanks, Mom." He took the muffin from her, gave her a tender kiss, and turned to go. Then he stopped himself. "Oh, but these papers."

"Leave them." Mrs. Durand smiled indulgently. "Jane can get them when she cleans."

But Leland wasn't having any of that. The thought of their pretty young housemaid seeing his pathetic attempts at writing was too mortifying. Jane was a bright girl and had done well in school, unlike Leland. She had been a playmate of his until her father's death forced her to earn her own way as a domestic. He raced back and scooped up the crumpled papers and threw them in the waste bin by the desk.

"Go now, or your papa will think you're a very lazy boy."

This last remark was a reference to a bone of contention between Mrs. Durand and her husband. For years, Mr. Durand had been frustrated by his son's academic struggles too. But, unlike Mrs. Durand, he stubbornly continued to believe that the boy simply would not apply himself.

"Just keep zee 'and moving," his father would say, breathing heavily over Leland's shoulder. "There's nothing wrong weet your brain—you *speak* fluently, don't you? Just move *le main comme ça*." Like this.

Often, when his father peered over him, Leland's hand trembled so badly that his pen would fall to the floor and stain the carpet with ink, which would only further enrage his father.

Well, but now there was hope that Mr. Durand's opinion of him would change. Indeed, Leland believed it *was* changing. In the way his father looked at him, there was now a glimmer of something like faith.

The post office was one block down on Front Street. As always, Leland's spirits lifted as he walked past Birch's Hardware, the McCrery Pioneer Milling Company, and all the handsome brick residences. The city was growing, prospering.

Leland entered the small post office and handed the letter to the old postmaster, who had been installed behind the window ever since Leland could remember.

"Another letter to Miss Eames, eh?" the old man asked.

"Yes, sir." Leland sighed. In this small town, everyone made everything his business. But then, he supposed a postmaster's business *was*, in fact, other people's business.

"Haven't seen one from her recently." The old postmaster didn't mean to make mischief, Leland knew, despite the insinuation. Then, noting the letter's destination, the old man exclaimed, "Why, this is going to a depot in Chicago!"

"Miss Eames boards a train on Monday and shall arrive in Chicago on Wednesday. She's coming here, in fact. We're to be married." Leland blushed.

"Oh, good news, lad. Excellent news!"

"Yes, yes, it is." And with that, Leland bowed and said, "A good day to you, sir."

• • •

It was, in fact, turning into a lovely spring day. Although already late, Leland crossed the street and stood a moment on the wharf, upon the rough wood planks. He rested his forearms on the railing and gazed past the waiting steamboats, toward San Francisco. He inhaled, then exhaled, letting the tension of the morning leave his body.

Only then did he realize that he still gripped the muffin his mother had given him. He brought it to his mouth and took a large bite. It was warm and berry-filled. Then he gobbled it down, licking the crumbs off his fingers, for he had no wish to dirty his clothes. He was not overly fastidious about such things.

As Leland gazed across the river, he thought, with a rising sense of exultation, *There is so much to strive for.* But as he turned away from the wharf, his greatest hope of all was that Miss Eames would not be too disappointed with him.

13

May 24, Chicago, midnight

SHEILA, WHO HAD BEEN CLINGING TO LOUISA like a monkey, suddenly released her grip, which sent the nanny tumbling backward, where she nearly fell on the pavement. Louisa then found herself summarily dismissed for the night by Mrs. Ridgewood, who admonished, "I'll have the hotel doctor come round in the morning. We'll have no need of you before then."

As the two young women rode side by side in the second carriage, Louisa finally said, "You're a very good liar, Miss Eames. Though you should know that I abhor lies or deceit of any kind."

"Liar? Nothing!" Hattie seemed entirely unmoved by Louisa's disapprobation. She pointed at the girl's bosom, now partly covered by her cape; lifted the collar with two fingers; and peered inside. "Oh, but wait. Are those freckles? I'm so sorry. I mistook them for bubonic plague."

Catching Hattie's merry eyes, Louisa frowned, though Hattie thought she could detect a little gleam of amusement there.

The Tremont House was a grand rococo-style building that sat upon an entire block at the southwest corner of Lake and Dearborn Streets. Two enormous gas lamps illuminated its entrance, and, as the young women stepped down from their carriage, a cadre of uniformed hotel staff guided them toward the entrance. The excursionists were encouraged to share rooms, and so, having no one else in mind, the young women decided to stay together.

Once in their room, Hattie took a long bath, sighing with pleasure as she lowered herself into the hot water. After drying herself, she brushed her teeth and fell asleep almost the moment she lay down upon the large, plush bed.

But Louisa lay wide-awake, eyes raised to the ceiling. Her delicate senses had been overstimulated, first by the long day, then by Hattie's extraordinary lie, and finally by the thrilling carriage ride through the romantic gaslit streets of Chicago.

Suddenly, Hattie began to snore. Louisa reached her arm out in the darkness and rested it on the girl's hip. At Louisa's touch, Hattie sprang into a sitting posture, eyes wide open. She snorted, then fell back upon the bed.

Louisa gazed up into the darkness, grateful for the silence. Her thoughts drifted to home. Not the shabby little room by the Roxbury schoolhouse, which she had recently called home, but to the long-vanished Alexandria of her childhood.

The parsonage had been a tranquil, comfortable place, and she was mostly left in peace there. Evelyn, their cook, minded her when she was not in school. Louisa recalled her vividly: a young Negro girl with dreams of going north. The girl was not particularly kind or affectionate with Louisa. But she was never unkind, except perhaps once, when she told Louisa, "No right-minded man ever gone marry you."

The words were hard but true, spoken to prepare Louisa for an uncertain future. "When dem Nordern soldiers come true town, dey'll run your daddy right out, and den you better know how to keep from starvin'."

"Oh, go on, Evie," Louisa replied, continuing to draw at the kitchen table.

"You mark my words."

Evelyn taught Louisa how to sew, cook meals, wash linens so that they smelled sweet and looked snowy white, and make tasty soup from bones and vegetables.

On April 12, 1861, Louisa's tenth birthday, Evelyn had promised she would make Louisa a jam-filled sponge cake. Louisa had waited patiently all week, and then the day finally came. The cake was on the table. Two of Louisa's school friends had joined her, no doubt more because of the cake than because they loved Louisa. None of the schoolgirls were so loyal to the invalid that a mocking word from another girl would not send them giggling and whispering. But now, eager for cake, they all sang a sweet birthday carol, and Evelyn was just about to cut it when from beyond the parsonage gates, there arose a sudden hue and cry. Two men, friends of her father's, came bursting through the door.

"They fire on Fort Sumter! Come quick, Reverend!"

"Who has, son?" Mr. Finch asked. He had been sitting in his study reading a book and avoiding the children.

"South Carolina. Colonel Chestnut—but do come! The men arm themselves and the women have gathered in the church. They're crying to wake the dead."

Louisa's father grabbed his hat and, as he did not ask his daughter to follow him, she made free to take a piece of cake and stuff it into her mouth. The other girls eagerly followed suit and were shocked to see Mr. Finch's arm suddenly fly over their heads and smack Louisa across the face, sending the piece of cake flying from her lips.

"Thoughtless girl! To eat cake at such a time!" He turned to the other girls. "I don't want to see so much as a crumb of this cake when I return."

"Yes, sir," Louisa said, fighting back tears. But her two "friends" let out a shriek of terror and fled through the front door, crying for their mothers. She never saw them again.

Louisa was left in the parlor, cake on her face and hands, tears streaming from her eyes and into her mouth, growing sweet upon contact with the icing.

But she didn't swallow them. And, apart from a little weak tea, she let nothing pass her lips for nearly a week. Mr. Finch thought she had taken ill and instructed Evelyn to give her Gentian root twice a day. It was so bitter that Louisa thought he meant to poison her.

Evelyn, knowing exactly why the girl would not eat, poured the contents of the chemist's bottle into the churchyard among the tombstones, muttering, "Dey dead already."

But she warned Louisa, "You'd better start to eat, girl, or you know what he'll do. He'll force it down you. I'm telling you the God's honest trut'."

No one had explained to Louisa the significance of Fort Sumter nor why her father, normally mild-mannered if cool, had struck her. And though a week later he apologized for striking her and admitted it was wrong to do so, she knew only that something had broken between them. Violence could never be taken back. Not really.

"When you go north, Evie, take me with you," Louisa said.

But Evelyn just laughed. "It's gone be hard enough without dragging no invalid white girl wit me!"

The following month, just as Evie predicted, on May 23, 1861, Union soldiers came down from the north and invaded Alexandria, one day after Virginians had voted to secede from the union. At dawn, thousands of federal troops rushed in from Washington to capture the city. What had been a quaint, sleepy town of stately Georgian residences, austere church steeples, and brick sidewalks, was replaced by a maelstrom of violence that Louisa still had no words for, only nightmares. Evelyn escaped soon after, leaving Louisa to suffer the war, her father, and her fate alone.

● ● ●

Just as Louisa felt she would never sleep, she heard a nearby church bell ring three, and then the high-ceilinged room disappeared. She slept deeply for several hours. Then she heard the screams of dying boys coming from a makeshift hospital, saw panicked crowds down by the depot, and a mile-long line of coaches piled high with Alexandrians' earthly belongings. A tall Union soldier, laughing merrily, picked her up in the middle of the street and set her down on the sidewalk, to become locked in a mob. And then, in July, there was Manassas . . .

Louisa cried out, finally waking herself. A brilliant crack of sunshine coming through the parted curtains hurt her eyes. "Miss Eames?" she called. But there was no answer. She looked over to the other side of the bed: the girl was gone.

Louisa peered out the window. The sun was just peeking between the buildings along the avenue to the east of the hotel. Why had Miss Eames not roused her?

She bathed and dressed quickly and had just opened her door when she nearly ran into the hotel doctor. He was a thin old man with a kindly face.

"Oh, Miss Finch, is it? I was just about to knock. I hear you're unwell. A rash?"

"Oh, no. I'm perfectly well this morning. I believe it was . . . heat rash. It's so awfully hot in the cars. D'you see?" Louisa proffered a pale, flawless inner elbow. Miss Eames must be casting a spell on her, for she had never lied before.

"Well, if you're certain. But perhaps I should examine you for good measure."

"I'm quite late—goodbye!" She curtsied to the old doctor and descended into the hotel lobby, where her knees grew weak at the fearful sight of Mrs. Ridgewood. She stood with her two children, narrow face pinched tight in anger. Seeing Louisa hurry toward them, Mrs. Ridgewood cried, "But all the carriages are *gone!*"

"I thought you were staying at the Sherman, ma'am," Louisa replied mildly.

"We walked over to fetch you. You don't think I would simply leave you to your own devices, do you?"

"I'm so sorry, ma'am. I had such difficulty falling asleep, and when I finally did . . ."

Mrs. Ridgewood was unmoved. "I knocked and knocked upon your door. I thought you were dead. And that girl who said you had a rash—where has she gone off to? Did the doctor find you or not?"

Louisa compelled her voice to remain steady. "I'm quite well this morning, ma'am."

The children meanwhile had come up to Louisa and begun tugging at her skirt.

"Let's *go* already!" Frank said. "We're missing everything!"

Louisa looked back longingly at the private rooms behind the lobby. There, she knew, a lavish breakfast had been set out for the excursionists. She could smell eggs, bacon, and coffee . . .

"If I may just take some refreshment—"

"You may not!" replied Mrs. Ridgewood. "I've gone to a great deal of trouble to arrange for another coach to join the others. It awaits us as we speak." But, seeing Louisa droop as if she might actually collapse, Mrs. Ridgewood added, "I'm sure we can find a place to stop for tea at Lincoln Park."

●   ●   ●

Without, it was a sunny spring morning. Though Louisa would always prefer the countryside, she appreciated the sweet air of a fine, cool day against the city's own sounds and smells, the bustling and murmuring of strolling people, the rumble of carts, and the clop of horses' hooves. They passed window cleaners, street cleaners, and boys selling sweetmeats. Louisa heard a symphony of human activity superimposed against the brightly benevolent silence of nature. But oh, where was that annoying Boston girl? Louisa would scold her roundly for allowing her to sleep away the morning!

They rode down Wabash Avenue and Michigan Boulevard, passing noble church spires and solid brick homes. Their coach passed beneath the river in a newly built tunnel, then up toward Lincoln Park. Along the way, they had a magnificent view of Lake Michigan, which looked just like an ocean, dotted with dozens of boats.

At Lincoln Park, they met up with several other coaches, but Louisa saw no Miss Eames. They finally stopped at an outdoor café, where she took tea and a biscuit. As they readied to depart, there was still no Hattie, and Louisa found herself looking about the park with growing concern. What if the girl had simply gone off? It would be like her. Yes, Louisa guessed, that was what she must have done. Well, but if that were her choice, to run off so foolishly, what concern was it of Louisa's?

Louisa hastily finished her tea and biscuit and, at the last minute, bought an apple before departing with the Ridgewoods.

They approached the depot about forty minutes later, but Louisa could perceive no trace of Miss Eames. As the coach finally came to a stop at the Chicago and Northwestern Railroad depot on Wells Street, Louisa saw a dapper, energetic little man pacing beside the train. He seemed mad, shouting to no one, his hands gesticulating wildly in the air. Then Louisa looked down and realized that Hattie was crouched beside the wheels of the St. Cloud car.

"But you see, miss, we've reduced the friction by changing the composition of the wheel itself."

"The Allen paper wheel is indeed a work of genius," Louisa heard as Hattie slowly stood up. "Oh, I've been just dying to do that for ages! I wish I could get fully *beneath* the train . . . It is one thing to read about them and entirely another to *see* . . ." Hattie wiped a stray hair from her face and painted herself with a streak of black grease. "But don't you think, sir, with regard to the journals themselves, that an improvement might be made simply by using some kind of ball bearing?"

The man took a step back, the better to look at the speaker.

"From whom did you derive this idea, child? Is your papa perhaps an engineer?"

Hattie stood tall at the affront.

"No, sir. It occurred to me when I read about the recent bicycle race from Paris to Rouen in *Scientific American*. The man who won that race did so on a Michaux bicycle fitted with Suriray ball bearings. It occurred to me only recently that those ball bearings might be used in the journal boxes of your train, to similar effect. Of course, I've no idea what material shall best hold up under such strain."

The man had little chance to express his astonishment before Hattie suddenly dropped down onto the platform once more, hoping to examine the train's brake mechanism. But flatten herself as she might, the space would not allow it. Just as Hattie stood up with a resigned sigh, Louisa stepped before her.

"Good morning, Miss Eames," Louisa said coolly.

"Morning, Lou," Hattie replied genially. "Have you met Mr. Pullman? Mr. George Pullman, this is Louisa Finch."

Louisa curtsied.

"Mr. Pullman and I have been discussing a few things. Did you know that these wheels are made of paper?"

"Paper? How can that be?"

Hattie went on to describe the virtues of the Allen paper wheel, and Louisa cursed herself for asking. The last thing she wished to discuss at that moment was the construction of the Allen paper wheel!

"This girl's got a man's head on her shoulders," Mr. Pullman said to Louisa. He turned to Hattie. "Do call upon me, dear, on your way back through Chicago."

"Oh." Hattie smiled, abashed. "That's very kind, but I've no plans to return, Mr. Pullman. My fiancé awaits me in Sacramento."

"Fiancé! Well, but I hope he's an open-minded fellow!"

And with that cryptic remark, Mr. Pullman tipped his hat to the young women and made his way back to the train. When he was gone, Louisa took Hattie firmly by the elbow and drew her close. "Miss Eames, what did you mean by disappearing this morning?"

"You speak to me as if I'm one of your charges," Hattie replied.

"Indeed not. I overslept—so much so that Mrs. Ridgewood came to the hotel and gave me a piece of her mind." Louisa suddenly recalled that she still held an apple in her hand, and she took a ferocious bite out of it.

Hattie grinned, almost as if she were pleased by Louisa's distress. "I'm very sorry Mrs. Ridgewood abused you. But you slept so deeply, I didn't dare wake you."

"I thought you'd gone off and gotten lost. I became . . . concerned."

"I did go off, but I didn't get lost. My sense of direction is quite compasslike, I assure you. And as for time—" Here, Miss Eames pulled her father's gold pocket watch from her trousers and showed it to Louisa. "Did you know, Miss Finch, that we lose one minute for every fifteen miles of longitude we travel?"

"I didn't. Did you know you look like a chimney sweep?" Louisa retorted, frustrated that she could not reply with anything like Hattie's technical acumen. "You should go wash up before all the water is gone from the water closet."

"Oh yes. Good idea! But we should rather call it just the 'C,' as I've yet to find any water in it."

"Then make haste before everyone else has used the water up."

Louisa moved into the car, but Hattie paused on the steps momentarily to watch the train's young fireman, who was polishing the car's brass fittings. He was a blond, fresh-faced young man without a trace of beard. Usually, the fireman was invisible to passengers, shoveling coals in murderous heat. It was a dangerous job. Polishing the brass must be a welcome change for him.

When he saw Hattie watching him, the fireman stopped what he was doing and nodded toward an adjacent wheat field. "Wouldn't think, would you, that this wheat'll be tall enough to hide a man on horseback come August! Well, if the Midwest kin beat us on corn, we easterners got the bulge on them in brains. Don't you think, miss? Me, I hope to be an engineer someday."

"I do think we've got 'the bulge' on them in brains, as you say." She curtsied and boarded the train, feeling a lurch of pity for this prideful young man.

• • •

The engine had already been fired up, and Hattie could feel the hot air wafting into the WC. She heard the steam huffing rhythmically from the smokestack. From the bathroom's tiny window, she looked out and saw the rest of the excursionists strolling down Michigan Boulevard. They appeared in good cheer, the ladies sharing laughter and the men smoking their cigars in the fresh morning air.

Hattie returned from the WC looking even worse than before. She had splashed her face and hair with water, but no water could remove the black oil spread across her forehead. Not finding a clean towel, Hattie had wiped her hands across her tunic, smearing black oil upon it as well.

Seeing her, Louisa frowned.

"What?" Hattie asked, placing her fingertips upon her chest in a defensive manner. "What's the matter?"

"You may want to change out of that thing."

"This tunic, you mean? Impossible!" Hattie shrugged. "I'll wait till they turn down the beds."

"Suit yourself."

The train had just begun to inch forward when a boy in wool breeches, no more than ten or eleven years of age, approached them.

"Miss Eames?" he called. "I've a letter for a Miss Harriet Eames!"

The girls said "her" and "me" simultaneously, and, after a moment's confusion, the boy handed the letter to Hattie.

"Thank you," she said to the boy, searching for a penny and not finding one. "But—did you mean to travel with us to Omaha?"

"Lordy!" the boy cried and, in another moment, had leaped off the train without his tip.

From the windows, the girls watched him, Louisa remarking, "It's a wonder he didn't break his neck, jumping like that." Then she turned to Hattie. "Who's the letter from?"

"It's from—"

They both heard the cry at the same time:

"Miss Finch!"

As Louisa rose, Hattie felt the girl's body stiffen, and she placed a consoling hand on her wrist. "Go on. I'll tell you later."

The whistle blew, and the train began to move once more.

14

Wednesday, May 25, 1:30 p.m.

SEVERAL HOURS AFTER LEAVING CHICAGO, THE TRAIN stopped in Sterling, Illinois, where yet another huge crowd awaited the train. Mr. Price stood on the platform and delivered a lofty speech in praise of the innovations of Mr. Pullman, who then regretfully took his leave. A "single brow of woe" accompanied his descent from the train as the excursionists all crowded the platform, the men removing their hats and sniffling women waving their handkerchiefs.

Immediately, a short, balding, barrel-chested man of middle age boarded. None of the executives came forth to greet him, though, and Hattie wondered whether the man had actually purchased a ticket. When Mr. Straight came around, the newcomer introduced himself as Silas Crockett. He handed Mr. Straight a grimy note with his thick fingers, which seemed to satisfy the old conductor.

"An unfair trade, I'd say," Hattie muttered with distaste as Mr. Crockett made his way past her. "And why must he sit in *our* car?" she added. He smelled of perspiration and, oddly, peppermint. He took a seat three rows down from her and proceeded to shove a dirty leather bag beneath it. Then he arranged himself so that his stocky limbs crowded out the man beside him, who sagely hid behind a two-day-old edition of the *Boston Daily Advertiser*.

Within moments of seating himself, Mr. Crockett looked around, but the excursionists in the Revere car seemed to have turned to stone. He said to his companion behind the newspaper, "Nice digs, eh?"

The man did not appear to hear him, and so Mr. Crockett fairly shouted to the entire car, "Nice digs we got, eh?" When no one replied, he answered his own question. "Absolutely incredible! Why, it reminds me of a steamboat I took once, back in '49 . . ."

"Ugh," Hattie muttered.

Mr. Crockett had stood momentarily to yank up a trouser leg when a bump in the tracks put him off-balance. He righted himself by planting a meaty hand on the shoulder of the man hiding behind the newspaper.

"Whoa!" Mr. Crockett exclaimed. "Guess Pullman's newfangled cars aren't everything they're cracked up to be!"

As no one made a reply, Mr. Crockett finally settled back into his seat.

• • •

It was nearly five when they approached Burlington, Iowa. Here, the fields of wildflowers gave way to soft, low hills covered by acres of willow saplings. Their pale-yellow-green leaves took on a vivid glow as the sun descended.

Suddenly, Hattie nudged Louisa in her side. "Oh, here's a good one! Who is pink and weighs a great deal?"

"I've no idea. Who?"

"A Pinker-ton!"

Louisa replied thoughtfully, "But you know, I've heard rumors that they ride these rails. Frankly, the notion frightens me. I knew men during the war who thought theirs was the only way of virtue." Then she murmured, "Perhaps we have a Pinkerton agent aboard our own train."

"And I know who it is," Hattie cried, eyes shining mischievously.

"Who?" Louisa asked anxiously.

"Mrs. Lovelace!"

Louisa laughed, revealing two dimples.

"You have dimples," Hattie remarked.

"Do I?"

"You mean you don't know?"

"Well, Papa thinks mirrors encourage vanity. Though I must admit I've looked at myself in shop windows."

"Ugh," Hattie grunted.

Louisa began another drawing, and Hattie continued to read the *Trans-Continental*. Then the train slowed and came around a bend, exposing an enormous iron bridge that spanned the Mississippi. Everyone raced onto the platforms to see the famed river ahead of them. Hattie, interested in the bridge, rose eagerly and made her way into the aisle when she noticed that Louisa had closed her eyes and braced her head upon the seat crest in front of her.

Hattie stopped. "What's the matter?"

The train had come to a stop, and Hattie saw that the bridge was open, its center portion forming a T to the rest. The engine driver waited as a loud whistle of steam heralded the closing of the bridge. Before long, a single smooth-looking track awaited them once more, and the train continued slowly over it.

"I'm frightened," Louisa managed in the voice of a little girl.

"Do not fret, Miss Finch. All is well."

"Oh, we're upon it now!" Louisa covered her face with her hands.

"Miss Finch, please." Hattie beckoned her. "Come see, and I'll explain it to you. We're nearly on the other side now. We're safe."

"No," Louisa said, reaching her hand out as if she might stop their progress.

She said, "Now, would you allow me to explain? Your ignorance preys unnecessarily upon your imagination. A little knowledge might cure you of such unwarranted fear."

"A little knowledge," Louisa repeated thoughtfully. "All right. If you think I can understand."

"Of course you can," Hattie said, sitting back down. She turned to the girl. "To begin with, this bridge is the first iron bridge ever built across the Mississippi. It is a masterwork of innovation."

"Innovation? That doesn't sound good."

Hattie smiled and looked down at Louisa's sketchbook, which was still locked in the white fingers of her left hand. "May I?" She reached for it.

Louisa proffered her sketchbook, and Hattie flipped to a back page. Then she paused.

"But perhaps I should begin with a bit of background on the river currents and composition of the riverbed. It will amaze you how they managed to figure out where, precisely, to build the bridge."

"Just explain how the bridge stays up, please."

Hattie began to draw, though she could not help but remark, "The construction of the foundation—these piers are double the size of most bridges. They are the very heart of the thing."

"Be that as it may."

Hattie sighed. Her strokes were tentative at first but soon grew bolder, until she had drawn a fair likeness of the swing bridge they had just crossed.

"I didn't realize you could draw," Louisa commented. "It's very good."

"Do you mean that it's accurate, Miss Finch? I hope so. For my aim is not an aesthetic one. Now, d'you see these? These triangles serve a purpose. They're actually a physical expression of important mathematical formulas."

"And how does a mathematical formula keep us from plunging into the icy depths?" Louisa challenged.

Hattie kept on. "Formulas are important because they predict the strength one can reasonably expect of certain materials under conditions such as heat, cold, or pressure."

"But that arch"—she pointed to the pretty swaglike cables above the bridge in Hattie's rendering—"surely that is decorative?"

"That? Oh, no. That's called a catenary arch. It's like a parabola but . . . not exactly." Hattie glanced at Louisa and was met with a blank stare.

"Now, what were you saying about the—the cat-and-canary arch?"

"Cat-and-canary arch!" Hattie laughed but not in a mean-spirited way. She began to explain the basic mechanical forces of pressure, tension, and bend.

After a few minutes, they both heard a slow, sleepy voice whine, "Lou-*eeza!*"

"I must go," Louisa said, rising. For once, Louisa was glad to be called by the Ridgewoods, for she thought that if she stayed to listen to Hattie's explanations, she would go mad with boredom.

15

AT SIX O'CLOCK, THE TRAIN SLOWED TO a stop. Alfred made an appearance at the far end of the car. "Dinner is served in ten minutes! Ladies who wish to change cars, please descend now!"

There was certainly no rush, but the excursionists sped down the narrow aisle as if someone had cried *Fire!* Hattie suspected that it was because no one wished to have Mr. Crockett among their foursome for dinner. She felt quite similarly, and indeed was the first woman to arrive in the St. Cloud car, where she took a seat beside Mr. Hunnewell. Julia arrived soon after, and Mr. Hunnewell addressed them both.

"Well, ladies, you might be amused to know that in New York, I picked floral samples, but I then stuck them in my *Crofutt's*, and now I daren't open my guidebook!"

"No great loss," opined Hattie.

"Why do you say that, Miss Eames?" Mr. Hunnewell frowned. "George Crofutt is a most excellent friend of mine."

"Oh, sorry! But, well, don't you find that he leans toward the hyperbolic?"

"Hyperbolic? Why, no, indeed. This country is full of marvels."

Julia came to Hattie's defense. "I agree with Miss Eames, Papa. Mr. Crofutt describes everything as if he wore rose-colored lenses: each locale is absolutely 'exquisite' and 'exceptional.' But that can't be so, for it would defeat his own argument."

JODI DAYNARD

"Exactly!" Hattie slapped the table, nearly upending her water glass. Fortunately, a waiter arrived just then to take their dinner orders. In his crisp white jacket, he looked at first glance much like Alfred, but upon closer inspection, Hattie decided that he was older than Alfred, but by how much, she didn't know.

Hattie ordered the roast beef in port wine sauce with parsley potatoes.

Then she asked, "What's your name, by the way?"

"Odysseus, miss."

Hattie grinned. "A fine name for a traveling man, I'd say! Odysseus, I'm Miss Eames."

"Yes, I know. We make it our business to know everyone in our car or commissary."

"You do? Lord knows, I couldn't keep us all straight."

Odysseus smiled briefly and went off to get their meals.

After they had finished their main course, Hattie ordered an apple upside-down cake with coffee, while Julia took tea. Mr. Hunnewell, unhappy at having lost an argument to the young ladies, took himself off to the smoking car with a great deal of throat clearing.

Once he had gone, Julia said, "I think Papa is homesick—at least at home, he has his garden and may read his books. Do you miss home, Miss Eames?"

Hattie replied thoughtfully, "I miss *some* things. Yet I can't say that all my memories are fond ones." Then she added lightly, "We have two homes, actually. One is on Beacon Hill and the other's in Easton. It is the Easton home I imagine when you ask me if I miss home. In winter, we look out over the Canoe River from the morning room. It's so light and cheerful! When I think of that room, I imagine my brothers clinking their forks against our china, impatient to run outside, and my parents scolding them as if they were not nearly grown men. We could play and run for hours without ever leaving our own property. And, oh, in summer—the lily pads upon the ponds . . ." Hattie trailed off.

108

Julia smiled. "It sounds delightful." She added wistfully, "My own siblings are grown and gone away. They were never my playmates. And though our property is large as well, I feel lonely there. Perhaps because I can recall when my siblings lived with us."

Hattie realized that she often felt lonely even with her brothers living there. But she replied, "We have a most excellent cook. Her name is Joy. She makes delicious creamed chicken hash and stuffed goose with apple fritters. On Sundays after church, we come home to mountains of waffles, and I am scolded for deluging them with maple syrup."

Yet the more Hattie went on about the delights of Easton, the more aware she became of all that she didn't say. She sighed.

"Does some thought trouble you, Miss Eames? I'm sorry if my prying questions are the cause."

"No, no. I've merely managed to make myself homesick," she said, knowing it was only partly true. "But that's because I shan't return. Hours go by where I forget this fact entirely."

"Oh, I see."

Julia's polite silence prompted Hattie to add, "As I mentioned, I'm to be married in California. And I nearly missed this train because my father and I were arguing about what I wore. He thought I was an embarrassment to him."

Julia's eyes shone with mischief. "Well, now that Papa's gone, you must tell me *everything*. If you would."

Hattie laughed. "I'll begin the story, though Lord knows if I can end in time for bed. I'll make a start at least." She took a deep breath. "One year ago, my father had nearly given up on the prospect of marrying me off. I can't tell you how many young men crossed our threshold." She paused to recall. "There was a bright young clergyman who kept coughing, and I thought he had a year to live at best. Then there was a student of law, a friend of my brother Robert's. He had about a *thousand* spots on his face. And, oh yes—the son of a steel merchant, who declined the offer of a perfectly good game of catch with my brothers and me. Imagine that!"

Julia asked, "So how did you happen to meet Mr. Durand?"

"Well, I've never actually met him. Papa received a letter from an acquaintance in California. Apparently, there was a young man gaining a name for himself in Sacramento. The boy was from humble but well-to-do stock, twenty-three. He sent me a carte de visite, and he looks very fine indeed."

"And you agreed to marry him?" It was Julia's first display of surprise at Hattie's narrative. "Sight unseen? I didn't know girls still did that."

"Of course not." Harriet frowned. "I rejected him outright. 'Papa,' I said, 'Am I one of your shovels, to be shipped across the country and sold in this manner?' But Mr. Durand wrote to me and—" Here, Hattie tenderly placed a hand to her heart. "He endeared himself to me almost at once. If you only knew how excruciatingly bad his writing is, you would love him too."

"I would?"

"What I mean is," Hattie added, "he is charmingly unconcerned with outward appearances. You should have seen his hair in the picture he sent."

What Hattie did not say was that, in the months that Leland wrote to her, she knew she was running out of options. Nearing twenty-one, she would either have to marry someone or remain a spinster, closeted within her father's estate. Alone, without her brothers, knitting by the fire.

"You sound most fortunate, now that you've explained it. You sound sincerely attached to him."

"Oh, I am!"

Julia sighed wistfully. "You've no idea how much pressure has been put upon me to make a good match. But I refuse to marry for mere material considerations. Nor considerations of class. I care nothing for these. And as for appearances," she continued, "if a man can't countenance the fact that I have a slight gap in my teeth, then, for goodness' sake, I don't want him!"

"I like the gap. It's quite charming," Hattie said. Suddenly, she asked, "Is your father a stockholder of the Union Pacific Railroad?"

"He is," Julia said, surprised by Hattie's shift in thought. "Is yours?"

"I'm not sure. He never speaks of it, but he's always heading off to meetings of one kind or another. He subscribes to all the railroad magazines. And I know he favors the railroads because he has voted in favor of subsidizing them. But I ask because I've begun to wonder about something."

"Yes?"

"Well, here is my question: How could these men have made money on an enterprise that has only just now begun to draw customers?"

"I've wondered the same thing myself," Julia interjected, "and I'm afraid I don't have a good answer."

Porters wishing to return the St. Cloud to its usual aspect shifted from foot to foot, and the two girls stood and made their way back to their seats. Hattie observed that, without the stultifying presence of her father, Julia was marvelously intrepid, leaping across the gaps with a giggle. When they reached the Revere car Hattie kept going, thinking she might finish her conversation with Julia in the Arlington.

"Perhaps it is like gambling," she finally said once they had reached Julia's seat. As the one across from Julia was empty, Hattie sat down in it. "Perhaps people have been willing to pay for shares of stock from a company that is not yet prosperous but might soon prosper. Speculation, I think one calls it."

Mr. Hunnewell, returning at that moment from the smoking car, looked stonily at Hattie. He was going to let her comment pass but then thought better of it. "I hardly think that the business dealings of the Union Pacific are an appropriate topic for two genteel Christian ladies."

Hattie bristled as she moved her knees to the side so that he could cross over her to his window seat.

"I don't understand, Mr. Hunnewell. Why should our being either genteel or Christian prevent us from discerning the truth?"

Mr. Hunnewell, having no ready answer, began to formulate one when Hattie continued, "I myself am ashamed of having so easily dismissed Mr. Adams's accusations of railroad corruption."

"Where, pray, did you read that?" Mr. Hunnewell looked alarmed. "Not *Peterson's*, surely?"

"*Peterson's*?" Hattie snorted at the reference to a popular ladies' magazine. "No, I chanced upon it in an issue of the *North American Review*. Papa gets quite a lot of subscriptions, and I enjoy—" She interrupted herself. "Well, anyway, I suppose I had no *wish* to know. But isn't that the way one always is, when one profits from a situation?"

Mr. Hunnewell now looked as if he were about to breathe fire in Hattie's direction. "Once more, Miss Eames, as your surrogate parent on this trip, I believe you will do well not to meddle in areas you can't know anything about."

"I will know anything I *choose* to know, Mr. Hunnewell," she replied heatedly.

"Hattie!" Julia placed a hand on her arm.

"Well, I *will*," Hattie continued, even as she found herself being nudged out of her seat by Julia.

Back in the Revere, Hattie was surprised to find Louisa.

"The children wished to retire early," Louisa explained, then pursed her lips. "Though I suspect they're playing 'doctor' beneath the bedcovers."

"Ugh. I don't want to know."

"So, from whom did you receive a letter?" Louisa changed the subject.

"Oh, it was from Mr. Durand. Would you like me to read it to you?"

"Yes, please."

Hattie retrieved the letter from her pocket and was about to read it when she said, "Here—you won't get the full effect unless you read it for yourself." She passed Louisa the letter. For several moments, Louisa squinted farsightedly at it:

> My Dearest Miss Eames, or Hattie, as you have said I must call you, though it does feel as if you allow me to take liberties.
>
> I am already late for work because you know how I suffer with these infurnal sentences. But rest assured my anticipation for your arrival and your remainder in California no's know bounds. I can hardly sleep at night for the thought of unteing with you at least. But I must leave off now for fear of saying something foolish.
>
> Your ever faithful Leland

Louisa placed a hand over her mouth to keep from laughing.

"See?" Hattie agreed. "Isn't he just *darling*?"

"He sounds most sincere. But—*unteing* with you at last? I've lost his meaning."

"I believe he meant to write 'uniting.'"

"Oh." Louisa glanced at Hattie and let out an involuntary snort.

Hattie frowned and tucked her letter back into her trouser pocket. She suddenly felt like a mother who, lovingly mocking her own child, would not tolerate his being mocked by anyone else.

After this exchange, Hattie made a great show of opening her new copy of the *Trans-Continental* while Louisa endeavored to draw the bright flowers—pink, cornflower blue, and chrome yellow—that she had seen growing alongside the tracks in Burlington.

Soon, Alfred came through the car and made up all the beds with fresh, inviting linens. Hattie bade good evening to Louisa and climbed up into her berth. She took out her *Crofutt's Guide* and began to swat the pages in search of a single infelicitous word. In the morning, she would prove her point to Mr. Hunnewell.

The gaslights dimmed. Holding towels and toothbrushes, the excursionists queued up for the WC. People undressed behind the semiprivacy of their curtains, poking them from within so that the berths looked as if they were possessed by spirits. Finally, everyone began to settle for the night.

Louisa undressed and then lay quietly in the dark. After some time, Hattie thought she could smell a faint, lovely perfume coming from below her.

"You smell good," she whispered.

"You're still awake?" Louisa replied.

"It's not very late. I'll go off for a smoke in a moment. What's that you wear?"

"Oh, something my aunt gave me for my eighteenth birthday. It's called Farina's Eau de Cologne."

"It smells like . . . wildflowers . . . in warm sunlight."

"That's very poetic." After a moment, Louisa added, "Papa was furious. He told me to throw it out."

"But why?"

"He said perfume was a frivolity."

"You didn't, did you? Throw it out?"

"Oh, goodness no."

Then Hattie sighed. "I'm an idiot. Of course you didn't." Then she felt around for her cigarettes and flask, ready to take her last smoke of the day.

"Miss Eames?" Louisa asked.

"Yes?" Hattie was perched on the edge of her berth.

Louisa hesitated. "Why *do* you smoke and drink?"

"Why? I don't really know. Habit, I suppose."

"Do you enjoy it?"

"Would I do it if I didn't enjoy it?"

"You might."

There was an uncomfortable silence, after which Hattie admitted, "I feel—I often feel that I don't fit in. With people, you know."

Silence. Then, "Do you *wish* to fit in?"

"Why, yes. I wish to fit in without—without changing myself."

Louisa laughed, but in her laughter, Hattie heard no trace of unkindness. Still, she felt as if Louisa saw right through her, even in the darkness.

"And what about you?" Hattie asked. "Do you feel you 'fit in'?"

"Me? Not at all. But then, I've been locked away like Rochester's mad wife."

"You seem anything but mad."

"Not my mind. My body."

"I saw you limping, but I didn't know the cause."

There was a silence, after which Louisa said, "Come look."

Hattie hopped down from her berth and pulled the curtains aside so that she could sit beside Louisa. From beneath her cover, Louisa lifted her right leg at the ankle and showed her foot: it was twisted inward like a handlebar, a shrunken appendage, small as a child's.

Hattie exclaimed, "Oh!"

Louisa slid her foot back beneath the cover. "I'm not unsociable by nature, but years of isolation have made me turn to more forgiving companions, such as art. And animals."

Suddenly, Louisa yawned and gave Hattie a shove. "Go now to your vices and let me sleep."

The car grew quiet; here and there, a snort or cough could be heard. Hattie lingered a moment, the better to inhale Louisa's intoxicating eau de cologne. Then she moved unsteadily down the aisle.

In the smoking car, Mr. Crockett was puffing on a cigar and playing cards with some young fellow. There were chips and cards on their table. When he heard Hattie, he looked up warily. She nodded but moved on.

No one was in the barbershop, but in the editorial offices, the editors were hard at work on the morning's paper.

"Evenin', Miss Eames," said Mr. Byrne.

"Evening," she said.

"Still waitin' fer dat introduction!"

"Which introduction is that?"

"You know. The one to your friend. Miss Finch, as is. I have a feeling we've a lot in common."

"Oh?" Hattie asked.

"We're both artists, you see."

Then she shrugged and said, "To varying degrees, I suppose."

Mr. Byrne's ready smile soured; at once, Hattie wondered why she had taken a dislike to him. He was not a good artist, but since when had she cared about that?

Hattie entered the baggage car, closing the door behind her. Then she sat down on a trunk, rolled her cigarette, and smoked between swigs of bourbon.

The sight of Mr. Byrne had put Hattie in a foul mood. But the smell of Louisa did precisely the opposite. She had to admit that she had begun to admire some things about Miss Finch, such as the acuity of her perceptions, which so belied her prim demeanor. Or the way she could sit so still as she gathered her impressions from beyond the window. And how, finally setting pen to paper, she drew without any hesitation at all, her strokes executed with etchinglike precision.

Eventually, Hattie stood up and dusted herself off. By the time she reentered the smoking car, the printers had packed up for the night. Mr. Crockett was gone. When Hattie arrived in the Revere car, it too was dark and silent save for a few flickering gas lamps shining softly behind closed, gently swaying curtains.

She saw the steady rise and fall of Louisa's blanket and once again smelled her intoxicating perfume. Hattie climbed into her berth as quietly as she could, changed into her night shift, and lay down in the darkness. Beneath her, she could feel the train's wheels run rhythmically across the tracks.

Hattie stretched herself out the full length of the bed and then rose onto one elbow to gaze up at the top of the car and through the narrow rectangular skylights: all was black save for the train's own eerie, conical beacon of light. Occasionally, she could see a distant kerosene lamp and, high up, thousands of winking stars.

"So did you have a good smoke?"

Louisa's voice startled her.

"I thought you were asleep."

"I was."

"I'm sorry if I woke you."

"Don't be."

"Well, yes," Hattie answered. "But Creepy Crockett stared at me as I passed him—I wonder who he is? Oh, and Mr. Byrne reminded me to introduce him to you."

"Really? What did you tell him?"

"I told him you didn't have much in common."

"That was not very kind," Louisa replied. "What's more, it may not be true."

"You're right," Hattie admitted, once again taken aback by the ease with which Louisa contradicted her. "I hardly know you, after all."

There was a long silence.

"Louisa?" Hattie said after a while.

"Yes, Miss Eames?"

"Do you feel better now? About bridges, I mean?"

Louisa yawned and said, "Vastly."

In the darkness, Hattie could not tell if Louisa was teasing her. Then the girl added, "No, truly. You've helped me a great deal, Miss Eames. And I would be remiss if I did not thank you for rescuing me from the Ridgewoods last night."

Hattie grinned, unaccountably happy. She suddenly decided that she liked Miss Finch. *My first real friend,* she thought. She had never had a woman friend. She liked Louisa's honesty too, even if it meant that she herself was often to be contradicted.

16

Thursday, May 26, Council Bluffs, 6:00 a.m.

WHEN HATTIE WOKE THE FOLLOWING MORNING, SHE found herself alone in the Revere car. Where was everyone, and so early? It was still dark, though the light of dawn already made the window curtains glow. The train had come to a stop. Disoriented, Hattie glanced at her father's pocket watch, then peered through the window as she searched for a clean tunic. They had arrived in Council Bluffs, Iowa.

Hattie was just pulling her tunic over her head when Alfred entered the car. When he saw Hattie, he squeezed his eyes shut and thrust out his hand. "Oh, so sorry, Miss Eames."

Hattie giggled. "I'm nearly dressed, Alfred. You may come in. I'm late to breakfast, it seems."

"I called and called, Miss Eames," he said plaintively, as if fearful that someone would accuse him of not doing his job. "An' I saw Miss Finch try to shake some life into you. But you was dead to the world." Then he said more cheerfully, "The commissary cars are open this morning. Most folk have already gone. But you'll get something to eat if you hurry." Alfred turned and closed his eyes so that Hattie could pull her tunic down. Then Hattie grabbed her stockings and boots and hopped down into the aisle. From there, she was able to see a large luggage shed, in front of which bundles of feather beds were tied up with blue check.

Red chests, corded with rope, were stacked one upon another, and murderous-looking miners kept a sharp eye on their rifles and bedding.

An emigrant train had pulled in just before them. The women wore calico dresses and bonnets or kerchiefs tied around their heads. Families pushed and shoved their way onto the platform along with pots and pans, crying children, and old people, all quarreling in foreign languages. The baggage men—no Pullman porters here—tossed the emigrants' trunks in the air as if they harbored a personal grudge against them.

"But must they be on the same platform as us?" Hattie heard one excursionist ask her spouse.

"There is only one platform, my dear," replied her husband. "Though I concur, they might have timed things more agreeably."

Hattie checked her father's pocket watch and realized she would miss breakfast if she wasted another moment. She raced off to the St. Cloud in her bare feet. Entering it, she saw Louisa, already sitting with the Ridgewoods, across the aisle in the far corner. Mr. Crockett sat in uncomfortable silence with a father and his son at the table closer to the kitchen. When he saw Hattie, he nodded, and she curtsied fractionally. The porters, now dressed in waiterly white, were already lifting plates from tables and topping up coffee for the lingerers.

Mr. Hunnewell had fortunately gone off, and Julia smiled at Hattie's bare feet.

"You'll be cold," she remarked.

Hattie tucked herself quickly into the booth, but, rather than ringing the service bell, she drew Odysseus over with an eager coffee-pouring motion.

"Here—if you're desperate, have mine," Julia offered. "It's my third cup anyway."

"Oh, aren't you an angel," Hattie said, grasping the proffered cup. It was still quite hot, and though it was sweeter than she took hers, she sipped it gratefully.

"Can you believe we're nearly in Omaha?"

"No," Hattie said. "It's only Thursday, and we're already halfway across the continent."

Odysseus finally reached her.

"I'll have eggs with sausage, a bowl of fruit, and some coffee, please." Then she added, "I'm sorry I'm late, Odysseus."

"It's all right, miss," Odysseus said, one eye twitching involuntarily at Hattie's familiarity. "But we're only serving a Continental breakfast this morning, so's you can make the ferry."

"What does that mean, a 'Continental' breakfast?" Hattie frowned.

"Rolls, pastries, fruit, and boiled eggs, Miss Eames."

"Well, yes. All right."

"Which, miss?"

"I must *choose*?" Hattie looked startled. "Well, all but the rolls, then."

"Coming right up."

Once he had gone, Julia said, "Well, I'm glad to see the train has not altered your appetite. It has mine, alas." Julia placed a hand across her stomach.

"Really?" Hattie asked, reaching for Julia's roll. "May I?"

Julia nodded, and Hattie took an enormous bite of Julia's abandoned roll and washed it down with a mouthful of Julia's coffee.

Just then they heard Mr. Crockett's booming voice shatter the hushed breakfast chatter. Someone must have asked him to keep his voice down, because he cried, "Why in hell should I? Stinking Injuns! Oh, they'll take our guns with a smile, but watch your back. They'll shoot you, slit your throat, and chop your scalp off for good measure! You don't see 'em, but trust me, they're out there." He nodded toward the Missouri River in plain sight beyond the window.

The young man sitting at his table frowned and said, "Oh, do sit down and eat your breakfast, Mr. Crockett."

Then the boy's father stood up too. "Yes, what do you mean by terrifying everyone with your spurious claims?"

"*Spurious*, you say?" Mr. Crockett laughed. Hattie thought he didn't know the meaning of the word. "Why don'tcha ask Mr. Price how *spurious* they are, if you don't believe me?"

Clearly, Mr. Crockett meant to insinuate something, but Hattie could not guess what it was. There had been talk in Boston recently about imminent Indian wars on the plains. Reports of new aggression arrived daily. But before their departure, the Boston Board of Trade had assured everyone that the "Indian problem" was entirely under control by government agents whose sole task was to protect the railroad and its passengers.

And it was true that the excursionists had seen many soldiers, glum and watchful, all along the route.

"Perhaps they fight among each other," the father offered.

"Yes. That too," Mr. Crockett replied. "But it's *us* they're all after."

Finally, Hattie stood up. She had had enough of Crockett and his fearmongering. Was he looking to sell them all insurance too?

"I do hope that's the royal 'we' you're using, Mr. Crockett."

Mr. Crockett barely had time to comprehend Hattie's insult when Mr. Price entered the car. Following directly behind him was his vice president, Mr. Bliss, another well-known UPRR stockholder.

"What's going on?" Mr. Price scowled at Hattie. Then he gestured for Mr. Crockett to follow him. Mr. Crockett hesitated, which gave Hattie the opening she needed.

"Mr. Price, who is this loudmouth, and what on earth is he doing aboard our train?"

A look of disbelief spread across Mr. Price's face, and undoubtedly only the fear of offending Congressman Eames prevented a ruder reply than he gave. "You needn't concern yourself with him, Miss Eames. He's an old acquaintance, and he has done much for the Union Pacific." Once more, he indicated for Mr. Crockett to follow him. Mr. Crockett angrily pushed his way past those who were standing in the aisle. When he neared Hattie, he loomed so close to her face that she could smell the coffee on his breath.

When Mr. Crockett had gone, Hattie fell into her seat. Louisa rose up from her place with the Ridgewoods and moved to her. Julia stood as well, ready to offer comfort.

"Oh, Miss Eames!" Julia cried, a hand over her heart.

"But you're actually mad!" Louisa added.

"Calm yourselves." Hattie touched their arms. "Mr. Crockett is loudmouthed, but I doubt he's dangerous. Hopefully Mr. Price will send him packing."

"Well, I for one nearly fainted when you spoke back to him," said Julia.

Just then Mrs. Ridgewood came up behind Louisa and tapped her on the shoulder.

"If you would, Miss Finch. Frank needs to use the WC."

Hattie wondered at Mrs. Ridgewood's civility until she realized that she must have considered Julia above her in social standing. Julia was the daughter of Boston's most prominent philanthropist, possessed of an estate known throughout America. Whereas the Ridgewoods, from what Hattie had heard, were merely wealthy—and new wealth at that.

Louisa looked sad to leave them. Then she suddenly brightened. "Oh, but look, Hattie, your breakfast!" Odysseus was heading up the aisle with a laden silver tray.

"At *last*!" Hattie said cheerfully, and proceeded to dig in.

17

Council Bluffs, 7:00 a.m.

IT WAS TIME TO BOARD THE COACHES that would take them to the
ferry to cross the Missouri River into Omaha. In the Revere car, Alfred
had climbed up onto a foot box with a dusting cloth and begun to clean
one of the hanging lamps.

Hattie remarked, "Alfred, I saw you clean that quite recently."

"Oh, we gotta clean 'em every day, Miss Eames."

"But what if they're not dirty?"

"Everything on this train be dirty after two minutes. But even if
they weren't, we clean 'em jus' the same. There'll be hell to pay otherwise, Miss Eames."

"I think this Hell fellow has grown quite rich off your labors,
Alfred."

"Miss?"

But Hattie just laughed and waved goodbye, touched that Alfred
had felt he might speak to her in his natural, unscripted voice. He
resumed his polishing, and she descended the train, then climbed up
into one of the coaches. Hattie looked about her. Rolling prairie had
given way to low bluffs—steep, brown, and infinitely wild. Off to the
left, upon a quiet little lake, floated a flock of wild ducks; swamp-fire

willow set the banks aglow, and herds of cattle and wild horses grazed peacefully.

Once at the river, the excursionists boarded two high-pressure steamboats. They cut so quickly across the water that some excursionists shrieked, thinking that the boats would run aground. Hattie wondered why they weren't able to remain on the train as they had in Detroit. The Missouri was the only river, as far as Hattie knew, that they would cross while not in the train itself. She thought it must have been an old bridge, not fit for the massive weight of Pullman's train. As they crossed the muddy, churning Missouri, someone cried, "Oh, look!"

Set against a dark forest and upon a hill, Omaha's capitol dome shone brightly.

The first stop on their tour of Omaha was at the machine shops and roundhouse of the Union Pacific Railroad. Hattie was impressed by the shops, but Louisa seemed bored. Mr. Crockett must have been spoken to in no uncertain terms, because he was meek as a lamb the entire morning. Still, he kept glancing at the other excursionists, eager to find someone to talk to. Finally, he blurted, "Well, I'll be damned! Would you look at that blacksmith shop!"

Hattie turned to Louisa and asked, "Why can he not just *shut up*?"

"I suppose some people aren't content unless they're the center of attention."

"Have you noticed that he smells of peppermint?"

"No. I've fortunately not placed myself so close to him."

"What could it be, do you think?"

"Hair oil?" Louisa guessed. "Perhaps a miracle growth tonic."

The young women looked at each other and laughed. Hattie stepped closer to Louisa, the better to smell the traces of her perfume. Then she said, "Well, but Mr. Crockett is right. These shops are most extraordinary."

Louisa yawned even as she nodded her agreement. "Most extraordinary," she said.

From the railroad workshops, the excursionists were taken by special train to the city center, where forty fine carriages, pulled by sleek horses, awaited them. In stark contrast, men in alligator boots and loose overcoats made of blankets, with wild, unkempt hair and beards, stared at them suspiciously, as if every excursionist were an adversary.

Seeing the carriages, Louisa said excitedly, "Come. Let's make sure we get places beside one another."

But Hattie hesitated for so long that Louisa winced.

"No, it's just that I—" Hattie stopped midsentence as the Ridgewood family surrounded Louisa and carried her off to one of the carriages. Mr. Ridgewood helped Louisa up, and they were soon rolling away from the depot, Louisa looking back at Hattie forlornly.

Hattie was dismayed that she had not had the chance to disabuse Louisa of her misunderstanding. She had no patience to sit with others in a carriage, to be told what to find worth observing. But she suffered to think that Louisa had thought Hattie indifferent to *her*.

Hattie made her way up Farnam Street toward Capitol Hill. She reached the summit after ten minutes, out of breath. She was rewarded with an inspiring view of the entire Missouri Valley and of Omaha City, nestled at the base of the hill. Beyond, the river rushed along the green bluffs of Iowa.

Hattie soon set off back down the hill, making her way to the Cozzens House Hotel. She sat at a table in the lobby. While she waited, she procured paper from the concierge and proceeded to compose two telegrams, one to her father and the other to Mr. Durand.

She had just begun the second telegram when Louisa Finch walked in holding a large bouquet of prairie flowers. Framed by the doorway, she looked like a work of art: her cheeks and neck were flushed from the outdoors, and her green eyes shone with delight at the sight of Hattie and then at the gemlike bouquet of purple phlox, larkspur, and green-gray spiderwort in her clasped hands.

"Here. I'm sorry." Louisa proffered the bouquet.

"Sorry? What for?" Hattie took the flowers and looked up at Louisa. She had no feelings either for or against cut flowers, but she was moved almost to tears that Louisa had thought to pick them for her.

"I'm afraid I was peevish with you when you wouldn't ride with me."

"Peevish? Not at all! It was I who felt badly for not explaining myself properly. I've always disliked tours of any kind . . ."

"I know." Louisa smirked. "It took me but a moment to remember Chicago, but by then we had already departed."

"They're *beautiful*, Louisa," Hattie said. To hide her tears of happiness, she went to procure a vase. The concierge gave her one—she thought he would have given her a grand piano, had she requested one. Then the maître d' picked up the vase and led them to a table in the dining room.

The women sat facing one another. Hattie was suddenly aware of feeling nervous. She looked down at the place setting and, for something to do, took a sip from her glass. The water was chilled, fresh, and very clear. Observing the glass from all angles, she asked, "So, what did you do this past hour?"

Louisa removed her sunbonnet and set it upon the carpet beside her. "They took us across the prairie, to a farm whose owner allowed us to pick what flowers we chose. Our carriages were pulled by very fine horses, as you saw. Well treated too, by the looks of them."

Just then a crowd of excursionists noisily entered the dining room. Many glanced enviously at the girls, who had procured the last free table. While they waited to be seated, the excursionists commented upon the hotel as if no one overheard them:

"Oh, would you look at this tin ceiling?"

"The curtains are very fine."

"A bit worn, though."

"I do hope they have good steak."

"*Crofutt's* says they do."

Hattie looked about the room. "By the way. How on earth did you escape the clutches of the Ridgewoods?"

Louisa was about to reply when the Ridgewoods entered, as if her words had conjured them. Spotting Louisa, Mrs. Ridgewood cried, "Lou-*eeza*! There you are!"

Louisa sighed and reached to take up the vase of flowers, but Hattie forestalled her. "Go on, sit with them. I'll take the flowers back with me. You know the children would only find a way to break the vase."

"All right. Thank you."

Once Louisa had left, Hattie devoured a massive steak, cooked just the way it should be: charred on the outside but rare within. As she was sipping the last of her coffee, Mr. Price appeared in the entrance to the dining room and said, "Ten minutes, ladies and gentlemen. Our carriages await."

Hattie paid her bill. Then, stopping first to reassure herself that her father's billfold was safely returned to her pocket, she moved around the side of the building to have a smoke. She enjoyed her cigarette and the odd elation that had come upon her after reconciling with Louisa. She stubbed out her cigarette with her toe and walked quickly to the train, arriving just as the carriages carrying the excursionists pulled up.

Hattie shouldered her way through the crowd and back to her seat in the Revere car. She had just realized that she had forgotten to post her telegrams when a post boy made his way through the aisles, crying, "Letters and telegrams! Post 'em here!" A whispering titter became audible and grew louder. Hattie looked out the window to see what was causing it.

Standing apart from the crowd on the depot platform was an old Indian woman. She was so still that at first, Harriet thought she wasn't real but a statue of some sort. Wax, perhaps. Her back was bent, and at her breastbone she clutched a red wool blanket that hung nearly to her ankles. Her hair, thinning and gray on top, had no part but receded like that of an old man's. On either side of her head, behind pierced and sagging ears, dangled two long pigtails bound in strips of buffalo hide.

Hattie could not tear her eyes from the woman's face, even when she felt Louisa's presence behind her: its oily dark skin, eyes obscured by a triple swag of pockets, crow's feet nearly to the ears, a prominent brow, and a mouth whose lips pursed together in a smile that bore no relation to happiness.

Several children heckled her through the open windows.

"Are you a good squaw?"

"Good Indian want money?"

"Have papoose?" one young man who might have been David cried. This made the other hecklers roar with laughter, for the woman was seventy if she was a day.

Mr. Crockett suddenly appeared among the hecklers and crooned gleefully, "I sure hope not! Nits make lice!"

"What does he mean?" Louisa asked.

Mr. Hunnewell, passing through the car at that moment, stopped to explain. "He means that one needs to exterminate the children too. They breed, you see. Colonel Chivington, who led the infamous attack upon the peaceful Cheyenne at Sand Creek, was vastly fond of that saying."

With a look of horror, Louisa exclaimed, "But she's an old woman!"

Mr. Hunnewell offered his open palms and shrugged, as if to say, *I'm only the messenger.*

Then Louisa asked Hattie, "Why does she just stand there like that?"

"I'm not sure," Hattie replied, "but I think she's waiting for permission to come aboard."

"Well, why don't they give it, then, instead of making her stand there to suffer such ridicule?"

"I imagine the railroad lets the Indians ride the rails to keep the peace, but that doesn't mean they *like* it."

"People are so cruel." Then, without another word, Louisa sat down, took out her sketchbook, and began to draw the old woman. At the same moment, Mr. Byrne, seized with his own artistic inspiration, hurriedly descended the train with his easel, exclaiming, "Now, won't this make a fine picture for our next issue!"

Suddenly, Hattie felt something she rarely felt: shame. Ashamed to be among these excursionists. Her father had taught her to care about those less fortunate than they, and this conduct was most unbecoming for members of her class. For any class, really.

Louisa sketched the woman as if her fingers were connected to that pitiful being by a fine silk filament.

A gust of wind lifted a wisp of the old woman's hair, but she didn't reach up to adjust it. For five minutes, she continued to stand there, buffeted by the sudden, fierce gusts of wind.

At last, Mr. Straight finally approached the old woman. He tapped her roughly on the back and stuck his thumb out in the direction of the baggage car. Then he turned away with a scowl, as if he had allowed many such Indians to board the train but would never grow to like it.

Mr. Byrne, lugging his easel under one arm, triumphantly boarded as well; he shared his sketch with those who were only too eager to see it and laugh.

Hattie took a brief glance as he proffered it to her: she started back at once. What a vulgar caricature! The woman's nose had been enlarged, her gray hair made even more gray and disarrayed.

Hattie then glanced at Louisa's sketch; it was a far truer likeness. And far more generous.

"But what have you drawn there, about the mouth?" Hattie asked her.

"Oh." Louisa half smiled. "Well, I see kindness in the midst of resignation."

"How honest your portrait is," Hattie was moved to say. "How I pity her!"

Louisa nodded, seeming miles away. "I feel I *am* her," she replied.

18

Leaving Omaha, 5:00 p.m.

THE TRAIN FINALLY SET OFF TOWARD THE giant red fireball that hovered above the horizon. It was impossible to read, and Hattie could do little besides gaze out the right side of the train, away from the setting sun. The light grew so bright that many excursionists were obliged to shut their eyes. Some dozed.

Several miles out of Omaha, rich, rolling prairie appeared, like an ocean of grass. Up the valley of the Platte, there were no trees save the occasional cottonwood grove near the river or a newly planted orchard near a farmer's dwelling. They passed several stations with windmills for drawing water.

The Great Plains rolled away on either side, clad in russet and tawny gold. Tender grass and moist black earth were close at hand, behind which, from the south, a wild mass of thunderclouds gathered.

Suddenly, all those on the left of the car moved to peer out at something, and Louisa stood up briefly to see what they looked at: it was the old emigrant track, now overgrown with tall grass. Every several hundred feet, a crooked cross poked up like a strange dwarf tree.

Murmurs of dismay flew through the car: *crosses for the dead! Crosses for the dead!*

"But this sight was not mentioned in *Crofutt's*!" they heard a woman cry.

Louisa said with pity, "Soon they shall all be concealed by the prairie, poor souls."

After leaving the crosses behind, the excursionists quieted. The sun descended upon the roaming cattle, the sod houses, and the tumbledown barns. Clouds of dust made their way through the train's open windows, and so the excursionists became ghostly too, half-hidden in them. Then they passed mountain sheep and antelope with pincerlike horns. Hattie had been on the lookout for buffalo, as Louisa was very keen to see them. But so far, only their bleached white bones shone in the rising moonlight.

When they reached Grand Island, many excursionists descended to stretch their legs. Hattie and Louisa descended as well, choosing an inviting-looking path that led to the river, where they paused upon an old wooden bridge. A mass of swallows, disturbed by the footfalls, swooped up from beneath the bridge with a noisy flutter.

"Oh!" Louisa cried out, shielding her head, thinking at first that they were bats.

Hattie moved closer, as if she would protect Louisa. After a while, she asked, "Did you notice how the others reacted to the crosses upon the old emigrant trail?" In a high-pitched voice like Mrs. Ridgewood's, she mocked, "We'd prefer the first-class landscape, please."

Louisa smiled. After a thoughtful pause, she murmured, "I wonder sometimes why Mrs. Ridgewood is so unhappy."

"I wouldn't waste my curiosity upon her."

They headed back toward the train. About a hundred yards beyond the bridge, in the still, dusky light, Hattie saw a small herd of buffalo. Two dozen or so grazed peacefully, their huge humpback forms easily recognizable. Several calves nuzzled their parents, red fur shining bright as oranges.

"Look, Louisa! Oh, look!" she whispered, hunching down.

When Louisa saw the buffalo, her mouth opened, and she clasped her hands together. Suddenly, they heard the sound of guns cocking through the train's open windows. The girls watched in horror as half a dozen men opened their windows and began shooting. At the first deafening crack, the buffalo began to run.

"Stop!" Hattie cried, and ran toward the Palmyra car. There and elsewhere throughout the train, the men kept shooting. Their wives stared out the windows at Hattie as she ran toward the train, waving wildly.

Louisa had turned away and covered her ears, and her eyes held tears. Hattie finally entered the Palmyra and moved towards several of the men, who were kneeling upon the seats and steadying their rifles upon the windowsills. She began to pull at their elbows, sending their shots into the air, once or twice even risking the bullets hitting the excursionists themselves.

Mr. Straight finally came barreling down the aisles, pushing everyone out of the way. "Halt! Stop shooting!" The poor man was red in the face and looked as if he might collapse. Then he fairly gasped to the stragglers outside, "All aboard!" and signaled his engine man to blow the whistle.

Once the train began to move, the conductor lit into the men. "We stop for shooting only at designated places. It is prohibited to shoot wherever you please! Do you want to kill somebody?"

Mr. Crockett lowered his gun and said, "I thought that was why we all paid a fortune for this excursion. So we could do what we pleased, when we pleased to do it."

"I doubt *he* paid a penny to come aboard," Hattie said, loudly enough for everyone to hear.

Mr. Straight sent Hattie a baleful glance before pointing to Crockett and saying, "Not another word, y'hear?" Then he moved into the next car.

Fortunately, the train had picked up speed and moved on. The buffalo had dispersed, but through the windows on the left side of the train, the women saw one calf, mortally wounded. It lay on its side, its legs twitching in the dust. As the train pulled away, Hattie saw one of the adult buffalo amble up to it and prod it to get up.

Louisa and Hattie returned to their seats in the Revere, and Louisa sat down heavily, ignoring Mrs. Ridgewood's calls. Hattie sat down next to her.

"It's too terrible," Louisa said. She buried her head in Hattie's breast and cried.

"Who was it?" Hattie growled. But though she glared at them all, she couldn't tell who had fired the fatal shot. She heard the sound of laughter from the few men who were still awake, enjoying the recollection of their hunt.

"I got 'im."

"No, that was my shot. Dead-on."

Louisa was in no condition to tend to the children or their nightly ablutions, and Hattie procured some hot tea from Alfred. On the tray, he had thoughtfully placed a small bottle of laudanum.

"Thank you," Hattie said. "That's very kind." She stirred a scant teaspoon of the colorless liquid into Louisa's tea, and Louisa was finally able to rest. She faced the window, knees drawn up, and Hattie placed a blanket over her up to her shoulders. Her breathing gradually slowed and deepened.

Hattie had begun to understand Louisa's love of animals. Indeed, Louisa now seemed to her more animal than human: in her sensitivity to movement, her keen sight, and in what Hattie perceived as a preternatural alertness to danger. Her rage grew as she felt, rather than understood, the depths of Louisa's suffering. It worked its way up to her throat just as Mrs. Ridgewood approached Louisa's berth and cried, "But what does she do, sleeping like this before the sun has even set?"

Hattie hissed at her. "Go away, Mrs. Ridgewood."

Seeing Hattie's mad eyes, Mrs. Ridgewood returned to her seat without daring to say another word.

Night soon descended, and many excursionists retired early. Hattie sat upon Louisa's bed. She placed a hand on the girl's blanketed hip and focused on the rise and fall of Louisa's breath. She breathed in, hoping to catch her perfume, but it was gone.

Hours later, after all the excursionists had gone to sleep, Louisa suddenly sat up, nearly cracking her head on the berth above.

"But have they called for me? They must have." She made as if she would rise to tend the children, but Hattie, who had been sitting there, staring into the darkness with uncustomary patience, stopped her.

"It's nearly midnight, Lou." The car was dark and silent. Out of the left side of the train, a half-moon shone bright and clear. "Everyone's asleep."

Louisa, waking more fully, glanced at Hattie. "What did you say to Mrs. Ridgewood?"

"Say? Why, nothing."

"Liar," she said. "Very well, but why aren't you in bed yourself?"

"I'm not sleepy."

"You stand guard, like Cerberus."

"Cerberus? Certainly not. I have but one head. I'll just go have a smoke and then turn in."

"A smoke and a nip from your flask, you mean," Louisa replied.

"There's little pleasure in having one without the other."

"Oh, go on." A small smile finally appeared at one corner of Louisa's mouth, and she pushed Hattie off the bed, a gesture she had begun to take pleasure in. "Enjoy your sins. But you must know, I dislike the smell of them."

Rather than take offense, Hattie felt oddly encouraged. She reached up to her berth and found her flask, her tobacco pouch, the tin of chewing tobacco, and a box of matches. She made her way through the Arlington and to the smoking car, which now was entirely empty.

The gaslights on the walls flickered dimly; the ceiling lights had been extinguished. After a moment's hesitation, Hattie sat down in one of the plush chairs and simply listened to the sound of the train *chukka-chukka* across the tracks. *Inexorable,* she thought.

Hattie removed her flask and took a sip; the burning heat traveled down her gullet, setting off a flare in her belly. She stared out the window: all without was darkness now, punctuated only by the lamps from within the occasional farm.

Hattie removed her tobacco from its pouch and rolled a cigarette. She had just put it to her mouth when she thought she heard footsteps and paused, the better to listen. But it was only an excursionist who had wandered out onto the platform of the Arlington car, perhaps to look at the stars. Within a minute, he reentered the car.

Hattie rose with a reluctant sigh. The bourbon had made her sleepy. She moved through the hairdresser's, then the printing office, and finally into the baggage car. She sat down as usual upon one of the trunks. It was dark save for the light of the half-moon that shone through the window. Hattie clasped her cigarette and matches, waiting for her eyes to adjust. When they did, she lit the cigarette and inhaled. The sudden red glow of the cigarette tip seemed to cause an equally sudden shuffling noise. Then one of the trunks budged, and Harriet exclaimed, "Hello!" She took another hasty puff of her cigarette as something to the side of the trunk flipped one eye open and stared at her. Hattie stared back.

It was the old Indian woman, sitting on her haunches. She must have been squatting there in the cold and dark since they left Omaha. That was nearly a dozen hours ago! In the moonlight, Hattie could now see the shine of the old woman's eyes. She raised the cigarette to her lips, then paused.

"Would you like it?" Hattie extended it toward the squaw.

An ancient hand with impossibly long, curled nails unfolded and then quickly snatched Hattie's hand and brought it to her nose. She smelled the cigarette. She nodded.

"Shall I light it for you?"

The woman extended her ancient hand once more, this time wanting the matches. Hattie gave them to her. With a practiced movement, the old squaw lit the cigarette and then inhaled deeply. Her cheeks sucked inward, revealing a toothless cavity for a mouth. She handed Hattie back her box of matches.

Hattie rolled another cigarette for herself, and the two smoked slowly, silently. The old woman puffed away with apparent contentment. Hattie took a swig from her flask. Then, after a moment's hesitation, she offered this to the old woman as well. As she had done with the cigarette, the old woman held the flask and Hattie's hand to her nose. She sniffed, then took the flask from Hattie and drank.

Hattie saw her swallow and lick her toothless gums before handing the flask back.

Hattie said, "I'm headed to Sacramento." Her own voice sounded strange to her in the dark, silent car, lit only by half a moon. "We expect to arrive on Tuesday. Where are you going?"

The old woman took the last puff of her cigarette and extinguished it on the floorboards. She opened her mouth, and Hattie unconsciously drew back as a sound came out.

"*Ogallala.*"

"Oh? I didn't know we stopped there."

The old woman nodded. Then, continuing to examine Hattie, her face cracked into a broad smile that swallowed her eyes in folds of flesh. She pointed at herself and then at Hattie with one long-nailed forefinger. Then she nodded again with deep respect and said, "*Winkdé.*"

"*Winkdé,*" Hattie repeated. She waited, hoping for an explanation. But none came.

"Strong medicine," the old woman added. Then she lowered her head on her folded arms. Very soon, she was asleep.

Hattie sat with her for a while. Then she stood up and began to walk away, when she recalled Louisa's words about disliking the smell of her vices. With a sigh of regret, she set her flask and tobacco pouch beside the old woman and returned to the Revere car empty-handed, casting a single mournful glance behind her.

Much later, before dawn broke, Hattie sat up, threw on her robe, and, in her bare feet and shift, she went to retrieve her beloved sins. But when she reached the baggage car, she found that they, along with the old woman, were gone.

19

Friday, May 27, Julesberg, Nebraska

LOUISA AWOKE WITH A WEDGE OF DAWN coming in through the window across the aisle. She had been dreaming of the Sunday she and her father rode to Manassas. Reverend Finch had been called to a hospital there, and no one was left in Alexandria with whom he could leave his daughter. All the bridges had been blown up, and they had been obliged to ride straight through rivers. All around them, swirling down the currents, floated the bloated bodies of dead horses . . .

Louisa jerked awake just as the train passed the Julesberg depot; at once, she checked above her for Hattie; she wasn't there. Julesberg must have been one of those ghost towns she had heard about. Gazing out her window, she saw no signs of life apart from two rough-looking men who held their cigars with incongruous delicacy, like women holding their lorgnettes at the opera.

Louisa rose quickly, dressed, and stopped for a quick ablution on the way to the St. Cloud car.

"Oh, *there* you are." Louisa smiled, seeing Hattie sitting next to Mrs. Lovelace. This time, unlike in Chicago, Louisa made no effort to hide her relief. As it happened, there was a free seat next to Hattie, Mrs. Lovelace, and David, and Louisa sat down in it. She looked around her, but as of yet, the Ridgewoods had not made their way to breakfast.

"Our excursionists are bristling with news this morning, Louisa," Hattie said by way of greeting. "Apparently, a party of one hundred Shoshone Indians, dressed in war paint, crossed the tracks at Ogalalla last night."

"What if they mean to attack us?" Mrs. Lovelace said tremulously.

David rolled his eyes. "You might sing to them, Mother. That should scare them away."

Mrs. Lovelace frowned and waved a hand in vexation. "I fear they'll kill every last one of us. Ravage us first, no doubt."

Mr. Crockett, who happened to be sitting across the aisle from them, hollered in a bemused tone, "Don't think you've got much to worry about, Mrs. Lovelace!"

"Oh, do be quiet, Mr. Crockett," Hattie spat.

"Or what?" Mr. Crockett challenged, rising from his seat.

But before Hattie needed to defend herself physically, Mr. Price entered the car.

"All right, now, what's all this about? Is it about the *Shoshone?*" His voice was conciliatory, like a husband calming a fretful wife. "The Shoshone have no interest in us. I've received word from the mayor of North Platte that they attacked a band of Paiute last night."

"Hallelujah!" Mr. Crockett cried. "They're killing each other. Saves us the price of bullets!"

Mystery solved, the excursionists returned to their breakfasts. But Mrs. Lovelace whispered to Hattie and Louisa, "You know, I'm not sure I believe a single word these gentlemen say."

"Oh yes, you know better, Mum," David said, dripping sarcasm.

"Why don't you just shut your trap, David?"

A wave of shock at Hattie's rudeness silenced them just as Mrs. Ridgewood approached.

"Louisa, please fetch some hot water and the Black Drop from my bag. Frank came down with a cold during the night."

Hattie recalled her mother giving her Black Drop on at least one occasion. It was a sweet, syrupy concoction that put her into a stupor almost instantaneously.

"And please notify Mr. Ridgewood that Frank is *quite* ill."

Hattie whispered to Louisa, "She behaves as if the child has typhus."

Louisa turned her face away to keep from laughing. Then she replied, "Yes, ma'am. At once." She stood up and went off to do her mistress's bidding.

The porters were still making up the beds, and many people, Hattie included, chose to remain in the commissary cars, sipping their coffee, conversing quietly, or reading the new edition of the *Trans-Continental*. Hattie gazed out the window, thinking about the old Indian woman and what she had said to her. Try as she might, she could not figure out what it meant.

Meanwhile, Mrs. Lovelace and her son excused themselves, David glancing through narrow lizard eyes at Hattie, who smiled falsely at him. As she stood up to let David pass, Hattie was surprised to find Mr. Hunnewell and Julia in the very next row.

"May I join you?" she asked.

"Of course!" Julia smiled up at her.

When Louisa returned ten minutes later, she took the fourth seat. Then she turned to Hattie and asked, "What happened last night? I don't believe you slept."

"I did—a few hours anyway," Hattie admitted. Then she said mournfully, "I gave up smoking and drink."

Mr. Hunnewell grew still behind his paper, and Julia ceased counting her knits and purls. But Hattie didn't mind if they listened.

"Did it take you all night to give them up or to indulge in them?" Louisa asked.

"I indulged them, and then I gave them up. I never said I was a saint."

"Well, no wonder your eyelids are purple."

"But the strangest thing happened—"

Suddenly, Sheila appeared. She grabbed Louisa's hand and began to pull. "Come play old maid with me!"

"Excuse me," Louisa said.

Once Louisa had gone off, Hattie addressed Julia. "Do you remember the old Indian woman on the platform, the one everyone teased?"

"Of course."

"Well, she was in the baggage car last night. I nearly died of fright."

"Did you speak to her?" Julia asked excitedly. "Did she say anything?"

"I offered her a cigarette and a sip of my bourbon. She said she was getting off in Ogallala. Well, she said 'Ogallala,' anyway."

Julia shivered. "Goodness! I don't know if I'd have been brave enough to stay in there with her."

"Oh, she was quite harmless. But then she did say something that puzzled me a great deal."

"Indeed?"

"She looked at me, pointed to herself and then to me, and said, '*Winkdé.*'"

"*Winkdé?*" Julia repeated. The word meant nothing to her.

"I wonder what it means. You should've seen the way she stared at me!"

"Why, I—"

"Two Spirits," Mr. Hunnewell interrupted. Then his long, solemn face appeared from behind the paper. "Fortunately, I recently read a narrative of the great geographer Mr. David Thompson, in which he recounts several stories of those who call themselves *Winkdé*, or Two Spirits."

"But what does it *mean?*" Hattie pressed. "My father says you're an Indian expert."

"Somewhat, somewhat," he demurred. "But to your question."

Here, Mr. Hunnewell set his paper down and crossed his long, thin legs. "The concept of two-spiritedness is not easy to comprehend and is perhaps too sensitive for ladies' ears."

"Father," Julia said, frowning. "We're not so delicate as you think. We shan't collapse."

"Besides," Hattie added, "it's not fair to reveal half the story and leave us in the dark as to the rest."

"Very well." He sighed and pursed his lips. "*Winkdé* is a Lakota word, though different tribes have different names for it. It is the name they give to someone who feels, who is . . ." He opened his hands.

"Who is?" Julia encouraged him.

"Who feels himself to be both man *and* woman. Not merely physically but spiritually, as it were. These plains Indians whose land we now traverse take the view that there exist at least four genders: Men, men-women, women-men, and women."

Here, Mr. Hunnewell paused, the better to give the young women's minds time to catch up.

"And . . . how do they feel about these 'Two Spirits'?" Hattie asked, all ears. "Are they shunned? They certainly would be in our society."

"Quite the contrary," Mr. Hunnewell replied, happy to display his secondhand expertise. "Two-spirited beings are thought to be uniquely endowed by the Great Creator, and they're held in the highest esteem. Some are clairvoyant as well. At least, that's what the Lakota and other tribes believe."

Hattie began to ask another question when Julia, to her surprise, abruptly ended the discussion by saying, "Thank you very much, Father," and returned to her knitting.

Hattie was disappointed, for she very much would have liked to continue the discussion. She didn't understand what had made Julia cut her father off, except perhaps to spare Hattie discomfort. But why should she think so? At once, Hattie excused herself and made her way to the washroom, where she distractedly removed her clothing and sat naked on the toilet hole. Then she poured a cup of lukewarm water from the spigot onto her head.

A paper-thin bar of soap hung from a slimy rope. Hattie grasped it and, leaning over, viciously scrubbed her scalp and long hair. Then she poured more lukewarm water over herself, stood up, shook herself like a wet dog, and toweled herself dry. Suddenly, she realized that she had no fresh clothing to change into. "Oh, for pity's sake!"

Hattie opened the bathroom door a crack and peered out. Alfred had nearly finished folding up the beds in the Revere car. Most of the excursionists had now returned from breakfast, but there was nothing to be done: Hattie squeezed the last drop of water from her hair, wrapped the grimy communal towel about her body, threw open the door, and streaked down the aisle.

She leaped up into her berth and closed the curtains. Only then did she realize that she had left her dirty clothes in the bathroom and that her clean clothing was beneath Louisa's berth. "Oh, *hell*."

"Miss Eames?" Alfred stood below her berth. Hattie peeked out of the curtains, holding them beneath her chin like the strap of a bonnet. His mild, curious face was directly in front of her.

"Oh, Alfred." She sighed. "Would you mind handing me that big bag beneath the lower berth? Yes, just there. And could you leave my bed unmade for a few hours? I hardly slept a wink last night."

Alfred glanced worriedly at the lower berth, concerned for Miss Finch.

"Miss Finch won't mind a bit," Hattie said, reading his mind. "The children keep her captive—why, I doubt she'll return before we reach Cheyenne."

"Very well, Miss Eames." Then Alfred added, "Allow me to shut this curtain." He reached over and shut the curtain of the window across from Hattie's berth, which then became enveloped in soothing shadow.

"That's marvelous. Thanks, thanks a lot, Alfred."

Hattie lay back and shut her eyes with a sigh, placing her tunic across her eyes. Almost immediately, she fell into a deep, dreamless sleep.

She remained in oblivion for some undetermined time before someone woke her with a cry: "Look! Longs Peak!"

20

Friday, May 27, Cheyenne, noon

THE PULLMAN HOTEL EXPRESS PASSED THROUGH THE outskirts of a village composed of primitive huts and tents. The train slowed, and soon Hattie could hear the sounds of a regimental band, so unreal in the wilderness surrounding them that Hattie thought she dreamed it. Far off to the south, the crest of Longs Peak was robed in snow.

They were at Cheyenne.

At the depot, a huge crowd elbowed each other to catch sight of the train. Soldiers stood with an alert and disapproving air, in slouched hats and villains' mustaches. Across their chests, wide belts of bullet cartridges, double-bladed knives, and clanging sabers were slung. Hattie thought the soldiers looked very much like the miners back in Omaha.

Beyond them, an array of bold black-and-white store signs competed for attention: BILLIARD ROOM, said one. SAMPLE ROOM, read another. MEALS FOR 50 CENTS. In case the signs weren't compelling enough, by each open door, a boy or woman clanged a bell.

As Hattie descended the train, she saw the foothills of the Rockies beyond the town, and a thrill went through her. Standing on a wooden platform and surrounded by a huge crowd, the governor of Wyoming Territory began to speak sonorous words of welcome. When Hattie saw

Louisa across the crowd, her heart kicked with delight, and she let out an indecorous four-fingered whistle.

Louisa grinned and slowly, painfully, wended her way toward Hattie. On the train, it was easy to forget that she was an invalid. But not here on the long, broad streets of Cheyenne.

Together, and with the governor still speaking, they set off down Main Street. Hattie noticed that the streets of the town all formed neat right angles, and several brick buildings lent an air of permanence, unlike the many shanty towns they had passed. They walked by a jewelry store with a splendid display of moss agates in the window. These were milky white stones with veins of yellow and gray. Trapped within the stone, feathery green patterns resembled tiny ferns or seaweed.

"How beautiful these are," Louisa remarked. "They must be thousands of years old."

"Millions, actually," Hattie corrected her. "Moss agate is a kind of volcanic rock, much of which was formed around—"

"But I don't like the ornate settings at all, do you? They gild the lily."

"Gild the moss, you mean." Hattie smiled, proud of her joke. But Louisa sighed, apparently weary of Hattie's constant cleverness, and Hattie felt chastened.

After walking another block, they came across two boys selling prairie dogs. One boy was older than the other, perhaps twelve. The younger one could not have been more than eight. Louisa bent down to look at the little creatures. Near a dozen prairie dogs were all crowded into a single crate. They darted back and forth, looking for a way out, chirping madly.

"Oh, look at them, Hattie," Louisa said plaintively, grasping the bars of the crate.

"Don't put your finger in there, Louisa," Hattie warned.

"Why, you think they'll bite? They wouldn't bite me."

"Well, by all means, do so, if you wish to avoid your servitude with the Ridgewoods."

Louisa cast Hattie an arch look, then asked the older boy, "How much for them?"

"For one, miss?"

"No, I mean for all of them."

"I don't have crates for all of 'em. Not just *now*, miss," he added, as if he were a true businessman.

"But how much anyway? I'm not a wealthy woman either, mind you. I'm just a nanny."

The little boy whispered into the ear of his larger companion.

"Five dollars."

"Five dollars!" Louisa laughed. "You must be mad. Have you food for them?"

The boys shook their heads as if it was the first time they'd thought of giving the animals food.

"Louisa." Hattie frowned. "What will you do with all those prairie dogs?" She was impatient to keep moving.

"All right. Four," the boy said, ignoring Hattie.

"One dollar," Louisa replied. "And that's my best offer. I've only got five to my name."

The boys assented and began to haul the crate toward the train when Louisa stopped them. "Oh, no. Would you just keep them where they are for a few minutes? We want to see the rest of the town."

The older boy scowled. "We ain't waitin' here all day!"

The younger boy poked him. "Not much to the rest of the town," he said.

"We'll only be a few minutes." Louisa handed him fifty cents and said they'd get the rest of the money when she returned. The older one shrugged, lit a cigarette, and threw the match onto the ground, grinding it deep into the soil with the tip of his thick-soled shoe.

"Well," Harriet said once they'd moved on. "That was interesting. How do you plan to feed them, I wonder? Or do you plan to let them loose to feast on the excursionists? I expect they'll make an insipid meal."

Louisa smiled but merely asked, "Where are you taking us, Harriet?"

"Nowhere in particular. Just having a look around."

"But what if the train leaves without us?"

"Oh, those men shall go on and on, congratulating each other. We have half an hour at least, I'd wager."

"If you think so," Louisa said uncertainly.

Beyond the downtown area, the streets became rougher and narrower. Hattie stopped to pick up something that glinted in the sun. "Look." She showed Louisa.

"What is it?" Louisa peered down at the small brass cylinder.

"A shell casing."

Louisa frowned. "Throw it away."

Hattie did, and they continued on, stepping over broken beer bottles and other refuse until Louisa placed her gloved hand on Hattie's arm. "Let's go back. This place gives me the shivers."

"Why, there's nothing here anymore. It's abandoned. Or rather, some group of people has abandoned it."

"Perhaps. But the spirit—the violence—it's still here. I can feel it. Besides," Louisa said, turning back, "I don't trust those boys not to take my fifty cents and bolt."

"I still don't see how you plan to—"

Hattie broke off when she saw, just off to the left in a narrow alley, something hanging from a branch, twisting in the wind that blew between the buildings.

It was a noose, dangling several feet off the ground. Beyond it lay a tall, thick slab of tree trunk that must have served as a platform by which the condemned met his Maker.

Hattie slowly approached the object, but Louisa pulled at her sleeve.

"The sight gives me such a bad feeling. It's a bad omen," Louisa said, unconsciously placing a hand upon her neck.

"Come away, Lou," said Hattie. "Let's go get your prairie dogs."

The boys were still there when they returned, though Hattie and Louisa received no greeting. The younger one merely stuck out his hand, palm up.

Louisa placed two quarters on his dirty palm. Then she looked at the young boy with a kind of stern tenderness.

"It is very wrong to cage and sell these animals as you do," she said.

"Huh?" The small boy screwed one eye shut. "No it ain't. Why, did you see bear they got over at Laramie? They got a big black one an' charge a nickel to see it too!"

"Go on home," Louisa replied. "Shoo!" She jolted after them in her black boot, which frightened them off better than any words could. Then Louisa turned to Hattie and said, "Help me with this crate, if you would."

Hattie sighed, lifted one end of the crate, and began to move toward the train when Louisa stopped her. "No, no, Harriet. Over there." She pointed with her chin to a field just behind a group of houses.

They dragged the crate some distance and then set it down, whereupon Louisa knelt and undid the lid. "All right, my beauties. Off you go."

At first, the prairie dogs merely craned their necks and pawed the sides of the crate. Then a few brave ones leaped out and scurried off at once. But one, a small young dog, actually climbed in Louisa's lap and curled up there. Louisa sucked in her breath and remained very still until the prairie dog, realizing that Louisa was not a nest, leaped off and scampered away.

Slowly, Louisa stood and dusted herself off.

Hattie didn't know whether to laugh or cry. She remarked merely, "I fear you're too good for this world, Louisa."

• • •

Many of the excursionists had already boarded when the two women finally returned to the train. Hattie went off to the washroom. While she was gone, Mr. Straight came down the aisles handing out telegrams, which had been given to him by the Cheyenne depot's telegraph operator. He handed one to Louisa. It was from her father. She had not expected anything from him so soon, and she tore it open at once.

Dear Daughter,
Hope trip goes well. I have found employment.
Should Ridgewoods situation not suit, make free to
come home. Send word.
Your father

When Louisa saw Hattie coming down the aisle, she stuffed the letter into her pocket.

Hattie noticed the gesture and, wiping her wet hands on her trousers, asked, "What was that?"

"Oh, just—"

But Hattie had already shifted her attention to the new edition of the *Trans-Continental*, which lay faceup on her seat. On first glance, it varied little from the first edition, save for one headline, which read in bold lettering, CHICAGO'S WELCOME. Hattie sat down and opened its pages with a smirk.

"Let's see. What great insights do they have for us today?" Hattie asked aloud. She read quickly, turning the pages in her customary manner by giving each page a quick swat. After a few minutes, she set the paper down and smiled. "All right, Louisa. Here's a good one for you. Why is a madman like two men?"

Louisa saw the mischievous gleam in Hattie's eyes, and she suddenly knew the answer. Not to Hattie's riddle but to the question of why she had balked at sharing her father's letter.

"Why?" she asked, looking at Hattie, so smug in her certainty that Louisa would never guess.

"He is a man beside himself. *Beside* himself. Get it?"

Louisa endeavored to look amused. But her sudden understanding coincided only uneasily with Hattie's gay mood. The truth was, she had no wish to leave this train. Even though her situation was appalling, someone made it worthwhile. And that someone was sitting right next to her. A corner of Louisa's mouth crept into a half smile. But Hattie, glancing at her, slapped the paper with exasperation. "Oh, but you're *very* dull today, Miss Finch!"

21

Friday, May 27, west of Cheyenne

IT WAS NEARLY SUNSET WHEN THEY BEGAN to ascend the Rocky Mountains. They had taken on a second engine in Cheyenne, and the throbbing puffs of the two engines sounded like giant creatures gasping for breath. West of Cheyenne, the landscape was eerie, grim: only the fantastical rock formations broke the dusty desolation. Louisa looked out the window as the tracks ascended ever more steeply to Sherman, the summit of the Rockies. Mrs. Ridgewood called to her.

"The children would like you to read them a story."

Louisa murmured to Hattie, "Look how the clouds change below us, like meadow mists."

But Hattie was reading about Sherman in her *Crofutt's Guide* and didn't notice when Louisa rose and left with Mrs. Ridgewood.

Although the plateau is covered with grass, and occasional shrubs and stunted trees greet the eye, the surrounding bleakness and desolation render this place one of awful grandeur. The hand of Him who rules the universe is nowhere else more marked, and in no place which we have ever visited have we felt so utterly

alone, so completely isolated from mankind, and left
entirely with nature as at Sherman, on the Black Hills
of Wyoming.

Upon first sight, Sherman looked like many of the shantytowns
they'd passed: two hotels with false fronts dominated the main street,
with saloons and provision shops, hardly more than shacks, on either
side. As they pulled in to the depot, Hattie closed her *Crofutt's* with a
smirk.

But when they crossed to the other side of the tracks, a grand vista
opened up of meadows filled with flowers and animals and everything
framed by distant mountains.

"Oh!" she said aloud, and took off at a run, her arms wide, as if she
wished to embrace it all. Larks, swallows, and yellow-headed blackbirds,
disturbed by her intrusion, fluttered up, filling the sky with flashes of
lime green and buttercup yellow.

Louisa, still at the end of the car with the children, caught sight of
Hattie through the window. Hattie suddenly stopped and lowered her
arms. Twenty yards off, a pronghorn antelope stood its ground, tail and
ears pointed stiffly toward the vast reddening sunset.

"Boo!" Hattie stomped her foot. The antelope started back, which
made her laugh.

"Don't frighten him, for goodness' sake," Louisa shouted.

"Come on!" Hattie laughed happily and waved back at Louisa.

"I'm coming!" And, abandoning her charges, Louisa hurried to
descend the train. The children cried, "But we want to come, Miss
Louisa!"

"Wait for your parents, children," Louisa replied.

The antelope sprinted away, and Hattie amused herself anew by
playing peekaboo with the prairie dogs. They scurried into their holes
and then popped their heads out. Then, at the sound of Hattie's voice,

they withdrew into their holes once more, only to pop back up when curiosity got the better of them.

The excursionists seemed unsure of where to go and stood in a clump to the side of the train.

"This way," Mr. Price said, waving them up a path to the right. He began to walk up a path leading to a rocky peak.

"Crofutt says we're more than eight thousand feet above sea level now!" Hattie heard someone exclaim.

"Amazing," said another.

The winds were strong here, and Louisa's hair flew out of its pins, wild and strikingly blonde. As she walked toward Hattie, she placed a hand upon her chest, rendered breathless by the thin air. Or perhaps it was the purity of the scene that took the breath from her: Hattie playing like a child with the prairie dogs, surrounded by such wild grandeur.

Hattie now stood with her arms akimbo, leaning into the wind as she faced south toward the Laramie Mountains. The outlines of her body glowed with a bright-red aura.

"Harriet," Louisa said, coming up to her.

Without turning around, Hattie rolled a shoulder forward, inviting Louisa to come beside her.

"Can you believe this place?" Hattie shook her head, still staring directly ahead toward the vast bowl of mountains plunged in limitless sky. "Crofutt wasn't kidding."

"Breathe slowly," Louisa cautioned. "Or it shall take your breath away, as it has done mine."

Hattie paused for a long moment. Then she said, "There's something special here, isn't there?"

Louisa stood very still, shutting out the jarring sound of the excursionists as they made their way noisily up the hill behind them.

"Yes."

They soon felt obliged to catch up with the others, and Louisa leaned easily upon Hattie as the two made their way up the path.

Atop the hill, the excursionists murmured their surprise: a small hotel stood with open doors, waiting to serve them refreshments. Hattie and Louisa remained outside while the others eagerly entered.

"You haven't gone off for a smoke today," Louisa remarked, peering over the summit ridge.

Hattie looked at Louisa with surprise. "Didn't I tell you? I gave them away. To that old squaw."

Louisa stopped walking and turned to Hattie. "What old squaw?"

"The one who got on—oh, but for goodness' sake," Hattie berated herself. "You'd already gone off when I told Julia and her father. She was in the baggage car when I went in for a smoke."

"Did you speak to her?"

"In a way. She told me she was headed to Ogallala. Anyway, I had resolved to give up my vices, and as she seemed keen to have them, I left them behind." Then Hattie confessed with a small smile, "Early in the morning, I desperately wanted them and went to fetch them. But they were gone—along with the old squaw."

"Poor you. That must have been hard."

"No," Hattie said, looking away. "It's a good thing. You were right."

Louisa paused. "Did you really give away your earthly pleasures just to please me?" Louisa turned, and Hattie felt those green eyes look straight through her.

"I did," she said.

The others emerged from the hotel just then and joined them. As the sun hovered just behind the Laramie Mountains, the excursionists moved onto the highest rock. Then they took each other's hands and sang "My Country, 'Tis of Thee" and "The Star-Spangled Banner." The songs' words were sung so earnestly, with America spread out in its vast glory below them, that many held tears in their eyes.

When they finished, a hush fell over the group. The excursionists moved back down the hill to the train, the bell clanged, and the whistle blew its hissing but harmonious chord. Mr. Straight shouted, "All aboard!"

Louisa and Hattie had hung back from the others, unseen. They were silent, each moved in her own way by the singing. They had just crossed the tracks in front of the train when the whistle blew a second time, and the train inched forward.

"Oh God. It moves!" Louisa cried.

Hattie, eyes glinting, made a calculation: they could not reach the other side of the engine in time to board. She waited a few seconds for the train to get closer. Between the cowcatcher and the caboose, there was a narrow shelf about two feet off the ground, where the workmen sometimes liked to sit. Hattie easily hoisted herself into it.

"You'll kill yourself!" Louisa said.

"Oh, no—come on. There's plenty of time!"

Hattie proffered her hand and Louisa took it, then sprang forward with a gleeful cry, just managing to clear the bench beside Hattie.

The train began to pick up speed, and the young women stared at each other in amazement. Hattie turned around and waved to the engine driver. He did not see her, and the train continued to gain speed.

Louisa and Hattie both began to scream and wave, and thankfully the alert young fireman, whom Hattie had spoken with back in Chicago, noticed them, grinned, and signaled to the engine driver. The latter scowled and was obliged to blow his whistle, signaling back to the brakeman. Then he stood and glowered at them through the caboose window. Seeing his face, the young women burst out laughing and gripped each other's hands in delicious terror.

By now, the sun was an orange fireball sitting low to the ground, blinding them to all but the prairie grass and the distant snow-covered mountains. The train slowed and then came to a full stop. The engine driver hopped down from the cab and pointed at them.

"You! Off! Get off!" He wildly waved his arms, as if they were a herd of cows.

Louisa and Hattie descended the cowcatcher, Louisa a bit unsteadily. Then they both stood up straight, like soldiers ready for their captain's reprimand. Louisa's hair was wild about her face, and her pale cheeks were flushed. But even as she braced herself for a scolding, she turned to Hattie and exclaimed exultantly, "What a thrill!"

"You're both crazy!" the engineer shouted at them.

Mr. Straight was now upon them as well.

"Miss Eames, I've a mind to send word to your father!" he bellowed.

"I'm very sorry, sir," Hattie said sincerely enough. But then she looked at the state of Louisa's hair and giggled. It didn't matter. Nothing mattered. Not even the engine driver's fury or Mr. Straight's threat to send a telegram to Mr. Eames. Because, for one perilous moment, Louisa had held her hand.

22

Saturday, May 28, Sacramento

LELAND HAD A LITTLE LIFT IN HIS step whenever he recalled Miss Eames's telegram from Omaha, which he had received two days earlier. "I look forward to meeting my new husband," she had written. The words echoed and echoed in his mind. Everything was coming into place.

Leland Durand had been searching for a suitable home for them for several months. Then, just three weeks earlier, when Widow Mackenzie died, and her house was put up for sale, Leland bought it. It was a grand but dilapidated mansion rebuilt decades ago by Mr. Mackenzie.

Mr. Durand Senior gave his ambitious son the earnest money, saying as he handed it over, "You've worn me down, *mon fils*, with your *optimisme!*" Which, Leland supposed, was almost the same as believing in him.

Now, having met with the estate's attorney and the banker for the closing, Leland raced directly to the property, key in hand. He would not be at the grocery that day, for now there was a very great deal to do. There were broken sash ropes in the windows and warped floorboards that needed to be nailed down or replaced. The kitchen—well, Leland shuddered to think of it. It had not been improved upon in the century since the home was built, and it remained a rough wooden shed, though the enterprising Mr. Mackenzie had rebuilt the rest of the house in solid brick after receiving a cash windfall in '49.

It seemed that Widow Mackenzie had used the kitchen only to make herself her morning tea, her evening's warm milk and biscuit, and a daily boiled egg. When the undertakers came to remove her body from the house, they found an egg still in its pan upon the stove.

Leland had no intention of having his wife spend time in the kitchen. They would hire a cook, but even so, it wouldn't do for the wife of a wealthy entrepreneur to suffer such a—Leland sought for the word—*discrepancy*. Yes, that was the word. Such a discrepancy between the elegant front rooms and a shamefully outdated kitchen. It reminded him of the shantytown buildings with fronts as false as they were grand, concealing one-story sheds behind them. That was not the style of life to which Leland Durand wished his wife to grow accustomed.

Widow Mackenzie's house (he must stop calling it that!) would soon be known as the Durand house. In twenty or one hundred years' time, he hoped, people would still be calling it that. Still admiring it. And yet, while desirous of joining the new western elite, Leland longed to appear not to care about money at all. That, after all, was the true sign of an aristocrat, wasn't it? At that moment, however, he could not help but think that Miss Eames's dowry of five hundred dollars would come in very handy, as contractors invariably underestimated the cost of things.

As Leland approached his new house on O Street, he suffered a blood-freezing moment in which he feared Miss Eames would be repelled by its proximity to his parents' home. *My wife shall be mistress of her own home,* he thought, standing tall. *I must have a conversation with Mom and Pop about it.* Yes, he would have them send word ahead if they wished to stop by. No more "come as you will" familiarity. Oh, but was that too cold?

Of course, for the first several months, they would need to live with the Durands while the repairs were being completed on the house. Leland suddenly had the uncharitable thought that Widow Mackenzie might have obliged him and died somewhat sooner than she did. For what was an extra month of eternity to her? Leland laughed at himself and shook his head at the crazy joy Miss Eames's letter had elicited in him.

Anyway, he hoped Miss Eames would not mind waiting; indeed, he secretly hoped that she would become imbued with the same hearty pioneer spirit that had served his own family so well. From all her letters, she seemed a sensible, down-to-earth girl. After all, no one too delicate would admit to climbing trees and wrestling with her brothers, would she?

In the early days of Sacramento, people thought Mr. Mackenzie wildly extravagant to rebuild his house out of brick. But when the fire of '52 razed most of the city, and the Mackenzie house stood intact amid the rubble, the townspeople began to rebuild their homes in brick too. Leland thought his new home's hearty origins a good omen. *I'd like to have many children,* he suddenly thought.

The house stood three stories tall and was built in what Leland had learned was the "bracketed Italianate" style. Ornate pediments adorned the twelve fronting windows, and the double staircase would be magnificently restored.

Within, he would install gaslights and several skylights. Six fireplaces would keep them snug. Leland hoped the chimneys didn't need too much repair, for that would be very dear.

The contractor was waiting for him on the steps, smoking a cigarette. He was a tall, wiry man not much older than Leland himself.

The young men shook hands. Leland fished for his new house key in a trouser pocket, then opened the door, which stuck a little from its many layers of paint. The contractor tossed his cigarette off to the side of the house, and together the two men stepped into the dark, musty-smelling manse. "I should think these balusters will need refinishing," Leland said, moving up the steps to the second floor. "And—oh, do you hear that creak? The joists need shoring up."

After his meeting with the contractor, Leland headed to the telegraph office. In addition to telling Miss Eames about the house, he needed to inquire about when the train would stop in Sacramento, for Miss Eames had failed to mention it. It had slipped his mind that the Pullman Hotel Express was not a regular train. Those invariably stopped in Sacramento before their terminus in Oakland.

Leland felt a twinge of guilt for not having yet told Miss Eames about the house. He hadn't wished to raise her hopes should the deal fall through. In the case of an estate, the banker told him, there were sometimes unforeseen delays and entanglements.

Now, only three days before Miss Eames was due to arrive, Leland considered that a telegram would no longer signal desperation but would convey his thoughtfulness and efficiency.

The Western Union office stood at the northeast corner of Second and J Streets. As Leland approached it, he recalled the first time he saw the new telegraph line and smiled at the memory. "Where do the words go?" he had asked his father.

His father had laughed. "Where do zee words go? Now that's a fine question." The truth was, Mr. Durand didn't understand the new technology any better than his son. But that did not deter him from using it to manage orders and shipments from all over the country.

Leland entered the office and smiled winningly at Madge Perry, whom he had known since childhood. She was a fetching black-haired girl of about seventeen, the little sister of one of his boyhood friends.

"Hello, Madge."

"Oh, hi, Leland. What's it to be today? And to whom?" she asked.

"Hang on, Madge—I must write it down."

Madge stifled a smile. "Here, have a piece of paper." She handed him some notepaper and a pencil, and Leland leaned on the wooden counter and licked his lips in an effort to concentrate.

> Happy news! ~~Have~~ purchased grand old house that shall be good as new by ~~Sum end of summer~~ summer's end. ~~You will love it.~~ Fervent hope it pleases you. ~~Hope you love it.~~ Please ~~wire~~ inform arrival time.
>
> ~~Love, fondly,~~ Your Leland

Twenty-six words. Four were owed to him, but Leland could not think of a single word to add. After several minutes of profound sighing, he added *Have* back to *purchased* and *the* before *summer's end*.

Leland handed the note to Madge, who laughed out loud. She looked up at him. "And you expect me to read this?"

Leland peered down at his note with dismay. "Oh, sorry!" He snatched it back, then read it haltingly, hardly able to make it out himself.

Suddenly, Madge blurted, "Whoever this Miss Eames is, I hope she knows how lucky she is!"

Now it was Leland's turn to blush.

23

Saturday, May 28, Green River, Wyoming Territory

WHEN HATTIE WOKE ON SATURDAY MORNING, THE train was just approaching the Green River depot. The river, which they soon crossed by means of a modern bridge, did indeed look green, and Hattie wondered at its composition.

Louisa had already dressed and gone off, presumably to mind the children. But when Hattie entered the commissary car, she saw her sitting with Mr. Hunnewell and Julia. Everyone was talking about the theater in Salt Lake, which they would attend that evening. Apparently, they were to spend two nights there, touring the city. They would even meet Brigham Young and attend his services in the great Tabernacle. If Hattie had known this, she had forgotten about it and was slightly dismayed. She disliked the theatrical arts, and the prospect of meeting Brigham Young did little to compensate.

Like everyone else, Mr. Hunnewell and his daughter were talking about the theater. Hattie greeted them and then proceeded to gaze out the window. The train stopped briefly at the depot, then ascended, passing dramatic red sandstone cliffs that reminded Hattie of ancient cathedrals.

No one else took an interest in the natural surroundings, having concluded that Wyoming was little more than dusty white desolation punctuated by sagebrush and greasewood.

Then suddenly, Odysseus appeared at the head of the St. Cloud car and announced, "Ladies and gentlemen. Allow me to draw your attention to the right side of our car, where the celebrated red sandstone formations shall certainly amaze and delight you. Just there, to the left, is one they call Pulpit Rock."

Everyone ceased talking about the theater and stared out at Pulpit Rock.

"It looks like a volcano," Hattie said.

"It looks like a breast," Louisa whispered, giggling.

Hattie glanced happily at Louisa, whom, she was shocked to discover, was staring directly at Hattie's ample bosom.

Hattie heard a waiter clear his throat. Alfred was standing beside her with a silver pot of coffee.

"Coffee, Miss Eames?"

"Oh, yes please."

As Hattie sipped her coffee, Julia looked over at her.

"Before you entered, the St. Cloud had been abuzz with your exploits last night."

"Julia, my dear, I hardly think . . . ," began Mr. Hunnewell.

Hattie smiled at Julia and then turned to Mr. Hunnewell. "It's all right, Mr. Hunnewell. The engine driver was annoyed, to be sure. But to jump upon a moving train was a great thrill, one we shan't soon forget."

Julia sighed. "I wish I were brave enough to do such a thing."

"And get your neck broken?" Mr. Hunnewell replied sternly. "It's a good thing you weren't harmed—or I should have had to answer for it, Miss Eames."

He continued in a more placating tone, "Now today, you ladies may look forward to doing something more suitable to your gentle sex:

in Wasatch, we have every hope of discovering hitherto-undocumented species of flora."

"Ooh!" Hattie nudged Julia and whispered, "Hitherto-undocumented species of flora. Imagine that!"

Julia giggled and nudged Hattie back. Then Hattie said, "Oh, but Louisa will want to join us. Won't you, Louisa? I hope Mrs. Ridgewood can spare you."

Mrs. Ridgewood, overhearing her name from the other side of the kitchen, cried, "Lou-*eeza*! I would have you sit with us!"

Louisa rolled her eyes, curtsied to the Hunnewells, and made her way down the aisle, clutching the backs of the seats to steady herself.

Hattie stood up. "Excuse me," she said to the Hunnewells. "I'll be right back."

She followed Louisa until she reached the Ridgewood party. Seeing her, Mrs. Ridgewood frowned. The children, who had been surreptitiously tormenting one another, looked at Hattie dully, then tried to resume their covert pinching as Louisa pried the children's fingers off one another. Louisa looked up at Hattie, her eyes bright with both delight and fear.

"Hello," said Hattie.

"Hello," Louisa replied questioningly, having seen Hattie moments before.

Mrs. Ridgewood murmured a greeting and then frowned. "Your exploits have been much talked about this morning," she said.

Ignoring the woman's frown, Hattie turned to Louisa. "We had a great deal of fun. Didn't we, Louisa?"

"I shouldn't boast of it if I were you," replied Mrs. Ridgewood.

"Oh, I nearly forgot," Hattie said, changing the subject. "Mr. Hunnewell leads an expedition later to look for flora and moss agates. He seems quite certain he'll find a new species or two. I believe Louisa would like to go."

"Can the girl not speak for herself?" Mrs. Ridgewood asked.

Louisa said, her voice hardly above a whisper, "I would like to go."

"Well now, I don't know . . . ," considered Mrs. Ridgewood. She broke off when she saw Alfred moving down the aisle.

"Telegram for you, Miss Eames." Then he couldn't help blurting, "Got to Green River in ten minutes!"

"A telegram? From whom?"

The porter looked down at it. "Doesn't say, not so's I can tell."

Hattie took it. "Thank you, Alfred."

She tore open the letter without bothering first to find a seat. As she read, she could feel Louisa's eyes upon her.

> Happy news! Have purchased grand old house that shall be good as new by the summer's end. Fervent hope it pleases you. Please inform arrival time.
>
> Yours,
> Leland

Hattie placed a hand upon her stomach as if she had a sudden cramp.

Louisa asked, "What is it?"

"A telegram from Mr. Durand."

"So I inferred. But what does he say?"

Hattie hesitated. Louisa, looking hurt, turned to Mrs. Ridgewood and said, "Excuse me a moment, won't you?"

Without waiting for an answer, Louisa rose and walked down the aisle. Hattie followed, but she hesitated long enough for Louisa to turn to her and remark coolly, "Never mind. I can see you want your privacy, and you're right. I'll give it to you."

"I'll read it to you later," Hattie said, shoving the telegram into her trouser pocket.

Louisa began to walk back toward her seat but could not sustain the pose of indifference. She turned back abruptly and blurted, "But why can't you just *tell* me? Why aren't you laughing at his poor spelling as you always do?"

Hattie's voice rose. "It's a *telegram!* There are but twenty-five words." She removed it from her pocket and perused it once more. "Twenty-eight, actually." Then she folded it up again.

"Oh, suit yourself," Louisa replied, not taken in by Hattie's sophistry. Then she moved to sit with the Ridgewoods.

For once, Hattie stood still, uncertain where to go or what to do. So he had bought a house. A grand house, not unlike the one she had just left. Such news would have delighted her one week earlier. Why did it not do so now? She had upset Louisa, and now she herself was upset.

The train slowed to cross a trestle bridge, a wooden one six hundred feet long. The river here was swift, muddy, and boiling. Suddenly, Louisa stood and said to Mrs. Ridgewood, "Excuse me. I feel unwell." She pushed past Hattie, then rushed past others in the aisle. Louisa disappeared from sight momentarily, and Hattie, catching up to her, found her frozen in place on the St. Cloud platform.

A bump in the tracks prompted Louisa to grab on to Hattie and squeeze her eyes shut. Hattie stole the moment to feel Louisa pressed against her, to smell for traces of her perfume.

"It's all right; we're over it," she said. Hattie had just released her hold on Louisa when she cried, "Oh, look!"

There, on the left bank of the river, stood an elk. He was so close to the tracks that they could see his enormous rack of buff-colored antlers, spongy as sea coral. A moment later, they passed a buffalo nursing a calf. The little one was bright orange and had no hump. Its face was obscured by its mother's flank, and its tail flicked happily back and forth.

Hattie thought back to the other buffalo, the ones the men had shot at in Grand Island. They had killed the animals for sport and left their carcasses to rot untouched and unused. Her gorge rose again now.

Just then Louisa propelled herself across the gap to the Marquette's platform.

"Wait," Hattie called, riffling through her pocket and proffering the telegram, which nearly blew away in the wind. "Here, you may read it. I'm sorry."

But Louisa was already inside the Marquette. Hattie stood there, bewildered. Then she too jumped across the gap and sprinted down the aisle in pursuit of Louisa, who now stood by the washroom door. Someone was within. Taking her by the hand, Hattie pulled Louisa onto the next platform. She said, "I'll read it to you now."

"You needn't."

At that moment, they heard a loud bang, and the train lurched so violently that Hattie was nearly thrown off it. Then it shuddered to a stop. She struck her thigh hard against the railing and let out a cry of pain.

Next Hattie heard shouts from within as excursionists flew into one another and Union Pacific china clattered to the floor.

"My God!" someone cried.

"What's happened?" shouted another. "Is it savages?"

Just then Alfred flew out of the St. Cloud car and hopped off the train. He sprinted to the engine. Meanwhile, Hattie and Louisa made their way back inside the Marquette, where many excursionists were crying in fear, convinced that Indians were attacking. Hattie, on the other hand, thought perhaps there had been a break in the rails.

Alfred reappeared within moments, out of breath.

"We've hit an ox," he said.

24

Near James Town, Wyoming, 9:30 a.m.

HATTIE BROKE AWAY FROM LOUISA AND JUMPED down off the train. She ran forward to assess the damage for herself, at the last moment calling back, "Stay where you are!" She knew the sight would be gruesome, and it was.

The ox's head had made it across the tracks but not the rest of it. The animal must have caught a leg beneath the cowcatcher and become stuck. Most fortunately, the engine and tender had only partly derailed. They leaned steeply to the left. The tracks beneath it, from what Hattie could see, had been pulled off their pins for at least twelve feet, perhaps more. On the far side of the derailed engine lay the head, shoulders, and a single foreleg. Its eyes were rolled back, tongue flaccid, neck tendons exposed. On the other side lay the rest of the body. The headless ox was on its side, legs peacefully curled, as if it were merely dozing. Hattie felt a lurch of pity for the poor beast and glanced back to make sure Louisa had not followed her.

Mr. Straight was giving out orders right and left. He needed to send for a crew to right and stabilize the engine and to replace the damaged tracks—though how he would accomplish this Hattie could not guess. The nearest town was Ogden, three hours away.

Her question was answered a few minutes later when the young fireman from the east shimmied up a telegraph pole. A long wire dangled from a loop of wire upon his arm, and a heavy tool belt threatened to pull his pants down below his hips. When he saw Hattie, he smiled as if to say, *These things happen.* She didn't know if he meant his pants or the derailment.

Meanwhile, many of the men, including the executives and the editors of the *Trans-Continental*, had arrived on the scene. Mr. Symonds, the new engine driver, had come aboard in Evanston with a new engine, leaving the two others behind. He pulled Mr. Price aside and whispered something to him.

Mr. Price announced with a reassuring grin, "Fortunately, this engine is not beyond repair. But I'm afraid we'll be held up."

"How long?" someone asked.

"Several hours at least, I'm afraid."

A communal groan erupted.

In the Revere car, women were tending to their crying children. Some excursionists peered out the open windows, from which they could see either the body of the ox or its head. Others actually moved back and forth, wishing to see both, making of the twin images a sort of stereoscope.

Hattie had just stepped back onto the platform of the Revere car to tell Louisa what had happened when Mr. Crockett came flying past her gripping a pen knife. She found Louisa sitting against the platform's iron railing with Julia. Both had their heads bent into their knees, and Hattie was unreasonably envious that Julia condoled with Louisa.

Hattie looked over at the body of the ox, when a glint of metal caught her eye. "Oh, but would you look at that *fool.*"

Julia and Louisa lifted their heads to look. Mr. Crockett was jabbing at the ox's flank with his pen knife, perspiration rolling down his face at the effort.

"Who's that?" asked Julia, straining to see.

"Why, it's Mr. *Crockett*," Hattie replied. "Oh God, he's trying to—" Here, Hattie interrupted herself to call out to him: "You'll never manage like that, you idiot!"

"Shall I go stop him?" Julia asked, ready to sprint from the car.

"No, wait," Hattie replied.

Mr. Crockett glanced up and saw Hattie standing in front of the other two women. The sight of her appeared to motivate him to jab at the ox even more ferociously. But after another five minutes, he was forced to give up hope of procuring his steak, as the pen knife was now bent at a right angle to its handle, no match for the poor ox's thick hide.

•   •   •

Eventually, a crew of railroad workers from Rock Springs, only twenty-one miles away, arrived in two horse-drawn coaches and got to work. Lunch was served early. Food was always an excellent distraction, the executives knew, and on this day, Mr. Price made certain that no expense was spared: there was fresh green salad and cheese, brook trout, and a trifle with berries. But few besides Hattie had any appetite, having just eaten breakfast. And some excursionists had been made thoroughly sick by the sudden jolt or the view of the mangled beast.

Sitting with the Hunnewells, Hattie joked, "No sign of steak, thank goodness."

"Oh, Hattie." Julia frowned.

Hattie ate quickly and then excused herself. She said she wished to observe the workers right the engine and relay the tracks.

As she watched the hale young men, they occasionally glanced at her with some brief curiosity but did not stop to speak to her. Their motions—repairing the damaged tracks and rails, righting the engine, and finally shimmying it closer to the tracks by means of makeshift wooden wedges and jacks—were practiced and coordinated, as if this was not the first time they had rerailed a locomotive car.

Finally, when they had finished and were packing up their gear, one of the men allowed himself to ask Hattie, "Interested in our work, are ye?" He sounded like Mr. Byrne but with a lighter spirit to him somehow.

"Very much so. I'm interested in this engine, actually."

"Oh, right—she's a beauty, in't she? Finest I ever did see. Shame to see her with so much as a nick on 'er."

"But she's all right now?" Hattie asked, making the engine female, as this worker had.

"Oh yes. Hard to break this one. Would take sumthin' more'n an ox to stop 'er, God preserve us."

Hattie smiled at the young man and curtsied; he nodded at her and wiped his brow with his sleeve. She felt unaccountably cheered that the fellow had spoken neither up nor down to her. Nor had he endeavored to flirt with her. Wistfully, she imagined a collegial world in which such was the usual case, not the exception.

• • •

It was about one in the afternoon when the Pullman Hotel Express was able to set off again. The terrain was fairly level at first but soon began to ascend into the Wasatch Mountain Range. They climbed with painful slowness.

Mr. Hunnewell had been looking forward to leading an excursion and was disappointed to learn from Mr. Straight that they would stop there just long enough to attach an observation car, the better to see those sights hailed by Crofutt as the natural "jewels" of the excursion.

They pulled in to Wasatch about two hours later, and the excursionists were told they could descend long enough to stretch their legs. A new observation car was attached at the back of the train. It had no roof and was fitted with stadium benches. Fortunately, the afternoon was quite warm, and many of the ladies raced to the car with their oiled bonnets and parasols to assure themselves a seat.

Within moments of leaving Wasatch, the train barreled through the longest tunnel of their journey, 770 feet, cut into the clay and sandstone cliff by nitroglycerine-bearing Chinese workers. Passengers shrieked at the sudden eclipse and then cheered as they emerged into a splendid sunlit valley. Soon, the train passed a signpost for the Wyoming-Utah border. The ground beneath them was covered with loose, broken rock, and all around them had sprouted needlelike red spires and oddly shaped rocks that now reminded Hattie of chess pieces.

As they approached Echo Canyon, the hills rose abruptly on every side, and the snow-clad Wasatch mountains appeared to the south. Towering rocks jutted from the steep hills on their right, and Hattie could see Echo Creek running through the gorge below. The train slowed at Castle Rock, at the entrance to the canyon. There was a vast wall of rock striated with red and gold. As it came into view, though, many excursionists were too busy searching frantically for these in their *Crofutt's Guide* for them to see the wonder firsthand.

But the slowing train discomfited a number of passengers.

"We shall miss the theater!" Mrs. Lovelace cried. "And they promised that we're to see a very renowned troupe from New York."

Murmurs of assent followed upon her exclamation, but then Mr. Crockett piped up. "If you wanna see somethin' from New York, why didn'tcha just go to New York instead of hoofing it out here to Hell 'n' beyond?"

Everyone began to boo him when Mr. Straight appeared. "Echo Canyon in twenty minutes!"

The train slowed to a stop on the edge of a desolate yet grand canyon. The excursionists descended still clutching their guidebooks. Once outside, Hattie and Louisa gazed out at the sandstone hills. After a while, Hattie, endeavoring to break the uncomfortable silence between them, remarked, "They look like hieroglyphs, don't they? Hieroglyphs from an ancient world."

Finally, Louisa looked up at the hills and said, "What if God has written something there? What if it's a divine message, and we simply don't understand it?"

Still looking up, Hattie frowned. "Why would God write a message and then not allow us to understand it?"

Louisa thought about it. "Perhaps that's what truth is: not what He reveals but what He conceals."

"Then how can we know it's the truth?"

Louisa smiled. "That's my point."

Hattie turned and narrowed her eyes at Louisa, suddenly suspicious. But Louisa continued to look at the sculpture upon the hills. Finally, she said, "Let's talk tonight."

Just then they heard a loud cough. It was Mr. Byrne, who said to them, "Amazin', isn't it?"

"It is," Louisa admitted.

Hattie scowled but said nothing. Mr. Byrne's words weren't meant for her. In the bright daylight, the artist's hair matched the sandstone cliffs. She felt a sudden revulsion for him and his red hair and wished she could swat him away like an insect.

"We were just discussing these cliffs," Louisa went on. "What do you think they look like, Mr. Byrne?"

"Oh, I—why, quite red and r-rocky," he stammered. "And . . . tall."

Hattie snorted, but a withering glance from Louisa silenced her.

"Yes?" Louisa encouraged him.

But Hattie interjected in an aggressive tone, "*I* thought they looked like ancient hieroglyphs."

"Now that you mention it, they do indeed." Mr. Byrne's fingers nervously played with each other.

He turned to Louisa and opened his mouth to speak just as Hattie blurted, "Louisa wondered whether God wrote a message in them."

But Mr. Byrne, ignoring Hattie, asked, "Miss Finch, I was wondering if you'd like to accompany me to the t'eater tonight?"

"Why, I—" Louisa began.

"Miss Finch has—"

"I would love to," Louisa interrupted Hattie. "But you must get permission from Mr. Ridgewood, since I am traveling with them. Thank you, Mr. Byrne." She curtsied.

"I will ask at once! Excellent!" He bowed, then slipped away before Louisa could change her mind.

"What a nuisance!" Hattie said once Mr. Byrne had gone. "Why on earth did you encourage him? Surely you don't really want to go with him?"

"But I do." Louisa looked at the ground and fondled the brim of her bonnet, which she held down by her thigh.

"But I thought you—"

Louisa turned to face Hattie. "I know what you thought, Harriet. And perhaps you're right. But he was well within his rights to ask, and I was certainly well within mine to accept."

"By all means," Hattie replied stiffly, nodding to her. "Go, if that's what you wish to do, and if Mr. Ridgewood will allow it. He probably won't."

"I shall."

Meanwhile, Mr. Hunnewell, knowing that he had only twenty minutes for his expedition, cut an absurd figure as he fairly sprinted ahead in search of flora and moss agates. Hattie saw Louisa limp off to join Julia, who was following her father.

Hattie turned and walked purposefully in the opposite direction, down a dirt path toward the Weber River. Close to the river, she rounded a desolate stone outcropping. On the other side of it, entirely hidden from the train, stood a young Shoshone boy of perhaps ten or eleven. He was alone and nearly naked, apart from an animal skin about his waist and feathers in his hair. His little brown body was hard and sinewy. He was shooting coins with a bow and arrow. The coins sat atop split stakes across the river, the sun glinting off them.

Hattie approached the boy as if he were a younger brother. "Give it here," she said, indicating the bow and quiver. When he hesitated, she took them from him and began to aim an arrow. He let out an angry cry of protest in his native tongue.

"Oh, go away. Shoo," Hattie said. The boy ran off, presumably to fetch a parent or sibling.

Hattie's aim was good, and she hit several of the coins. There were times when her brothers had let her play Robin Hood with them in exchange for doing their homework. But now the activity, far from releasing her misery, only fueled it. She began shooting at other far-off targets, things she couldn't possibly hope to hit. Was it Mr. Byrne who had upset her, inviting Louisa to the theater? Or was it Leland's telegram and his happy news?

She was on her seventh and last arrow when Louisa came limping toward her with two fistfuls of moss agates, which she was struggling to fit in her petticoat pockets. When she saw Hattie, she dropped the stones on the path.

"What are you doing?"

"Shooting arrows, as you see."

"Everyone's returned to the train. They can see you, you know."

"Let them. I don't give a damn."

"Yes you do. And don't swear—it's . . . *common.*"

But Hattie returned her attention to the bow and arrow, and Louisa moved closer. "Harriet, please. Please stop."

She came to stand next to Hattie, but when Hattie ignored her, she moved around to face her. Hattie's bow was still tautly extended. For a moment, it seemed as if she might release the arrow into Louisa's breast. But Louisa stood tall and unmoving.

It occurred to Hattie that for such a rational person, someone who lived very nearly by the mechanical rules she understood so well, she harbored something quite untamed within herself. And yet, Louisa, far from cowering, stood even taller.

Hattie lowered the arrow, dropping both it and the bow. Tears sprang to her eyes. Then she turned to see the boy returning with his entire family of angry Shoshone.

Three boys and a young man approached her. Their hair fell to their waists. All of them wore strings of white shells draped to their breastbones. The young man, holding a rifle as tall as the children, scowled.

Hattie and Louisa moved off in the direction of the train as the family carefully watched them retreat. Once they were safely out of range of the boy and his family, Hattie turned and glared poisonously at Louisa.

"All right! He has bought us a *house!*"

25

HATTIE'S NEWS HAD COME AS NO SURPRISE, but the viciousness with which she informed Louisa of it brought tears to Louisa's eyes. What had she done to deserve such unkindness? Well, but she knew the answer, didn't she? That did not make it any less painful. *Knowing,* Louisa thought, *is no cure for understanding.*

Meanwhile, the train passed along a thousand-foot ledge, and the excursionists all screamed in terror as they leaned into the mountainside.

Hattie spat, "Regard how everyone leans to the right. How stupid they look, leaning in such a way. You'd think they believed they kept the train on the tracks by force of their own pressure."

"You mean we don't?" Louisa replied, a knowing smirk playing at the corner of her mouth.

Hattie glanced warily at her friend, but Louisa's face had turned to alabaster.

The canyon narrowed so that one saw only the river below or the sky above, and the excursionists, feeling more secure, righted themselves.

Louisa suddenly turned to Hattie. "Oh, Hattie. Let us speak honestly with one another."

"Fine," Hattie snapped back. She added with a cagey glance, *"When?"*

"When we have a moment to ourselves. Don't be afraid," Louisa added.

"What makes you think I'm afraid?" Hattie laughed drily.

Louisa sighed. Meanwhile, the train maintained a slow, almost leisurely pace as it ambled along the banks of the river, and Louisa's attention was drawn to the landscape. She said, "The sagebrush looks like tiny olive trees, doesn't it?"

"I wouldn't know."

"You would if you looked." Louisa nodded to the window.

Hattie pressed her face to the window but saw nothing. It was all a blur. Not because they were moving too quickly but because she was blinded by a wholly irrational and all-consuming anger. Louisa wanted to destroy their illusion; very soon, she would have to do so as well.

The train now passed through even taller walls with huge serrated ledges. They passed the famous Thousand Mile Tree, which told the distance from Omaha. Sandstone formations continued to loom up like totems to a lost God.

After about six miles, the engine driver slowed the train so that everyone could observe the Devil's Slide. These were two enormous rock ridges that ran up and down the hillside. The space between the ridges spanned about one hundred yards and was filled with wildflowers and a profusion of strange vines. Beyond the Devil's Slide, on either side of the canyon, pale-yellow and red rocks were heaped on top of one another in a majestic confusion.

After passing through Weber Canyon, they came to more fields of grain, great patches of blue lupine, and a resting river. The train crossed the river, and then all went dark as they entered a long tunnel. Louisa grabbed Hattie's arm, which Hattie tolerated stiffly. On the other bank, Hattie noticed a stranded immigrant family. The miserable-looking group sat upon the edge of their wagon as the man hammered at a wheel and a horse swished flies with its tail. Hattie had nearly forgotten that people had been passing this way by cart and on foot for decades. From the comfort of their Pullman Hotel Express, wagon travel was a sad, atavistic spectacle.

Next, the train descended, turned a sharp corner, and emerged upon a broad plain. They had entered into the great Salt Lake Valley. It was dotted with one-story farmhouses, all having two or three front doors. What were they for? Ahead of them just a few miles were the smoke plumes of Ogden and, beyond that, the silver spill of Salt Lake.

At last, they arrived in Ogden, Utah. It was now late in the afternoon, and the directors of the Boston Board of Trade had to rush through their pomp and circumstance. The depot had been built on a mud flat by the edge of the Weber, and in order to arrive at the depot itself, the excursionists had to traverse a boardwalk nearly half a mile long. Neither Hattie nor Louisa left the train.

About an hour later, they pulled into Salt Lake, in time for the excursionists to take a fine, if slightly rushed, meal before setting off for the theater.

Mr. Ridgewood joined his family for dinner, which meant that Louisa was able to sit with Hattie, Julia, and Mr. Hunnewell. Louisa wore a new gown, which Hattie thought looked lovely on her. But she didn't say so. Their booth was relatively quiet, Hattie and Louisa apparently having little to offer by way of conversation. But the rest of the excursionists were already voicing their first, favorable impressions of Salt Lake itself.

"Oh, but did you regard the broad streets?" exclaimed Mrs. Lovelace from across the aisle.

"The air, I must admit, is very fresh," said David grudgingly.

"Its situation is idyllic, surrounded as it is by mountains."

"The houses are all tidy," Hattie remarked. "One must give them that. But I noticed a number of farmhouses with more than one front door. What is their purpose?"

"Multiple wives," pronounced Mr. Hunnewell.

"Each wife needs a separate door?"

"Precisely."

"But don't all the doors lead into the same room? The houses seem awfully small."

Julia endeavored to keep herself from laughing.

Mr. Hunnewell replied, "I suppose each woman is meant to feel as if it is *her* home. It may also signal the prominence of the man within."

"Gosh," Hattie said. "How imbecilic."

"But Hattie," Julia interjected, "you must admit that they have worked very hard. Created plenty out of drought. Surely that's no easy feat."

Mr. Crockett suddenly piped up from across the aisle. "By all means, let's go visit the great polygamist!"

Hattie noticed that Louisa had grown very quiet, and her simmering anger cooled a moment. "What's the matter, Louisa? Are you unwell?"

"Oh, no. But . . . I have this bad feeling." She placed a hand to her heart. She continued, "Did you notice the trees upon our approach? The oaks?"

"No. What about them?" Hattie, relieved that Louisa was not ill, went back to being cold to her.

"Compare them to what we saw earlier today, to the natural grandeur of Echo Canyon. Yes, these settlers have created life, but it seems . . . deformed."

"Deformed?" Hattie frowned.

"Yes. Like . . . something made up of dead parts." Louisa shivered, her disgust deepening. "Something Victor Frankenstein might create. Not *natural* life."

"Victor Frankenstein? For goodness' sake, Louisa, what are you going on about?"

Louisa looked up at no one in particular, her eyes fearful. "When I was a child, my father took me to an exposition. It was at the Willard Hotel in Washington. There for the viewing were all the volumes of the government land surveys for the railroad. I couldn't read at the time, but the drawings—oh, how they took my breath away! They were the most exquisite drawings of a land I had only dreamed about: mountains, rivers, deserts. Indians, buffalo. Elk. Birds that few men had ever seen before. The colored plates revealed God's land untouched by man. Oh, they gave me such reason to hope! Such reason!" But far from sounding hopeful, Louisa's voice was despairing.

Julia and her father could only glance at each other in morti-fied silence; Louisa's confession seemed to have little to do with the Mormons or even oak trees.

"Well," Julia offered. "While the results here may not be perfect, it does seem as if they've been remarkably clever, creating such an Eden in the desert."

"Exactly!" Hattie said with malicious triumph.

Louisa, to the astonishment of everyone, rose from her seat and burst into tears. Then she turned and ran out of the St. Cloud car.

"The long day has been too much for her, I expect," said Mr. Hunnewell mildly. "She's a very sensitive girl. Perhaps because of—"

"Indeed," Julia forestalled him. "And the ox this morning—"

Mr. Hunnewell nodded. "I hope and pray the theater will take everyone's minds off that unhappy event."

Hattie stood abruptly. "I must go to her."

Julia glanced up at Hattie but said nothing.

Passing through the Revere car, Hattie called, "Louisa!" but heard no reply. She looked out at the platform, but Louisa wasn't there either. Finally, at the very end of the car, she heard a noise coming from the washroom.

"Louisa?" She knocked. "Louisa?"

A feeble voice replied. "Oh, I'm sick." Louisa made retching sounds, and the WC's already foul odor wafted up from beneath the door. Clearly the porters had been too busy after the ox incident to complete their regular tasks.

"It's revolting in there. I'm sick myself. Come out."

There was silence for several moments, and then the door opened, releasing the most awful stench. Louisa emerged as white as if she'd been bled by leeches.

"Come away. Come," said Hattie, covering her nose with one hand. "You must have fresh air at once." Whatever anger or resentment Hattie had felt vanished at the sight of Louisa.

Hattie led them onto the platform. There, the air was better, but now they were obscured by billowing steam from the cooling engine. Hattie grimaced. "Let's get off this wretched thing."

She hopped down onto a broad, neatly groomed dirt road. To her left stood a bizarre, ugly sort of roundhouse that wasn't quite round.

"That must be the Mormon Tabernacle," she said as she helped Louisa down the stairs. But the girl, weak from illness, caught her foot at an inauspicious angle and fell onto her hands and knees in the middle of the road.

"Louisa!" Hattie cried. "Goodness! Are you—"

Louisa grimaced in pain, held her ankle, and then burst out laughing. "Oh my God!" she cried, weeping with laughter.

"Why, why are you laughing?" Hattie asked, alarmed.

Louisa dried her eyes and tried to compose herself, still hiccupping with laughter. She finally managed, "Things are such an incredible mess."

26

AT FIRST, HATTIE HAD NO IDEA WHAT Louisa was talking about. Hattie's emotions swirled about her without words or clear borders. She was like a child who knows that she is angry and frustrated but not why. She had been angry when Mr. Byrne asked Louisa to the theater, and she had been upset when she read Leland's telegram about having purchased a home for them. But she found it hard to extrapolate meaning from these feelings the way one could from mechanical formulas.

Along the gate that fenced off the Tabernacle grounds from the street, the curb had a granite edge raised some inches off the sidewalk. Louisa sat down on it and faced Hattie, who sat down right beside her, though she did not look at her. She feared she might never look at Louisa again.

"You have no idea why I accepted Mr. Byrne's offer, do you." It was not a question.

"Don't I?"

"No, you don't, in fact. You think I did it to get back at you."

"For what?"

"For not sharing the contents of your telegram."

Hattie scowled. "That's ridiculous." Still, she did not look at Louisa but edged slightly away.

"I agree," Louisa said. "You're angry that you're unhappy about Mr. Durand's news, and you invest me with your own spitefulness. But I have none whatsoever. And yours hurts."

"Oh, Louisa, I'm—" Hattie felt her first lurch of remorse, but Louisa forestalled her.

"If you allow me to explain, I think it will put your mind at ease."

"Very well," Hattie said.

"First of all, I like Mr. Byrne. He's rough around the edges, but he's hardworking—and lonely, I suspect. Don't you see how hard they work him? Why, it's almost as if he's their indentured servant. Only think too how such an immigrant must feel among all these wealthy businessmen."

"But his art." Hattie shuddered.

"No, clearly art is not his calling," Louisa agreed. "But his drawings are appropriate for the newspaper. They're no doubt what they ask him to draw."

"Inaccurate—" Hattie began to say, then stopped herself. She suddenly realized that this inaccuracy bothered her. It wasn't just writing "Niagara Falls" when they had printed the issue elsewhere. It was a multitude of exaggerations that offended her—far more than an outright lie, which at least bore no relation to truth and thus could not taint it by proximity.

"Hattie." Louisa looked exasperated. "Have you considered that Mr. Byrne's work, though commissioned by Mr. Steele and the executives, may also be an honest reflection of his own enthusiasm for his new country? You give little credit to his idealism while forgiving your own absolutely."

"I—"

"Anyway," Louisa cut in, "as to why I wished to go: I've never been to the theater before—or, not really. I realize you know very little about me and, therefore, I must make allowances for the false judgments with which you fill your gaps of ignorance."

Taken aback, Hattie asked, "What do you mean, not *really*?"

"At first, Papa didn't approve of it. He said the theater was frivolous and encouraged licentious behavior. But then, one day, he said we could go. A parishioner had begged him to bring me to a children's show. When Papa assented, I was giddy with excitement. It promised to be such a special evening. I was so proud that Papa thought I was worthy of going to the theater, of being seen with him in public. But when we got there, he moved toward the very back row. I could see nothing from there. Nothing at all. I soon realized why he had brought us to the back row with all the workers and their families."

"Money?"

Louisa shook her head. "It was because Papa didn't want anyone he knew to see me."

"Oh, Louisa. Surely that's not true. That was only your childish impression."

"Not at all," she said firmly. "He admitted as much later."

"So what did you do?"

"I asked him to take me home. I told him I was unwell. And at home, he paced and fretted and then told me, finally, 'Deceit is against my faith, child. Your foot is not merely ugly, not merely deformed, but a symbol of my cuckoldry.'"

"Did you know what 'cuckoldry' meant?"

Louisa smiled. "I didn't, but I got the gist. There had been rumors about my mother's transgression, and Alexandria is a small town, or was then. He couldn't bear the whispers."

Hattie said, "Oh, Louisa!" and hugged her impulsively. "I'm more and more convinced your mother had good reason to take up with someone else."

"I don't know. I stopped hating him after that, though. I could feel the pain he suffered, to be an object of such ridicule in his own parish."

"And so he made *you* one." Then, after a minute of silence, Hattie finally summoned the courage to ask Louisa the question that had been on her mind. "Louisa, what happened to you during the war? I sometimes have the feeling that you suffered very greatly."

Louisa smiled and shrugged. "Everyone did. I perhaps least of all."

"But why compare your suffering to that of others? You were a child. What happened? What did you see?"

Louisa looked down and whispered, almost to herself, "What *didn't* I see."

"Tell me."

"What do you wish to know?" Louisa asked, still holding back.

"Well, did you see it?"

"See what?"

"The war."

"Of course."

"No, I mean—the fighting."

Louisa turned away from Hattie. Her voice was hard when she replied, "I haven't spoken of that. Not to a soul."

"What is it you haven't spoken of?" Hattie pressed.

Louisa sighed. "Well, you know that I lived in Alexandria. After the Union Army invaded, everyone fled who could. But Papa stayed on— he still had his 'flock,' he said. He was stubborn. And he wouldn't sign the Oath of Allegiance, and so soon enough he lost his position at the church. There were soldiers all about and camps upon the hill. When the fighting began, the wounded were brought to us. To the hospitals. They were all over the town. In people's houses, in our church . . ."

Hattie waited for Louisa to go on, but Louisa grimaced. "My ankle has begun to throb."

"Here. Rest it upon me."

Louisa raised her leg and placed her calf across Hattie's lap. Hattie gently rested one hand on Louisa's leg.

"When we go in, ask Alfred for some ice."

"That's a good idea."

Suddenly, a shadow fell where light from the Tabernacle had shone upon them. It was Mr. Byrne, standing over them, blocking the light.

"Dere you are," he said to Louisa. "I was looking for you." Then, noticing her leg raised upon Hattie's lap, he said, "But are you all right?"

"I'm very well, I assure you." Then Louisa remembered their rendezvous. "But, oh, I must ready myself." She stood up, dusted off her petticoat, and went to change into her evening clothes.

Mr. Byrne followed behind, calling, "Allow me to assist you up the stairs!"

After ten minutes, Hattie moved back to the train, now empty of excursionists. They had gone off in a swarm, no one wishing to get separated from the group. "Safety in numbers" was Mr. Price's motto, and he repeated it often.

She sat down, removed *Crofutt's Guide* from her bag, and began to read the section on Salt Lake. Growing bored, she set that down and picked up Louisa's sketchbook. She opened it gingerly and perused its pages, feeling slightly guilty at the intrusion, though not guilty enough to close it. Alfred came through the car to make up the beds and Hattie asked him, closing the book, "Alfred, may I have a cup of tea, please?"

"Certainly, Miss Eames."

"I'll be in the smoking car."

Hattie set down Louisa's sketchbook and made her way into the empty smoking car. She sat down in a plush chair and sniffed the air, still redolent of cigar smoke. She wished she had not given up her sins.

Alfred arrived with her tea, and she thanked him. Then she looked into his blank, dark face and asked, "Actually, Alfred, have you got anything stronger?"

"Stronger, miss?" He feigned ignorance.

"Yes. You know, perhaps a good brandy. I'd very much like to . . . numb this . . . toothache." She touched a finger to her lower jaw. "And maybe some peanuts to go with it. Dull the taste, as it were."

Alfred grinned, but so briefly that Hattie thought she imagined it. "Certainly, miss," he said.

He left and soon returned with a generous glass of amber-colored brandy and a bowl of peanuts, still in their shells. "We like to eat 'em this way, Miss Eames. But I can shell them for you if you wish."

"Shell them for me? Goodness, no—thank you, Alfred." Hattie found the idea of another person shelling nuts for her, even a paid servant, repulsive in the extreme.

Hattie set her tea aside at once, sipped her brandy, and sighed, "Ah!" Then she removed her shoes and curled her stockinged feet beneath her. She began breaking apart the peanuts, tossing the shells toward the spittoons but mainly missing them, as the hollow shells were too light to travel very far.

From a distance, Hattie heard laughter. She was glad of it, because unwelcome thoughts had begun to accost her: thoughts of Leland and his new house and Louisa enjoying the theater for the first time. A notion was taking shape in her mind, heavy, incontrovertible, and possibly catastrophic.

Hattie grabbed her shoes and, leaving her teacup and brandy snifter where they were, dusted off the peanut shells and made her way back to the Revere car. She peered through a window: bathed in the warm yellow glow of the Tabernacle, a swarm of excursionists, all happily conversing, headed toward the train.

Louisa stood beneath the Tabernacle, her hand resting lightly upon Mr. Byrne's arm. They were chatting animatedly and laughing. Every time he laughed, Mr. Byrne bent toward Louisa as if he might just fall onto her. When Louisa looked up and noticed Hattie in the window, her smile tightened.

Mr. Byrne offered to help Louisa up the steps, but Louisa shook her head, curtsied, and indicated that she wished to remain outside to take the night air. He bowed, tipped his hat, and then whispered something in her ear.

Hattie flushed with anger. Whispering in her ear! Of all things! Hattie waited until all the excursionists had boarded the train and then descended.

Approaching Louisa, she asked, "How was the theater?"

Louisa seemed lit from within, her eyes shining like gleaming peridots in the Tabernacle light. "Oh, it was so wonderful! They performed *A Midsummer Night's Dream*. It *was* a dream. A pleasant one, for once!"

Louisa chuckled, but Hattie was not pleased. She scowled, paced the sidewalk, and turned back to face her. Suddenly, she *saw* Louisa: in her evening dress, her blonde hair neatly curled in corkscrews at her ears, the rest swept back into a sleek bun, and she said miserably, "You look beautiful."

"Thank you," Louisa replied gravely.

Unaccountably, Hattie felt herself near tears, and she blurted, "I'm very sorry I was spiteful to you earlier."

Louisa nodded.

"And about Mr. Byrne too. He's a talentless fool, perhaps, but not malicious."

"It's good of you to say so."

"And I'm sorry I got angry with you for accepting him. I had no right."

"No, you didn't," Louisa said, leading Hattie away from the train. "But tell me, Harriet—I've been meaning to ask. Back in Echo, why were you so angry then?"

"Oh, *Echo*." Hattie sighed. "That seems ages ago, doesn't it?"

"It does. But that's no answer. You were angry with me. Why?" Louisa persisted, looking directly at her. "Remember? Shooting arrows? You could have gotten yourself killed."

Hattie shook her head. "It doesn't make sense, not even to me."

"Not everything needs to make sense," Louisa said.

They heard a rustling sound and stopped speaking. Mrs. Ridgewood peered fretfully about in the darkness, her flouncy petticoats swishing as she moved.

Mrs. Ridgewood moved into the conical light coming from the Tabernacle and made a few disoriented circles, coming within feet of the two young women. She cried, "Oh, that girl! I don't know what earthly use she is!" Then she stepped back onto the train with a loud sigh.

Once Mrs. Ridgewood had gone, they giggled, releasing some of the tension between them. Louisa said, "But let us move somewhere out of this light and the snooping excursionists." She took Hattie by the hand and led her through the gate of the temple grounds, into the garden. She found a bench, and they sat down.

Hattie, still holding Louisa's hand, admitted in a low voice, "I have so many unaccustomed feelings, Louisa, which I now seem to notice as never before. I've been rendered most uncomfortable."

Louisa hid a smile. She said gently, "Yes, without their usual habitat, our thoughts and feelings have nowhere to hide. At least, I find it to be so. What's more, you're far from home, you've given up smoke and drink, and you've none of your usual pursuits to occupy your thoughts. Well, why don't you tell me what you feel? Perhaps that will help."

Hattie looked up at the sky. The night was clear, the sky powdery with stardust. She could almost imagine that she and Louisa were alone in the universe. Hattie was wondering where to start when Louisa added, "It shall perhaps be easier if you don't try to order them. Your feelings, I mean."

"All right. Mr. Crockett—ugh! To have the temerity to upset everyone the way he does! What an ass! And yet, I can't help but feel there might be some truth to the things he says. Frankly, I've become somewhat curious about him."

Louisa nodded encouragingly. "Go on."

"I'm uncertain about poor Mr. Durand. My feelings have changed somehow."

"Somehow?"

Hattie could say no more on that subject at present, for as she began to reply, she felt a vast upheaval of grief that threatened to overwhelm her.

Moving on, she said, "I'm truly vexed that Mrs. Ridgewood abuses you and yet you don't stand up to her. If you don't, I swear I'll punch her one of these days."

"I don't recommend it."

"You see? And that's another thing." Hattie warmed to the subject of Louisa's faults, finding it a far more comfortable topic than her own. "That resignation, that stoic calm! It drives me mad! Sometimes I think you have no feelings, and at other times I think you're *all* feeling."

"And what about now?" Louisa leaned closer to her.

Hattie looked at Louisa in her fine gown and the soft glow of the Tabernacle's light a dozen yards off. Louisa's eyes glistened. Were those tears?

"I've had thoughts about you. About . . . holding you."

"Like this?" Louisa leaned over and kissed Hattie on the lips. Hattie replied by wrapping one arm about Louisa's shoulders and grasping Louisa's other hand more tightly, feeling Louisa's delicate yet strong fingers. Then, moving to hold her wrist, Hattie felt the pulse of Louisa's life beneath her thumb, and her own heart skipped to feel it. She reached around Louisa's small waist and grasped her tightly.

Hattie's voice was a whisper when she managed at last to say, "In three days' time, Leland will meet me at the depot in Sacramento. What will I do?"

"Do? Why, descend the train," Louisa replied. "There is nothing else *to* do, except to know at last how you feel."

"But that can't be enough!"

Louisa continued with almost cruel calm, "Though we ride together, you know—have always known—that we're on different paths. Yours leads to Leland and mine leads to—"

"A slave pen!" Hattie cried. "A fate far worse than mine. You must—that is," Hattie amended, "you *shouldn't* allow them to treat you poorly."

Louisa, continuing to hold Hattie's hand, glanced away. She murmured, "If it's my fate, then there's nothing to be done."

"Fate?" Hattie scoffed. "There's no such thing."

Louisa calmly added, "But there was something I meant to tell you, Hattie, back in Cheyenne. I had a telegram from my father."

"Cheyenne?" Hattie looked confused. "That was yesterday."

Louisa nodded. "My father wrote to say he'd finally procured regular employment in Boston and that, if I wished, I could return home. I couldn't tell you. You see that now, don't you? Not until I myself had decided what to do. I know how little you think of him."

"It's not about how little I think of either him or the Ridgewoods but what I wish for you. But—what do *you* want, Lou?" Hattie's question, much to her own surprise, was perfectly sincere. "There's probably a train leaving for Boston in the morning right from here. From Salt Lake."

Louisa shook her head. "I can't go back." Hattie exhaled the breath she had been holding, and Louisa added, "But I don't see a way forward either."

Hattie was thoughtful. Surely there was a way. Her face brightened. "Maybe you could descend in Sacramento!" she exclaimed. "You could teach at a local school. I bet they're eager for teachers."

But Louisa winced at this idea. "So that we could nod to each other at the market? So that I could read about your lavish soirees in the newspapers? So that, one day, I could teach your children?"

"Oh, Louisa, I don't know!" Hattie admitted. "Can we—can we just be happy now, for a little while? I've never felt so happy in my whole life. And have no fear—I know it won't last."

Once more, Louisa heard the cruelty in Hattie's voice, which she now knew to be her voice of despair. She said merely, "Yes, of course."

They ceased talking for several minutes and held each other. Then Louisa felt Hattie's shoulders shaking.

She pulled away and asked, "Why are you crying?"

But Hattie was laughing—so hard now that tears streamed from her eyes, as if her body was releasing the tension it had held in for so long. She wiped her eyes and looked at Louisa. "When I saw Mr. Byrne flirt with you, I wanted to rip his Irish blue eyes out of his head!"

"It was evident to everyone, I fear."

"Perhaps he shall propose to you."

"No."

"Why not? That might be a good thing."

"I wouldn't accept him. Surely you can imagine how it would ruin his life to have a wife such as myself. No, it's most likely I'll continue with the Ridgewoods."

Hattie changed the subject. "But answer me one thing, Louisa, for now that I know some things, I must know everything about you. You seem to have so little . . . doubt. So little anxiety about—" Hattie broke off.

"About *us*?" Louisa asked bluntly.

Hattie nodded.

"I've never been attracted to men. Oh, I've never known absolutely, though, since they have seldom shown any interest in *me*. I had a terrible crush on a schoolmistress once. But this is quite different, isn't it?"

Once again, Hattie felt as if Louisa saw right through her. "I always liked boys." Hattie shrugged. "I was a tomboy. When Papa began his parade of paramours, I wanted them to join our outdoor games not to propose to me."

Then, without warning, Louisa embraced her. "Oh, Hattie. I feel such tenderness. Such unbearable tenderness sometimes!"

When Louisa finally pulled away, she was grinning guiltily.

"Now, what are *you* grinning at?" Hattie asked.

"I fear that all of Papa's talk about fire and brimstone has failed to . . . take. If there really is a Hell, Hattie, I'm in a great deal of trouble."

"If there really is a Hell, Louisa, I'm going with you."

27

THEY BOARDED THE TRAIN; IT WAS ALREADY quite late, and the excursionists were asleep. As Louisa sat on her berth and began to pull the curtain closed, Hattie stole a quick kiss good night and then hoisted herself up into her own berth.

There was little chance she would sleep. Never had she felt such exhilaration or such fear. Her feet tapped against the edge of the berth, kicking at the curtains to distract herself from the kick of her heart. She felt humbled somehow. Why had she always believed she was strong? Because she climbed trees like her brothers did? Because she dared to wear trousers? Because she stood tall before all those mocking girls or traveled across America toward a stranger and a strange land? These were nothing at all compared to the courage she needed now.

She felt like a train, barreling through a tunnel at forty miles per hour. Blind, deaf, with nothing but sheer locomotion to aid her. What lay on the other side? A wall? A canyon? A cliff? Sacramento and smiling Leland Durand? No guidebook on earth could tell her what lay ahead.

But there was excitement too. Her body had awakened; she felt an ache in her breasts, as if they were calling out to be touched. She wanted to press herself against the young woman sleeping beneath her . . .

Hattie poked her head out of her berth and bent over to catch a glimpse of Louisa. She saw a sliver of Louisa's shoulder rising and falling. She tried to breathe in that same rhythm, anchoring her breath to Louisa's and with the rhythm of the wheels across the tracks . . .

Louisa was already gone when Hattie awoke, and she had to race to make breakfast. There was no time to wash. When she arrived at the St. Cloud car, it was already completely full. Hattie spotted Julia, sitting with her father. Everyone was talking about the theater the night before.

"Oh, but what a delight!"

"Stellar!" It was the operatic voice of Mrs. Lovelace. "I, for one, was exceedingly impressed."

"Agreed."

"Now, who was that actor, the one who played Puck? He was very amusing."

Louisa stood in the far corner of the car, her back to Hattie. Her head was bowed submissively before Mrs. Ridgewood; the latter's face was ugly with rage, and Hattie thought with a smirk, *How predictable she is.*

"What could you have been thinking, Miss Finch?" Mrs. Ridgewood was asking. "I searched high and low for you. In the end, I was obliged to put my own children to bed. What *were* you doing, anyway, that you could not at least inform me of it? Something very bad, I'm sure. Were you off smoking with that other girl? Oh, don't pretend you don't know who I'm talking about."

Her voice was quite loud, as if she wanted everyone in the car to hear her, the better to humiliate Louisa. Louisa lifted her head as if she would speak. She had begun to apologize when Mrs. Ridgewood waved her hand dismissively. "Never mind. I don't want to know."

Hattie came up behind Louisa and touched her shoulder, which made Louisa jump. Then she turned to Mrs. Ridgewood. "I should think you *would* want to know, Mrs. Ridgewood, if only you *knew.* Come, Louisa."

• • •

"Well, that was brave of you," Julia said, looking up as the two other girls sat down across from her.

"You heard us?"

"Everyone did, I fear."

"Julia," Mr. Hunnewell admonished, "do leave well enough alone."

"That woman, Papa—she positively tortures poor Louisa." But then Julia asked Louisa, "Why did she not insist you sit with her?"

"Oh. Papa told her I was to have Sundays off."

"Well thank goodness for *that*, at least."

Alfred swept over to their table with pencil and pad in hand. Hattie had memorized the bill of fare, but still she pulled it from her pocket with a flourish, scanned it lovingly, and said, "Alfred, I'll have the cod-fish balls, a hot biscuit, and the country sausages, please."

But Julia's face was still pinched with anger. Once Alfred had gone, she said, "Honestly, I'm sick and tired of that woman taking her misery out on poor Louisa, as I'm sure everyone is."

But instead of snapping back, Mr. Hunnewell nodded thought-fully. "I suppose such unhappiness is the risk of marrying so far above oneself."

"What do you mean?" Julia looked puzzled.

"Yes, Mr. Hunnewell, what do you mean?" Louisa echoed.

"Why, didn't you know? I thought all of Boston knew."

"Knew what? Please don't keep it from us, Papa."

Mr. Hunnewell held his edition of the *Trans-Continental* to his ear to create a wall between the next table and theirs. "Before she married Mr. Ridgewood, Mrs. Ridgewood was a shopkeeper on State Street. A millinery shop, I think. And some say *more* than that, though I cannot confirm the rumor absolutely."

"A woman who wears many hats," said Hattie.

Julia and Hattie looked at each other with a mix of incredulity and amusement. Louisa blurted, "Oh, poor Mrs. Ridgewood!"

Hattie frowned. "Louisa, you can't possibly pity her!"

"But I do. I was thinking about it: to lie beside such a cold, unfeeling man each night! I can imagine it just as if it is *I* who must perform that miserable chore." She shivered. "And how painful it must be to mix among Boston society when everyone knows your lowly origins. She might dress in the finest gowns, live in the finest house—yet nothing would prevent their cruel derision."

Hattie began to object, but Julia intervened. "I agree with Louisa, Hattie, though I don't like her any more than I did. But I do pity her now."

Five minutes later, the Ridgewoods entered the St. Cloud car from the St. Charles. They were having an argument.

"What? Have you lost your taste for playing the jolly family?" Mr. Ridgewood was saying.

"I'm tired," she replied, sounding near to tears.

"But what am *I* to do with them?" he objected. "You know full well they won't mind me."

"It's about time they learned to mind you, Henry." He leaned in to her and said something inaudible, to which Mrs. Ridgewood cried, waving her arms, "You may all go jump in Salt Lake for all I care." With that, she fled back to her stateroom, abandoning her children to their father.

"Alas, they shall float," Hattie remarked to her companions. "It's very alkaline."

Mr. Ridgewood took himself off to the smoking car, dragging his unwilling children behind him.

"Ow! You're hurting me!" Sheila cried.

Mr. Ridgewood looked about him to see who had heard her. Then he said in a sweetly conciliatory voice, "Mind me today, and you shall each get one dollar at the end of it."

Julia and Hattie looked at each other in astonishment, but Louisa only shook her head sadly.

Just then Mr. Crockett, whom no one had heard from in some time, stretched his arms out with a loud and satisfied groan. Then he stood up, slapped his belly contentedly, and announced, "The dramatics on this train are better than at the theater!"

· · ·

Apparently, the bribe didn't take, because none of the Ridgewoods was to be seen at church. As they passed through the gates leading into the Tabernacle grounds, Louisa and Hattie discreetly diverged to the right as the other excursionists turned left toward the Tabernacle. They strolled through the garden, close but not touching, Louisa bending occasionally to admire the bud of a rose or the fresh, tender leaves of the honeysuckle trees. The ominous mood that Louisa had felt coming into Salt Lake seemed to have passed, and Hattie thought that it would be hard for anyone to deny the beauty of these gardens, with their pink, white, salmon, and red roses just coming into bloom.

When at last they stood before the Tabernacle, Louisa turned to Hattie. Hattie thought she was going to remark upon the garden and was surprised to hear Louisa say, "But you do know I can fight my own battles?"

Hattie knew at once that she referred to her argument with Mrs. Ridgewood. "Can you?" Hattie shot back. "Why, you're like the Green Knight. Had Mrs. Ridgewood threatened to chop off your head, I believe you would not have flinched."

Louisa smirked. "Not true. You of all people know that who I am and who I seem to be are not one and the same."

"No," Hattie admitted. "But I couldn't take it anymore. Really, I couldn't."

"I know. But, Hattie, I cannot turn my back on my only means of independence." Louisa sounded truly worried. "At the moment, it seems as if Mrs. Ridgewood wants nothing more to do with me."

"Give Mr. Ridgewood an hour alone with the children, and that will change."

Louisa smiled.

"Goodness, those dimples!" Hattie suddenly exclaimed. She leaned toward Louisa as if she might kiss a dimple there in front of the Tabernacle, but Louisa gently nudged her away.

Just then Julia appeared. "May I join you two?"

"Of course," Louisa said, and the three women walked into the Tabernacle together.

Hattie thought the interior nearly as ugly as the exterior, although the size was impressive. She estimated it to be about 250 feet long, 150 wide, and 80 feet high. It could probably hold two thousand people. At its center stood a massive organ with columnlike gold pipes. A great star with pendants of artificial flowers hung from the ceiling, and the galleries surrounding the entirety were supported by pillars painted to imitate marble.

Several hundred people were already seated when the organ suddenly pealed forth, and the choir began to sing "On the Mountain's Top Appearing." The voices rose up, blending together in such beautiful harmony that Hattie shivered. She had to admit that the acoustical properties of the building were very fine.

After the hymn, a tall, square-jawed man approached the podium. Though in late middle age, he appeared remarkably energetic, both in body and in spirit. This was the great Brigham Young.

He delivered a long, impassioned address upon the topic of salvation. Louisa's head was bowed the entire time, her hands clasped together, her eyes closed.

But Hattie hardly heard a word of the sermon. After a fiery flare of devoutness had consumed her when she was about six, she had discovered Darwin. Since then she believed exclusively in the theory of evolution, with only a very slight, uncomfortable doubt regarding where those first living creatures came from—about the origins of the *Origin*, as it were.

When the service was finally over, the excursionists exited the building; everyone was unusually quiet.

Hattie, Julia, and Louisa had gone about fifty feet when two girls in old-fashioned calico skirts ran after them, carrying stacks of the *Book of Mormon*. They were plain brown books, well used.

"We meant to give you our book. Here." One girl extended a book to Hattie, who shuddered and backed away as if it were a writhing snake.

But Louisa said, "I'd like one very much, thank you."

The girl curtsied. "The wisdom of the prophet is very great. It will change you, I hope, as it has us." Then she glanced blissfully at her young companion.

Once they had gone a few yards, Julia began to giggle.

Hattie snorted. "Prophet, indeed! Why, those foolish girls."

"They seem happy," Louisa remarked.

"They're deluded. Well, I suppose many deluded people seem happy. But Mr. Young—ugh! Fashioning himself a modern Christ. Why, they're all stark-raving mad!"

Julia giggled, but Louisa didn't seem to find Hattie's tirade amusing.

"What's the difference between being deluded and happy and being truly happy?" Louisa inquired.

"One is based in reality; the other is not."

"But *whose* reality?" Louisa pressed. "Surely you must agree that happiness is determined almost entirely by internal conditions. One may be happy while sitting on a sidewalk in the dark, for example."

Hattie harrumphed.

"And besides"—Louisa pressed her advantage—"each of us loves God in a different way. Who are we to stand in judgment?"

"But Louisa," Hattie objected more gently, "no one can know God the way these people pretend."

"That's just it. They *believe*. Just as I do, despite—despite everything." She blushed.

Hattie noticed that Julia bent over to tie a shoelace that had not been loose, to give them privacy. *She knows,* Hattie realized. Julia stood up and said with an arch smile, "Well, Hattie. Since you're so fond of him, I'm sure you'll be pleased to know that the Prophet joins us for dinner."

•   •   •

That afternoon, while everyone either toured Salt Lake or pursued their own activities, Hattie wrote a telegram to Mr. Durand. Her feelings for Louisa, she had decided, were just that. Feelings. Of what substance were feelings? Iron? Steel? Of no substance at all.

Hattie's future was her lodestar: to become an educated woman whose ideas were valued by others, surrounded by other strong, innovative minds. And, of course, to help her equally ambitious husband. In this bold dream, if nothing else, Hattie had faith.

> Excellent news regarding house! ~~I should like to help with the work.~~ Do not worry if not finished. I ~~shall enjoy~~ relish the idea of having a ~~this~~ project. Arrive Sacramento 6:00 p.m.
>
> Till very soon—H.

It was short, but that, thankfully, was the nature of the telegram. Hattie was vaguely aware that she had become the heroine of two diverging stories. In one story, she meets a woman on a train, and nothing is the same; in the other, she travels by train to meet Leland Durand in Sacramento, and nothing has changed. She had chosen to live the second story. But was it really a choice?

Hattie stood up and moved off to the editorial offices of the *Trans-Continental*. There, she found a box filled with telegrams waiting to be sent. With a pang of dismay, she realized that the box was full because it was Sunday. None of the telegrams would go out until the following morning. Well, at least she had dated hers, so Leland would know that she had not delayed overly in replying to him.

While the editors were out touring Salt Lake, Hattie took the opportunity to snoop about the editorial offices. Her eyes soon lit upon an unfolded sheaf of pages that lay upon one of their desks. She picked it up.

Salt Lake City, Utah. Monday, May 30

The first article was called "Through the Wasatch," and it was about the Thousand Mile Tree:

> It stood a lonely sentinel, when all around was desolation: when the lurking savage and wild beast claimed supremacy and each in turn reposed in the shade of its waving arms. How changed the scene! The ceaseless bustle of an active age, the hum of labor, the roar and rush of the passing locomotive, has usurped the old quiet, and henceforward the lone tree will be, not a guide to the gloomy past but an index of the coming greatness of a regenerated country.

The coming greatness of a regenerated country. One week earlier, Hattie would have believed this sentiment, even if she made fun of its earnestness. Now it struck her as bombastic and self-serving.

Without, the day had grown warm, and Hattie suddenly felt the effects of having had so little sleep the night before. Pulling two plush seats together in the smoking car, she stretched herself out upon them and fell asleep, curled up like a wayward immigrant.

28

Sunday, May 29, Salt Lake, 5:00 p.m.

A GREAT RUCKUS WOKE HER. THE LAST thing she recalled was having pulled two plush seats together and stretching herself out upon them. She had been dreaming that the train moved, and so it was jarring to discover that they were still in place, just outside the Mormon Tabernacle.

The excursionists were back from their tour. For some reason, they all boarded directly onto the smoking car where Hattie was napping.

"Why, there you are. Curled up like a cat for an afternoon nap," teased Louisa, in good spirits. Then she whispered, "Here he comes."

The Prophet was making his way down the aisle when he glanced at Hattie, who ducked behind her chair like a shy child. He turned to Louisa. "They said I'm to go to the Palmyra car, dear. Would you kindly point the way?"

"Oh, yes, sir. Certainly." Louisa curtsied. "It's three cars down— that way." She pointed to the back of the train.

"Thank you. I'm much obliged, Miss—"

"Finch. Louisa Finch." She curtsied again.

And off he went, followed by a great many passengers who chose to follow behind him across the gaps. Hattie popped up from her hiding place. "Phew—that was close. He might have asked you to be wife number forty-seven!"

"Hattie." Louisa scowled.

Once the crowd thinned out, the mail boy appeared carrying a telegram. He looked about him and called, "Miss Eames? Is there a Miss Eames? A telegram for you!"

Hattie took the telegram from him, puzzled. None of the other mail had gone out, so how had this one come in? Had they made an exception for her father? She was just fishing for a penny from her pocket when Alfred stepped into the smoking car and announced, "Dinner is served!"

"Are you coming?" Louisa nudged Hattie.

"I'll just read my telegram first and wash up. It's from my father," Hattie was careful to add.

"All right. I'll see you in the St. Cloud."

As Louisa went off with the rest of the excursionists, Hattie unfolded her telegram.

May 29, Ogden, Utah. 3:00 p.m.

Dear Daughter,
I know you will be relieved to hear that your mother
is on the mend and that it was not diphtheria from
which she suffered. The unlucky woman had, rather,
an infected tooth that, once pulled, relieved her greatly
and resolved the fever . . .

Hattie rolled her eyes. Though indeed relieved for her mother, her conviction deepened that Mrs. Eames had not been, and never would be, truly ill. Even her eventual death would have to result from some grievous accident. But the telegram wasn't finished:

Mrs. Eames then said I might go. I thus made free to depart on the Pioneer. While not as luxurious as your Pullman Hotel Express, it is most comfortable. We have now reached Ogden and have no plans to stop in Salt Lake City. Therefore there is every reason to hope we shall arrive as scheduled, on the 31st of May, in Sacramento. I hope this finds you well.

Your loving papa

Hattie was amused that her father could not find a shorter way of explaining himself. She counted the words. Poor Papa—the telegram must have cost him a hundred dollars if it cost a penny!

Before joining the others, Hattie stopped to wash her face and brush her teeth. She glanced in the mirror above the sink and was dismayed at her own appearance. She had forgotten to brush her hair, and her dark eyes held a worried expression that no amount of smiling could conceal. Her father's assurance of a timely arrival in Sacramento had been little comfort to her.

By the time Hattie finally reached the St. Cloud car, nearly all the seats were taken. Fortunately, Julia had saved one for her.

"Over here, Miss Eames!" Julia waved happily. Hattie smiled and was about to sit down when she saw Louisa sitting at the very next table—not with the Ridgewoods but with Mr. Byrne. Mrs. Lovelace and her son took up the other two seats. Louisa was chatting amiably just as if she'd not said to Hattie, "Are you coming?" or "I'll see you in the St. Cloud.'"

Just then Mr. Byrne touched Louisa's hand. It was only for a moment, to punctuate a comment. They laughed. It was a small thing. But it didn't feel small to Hattie.

Without acknowledging Julia or looking in Louisa's direction, Hattie passed directly into the second commissary car, where she found all the tables crowded to bursting. Mr. Young was standing in the aisle

holding forth on the history of the Mormons. "My people have suffered, have toiled night and day . . ."

Hearing Hattie step into the car, Mr. Young stopped speaking and
glanced at her. Their eyes met for a moment before she turned on her
heels and retreated to the St. Cloud.

Julia was now looking inquiringly in her direction, and Hattie
made a show of seeking out the waiter. Seeing Alfred at the other end
of the car, she waved him over. Then she leaned in to Julia and said, "I'm
not feeling well. I'll ask Alfred to bring me tea in the Revere."

"Oh," said Julia sadly. "I'm very sorry to hear it. I wondered why
you passed over us. I thought perhaps you preferred to get a glimpse of
the great Prophet."

"It's my third glimpse, and I find he does not improve upon sub-
sequent sightings."

Julia glanced at her father who, fortunately, was studying the menu,
deaf to their conversation.

Just then Alfred appeared in front of Hattie. He smiled broadly.
"We have a most excellent rib of beef today, Miss Eames," he said.
Alfred knew that rib of beef was her favorite.

But Hattie replied mournfully, "Oh, I'd simply like a cup of tea and
a biscuit. Alas, I'm not . . . feeling very well." She placed a hand upon
her stomach for effect, and it then growled so loudly that she feared
everyone would hear it.

"Perhaps you'd like some salts of bismuth."

"Yes, that should do the trick." Hattie gave Alfred a stiff smile, all
the while thinking, *I'm to have salts of bismuth rather than roast beef.
What an ass!*

"I'm very sorry you're unwell and won't be joining us," Julia said. "I
was going to ask you your impressions of Salt Lake."

"I wanted to hear yours too," Hattie replied.

Hearing Hattie, Louisa turned in her direction and endeavored to
catch her eye. But Hattie would not return the look, and Julia said, "It

seems Louisa has acquired an admirer." She glanced questioningly at Hattie.

"Really? I hadn't noticed. But I think I must wait for my tea and bismuth in the other car."

Hattie curtsied and moved off with an inelegant lurch forward. She finally sat down in the empty Revere car with a disgruntled snort, and Alfred soon brought her tea.

Staring down at her penance, she felt a pang of self-pity. "You know, Alfred, I suddenly feel . . . much improved. Do you mind if I take a meal just here, in my seat? The dizziness remains. Indeed, it seems to worsen when I stand."

Alfred, obviously no stranger to subterfuge, smiled with his eyes even while his mouth frowned condolingly. Then he stood aside to reveal a folding stand behind him, upon which sat a dish covered by a silver dome. He lifted the dome to reveal a redolent plate of roast beef. "I took the liberty, miss. I feared they would run out when—er—if you felt hungry later."

"Oh, Alfred!" Hattie grinned. "You are the best! And isn't it fortunate that my hunger has returned at just this very moment!"

"Indeed, it is. Most fortunate."

Alfred fairly skipped away, apparently pleased with himself. Once he was gone, Hattie released her frustrations on the poor slab of steak that, fortunately, was already dead.

Salt Lake, 7:15 p.m.

HATTIE HAD NO WISH FOR JULIA TO discover that she had been lied to. So when she finished her meal, Hattie carried her dishes to a seat several down from hers. Then she began to move off toward the baggage car, realizing only belatedly that she had neither the flask nor her tobacco.

Across the gap, however, on the Arlington car's platform, Alfred was having a very fine smoke. He was standing close to Odysseus, who was also smoking. Hattie had never seen them at rest before. She stopped and listened. They were having an argument, and Hattie backed into the shadow of the Revere's roof so that she could eavesdrop unperceived. Alone together, their speech was vastly different from that which they used with the excursionists. While southern, it was different from Louisa's languorous drawl. Still, Hattie understood it perfectly.

"Dey *queer.*"

"Dey *ain't* queer."

"Dey *is.*"

"Dey is good-hearted women, I tell you."

"Good-hearted, maybe. But queer as blue milk."

"Ain't no such *thing* as blue milk, Oddie."

"Dat's what I'm *talkin'* 'bout."

The two young men laughed and inhaled their cigarettes. Hearing Alfred defend her, Hattie felt tears come to her eyes. Still, she was not moved enough by Alfred's gallantry to forego the satisfaction of her own desires. Hattie wiped away her tears and called out, "Oh, Alfred! What a fine cigarette you've got there!"

Alfred looked at his cigarette forlornly.

"Alfred, you're an angel!" she cried, leaping across the gap.

Hattie took the cigarette and placed it between her lips. Then she inhaled deeply and exhaled with an audible sigh.

"Thanks." She grinned. "Thanks a lot."

Alfred nodded, while Odysseus sent him a knowing glance.

Hattie bade them goodbye and made her way into the baggage car, welcoming the darkness if not the cold. She puffed away contentedly on her ill-gotten cigarette and was just wistfully stomping out the butt when a crack of light appeared from the door, followed by Louisa.

"I thought I might find you here."

Hattie scowled.

"You're smoking again."

"Excellent deduction."

Louisa sighed and sat herself down on one of the trunks.

"What's going on?"

"You tell me."

"Why, very little—goodness, it's freezing in here!" Louisa had donned a short-sleeved frock that morning and now wrapped her thin arms around herself. "Well, we toured the city, and then we returned for dinner. I thought you would sit by Julia, but it seemed you were . . . unwell." Her voice was full of concern. "Are you better now?"

"Oh yes, *vastly*. Just as Mr. Byrne must be, now that he has enjoyed your full attention."

"Is that what this is about, Harriet? Mr. Byrne?" In the scant moonlight, Hattie caught sight of Louisa's knit brow.

"You were laughing and smiling," Hattie said petulantly.

"He sat himself across from me. Then he said something amusing, and I laughed. Is that a crime in Utah Territory?"

"It appears that nothing's a crime in Utah Territory. Except monogamy."

Louisa wasn't amused. She leaned across a trunk to touch Hattie's hand. "Oh, Hattie. Why can't you be *honest*? Why must you always hide your feelings behind so much bluster? It's exhausting."

"I'm to have all the feelings, yet you're exhausted? How does that work?"

Louisa didn't reply. She laughed despairingly and raised her arms into the air. "First you pretend that nothing has happened. Then you fly into a rage, as if you own me. Oh, Harriet, you cannot have it both ways. You cannot insist that nothing has changed and also be madly jealous. You must *choose!*"

Hattie scowled. Then she asked, "Do you have feelings for Mr. Byrne?"

Louisa laughed easily, but seeing Hattie so upset, she reached out to her. "My poor darling. How can you imagine that I have any feelings for Mr. Byrne when I'm in love with someone else?"

They emerged from the baggage car a quarter of an hour later, a great deal warmer than they had been when they entered it. When they returned to the Revere car, it was eerily quiet.

"Where did everyone go?" Hattie asked.

"To hear Brigham Young, probably."

The women pushed on until they found the missing excursionists in the Palmyra. A service was being held, and everyone had crammed in, either standing or spilling out the doors onto the platforms. A few people managed to place their faces near the windows to breathe, as the cramped car had grown quite hot.

Everyone began to sing "Thus Far the Lord Hath Led Me On."
Then the train's pastor stood up and read a psalm:

> O Lord, thou hast searched me and known me.
> Thou knowest mine downsitting and mine
> uprising,
> Thou understandest my thought afar off . . .

Hattie looked on from the platform without singing. Louisa's eyes
were closed as she murmured the words. After the service, Mr. Young
remained in the Palmyra. Someone in the audience asked about how
they had managed to build such a flourishing city in the desert.

"We find great consolation for our sins in hard work," he replied.
"You've seen our streets and gardens. But have you tasted our fresh
water? It's delightful. Yes, from the parched desert we have created all
this, thanks to the Lord."

Another excursionist asked about the local Indians; several excursionists murmured their disapproval, whether of the topic or of the
Indians themselves, Hattie didn't know. She had heard that when the
Mormons first came out to Utah Territory, they had attacked and killed
white settlers and then blamed it on the local Indians. Now Mr. Young
seemed to be claiming a deep and loyal friendship with them, present-
ing himself as a keeper of the peace. She whispered to Louisa, "This is
just one big act." Then she added, "Like everything else."

"Shh!" Louisa's brows knit, and she put a finger to her lips. Julia,
who stood on her other side, grasped Hattie's arm.

Mr. Young went on to discuss his attempts to broker a treaty
between the government and the Ute tribe. "I tried to get them to sell
their land to the government. I said to them, 'If you don't sell them
your land, they will take it anyway. Go to Uintah. They will build you
houses, make you farms.' Well, they signed the treaty and then nothing happened. Six years have passed, and all they've received are a few

trinkets. They believe the Great Father in Washington has abandoned them. And it's true," he said mournfully. "The Great Father and his advisers now have other ideas. They mean for the Ute to assimilate."

Mr. Crockett stood up. "Assimilate, my eye! They'll never assimilate!"

"Sit down, Mr. Crockett," someone barked. Hattie saw a dapper little man in a fine suit wave his hand in the air, as if waving away a bad smell.

"Who'll make me—you?" Mr. Crockett snickered.

Then Mr. Byrne stood and approached him. "This is a great country, sir," he said, standing tall.

Louisa sent Hattie a knowing look.

"And if Grant thinks he can assimilate them, then he'll do it. By God he was a great general. I met the man himself at Appomattox, and he led us to victory."

"Us?" Mr. Crockett laughed again. "Why, I figured you were just a two-bit Irish shop boy back then. Anyhow, you don't know about these Indians. Not like I do."

Mr. Byrne took another step forward, and Mr. Bliss and another man rose to intervene.

Mr. Byrne pointed a finger at Mr. Crockett's chest. "What did *you* do during the war?"

"Do? Why, sent someone in my stead. Just like Mr. Pullman and the rest of these men. And you know what? He died for our side as I would have, had I been a poor sod like you."

Mr. Byrne lunged for Mr. Crockett then, but the two men quickly held him back.

Mrs. Lovelace stood up, her large presence easily brushing off this argument as having no bearing to the issue. "If the Ute are angry, Mr. Young, doesn't that make them dangerous?"

Murmurs of assent flew about the crowd.

Brigham Young replied, "The Ute are a very peaceful people in general. And to answer this gentleman's comment—"

"Gentleman." Hattie snorted derisively.

Brigham Young glanced at her before continuing, "The Ute are ready to till their plots of land, to grow their own vegetables and grains. But it hasn't happened, and they're starving. They grow desperate . . ."

Here, Mr. Price finally stood.

"I feel obliged to say that we haven't had a single report of depredations in this area. None. What's more, the government is well aware of the need to relocate these people."

Mr. Young assented. "Indeed. I feel they shall be patient awhile longer. They're a patient, gentle people and certainly won't fight without an excellent reason. I'm proud to say they count me as their great friend and benefactor, and they've sworn to remain peaceful among us."

"Us? Who's us?" Mr. Crockett cried. "We ain't you—we ain't Mormons! You must be smoking their peace pipe! Why, I for one think we should vamoose. This place's a death trap!" The sudden look of terror on Mr. Crockett's face sobered the crowd at once.

Hattie whispered to Louisa, "Look at how frightened Mr. Crockett appears. I must admit, I'm now very curious about him. Who *is* he, I wonder?"

Before Louisa could reply, Hattie stepped from the open doorway into the car.

"Mr. Crockett." All eyes swiveled toward her. "Who are you, if I may ask? I think I speak for many of us when I say we're curious to know what business you have upon this train. Are you connected to the railroad?"

If Hattie had expected Mr. Crockett to take offense, she was soon to be disappointed. He was only too eager to tell his story.

"Me? Connected to the railroad? Why, no. Not exactly. I'm a trader. That's my trade—hee-hee! Been doin' business with these Indians goin' on twenty years. Doesn't make me trust 'em any better, though. Done some trapping in my day too—back in the day. But that's all over with—heading to California to seek my fortune like everybody else. I'd as good's go there than stay here! I'm finished with these godforsaken plains! Everybody says they're safe, but they ain't safe. You think these redskins are goin' without a fight?" He glanced challengingly at Mr. Young.

But Hattie remained calm when she said, "Trapping and trading. I see. What did you trap, Mr. Crockett?"

By now, even Mr. Young was watching Hattie with amazement. Julia nudged her, fearful that she would cross some scandalous line.

"Beaver, mostly," Mr. Crockett replied, suddenly looking wistful. "Deer too. Had a year of buffalo hunting. Made a good deal of money. Hard work, trapping. Trading's easier. But Indians are worse than buffalo for watchin' your back."

"What did you trade and with whom?"

"Oh, Navajo, Sioux, Ute. Made away with mountains of skins and fur, easy—just got to give 'em a trinket! They love trinkets! Anything shiny. Fool's gold, and they sure is fools."

"And do you work for someone?"

"Work for? Ain't worked for nobody but myself in my life. But even so, the railroad"—he shot a glance toward Mr. Price and Mr. Bliss—"has me to thank for keeping this road as safe as it is." Then, as if compelled to tell the truth in spite of himself, Mr. Crockett added, "Sold the Indians guns too. So they gave me a free ride for my labors." He shook his head disbelievingly. "Guns for promises—maybe not the best idea, now's I think of it."

Mr. Price, who had been keenly observing this exchange, now quickly moved to take center stage. "Ladies and gentlemen. This has been most fascinating. But I'm sure our esteemed guest is fatigued after such a long day. If there are no further questions . . ."

Suddenly, David Lovelace shot his hand up but, not waiting to be recognized, blurted, "How many wives have you got, sir?"

People tittered, but Hattie felt the relief in their laughter.

"Why, I've nineteen wives, young man. And *forty-three* children," Mr. Young answered with obvious pride.

Hattie leaned in to Julia and remarked, "Well, hasn't *he* been busy!"

Julia pulled her lips tight over her teeth. She grabbed Hattie. "Come on, *you*." Louisa, Julia, and Hattie fled onto the observation car, where they burst out laughing. In the open evening air, the laughter had an eerily thin sound, and it soon died out.

The benches were covered in a thin film of ash. None of the ladies wished to sit upon them. They climbed to the top, Julia and Hattie helping Louisa. The highest bench afforded an unobstructed view of Salt Lake glimmering like a spill of liquid mercury in the moonlight. The sky above was filled with stars.

Suddenly Louisa, gazing up and pointing, cried, "Oh, look!"

A shooting star sent a flaming trail westward, as bright as it was fleeting.

"Oh!" Hattie just managed to catch sight of it before it vanished.

Julia said, "I'm afraid I shut my eyes for a minute." She yawned. "I'm exhausted. Good night, my dears."

"Good night, Julia," they replied.

Neither Louisa nor Hattie seemed inclined to leave. Here, at least, they could be alone. Once Julia had gone, they kissed, and held one another, and for nearly a quarter of an hour, Hattie watched for another shooting star to appear, but none did.

Finally, Louisa asked, "Do you really think there's any danger?"

Hattie shook her head. "I don't know. I'm inclined to agree with Mr. Young, that they would need to have a very good reason. It would be suicide to attack us. Every man on this train is armed to the teeth."

"Oh yes, I'd forgotten." After a minute of silence, Hattie heard Louisa yawn. "I'm sleepy too. Let's go to bed."

By the time they made their way back through the cars, Brigham Young and his coterie had gone, and the excursionists had all retired. Checking to see that no one observed them, Hattie leaned in and kissed Louisa. "Good night, my dearest girl. Sleep well."

"My love." Louisa nestled her head in Hattie's neck before climbing into her bed and falling into a dreamless sleep.

30

Monday, May 30, Sacramento, 2:00 a.m.

LELAND WAS HAVING DOUBTS. HE HAD AWAKENED in the middle of the night with the thought that perhaps it had all been a huge mistake to place his faith, his entire future, in a woman he had never met. Never before had he wavered in his belief that it was his destiny to marry Miss Eames.

But now, at two in the morning, with the entire city asleep and its lights extinguished, he sat bolt upright in bed with the appalling understanding that he had been living in a dream from which he had just now awakened.

The home, the chain of grocery stores, the beautiful yet useful wife—all a dream! A shadow of a shadow! His heart pounded, and for a moment, he actually felt short of breath. He grasped his throat with one hand and thought, *Perhaps I'm dying!*

Leland rose. He threw on the same clothing he'd worn the night before and had tossed carelessly upon his chair. Rising, his chamber lit only by the moon, he searched for his socks but could find only one, so he laced up his shoes without them. Then he quietly descended. The old stairs groaned underfoot, threatening to wake his parents. He stopped a moment, grimaced, and then held his breath as he raced down the final steps onto Front Street.

Leland left the house, but his terror followed him. His fists were tight by his sides as he made his way—where? Where to go?

He walked toward the Mackenzie house. All the while, a persistent devil taunted him: *What* are *you, Leland Durand? A grocer's son. A grasping creature.*

Leland pulled his thoughts toward something tangible. Madge. The thought of her bright eyes, dark skin, and familiar smile calmed him; the corners of his mouth curled upward. Yes, better to court Madge, who was at least real, than to marry this figment barreling toward him at thirty miles per hour.

But the thought of Madge soon made him sigh. Madge was a sweet girl and very real. He had known her for many years. But she was like a sister to him. She did not excite him with thoughts of his future.

In the distance, he heard a barge horn. Then a dog began barking. Without the sun, the air was chilly, and Leland realized that he was cold. He walked faster.

What had he achieved? Nothing. What did he own? Nothing. What did he actually know of the world? Leland had been to San Francisco half a dozen times. Twice to Santa Cruz. He had barely made it through school and could not have told you when the American Revolution had occurred.

At last, Leland reached the widow's house. The moon was a crescent high in the sky. In the distance, he heard the rumble of a cart. The streets smelled faintly of vegetables left to rot on the grounds of the farmers' market one block away.

As he stood before the old house, which only the day before had looked so grand to him, tears came to his eyes. His occupation with the Mackenzie house, he realized, had shielded him from his own smallness. It had given him a physical place to expand his dreams, when before him stood only a broken-down eyesore. Maybe it would be best to light a match to it and burn it down!

The workers had left the scaffolding up, and through its boards he could see that several of the windows had been removed, to be scraped down back at the shops. The pedestals on the landing of the once-grand staircase had been removed as well, as workers repaired the crumbling treads beneath.

It was all so ugly, this work in progress! In a moment of frustration, Leland bent down and grasped a rock from the overgrown lawn. He threw it at one of the remaining windows. The rock cracked a windowpane but didn't break it. No, nothing would break this blasted brick house!

Leland yawned, suddenly exhausted; he turned and began to walk home. It was very early on Monday morning. He entered the dark, silent house and crept upstairs, cringing at the telltale squeak of the old stair tread. Once in his room, he stripped out of his clothing, donned his nightshirt once more, and knelt by his bed to pray, just like he used to do when he was a small boy.

"Dear Lord," he began. "Give me the grace—" Crouching there in the darkness, Leland suddenly found himself to be an absurd creature. He smiled, and the smile sent a thin breath of hope through him. *Perhaps,* he thought, *there is solace to be found in this absurdity, the absurdity of man and his ambitions.* But at the moment he couldn't find solace. He prayed he would find it by Tuesday.

31

May 30, Promontory, Utah, 2:00 a.m.

HATTIE WOKE, IMAGINING SHE FELT A JOLT. She sat upon her berth and listened intently, but all she heard were sounds of the night: a cough; several low, steady snores; and the screech of an owl. She wrapped her robe about her, rose quietly, and made her way to the observation car. The train was now moving slowly past Promontory, Utah. One year earlier almost to the day, the Union Pacific and Central Pacific lines joined up in Promontory, to great national fanfare.

Hattie peered out into the darkness. A short distance beyond the promontory, Salt Lake glittered with myriad tiny sparks of light. Above her, crushed diamonds lit the sky. They reached a plateau and then descended, the tracks curving gently around the northern tip of the lake, lined with cottonwood trees.

The moon was rising, and Hattie perceived movement. A jagged row of prairie grass inched toward the train, and at first, she thought it was a trick of the eye. But instead of moving away from the train, as such an illusion would, the prairie grass continued to move toward it.

Then something made the train leap like a bull, and Hattie was thrown back against one of the benches. The car tilted violently and flipped over. As it did, Hattie was propelled to the ground with such force that the impact crushed the breath from her body. She was rendered unconscious for perhaps a few seconds, and when she opened her eyes, the observation car was lying on its side. It had twisted off its pin and become separated from the rest of the cars. The slats of the wood benches had broken into treacherous spears, and through the spears that jutted up like a ruined picket fence, Hattie saw a swarm of Indian warriors running toward the train. The ones behind the prairie grass had thrown off their disguises, but there were others on horseback who had appeared from the cover of the trees. These men held weapons of all varieties: rifles, revolvers, knives, and a few bows with arrows in pouches fastened to their vests. They were screaming to wake the dead.

A sudden pain in Hattie's temple made her vomit at her own feet. The Indians encircled the train. Several had rifles and had begun shooting. Others had bows and arrows and began to unleash them. It was difficult to see anything, but Hattie could hear women screaming and men's voices yell, "Get back! Get down! To arms!" But she saw none of the excursionists, only the Indians' dark figures through a pile of broken wood.

She thought the Indians must have rigged a device upon the tracks, for the explosion had blown the engine up and off them. A lone torch briefly illuminated a great hellish swirl of ash and dust. In that vivid flash, Hattie saw the overturned engine and tender lying on their sides to the left of the tracks, smoke pouring from them. The engineer and the brakeman emerged from behind the overturned cars with pistols drawn. They began shooting.

The torch was just as suddenly extinguished, and then the tender box exploded with a great *whoosh!* Tall flames leaped from it, licking the sky.

The shooting seemed to go on forever. When it was over, and Hattie was certain the Indians had galloped off, she crawled on all fours through the overturned wreck, which now stood like a ruined wall. Slowly, she scanned the carnage around her.

Several Indians lay dead upon the ground. One Indian, a young man about Hattie's age, wore buffalo-skin britches and a red buckskin tunic. He was curled on his side, his legs in a fetal position. A bow lay near him, and his hand still gripped an arrow. Hattie could see his painted face, eyes and mouth wide open as if he'd been caught by surprise.

Farther off, to the side of the Revere car, one horse lay dead, and three others lay grunting and writhing. The gas lamps within the train cast a lurid light upon them.

"Oh God! Someone!" Her voice quavered; she was not sure if it had even been audible. No one replied. Did no one hear her? They could not all be dead. Suddenly, someone's foot disturbed a twig, and Hattie darted back behind the cover of the overturned car.

Mr. Crockett emerged into the canopy of light coming from the Revere car's dimmed gaslights. He glanced about him, pointing his pistol in the direction of the trees. Then he muttered, "Damn nits!" and proceeded to shoot the wounded horses dead.

Then he came to the last horse. It was a young white Andalusian. Its eye shone brightly, and Hattie realized that it was unharmed, merely stunned. The horse looked up at him with that wild, entreating eye and began to rise. Mr. Crockett took aim nonetheless. He inhaled. "Nits make—" he began to say once more when, out of the gloom, Louisa appeared.

She stood phantomlike in the hellish death field. Hearing her, Mr. Crockett turned to look in her direction.

Hattie turned back to Mr. Crockett just long enough to see his look of surprise when Louisa raised a great granite rock over him and then dropped it squarely upon his head. He fell like a stone, dead.

From the dark depths of the grove by the river came a short whistle. Then a young warrior stepped out of the darkness. He wanted his horse. Suddenly, he crouched down and disappeared into the brush, and Hattie caught her breath when, a few seconds later, he reappeared quite close to Louisa. His gun was pointed directly at her. Louisa stared at him but didn't move. He stared back and took a step toward her, as if he would kill or capture her. Then he looked up at the moon and lowered his gun, suddenly doubtful.

Was she real? Or was she some strange pale demon from the Spirit World? What real woman, white or otherwise, would stand so tall and fearless? He called to his horse, which rose unsteadily to its knees, swished its tail, and then stood. The boy mounted him at once. Then they disappeared back into the cottonwoods with hardly a sound.

• • •

Louisa stood just beyond the awning of light from the gas lamps, among the dead horses and the dead men.

Hattie glanced at Mr. Crockett, who lay splayed on his back, arms akimbo. His pistol had tumbled and come to rest a dozen feet away, and for a moment, she considered picking it up.

Hattie took a step toward Louisa and felt a pain in her back where a splinter of wood had poked through her tunic.

"Louisa!" she called.

Louisa stood, unseeing, as several excursionists now poked their heads out the windows and peered cautiously around. Hattie moved to embrace her, but Louisa pulled away. She looked at Hattie, but hers were the eyes of a stranger.

"Is he dead?" she asked.

"Yes," Hattie replied. "We're safe, though. Come back to the train—you're trembling. Let's get you warm."

Hattie put her hands upon Louisa's shoulders; Louisa grew rigid.

"I wanted to stop him. He had to be stopped. D'you see? I never—"

"Yes. Of course," Hattie quickly replied. "Now, come in."

The heads hanging out the windows began calling their names and other phrases she could not make out. Finally, the voices formed themselves into distinct words: "Where is Mr. Straight?" Hattie heard. "People are hurt in here!"

Without letting go of Louisa, Hattie moved toward the front of the train. She found the conductor already there. He stood beside the engine driver next to the overturned engine. They had been searching for the fireman, and now they had found him: the boy from the east who hoped to be an engineer someday. He was pinned between the boiler and the tender. His face was pink, his mouth melted to expose his teeth and jaws, his once-blue eyes boiled from their sockets.

"Oh, Louisa. Come away; come away!" Hattie placed her hands across Louisa's eyes. Then she remembered her task. "Sir," Hattie addressed Mr. Straight, "you're wanted in the cars. People are injured."

Hattie was gently leading Louisa onto the train when suddenly the latter exhaled, her eyes rolled into her head, and she collapsed at Hattie's feet.

"What is it? Is she wounded?" In the darkness, Hattie felt for the wetness of blood upon Louisa's body, but she found none.

Mr. Straight bent down to listen to Louisa's breath. "It's shock. She needs attention. Mr. Symonds!" he shouted to his engine driver. Symonds helped him carry Louisa back to the Revere car.

Hattie followed behind the men, dreading what they would find within. One of the first people she met was Julia, who, thankfully, was unharmed. "Mr. Fogg arrives," she said, referring to their resident doctor. "I shall go fetch blankets," she added, and hurried off.

Hattie could hardly breathe until Mr. Fogg had examined Louisa. When Hattie saw him, she recognized him as the man who had told Mr. Crockett to sit down during their argument the night before. He was a small, dapper man with a neatly trimmed beard and an unhurried, thorough touch. He put his ear to her chest and listened to her breathing. Then he took her pulse.

"She is unharmed physically, but her shock is profound. Keep her warm. Her feet must be elevated." Then, suddenly suspicious, Mr. Fogg asked, "Was she outside?"

"Oh, no." The lie felt thick in Hattie's mouth.

Mr. Fogg frowned. He turned to attend the others when he noticed the blood on the back of Hattie's tunic.

"Miss Eames, you're bleeding."

"Am I?"

"Your hands are scraped too, but I must see to this cut on your back. Allow me to examine it." He began to lead her toward the dressing room, but Hattie wouldn't go.

"You may examine me here. I shan't leave her." And with that, Hattie ripped off her bloodied tunic and pressed herself into a seat, her back exposed. Fortunately, most of the people in the Revere car were attending to their loved ones and paid little attention to Hattie or her exposed back.

Mr. Fogg looked at the wound and then examined the skin around it. He asked dubiously, "How did this happen?"

"I was in the observation car when it overturned."

"At such an hour?"

"I couldn't sleep."

Mr. Fogg frowned, as if to say that women had no business being up and about in the middle of the night. "Well," he resumed, "I need to clean and stitch it. Boy!" Mr. Fogg called to Alfred, who had been tending to another passenger. "Fresh water, please, and towels."

Alfred nodded and went off to procure the requested items but not without first sending Hattie a sympathetic look.

Hattie felt nothing when Mr. Fogg sewed her wound; her eyes were on Louisa, who lay back on two seats with her eyes open, not seeing. She began to tremble almost violently.

Hattie stood up straight, exposing her voluptuous breasts, which sent the prim Mr. Fogg flying backward with a cry.

"Where in hell are those blankets?" she shouted. Just then Julia appeared and rushed over with several to cover Louisa and Hattie both.

Meanwhile, Mr. Fogg had managed to finish his work. "Keep this dry," he said. "We'll change the bandage tomorrow."

Hattie nodded. Then she mouthed to Julia, *Sorry*. Turning to Louisa, she said, "Come on, darling. You're all right now. You've nearly ceased trembling. Are you quite warm?" Hattie took her hands, which were limp and cool. "Oh, look, your tea arrives!"

Louisa nodded. But if there was a convention that required one to speak when spoken to, she seemed to have forgotten it.

"I heard an explosion. Is it wartime?" she asked Hattie.

Alfred came toward them with a tray raised above his head. He moved deftly, nearly as focused on Louisa as Hattie was. Behind him, moving with an air of united authority, came Mr. Price and then Mr. Bliss.

Louisa stirred when she smelled the tea being poured. She looked about, suddenly roused from her state of semiconsciousness. Then she jolted up, frightened and confused. From the other end of the car, Mr. Byrne appeared.

"Is she all right?" he called worriedly.

"Oh yes. Or she soon shall be," Hattie replied.

He approached Hattie. "Well, is there something I can do?"

"You could send a telegram to her father. I don't dare leave her side just now. His name is Reverend Finch, and he is from Roxbury."

"Yes, of course." Mr. Byrne nodded and began to walk toward the smoking car.

But at the mention of a telegram, Mr. Price's body grew rigid, and he exchanged a glance with Mr. Bliss.

"It would be wise, perhaps, not to inform anyone of this occurrence just *yet*." Then he looked intently at Mr. Byrne.

Mr. Byrne bowed slightly.

Confused, Hattie started back. "Surely telegrams must be sent? I myself shall send one to Papa as soon as I can."

Mr. Price closed his eyes momentarily. Then he said, "Certainly, Miss Eames." He turned and gave a hard stare to Mr. Byrne. "I'd like to have a word, if I may."

Just then Mr. Ridgewood came running through the car with bloodied hands raised above him. He was still in his nightshirt, which was stained almost completely red, as if he had been stabbed. Yet he seemed unharmed. "Where are my children? For God's sake, where are they?"

"They're not with you?" Mr. Price asked.

"No!"

Mr. Ridgewood approached them. The excursionists stopped what they were doing and turned toward him as he froze in place outside the stateroom. Mr. Fogg moved toward Mr. Ridgewood, then stepped into the stateroom and looked down in horror: a dark stain had begun to spread out across the carpet and into the aisle. People gasped and then scrambled to back away from the river of blood.

Hattie whispered to Louisa, "I'll be right back." She got as far as the door but was prevented from entering by the presence of Mr. Price. Hattie peered in: Mrs. Ridgewood had rolled onto her side and nearly disappeared between the edge of the berth and the open window, from which her head dangled.

"Dear God. What has happened here?" Mr. Price said. "Someone cover her. A blanket, George!" he called to Alfred, using the railroad's generic name for porters. "At once!"

Alfred, perspiration now making pale rivulets down his face and neck, ran to find a blanket to place over the body of Mrs. Ridgewood.

Mr. Fogg pushed past Hattie and entered the cabin. Out of an excess of caution, he turned the body over: Mrs. Ridgewood's startled eyes stared up at him. A bullet hole had made a small flower on the left side of her forehead.

As Hattie made her way back to Louisa, she could not prevent herself from thinking that if only Mrs. Ridgewood had remained in her original berth with the hoi polloi, she might still be among them.

Mr. Ridgewood began calling, "Children! Frank!"

Everyone began to look for the Ridgewood twins. Mr. Byrne reappeared, his eyes wide blue discs. They sought out Louisa, then Hattie, and Louisa again, as if Mr. Price had told him something he refused to believe. Finally, he ran off to join the search for the children and soon returned with them unharmed: they had been cowering in the men's washroom. In their terror, they seemed to have fallen mute, for when Mr. Fogg asked if they were all right, they just stared up at him without blinking. Seeing them at last, Mr. Ridgewood reached out eagerly and cried, "Oh, my precious ones!"

But instead of running to him, they ran to Louisa and buried their faces in her petticoat, gripping her legs. Hattie noticed droplets of blood upon the left sides of their nightshirts, as if it had dripped upon them as they slept on their sides.

Louisa held the children to her and said, her voice tender yet firm, "Oh, but you're not in bed? It's very late. You must go back to bed at once."

The children screamed. Hattie stared confusedly at Louisa as they sprang away from her. Was it possible she didn't know that Mrs. Ridgewood was dead? Or that the bed beneath which the children had been sleeping contained their mother, lying in a pool of blood?

Soon, Alfred and another porter removed the body, and the crowd around it dispersed. But no one returned to sleep. The porters, realizing that the berths only impeded movement between and among the cars, hastily folded them back into the walls—all except Louisa's and Hattie's, which Hattie requested they leave for the time being. Then they worked quickly to bring all the shocked excursionists tea, biscuits, and blankets. Some asked for stronger stuff, which the porters obliged them. Receiving these, the excursionists grew oddly docile, nodding and thanking Alfred, Odysseus, and the others as if they were dear friends.

In the aisle, pistols still visible at their hips, Mr. Price and Mr. Bliss stood speaking to Mr. Straight. Every once in a while, Mr. Straight's gruff voice rose, and Hattie could hear him object, "But that's not the procedure!" Each time he endeavored to move off, presumably to send his report, they held him back and spoke to him in low, insistent voices.

Eventually, Mr. Straight nodded exhaustedly, then moved off into another car. The two executives left the car as well but returned in a few minutes with their overcoats on. Then they exited the train.

After several more minutes, Hattie heard voices and the sound of metal hitting rocks. People were digging by the side of the tracks. Digging graves. Hattie wondered if, in digging the graves, the men grasped handles that read EAMES SHOVEL MANUFACTORY in blue paint. It was likely. Straining her neck to look back behind their car, Hattie could make out the red tinge of Mr. Byrne's hair, but the others were obscured in the darkness.

For the rest of the night, Hattie remained with Louisa, never letting go of her hand. But even as she spoke to her of everything and nothing in particular, she thought, *Whatever happened out there wasn't something that only* just *happened.*

Hattie looked through Louisa's drawing kit and remarked, "Your pastels are quite marvelous. Why, I've noticed nearly every color of the rainbow! I wonder where one buys such supplies?" Then, looking at Louisa's imagined scene, "Oh, those silly prairie dogs! They're so very inquisitive, aren't they? They simply *must* know what's going on, even when they're too frightened to look."

Louisa nodded. Once or twice she smiled. Hattie was speaking to her about trivialities, as if those mundane activities might attract her now.

Hattie realized that Louisa had not said a word since telling the children to go back to bed, and, eventually, she fell silent.

• • •

Dawn broke upon a changed scene: all looked quite peaceful and natu-ral beyond the window. The watery light of an early sun dappled the young leaves of the cottonwood trees. Mr. Crockett's body was gone. The Indian boy was gone, as were the other fallen Indians. The dead horses had been dragged off toward the river, beyond the trees, and lit on fire. *Why,* Hattie wondered, *did they bother to drag them off like that?* She could smell them burning. Even after the flames had gone out, smoke continued to issue from the burned carcasses. The stench permeated the car, waxing and waning with the shifting night breezes but never entirely dissipating.

The men seemed to have disappeared, and Hattie doubted whether any had managed to sleep. *It was a busy night for them,* she thought mordantly. She sat down beside Louisa and closed her eyes.

"What's the matter, Hattie? Are you ill?"

Hattie was surprised to hear Louisa speak. She sounded like herself.

"The smell," Hattie replied, swallowing hard. "But I'm all right."

Soon, the thin orange line of dawn rose up into a pinkish, blood-orange light. Hattie, dressed only in her night shift, shivered with the cold. She stood up and was about to climb into her own berth when Louisa grabbed her hand.

"Come here. You're cold."

She lifted the blanket and pulled Hattie next to her, then pulled the blanket over them both. Hattie shut the curtains behind her and huddled close.

"That's better," Hattie said.

Louisa's body began to warm her, and Louisa murmured, "Oh yes. That's good."

As dawn grew bolder, Hattie heard the voice of Mr. Waterston, the train's clergyman, beyond Louisa's window. She sat up and looked: a makeshift service was being held by the graves. Mr. Price, Mr. Bliss,

Mr. Ridgewood and his children, and several others, hastily dressed, formed a motley group around the graves. Their heads were bowed, and they now murmured a prayer.

Hattie knew that Louisa heard the service, but neither said anything about it. There was nothing to say. She wrapped one arm around Louisa, finally warm.

Then they both slept.

32

THE BRIGHT MORNING LIGHT WOKE HATTIE. PORTERS busily scurried back and forth, carrying folding tables, fresh white linens, and the special railroad china just as if nothing had happened.

Hattie sat up and peeked through the window curtains. The train hadn't moved; they were still in Promontory. Hattie thought that by now, word must have spread about the attack, since no other trains came upon them. They would be blocking the route for several more hours at least.

Louisa continued to sleep, her long, slender form beneath the blanket turned toward the wall. Hattie let her sleep while she grabbed her robe and went to the washroom, where she cleaned her teeth and stripped out of her bloodied clothes and scrubbed her filthy body with a cloth, which she then threw out the window. The wound on her back had now begun to hurt most devilishly. The cuts on her hands were unsightly but fortunately shallow; she had no memory of breaking her fall with them. After her ablution, she wrapped her robe about her and sprinted back to her berth.

She found Louisa lying on her other side now, facing the aisle. Her eyes were open. Seeing Hattie, she smiled. Hattie, encouraged, smiled back.

"Oh, good. You're up. Let's go get something to eat. We'll both feel better for it."

"All right."

Hattie watched Louisa walk slowly to the washroom, returning five minutes later. Then they descended and made their way to the St. Cloud car. Was it her imagination, or were the excursionists watching them from the windows?

The St. Cloud car was eerily quiet. Julia was alone, sipping her coffee. When Julia saw Hattie, she sent her a questioning look about Louisa. Hattie shook her head almost imperceptibly and sat down. Only at that moment did she realize that Louisa would not go off as usual to sit by Mrs. Ridgewood and the children. They would not see Mrs. Ridgewood sitting there with that scowl, would not hear her call, "Lou-*eeza!*"

They sat down together, and as Hattie looked about the car, she was struck by its stunning normalcy: the bright-white tablecloths, steam rising from the coffee being poured, and the gracious porters in their white jackets fetching food. It was all strangely beautiful.

"That's odd!" she suddenly exclaimed. "Where are all our men?"

"My father said there was a meeting he needed to attend before breakfast," Julia replied, then glanced about her. "Goodness—you're right. Where are the others?"

"Stay here a moment," Hattie said to Louisa, placing a hand on her shoulder. "I'll be right back."

Hattie made her way to the St. Charles car, which was where many of the men, particularly those traveling without their wives, usually took their meals. It was empty. She returned to the St. Cloud.

"Were they in the St. Charles?" Julia asked when Hattie returned.

Hattie shook her head. "Perhaps they're meeting in one of the saloon cars."

Their breakfast arrived. The coffee seemed hotter, and the eggs even more nicely cooked, than usual, but they could only pick at them. Hattie watched a team of railway workers haul the broken observation car away. As she observed their progress, she began to doubt her own recollections of the night before. Had the three of them stood in that car? Had Louisa really pointed to the sky and said, *"Oh, look!"*? And later, had she returned to find herself part of some cataclysmic failure in which the car had flipped sideways and broken away from the others? The memory was like a lurid dream.

"I find it odd that no one has come to speak with us," she suddenly commented. "Do our families know that we're safe?"

"Do they even know what happened?" Julia asked. "Perhaps nobody knows yet."

Hattie whispered, "Did you see it, Julia? The attack, I mean?" Her eyes flitted toward Louisa, who continued to stir and stir her tea, now cold.

Julia nodded and began to tremble. She gripped her coffee mug.

"I'm sorry," said Hattie, reaching to steady her.

"The men were shooting, the ladies crouching or cowering beneath their covers. But I wished to know what was happening. So I glanced out the window and saw the Indian boy fall off his horse."

Hattie whispered, "Did you see Mr. Crockett?"

Julia nodded.

Louisa spoke, her voice perfectly audible. "She wants to know if you saw me kill Mr. Crockett."

"Shh!" Hattie hissed.

"Well, I saw you standing there, and I saw Mr. Crockett with his pistol. He was about to shoot that poor horse. I ducked at a sound, and when I looked again, he was on the ground."

They let the subject drop. No one ate; even Hattie had lost her appetite. She took only coffee and a bite of her eggs before pushing everything to the far side of her plate. The smell of burning horses was fainter now but still present. Hattie thought she would always smell them.

Hattie chose to jump the gaps back to the Revere car while Julia and Louisa descended the train. She got as far as the Palmyra when, opening the door, she was assaulted by fifty pairs of male eyes turned to stare at her. There was nothing friendly about the stares.

"Ladies are to descend the train whilst perambulating," said Mr. Price.

"To do otherwise is quite dangerous," Mr. Bliss added. Then he smiled.

Hattie glanced at Mr. Hunnewell. He met her eyes briefly, then pretended that something caught his attention beyond the window.

"Excuse me," she said. She curtsied and left the car, then descended. For once, no clever riposte had come to mind. Their cold looks had frozen her tongue.

Hattie met Julia and Louisa just as they were about to enter the Revere car.

"They're in the Palmyra. The men, I mean," Hattie said.

"Did they say anything to you?"

Hattie nodded. "Mr. Price told me I needed to descend the train. Their looks were . . ." Hattie shivered.

But the women in the Revere car were hardly friendlier. As Hattie passed them, she felt that all eyes were upon Louisa: silent, judging eyes. What did they know or think they knew? Hattie wondered. Then, the young women passed by the room where Mrs. Ridgewood had slept with her children. Julia shivered and nudged Hattie in the back, entreating her to move more quickly. The lake of blood on the floor had been washed and scrubbed; the berths had been folded, and what remained of Mrs. Ridgewood herself was now buried in the ground beyond the tracks. Only a wood board nailed over the broken window suggested that there had ever been a disturbance.

Their own seats farther back in the car had been cleaned, the window curtains opened to let in the sun. The windows had been washed, and through them the sun shone brightly. No trace remained of the chaos and terror of the night before.

Through her window, Hattie heard several of the workers.

"Helluvan accident, I'd say."

"An explosion, looks like."

"They tol' me it war them tracks, not set right or some sich, but looky what I found over by the wrecked-up car." The first worker, a young, swarthy man, possibly a "mixed blood," proffered a feather, which was attached to a broken string of beads, and the other man's eyes widened in wonder.

"They ain't said nothin' 'bout Injuns, have they?"

"Naw. An' I bet they won't if it war!"

Hattie turned away. Pensive, she took a piece of foolscap from her bag and began to compose a telegram to her father. Louisa looked ahead but not at anything in particular. Julia remained with them, a silent helpmeet to Hattie. She had taken up her knitting once more, and the green sweater was nearly finished.

"I'm amazed you have the presence of mind to finish that sweater, Julia."

"Well, if I don't finish it, then something else is lost as well."

Hattie was surprised by Julia's philosophical comment.

"Right you are. And not merely that sweater but your admirable— what's the word? *Persistence*, perhaps. I've noticed it for some time now. In the way you stand up to your father. Or last night, when you didn't cower or cry like the other ladies but ran out to see if you could help."

They had turned their seats to face one another, though the porters had not yet brought the tables back. Julia was obliged to set her knitting down upon her lap before looking at Hattie with amusement. "You flatter me," she said.

"Not at all. I'm moved to speak my mind." Then Hattie turned to Louisa. "Louisa, it occurs to me . . . shouldn't you send word to your father?"

"Did Mr. Byrne not already do so?" Louisa asked indifferently.

"No. If you recall, Mr. Price asked him to wait."

"Write him if you like." There was a pause before she added, "What shall you tell him?"

"I'll say the train was attacked but that you're perfectly all right. I should think the news will soon be in all the papers, and it's better if he hears the truth from you first."

"The truth?" She flashed a cryptic smile.

"Some version of it, at least."

"Some version," Louisa echoed. "You know, I feel like I'm a dragonfly upon still water."

Hattie and Julia looked at each other.

"Yes, a dragonfly," Louisa asserted. "Or perhaps a *damselfly.*" Her eyes glittered knowingly. "Someone threw a stone onto the water—oh, how long ago that was!—and it finally reached me, made me jump. Yes." She nodded. "That's the truth. Or *some version of it.*"

Neither Hattie nor Julia replied. Hattie felt that Louisa was not in her right mind. She finished the telegram to her own father and then wrote another to Reverend Finch, struggling over what to say. In the end, she chose to say only that Louisa was well. After Hattie had finished, she made her way to the offices of the *Trans-Continental.*

Things had been moved about since the last time Hattie had come through. The newspapers that had been printed on Saturday had been thrown into a wastebasket, the overflow set in a pile next to it.

The letterbox was not in its usual place either, and when Hattie searched for it, she found it beneath Mr. Steele's desk. It had been placed upside down and was covered by another stack of old newspapers. The box was empty. Where had the mail gone? It was now Monday, and no mail or telegrams had gone out the day before. There would be a pile somewhere.

Hattie's heart began to pound. She looked around at the dimly lit offices, then peered out the window to see whether a line had been attached to the telegraph poles beside the tracks. She saw none. She began to open the desk drawer and even peered behind the desk.

Nothing there but some dusty foolscap that must have slipped behind there days ago.

Hattie turned back with a sudden thought. She passed through the office and across the gap into the baggage car, now the first car of the train. Light came in from both the front of the car and the side window. Hattie glanced at the printing press in the corner, which previously had been shrouded in darkness. Next to it, a mass of old newspapers was piled upon a small wooden barrel. She approached the barrel. It struck her as odd that the editors chose to put such a heap of paper in a receptacle so obviously inadequate to hold it, especially when, nearby, there were several wooden packing crates.

Hattie lifted the pile of newspapers with both hands, expecting to find the usual trash. But there, lying beneath the newspapers, were all the excursionists' letters and telegrams. Someone had torn them to pieces.

33

THE REST OF THE WOMEN IN THE Revere car had shut their eyes and covered themselves with blankets, hoping to pass the time in the oblivion of sleep. No one endeavored to read her guidebook. Someone had even gone so far as to toss hers out the window; its pages fluttered in the sagebrush alongside the tracks, like a strange dead bird.

Louisa was not in her seat, and Hattie assumed that she had gone to the WC. The men were still nowhere to be seen, although Hattie now presumed they were in the Palmyra car. She realized that she had not seen Mr. Straight either. Not since the night before, when she saw him arguing with the executives.

As Hattie waited for Louisa to return, she heard the new engine being fired up. After several minutes, Hattie stood and looked about the car: no Louisa. Quickly, she walked to the WC and knocked. Then she opened the door; the bathroom was empty.

She continued through the cars, and when she reached the Palmyra car, she paused, her heart pounding. She pulled it open to find dozens of men crowded into an oval. There were not enough chairs for them; some knelt, others sat cross-legged. But all of them fell silent and stared at Hattie with open hostility.

"Excuse me," she said. Then she cursed herself for the years of training that made her say "Excuse me" when she had nothing to excuse herself for.

Hattie descended the train and gazed down the lonesome rail lines. Then her eyes lit upon the three freshly planted crosses that poked out of the salty white earth.

Louisa was kneeling beside one of the graves, her hand clutching a bouquet of wildflowers. Her eyes were shut tight, her head bent in abject misery, her lips murmuring a prayer.

"There you are!" Hattie called.

Louisa looked up but said nothing.

Hattie knelt beside her.

"They're not marked," she observed. "How do you know you've got the right one?"

There was a slight irony to her words, but Louisa replied simply, "I'm praying for them all."

Hattie waited while Louisa finished her prayers. Then she said, "The train is leaving soon. We should get back."

She helped Louisa to her feet, and together they returned to the train. They sat themselves across from Julia, who was sewing buttons on her sweater. Hattie and Louisa had been in their seats for perhaps five minutes when the whistle blew, the first slow *chug* of the wheels sounded, and the landscape beyond the windows began its magical backward motion.

"We move!" Hattie cried.

After Promontory, there were no trees but only barren alkali plains. Then they passed a river where a flock of pelicans took flight at the sound of the train, blackening the sky with their primordial forms. Hattie nudged Louisa and said, "Look at the pelicans."

Louisa glanced in the general direction, then turned back to stare at a wall of air between herself and Julia.

"Pelicans in flight," she said. "What are they but a fleeting disturbance of air?"

"They're very remarkable," Hattie continued, endeavoring to pull Louisa out of herself. "When I look at them, I can imagine a world entirely before man."

"If only," said Louisa.

Then they fell implacably silent.

•   •   •

The Pullman Hotel Express reached Palisade, where it stopped briefly, and a few women descended to stretch their legs. The Palmyra car finally disgorged its crowd of somber men. Mr. Price and Mr. Bliss remained behind. They stood sentry on the stairs, carefully watching everyone, their pistols visible at their hips. Mr. Price had dropped his guise of geniality, and Mr. Bliss's rosaceous face now looked positively leprous.

As the men passed her by, Hattie smelled tobacco smoke, mixed with the putrid reek of horse fat. The men remained among themselves and didn't mingle with the ladies.

Julia searched the crowd for her father. Finally, she blurted, "I'll go find Papa. Perhaps *he* can tell us what's going on."

Julia went off, and Hattie, taking Louisa's arm, said, "Let's walk a ways."

Louisa nodded distractedly.

The young women strolled along the stream. The day was warm and sunny, and the palisades on their left shone red and yellow. The stream wended its way back toward an old wooden bridge, and Hattie thought it odd that the trees' leaves along the river had turned to gold, until she realized that these were not leaves but a flock of yellow-headed blackbirds, hundreds of them.

Hattie had always been indifferent to nature, apart from Darwin's theory about it. Nature had nothing to do with her, nor she with it. But now, she found the pelicans and the golden-headed creatures as beautiful as if Louisa's soul had moved inside her. Or as if she had appointed herself guardian of it, until such time as Louisa returned to claim it.

The stream broadened into a river, and a snowy white swan floated down the current.

"Oh, look, Louisa! A swan!"

Louisa smiled. The white creature moved with no visible effort as it bobbed and balanced itself on the river's quickly moving surface. Encouraged, Hattie stopped walking and turned back to gaze at the red and yellow striations of the palisades. "Don't you wish to sketch these palisades? They're very beautiful."

Louisa smiled indulgently, and for a moment, Hattie's hopes rose. But in a barely audible voice, she said, "No, Harriet. Nothing is beautiful to me anymore."

"But that's not true!" Hattie cried. "I see it now. Everything that you do. Nothing has changed."

"Everything has changed."

Hattie grew frantic and said in a child's voice, "Oh, Louisa, don't abandon me!"

But Louisa looked at Hattie as if she'd spoken in a foreign language.

The train whistle blew, and all those who had strolled down the river now hurried back.

Leaving Palisades behind, the Pullman Hotel Express proceeded down a valley, along a river fringed with gossamer willows. Hattie saw Mr. Ridgewood walking toward them from the washroom. Sheila and Frank walked several paces behind him. On his arm he wore a black armband. Apart from the armband, little sign of grief was visible. Instead, he looked annoyed that the children had taken so long in the washroom.

Louisa stopped, as if she would speak to him, but Hattie pushed her forward.

"But I must say something, surely."

Hattie shrugged. "If you want."

But it seemed the impulse had passed, for Louisa said nothing, although the children looked at her as if they would speak to her before being pushed forward by their father.

It was soon time for lunch. Louisa told Hattie that she would remain in the Revere and take some tea. The other excursionists made their way to their usual dining cars—all except for the executives, who, for a reason Hattie could not fathom, now sat directly across from her, where formerly Mr. Crockett had dined. Mr. Price, Mr. Steele, Mr. Bliss, and Mr. Hunnewell conversed, smiled, sipped wine, and poked silver fork tines into small, firm potatoes. In the booth directly behind them, at Mrs. Ridgewood's table, sat Mr. Byrne and the two assistants, whose names Hattie did not know.

"Mm. That's an excellent piece of meat," Hattie heard Mr. Steele remark to Mr. Price.

"This Bordeaux has achieved an impressive depth," added Mr. Bliss.

"Indeed, it has," agreed Mr. Hunnewell. Next to them, Mr. Byrne ate in silence, looking at no one.

Hattie whispered to Julia, "Were you able to speak to your father?"

Julia shook her head. "He made as if he was far too busy. I think he's avoiding me."

Suddenly, Mrs. Lovelace exclaimed, "How can they expect us to eat? I myself cannot touch a morsel!"

Her son nudged her. "You may fast till we reach California, Mother, for all anyone cares."

Hattie stood up; Julia placed a forestalling hand on her arm. "Where are you going?"

"I'll be right back." She approached the editors. "How was your meeting this morning, Mr. Byrne?"

Mr. Byrne glanced over at Mr. Steele, whose expression made good his name. At the sound of Hattie's voice, Mr. Price, Mr. Bliss, and Mr. Hunnewell all turned to stare at her. But Mr. Byrne would not look at her when he replied, "It was all right."

"You men were gone a long time."

Hattie had not thought that such a pale, freckled man could look any paler. Now even his lips appeared whitish as he began to speak. "We were—"

But before Mr. Byrne could finish his sentence, the other men's poisonous looks made him stop. He stood up momentarily and peered out the window, his hands pressed to the glass, as if he might be thinking of jumping.

Hattie turned to Mr. Hunnewell. "Mr. Hunnewell, maybe you can tell us what the men spoke about all morning?"

He sighed wearily. "As you say, it was a long meeting, Miss Eames. You needn't concern yourself with it."

"But I *do* concern myself with it. What has the Boston Board of Trade decided to do about last night?"

The Boston Board of Trade was sitting right there before her, as were the major stockholders of the Union Pacific. Mr. Hunnewell crossed his legs and set his paper down with deliberate slowness. His hand trembled slightly.

"Do? Why, nothing. That is, nothing's been decided. Though we did learn that the editors of the *Trans-Continental* have chosen to print one final issue." He glanced back at Mr. Byrne and smiled thinly. "We must praise their tenacity."

Hattie's voice rose as she asked, "So we're free to write our families? To say we are safe after last night's attack?"

"My dear Miss Eames, you are free to do what you wish."

"I shall tell my father you said so."

Hattie turned without curtsying and pushed her way past porters carrying their cleaning supplies until she reached the Revere car. Louisa was not in her seat. Hattie moved on to the Arlington, where she found Julia sitting alone. Louisa was not with her. Alarmed now, Hattie asked, "Where is she?"

"I don't know. The lavatory, perhaps?"

"Oh, of course," Hattie replied with some relief. " But . . . come with me to the baggage car for a moment."

Julia rose and followed her across the gaps, through the smoking car, where several men stared at them from under dark, solemn eyebrows.

When they entered the baggage car, Julia cried, "It's freezing in here. Be quick!" She crossed her arms over her bosom and clasped herself around the shoulders.

"I will be. But sit a moment." Hattie felt the train slowing. The whistle blew, and the bell clanged, signaling that they were coming into a station. Then she placed a hand on Julia's arm, inhaled, and said, "They mean to cover it up. Like it never happened."

Julia was caught off guard. "Who does?"

"The men. Or rather, the executives. I have the impression that there are dissenting voices, though."

"Oh? Who?"

"Well, last night Mr. Straight was not happy to be told he could not send his report. And Mr. Byrne offered to send a telegram to Louisa's father, but Mr. Price stopped him. Poor Mr. Byrne," Hattie added. "I never thought I'd pity the man, but he looked like, well, like a trapped prairie dog."

"If this is true, Harriet, that they wish to act as if nothing happened, isn't that good news for Louisa?"

"I thought so at first," Hattie said, reaching into her pocket for cigarettes that were no longer there. "But now I'm not sure. It's possible that someone saw it. Likely, even. Every time we walk through the cars, I feel eyes on me and on Louisa."

"That could be your imagination."

"It could." Here, Hattie stood up and began to pace the very short distance between one trunk and the next.

"I've been thinking, though. If I were Mr. Price or Mr. Bliss, I should say that something fell upon the tracks. Something so big, it entirely derailed the train. Mrs. Ridgewood hit her head."

"And Mr. Crockett?" Julia asked, an eyebrow raised.

"Heart attack?"

"Oh, the whole thing's ridiculous!" Julia cried. "Children around a campfire wouldn't believe it."

"I know."

"But, Hattie, even if they do concoct such a tale, how will they prevent the excursionists from telling the truth once they've reached San Francisco?"

"Pay them," Hattie said with conviction. "A lot."

34

Monday, May 30, Sacramento, 11:00 a.m.

THE SUN WAS SHINING BRIGHTLY BEYOND HIS window when Leland woke to knocking upon his door.

"Leland, are you alive in there? It's nearly eleven!" It was his mother.

"Of course I'm alive, Mom. I'll be right down. I had a late night."

"I thought I heard you on the stairs at some ungodly hour. What's going on?"

Leland rose and searched for something clean to wear. "Five minutes! I'm just dressing!"

In the dining room, Leland's mother handed him coffee: sweet, no milk, just as he liked it. Leland took it and sipped it gratefully, avoiding her eyes.

"Leland, why do you avoid looking at me?" she asked from across the table. "Has something happened?"

He sighed. He could put nothing past her. "I'm sorry, Mom. It's not important. I couldn't sleep last night, and I walked over to the house. Everything suddenly felt—I suddenly had . . . doubts."

"Well, it's natural to have doubts." Her voice sounded relieved that it was nothing more serious.

Leland nodded. He would not say he had doubts about his entire existence. Under the circumstances, it was easier to talk about Miss Eames.

"Mom," he hazarded, "what if—what if she's not—?"

Mrs. Durand smiled tenderly at her son. "You'll know soon enough. Why, I knew the moment I saw your father that he was the right man for me. But if she isn't the right woman for you, Leland, no one will force you to go through with it. These aren't medieval times, after all. And recall that she has means of her own."

"I couldn't renege on a promise." He frowned and took a sip of his coffee.

Mrs. Durand set her cup down on its saucer and looked pointedly at her son. "You could, if that promise spelled misery for both of you. Indeed, I expect you already think more of her feelings than you do of your own. You've always abhorred disappointing people."

Leland looked at his mother and realized the truth of her words. Still, he doubted. How could a person, set hurtling in one direction, suddenly fling himself in another?

"Well, thanks, Mom," he said, setting down his mug. "You're a dear. I'd better be off though. Papa will wonder what on earth is keeping me."

• • •

Leland reached the grocery store out of breath. He paused on the sidewalk before entering and looked up at his father's thriving, hard-won business. Seeing it now through jaundiced eyes, optimism turned to doubt, which congealed into a sort of thick-blooded dread.

What he saw was a tidy little grocery store with clean windows and freshly painted iron columns. A woman stood beneath a giant awning, selling currants, figs, barley, oats, Sunrise Stove Polish, and flour, among other items. This was his father's "shopgirl," forty if she was a day, also French, with graying red hair. His father's shadowy, hunched figure moved about within, setting down boxes, arranging signs and displays, and coming and going from the back entrance to unload the morning's deliveries. For a moment, Leland felt a clutch of pity for the old man.

Seeing his son standing on the sidewalk, Mr. Durand Sr. came out to greet him. "Why, what's the matter, son? Cold feet, eh? Well, zat eez nor-*male*," he concluded.

"Oh, Dad," Leland cried. "What if—?" At the look on his father's face, Leland stopped midsentence.

"You ashamed of your old father, Leland? *Pas haute société?*" *Not high society?*

"No, Dad. That's not what I meant." But it was.

"Why, just look at these chickens!" Mr. Durand Sr. pressed his fingers upon a roast chicken by the till. As it was nearly lunchtime, a line had already begun to form for the crisp, redolent chickens, still warm from the oven.

Several years earlier, it had been Leland's idea to make them. At first his father had laughed. "What woo-man wants to bring home a meal cooked by somebody else?"

"Not a whole meal, Dad. Just the chicken." Although Leland had thought that preparing other items was not at all a bad idea. "Only think of the time and effort saved—especially on summer days, when kitchens grow so stifling."

Mr. Durand had agreed to try it for one week, sanguine that his dollar bet on the proposition would be an easy win.

He had lost. In fact, the experiment was such an immediate success that they could hardly wring the chickens' necks quickly enough.

Leland recalled his youthful triumph over the chickens now, deriving little of his usual pleasure from the memory. But his father continued proudly, "I built the grocery up from nothing. And from it, you'll make a fortune, with the railroad and the telegraph expanding the markets. Why, if she iz too good for that—"

"No, no. I'm very sorry, Dad. She's not too good at all." Leland added sheepishly, "I suppose it's just nerves, as you say."

"*Eh, bien,* lad." Nerves were something his father understood. Mr. Durand patted his son on the back. "Did you eat? You look pale as a ghost. Did you have nothing *à la maison*? I bet you didn't, did you?"

Leland smiled wanly. "No."

"Come on back and I'll feed you." His father hurried to retrieve a strudel from the back of the shop. "Here you go."

Leland bit into the warm, flaky pastry; its ripe, juicy fruit burst and ran down the corners of his mouth. He shut his eyes, feeling the pleasure move from his tongue to the roof of his mouth, then to the back of his throat, descending to warm his belly.

He thought it nothing short of miraculous that a man could be revived by the consumption of a good fruit pastry. Or rather, two good pastries, washed down with another strong, hot cup of coffee.

But the pleasant sensations didn't last. As he set to work at his tasks—unpacking crates, arranging fruits, operating the till when the shopgirl took her break, locating items for customers—Leland was aware of finding no meaning in any of it. He didn't know how his father could get up every morning and perform these same mundane chores day in and day out. Still, he dutifully fell in to the rhythm of his tasks until the sun was low in the sky and the last customers had been served. Then he swept and washed the floors and set the garbage out into the alleyway behind the shop. Finally, his father locked the doors, and together they walked home, a beautiful, soft light surrounding them.

"So, *demain*, it's the big day, eh?" Mr. Durand asked.

Leland nodded.

"Well, I hope it all works out, son."

Leland stopped walking and turned to his father. "You *hope*?"

Mr. Durand smiled. "Yes, of course. I hope. Your mother and I were very lucky. Not everyone is so lucky."

"Are you saying you don't think I'll be as lucky as you?"

His father looked at him, baffled. "No. I'm saying you need a bit of luck too. Everyone does. No matter how hard you work. And even then, even with luck, *il n'y' a aucune garantie.*" *There are no guarantees.*

In his current mood, Leland did not trust himself to reply. Why did his father choose this very moment to caution him about the uncertainty of life? He nodded, and they walked the rest of the way home in silence.

• • •

"Leland? Ernest? Is that you?" Leland's mother appeared in the hallway, looking particularly fine. She wore a new gown with pale-blue and brown stripes that brought out her very blue eyes.

"Long day?" she asked them as they hung their hats upon the coat pegs.

"No, not especially," Mr. Durand said.

"Yes," Leland replied at the same time.

As her husband rarely drank, Mrs. Durand turned to her son and asked, "Would you care for a drink, dearest? Bourbon or sherry, perhaps? Dinner will be ready in half an hour, and I've asked for something special."

"Why?" At once, Leland realized that he sounded rude and added, "I mean simply that nothing will change tomorrow."

She looked at him and smiled a bit sadly.

"Everything will change tomorrow, Leland."

• • •

A fire had been lit in the fireplace, and Leland stared at it as he sipped his bourbon, unaware of the glances being sent back and forth between his parents. He thought it was late in the season for such a fire but said nothing. It was his mother's handiwork, creating ambiance for their last night as a threesome. And she succeeded, he had to give her that. This had been a good home to him, a loving home; his parents had been good parents. So why did he feel as if everything was ending not beginning? Leland sat farther back in the leather wing chair and sighed.

Just then Jane entered the room and announced, "Dinner is served!" She smiled shyly at Leland, and the family moved into the dining room. There, upon the table, sat small bowls of fresh melon—pale-orange cantaloupe and pale-green honeydew—cut into neat round balls.

Mr. Durand nodded for Mrs. Durand to sit, and Leland followed suit. He had just lifted a small serrated spoon and speared a melon ball when they all heard a sudden pounding on the door.

Mr. Durand sighed. "Who could that be?"

Annoyed, he motioned for his family to remain seated. But Leland stood up and moved to the entrance of the dining room, from which he had a view of the front door.

The pounding had resumed by the time Leland's father finally opened the door. Standing beneath the gas lamp were two boys, their faces smeared with ash, holding buckets.

"Please, sir. Come quick." Then, seeing Leland behind his father, they cried, "Oh, Leland, hurry! It's the Mackenzie house!"

35

Monday, May 30, West of Palisade, Wyoming

HATTIE AND JULIA HAD BEEN SO VERY busy, scurrying and whispering. Everything done so covertly, as if they would hide their knowledge from her. But Louisa knew what they knew and more. She could feel the silence all around her. Not only that, but she could feel the *kind* of silence it was. Not peaceable or resigned. Not even the silence that comes with shock. No, it was the treacherous silence of complicity.

Louisa felt it in all the men, but in no one more than in Mr. Ridgewood.

Lunch had just concluded, and the porters were cleaning up. She suddenly wished Hattie would return to her seat beside her. Just then Mr. Ridgewood entered the car from the Arlington. He saw her sitting there alone and hesitated.

Louisa felt his hesitation like a silent gathering of internal power. Like the train itself after it had been stoked for hours. Louisa knew absolutely that he would ask for something that she could not afford to deny him. And yet, despite this, she felt compelled to stand up and say, "I'm very sorry for you, Mr. Ridgewood. I've been meaning to say so."

"Thank you, Miss Finch." He bowed gravely. His eyes sought hers and found them: *They are such a beautiful color,* Louisa thought. *Cerulean.* But they looked at her as if they observed a burning building or a sinking ship. Wondering not whom but what might be salvaged from the wreckage.

Without warning, Mr. Ridgewood leaned in and took her by the arm. "I would like to speak to you later, Miss Finch." He added, "It's in your interest, I assure you."

"Of course." She nodded.

He bowed and said, "Until later, then."

Louisa patted her arm: it was tender where he had held it. Once Mr. Ridgewood had left the car, she wondered what had bound her to such false civility. What thrall had possessed her to say "of course" and "thank you" and even to curtsy to such a man?

Hattie came through the Revere car a few minutes later and was surprised to find Louisa back in her seat. "There you are," she said.

"Mr. Ridgewood just paid me a visit."

Hattie scowled. "What did he want?"

"It was all right," Louisa lied. She turned to look out the window, because she could lie with her mouth but not with her eyes. She opened her sketchbook as if she were going to draw. Then, without turning around, she asked, "Did you have a good chat with Julia?"

"Why . . . yes. We discussed the men and what we believe they mean to do."

"Do? About what?" Louisa's question sounded perfectly sincere.

Hattie sighed as if all the energy had gone out of her. "We believe they mean to cover everything up."

Louisa shrugged as if it were of little consequence. Did the fact that they would endeavor to cover up the truth mean that she was safe? She didn't think so. But she didn't know and now believed that she could *not* know. Nor could Hattie, no matter how strong her powers of deduction.

The women settled into their seats. Louisa stared out the window at the desolate, treeless land. The rich fields of Illinois had gone, the wild rock formations of Wyoming had passed, and now all seemed lifeless, barren. Hattie took out a magazine, but she was not swatting pages as she usually did, and after a while, Louisa noticed that she was watching the excursionists. A pattern had begun to emerge among them: every ten minutes or so, one of them rose from his seat, moved off toward the back of the train, and returned to have another person rise from his seat and move off in the same direction. After reading the same page for nearly half an hour, Hattie finally stood.

"Where are you going?" Louisa asked.

"To speak to Alfred. I'll be back soon," she replied.

With Hattie gone, Louisa sank back into herself. So much had been set in motion. She felt the yearning, the wanting, all around her. Perhaps this was what Fate was: a tangle of warring desires. Was it her fate to be arrested or something else entirely? She supposed it depended upon whose desire was strongest, whose won out.

Eventually, Alfred appeared at the head of the car and cried, "Dinner will be served in ten minutes! Ladies, please descend!"

When Hattie returned, Louisa asked, "Did you speak to Alfred?"

"Yes."

"Well, what about?"

But Hattie merely said, reaching for her, "Come, or we shall miss dinner. I'll tell you later."

At dinner, they sat with Julia and Mrs. Lovelace, who for once had nothing to say except to express her concern for Louisa. "But, my dear, you look not at all well. Should we fetch Mr. Fogg?"

"Oh, no. I'm perfectly well," Louisa replied.

Mrs. Lovelace frowned. "You look as if someone has leeched you of all your blood."

"Mrs. Lovelace, *please*," implored Julia.

"It's all right, Julia. Thank you." Louisa smiled. In her meditation upon Fate, Louisa had found a measure of peace. Her conclusion was that Fate was not knowable. Just as Truth was not knowable. Then, to everyone, she said, "Harriet has been speaking to Alfred. I think she has found something out."

Hattie had not been intending to share what she knew just then and was at a loss for words.

"Oh?" said Mrs. Lovelace. "Do tell us if you know something."

"Yes," Julia agreed with some eagerness.

Hattie explained that she had persuaded a reluctant Alfred to enter the Palmyra car on some pretext, to find out what was going on.

"And? What *was* going on?" Julia asked.

"But *I* can tell you that, my dears!" Mrs. Lovelace moved close and leaned in to them. "It's quite daft, really," she whispered.

Mrs. Lovelace paused for dramatic effect. Then she said, "They paid us. Paid us for our silence regarding the attack. Quite handsomely too. Mr. Bliss sat there with an enormous ledger and wrote checks, just as if he were back at his bank."

"And did you accept their money?" Julia asked incredulously.

"Certainly, my dear."

"Do you plan to keep silent?" Louisa inquired.

"Of course not. They're really rather fools, these men, aren't they?" She added, "But what about Alfred?"

"Oh, I made him go look to see what they were doing. He was very afraid. Had I known you—But anyway, he returned saying much the same thing you have."

"Of course he did. But I wonder why they didn't endeavor to bribe you as well." She looked doubtfully at the three women. "Or—did they?"

Hattie had wondered the same thing.

"No," she replied as both Julia and Louisa shook their heads. "They must know that nothing on earth would compel me to keep silent about something I wish to reveal." But even as Hattie said the words, she glanced at Louisa and knew her words weren't entirely true.

They ate their dinner in silence, each woman lost in her own thoughts. When the last of their tea and coffee had been drunk, Louisa stood and turned to the other women. "I'm afraid I'm very tired. I think I'll return to the Revere. Perhaps they've made up the berths by now."

As she moved away, Louisa heard Mrs. Lovelace say, "Well, I for one still think we should call for Mr. Fogg. She looks not at all well."

The train soon stopped, and Louisa descended. She limped away, mounted the stairs to the Revere, and nearly walked straight into Mr. Ridgewood, who was standing at the entrance to the car, blocking it.

"Mr. Ridgewood." She curtsied, then endeavored to move past him. But the man forestalled Louisa's retreat with a hand that nearly touched her breast.

"I shall be true to my word, Miss Finch, and detain you only a moment." He cleared his throat. "The children simply won't mind me. But they've developed a clear regard for you. I should be very glad if you would join us in San Francisco and back again, to Boston, where you may take up residence in Cambridge with us as the children's nanny."

Louisa inhaled but said nothing.

"In a word, I simply must have you." Mr. Ridgewood smiled in a way that was meant to impart a self-deprecating humor to his words.

At once, she made a decision. "That's very kind of you, sir, but I've decided to return home. Papa has only recently sent word that he has procured regular employment and that I might make free to join him. I believe he misses me," she lied.

But Mr. Ridgewood, though he allowed her to finish speaking, appeared unconvinced. He grasped Louisa by the elbow and said, "Allow me to speak plainly: I *will* have you."

"And how will you do that, sir?" she asked softly, looking up into eyes she had once found beautiful.

"I shall appeal to your generous heart." Mr. Ridgewood smiled at her, but a clenched jaw belied his soft words. "My children have lost their mother. And there is a guilty look in your eyes that makes me believe you have regrets. Though I shan't press you upon that point. You're a devout woman, I believe?"

"I am."

"And have we not been taught that good deeds lead to salvation?"

"Yes," she murmured, tears coming to her eyes.

"Then you know it's the right thing to do."

Louisa was silent for so long that Mr. Ridgewood began to fill the silence. "Furthermore, I would—"

"Enough," she interrupted him, wresting her arm out of his grip. "I accept, if the children will have me."

36

Monday, May 30, Sacramento, 7:00 p.m.

WITHOUT WAITING FOR ANYONE, LELAND RAN. HE thought he heard his mother calling him from behind his back. Then he heard his father. But he would stop for no one. He raced past the two boys, and, as he neared the house, he heard the blasting horn of Engine No. 3 peal out from the fire station on Second Avenue. Men were running with buckets, and women were peering out the windows of their homes as Leland continued to run.

When he arrived, a crowd had already gathered. The sun was beginning to set, and the light was harsh; everything caught in its dying beams was either glaringly bright or obscured by shadow. The kitchen lean-to was ablaze, the flames illuminating the sky; fragments of what had once been wood curled delicately in the air and drifted about on invisible currents like strange moths.

Leland cried, "A bucket! Someone hand me a bucket, for God's sake!"

Someone did, and he set to work. Engine No. 3 arrived, and soon hoses, drawing water from the nearby plaza reservoir, were spraying fountains of saving liquid across the flames.

Darkness descended, then fire sprang up out of nowhere, to general shouts and cries, then darkness again. Leland felt his heart stop and start with the flames. Back and forth the battle went, until, after nearly forty-five minutes had passed, the fire was extinguished. Only a few small, stubborn orange flashes remained beneath the rubble.

The firemen continued to fight the last flames for half an hour, and the crowd thinned out. Many stopped to pat Leland on the shoulder and offer their condolences. Nearly everyone in Sacramento knew how it felt to lose a property, whether through flood or fire. Some had lost their homes. Others had lost their livelihood and had to begin again. And many had lost loved ones too. "To be alive is the victory," they said as they patted Leland condolingly.

When most everyone had gone, Leland collapsed onto the lawn and placed his black hands over his forehead. All that effort, and for what?

Nothing remained of the kitchen save a smoldering pile of sodden sticks. The windowsills and trim and all the doors of the brick structure had been licked clean, like a naughty child eats the frosting off a cake. Leland didn't know what remained of the home's interior.

His parents stood by his side, as did Madge, the old postman, and the banker who had closed the property for him only three days earlier.

"Good thing you're insured, son," said the banker.

"Oh, Leland!" Madge cried. "What will Miss Eames think?"

"My dear child," his mother murmured sadly.

Leland finally lifted his face from his hands and looked up at those around him. Tears had washed light runnels down his sooty face, but they weren't tears of grief.

No, Leland was laughing.

37

Tuesday, May 31, Reno, Nevada, 8:00 a.m.

CURLED IN HER BERTH, LOUISA WAS A tiny creature, a blind creature with its eyes shut against the cinder and ash that blew in through the window. The train followed the Humboldt River, which dried up past Lovelock, never reaching the sea. As the night deepened, Louisa sank into a state one could not call either sleeping or waking. In this state, she wandered through the abandoned streets of Alexandria toward home. The parsonage by the church was empty, her father long gone. But she moved toward it nonetheless, as if it could shelter her from the menace she felt so palpably.

Louisa was awakened by a gentle shake of her shoulder. Opening one eye, she did not at first recognize Hattie, who looked quite different dressed as she was in a hyacinth-blue gown and a tall, beribboned blue hat. The hat had a lovely flowing train of blue silk at the back, which cascaded over Hattie's shoulder like hair. Atop the hat, which dipped fully down to her dark eyebrows in front, was a tastefully arranged gathering of silk flowers and feathers. Hattie whispered, "Louisa, we're in Reno. I'm going to leave the train. I'll send word to Papa. I don't believe any of our communications are being dispatched. The ladies have been encouraged to remain on the train, but I'm afraid I was not encouraged. I *shall* descend."

"What time is it?"

"Not yet eight. But we've picked up another engine, and the men have already descended. You should see the crowd out there—look."

Instead of looking out the window, Louisa looked at Hattie. "Hattie, what on earth are you wearing?"

Hattie glanced at herself as if she had forgotten what she wore. "Oh, something my mother bought me before I departed. To impress— now I think perhaps to fool—Mr. Durand."

Louisa replied, "You look very beautiful. But I still don't understand."

Hattie said, "They've torn up all the telegrams, Louisa. I shall send one to Papa if it's the last thing I do. I don't want any members of the Boston Board of Trade to recognize me."

But Louisa, far from reassured by Hattie's plan, looked up wildly at her. "And what shall you say to him? Oh, I'm afraid. Don't go." She peered out the window and saw Mr. Price standing beside the governor of Nevada Territory. On the other side of him stood a young man who was decidedly not Mr. Straight, yet he wore a conductor's uniform and cap. He grinned painfully beneath Mr. Price's tight embrace.

"Who's *he*?"

"Not Mr. Straight. Probably Mr. Crooked." Hattie smirked.

Louisa didn't smile.

A crowd of hundreds of eager Nevadans waved and shook hands with the men. Behind them, the air wavered with palpable heat. A band was setting up, and sleepy-looking children yawned and prepared to sing a well-rehearsed song.

"But isn't that the telegraph office?" Louisa pointed to the office on the other side of the platform. It was open, and there was a girl within, busy at work.

"Look more carefully," Hattie said, nodding to the office.

Louisa pressed her palm to the window and suddenly exclaimed, "What are *they* doing there?"

Mr. Ridgewood and Mr. Bliss stood sentry in front of the telegraph office. Their attitude was casual, as if they merely waited for Mr. Price to finish speaking. But their coats were open enough so that any onlooker could see the pistols on their hips. "Don't go," Louisa begged.

"Do you think they'll shoot me? If they do, what will they tell my father?" Hattie winked, squeezed Louisa's wrist, and said in a more sincere tone, "I'll be careful." Then she moved toward the dining cars, calling, "Alfred? Oh, Alfred!"

•   •   •

Once on the platform in front of the St. Cloud car, Hattie quickly descended the train. She then moved off to the side of the depot, in the direction of the foothills. From a distance, their gently overlapping layers of brown, black, and taupe looked as soft as suede. Above her head, a flock of starlings pursued a hawk. It was sunny and clear, a beautiful day. So clear and beautiful that the black monster that stood huffing upon the tracks looked grotesquely out of place.

Hattie circled behind the depot as the crowd of people clapped, and the governor welcomed the excursionists to Nevada Territory. Then she headed back toward them. She stood proud, her posture erect, the feather in her hat dancing in the wind. The crowd began to disperse, and their new conductor cheerfully rang the bell to warn the men that departure was imminent. "Five minutes, gentlemen! All aboard!" In a moment, Hattie would hear the whistle and see the steam begin to billow out of the engine's smokestack.

At the sound of the conductor's voice, Mr. Bliss and Mr. Ridgewood turned, and Hattie ducked quickly into the telegraph office.

The girl behind the desk was younger than Hattie, with a face as round and flat as a plate. She wore a simple gingham frock, and her eyes widened at the sight of Hattie.

"Oh, aren't you a sight to behold!" she cried. "You must be one of the passengers. I've never seen such a splendid train in all my life, though trains come and go here all the time now."

"Yes, indeed." Hattie glanced nervously behind her. Mr. Price had returned to the train, but Mr. Bliss and Mr. Ridgewood were still keeping guard. "Well, I'd like to send a telegraph. Without delay, please. I wouldn't want the train to leave without me."

"Oh, of course! If you'd just write the name and address here, and then your message, the rates are on the wall." She glanced behind her shoulder at a handmade sign.

Hattie wrote quickly and had just finished when the train whistle blew.

"It's leaving!" the girl cried. "Oh, do hurry, miss!"

Hattie held out the paper at the same moment she realized that nothing one said in a telegram could be held in confidence. This woman would know at once what she wrote to her father, and then the world would know.

Hattie felt a presence behind her. She turned to see Mr. Bliss, who had entered the office.

"No need for that, Miss Eames," he said, plucking the telegram from her gloved fingers. "I can assure you that your father has been apprised of everything." Then he cleared his throat as if he knew he had made a blunder and added, "He knows you're safe."

But Hattie was already wondering: If they meant to keep the attack a secret, why had they told her father everything?

38

THE IRONY WAS NOT LOST ON LOUISA that, in her darkest hour, God had placed her in the finest land she had ever beheld. The barren alkali desert had fallen behind them; now mountains blanketed in pine forests towered up on either side of the tracks as they crossed and recrossed the foaming current of the Truckee River. Close to the river's edge, antelopes grazed on strips of meadowlands. Several bright-yellow birds had perched on them, feeding on insects that had lodged in their dry, dusty coats. The air smelled of pine.

Soon, the pale foothills of black oak and manzanita gave way to the snow-covered peaks of the Sierras. Along the tracks lay huge piles of boards and timber, poised to change the landscape irrevocably.

They were in California.

"Look," said Hattie, breaking into Louisa's stony silence. "We're arriving in Truckee." She had mentioned nothing about the telegram.

It was a handsome little village, despite its having many saloons. The main street had an arcade that spanned a dozen shops with iron columns and huge black-painted doors, suggesting permanence in the way the brick facades did in Omaha. Several ladies strolled past the shops holding sacks for parcels, and a steady stream of men staggered from one saloon to the other.

A small crowd stood at the Truckee depot, wishing to greet the excursionists, but Mr. Price came through the cars, calling out, "We stay only five minutes. Please remain where you are."

Most of the excursionists did as they were told, but a few descended despite Mr. Price's request. One man hopped off the train, glanced cautiously about him, and then sprinted off down the road—preferring to take his chances on his own than to spend another minute aboard the Pullman Hotel Express.

Louisa thought that he would not be the last excursionist who would rather disappear than suffer the return journey on this train.

Mr. Bliss, getting word of the defector, came barreling through the car in search of the new conductor. The young conductor was at the end of the Revere car speaking to Alfred, whose head bobbed up and down in numb agreement. Mr. Bliss caught up to them. "Oh, for goodness' sake," he cried. "Let's go! Why this delay?"

"We're taking on another engine, Mr. Bliss," said the conductor, jarringly cheerful in his ignorance of past events. "We won't get to the summit without it."

Outside, several men were helping the engine driver attach an engine, which would help them up the steep grade.

At last, the Pullman Hotel Express pulled slowly out of Truckee.

As they cleared the depot, it began to snow. It was a strange sight: soft snowflakes drifting down upon the young green trees and blooming wildflowers.

Louisa looked out the window as they passed along a bold series of curves, the train directly ascending the entire time. She said, "The train feels quite heavy."

"Are you afraid?" Hattie asked. She realized she still wore her hat and reached to remove it, setting it gently beneath her seat.

"Oh, no," Louisa said. She thought she would never be afraid again. Not for her physical self anyway.

Beyond the alkali sand hills, the women could just make out Donner Lake through the swirling flakes. They were so big and soft, so benign-looking. Hattie recalled the story of the Donner party. All those unspeakable acts, committed in a vain endeavor to survive. And all the while, the beautiful snow continued to fall . . .

Since their stop in Reno, Hattie could not cease wondering what the executives had told her father. But the more pressing question was: Why? Why had they sent word to her father, among all those they might have sent word to? She could not know with certainty that they had singled him out, but her suspicions had been aroused.

The train approached Summit Tunnel. From the distance of several hundred feet, it looked far too small for the train to fit through. Louisa started when Hattie touched her shoulder. "We'll reach the summit in a few minutes."

The train slowed and entered the tunnel. For a minute, all was pitch dark, and only the train's gas lamps allowed them vision. Then a burst of light made the excursionists squint at the mountain gorges that suddenly appeared, their eyes drawn down into an infinite green regress of spruce and fir. To the east rose Rattlesnake Mountain. The porters began their usual routine of preparing the commissary cars for lunch, and when the train finally stopped at Summit Station, the men descended. Outside, a team of workers unhooked the second engine, as it would not be necessary on their descent.

•   •   •

At Summit, the crowd was small. There was no band, no official greeting, no telegraph station, just a group of schoolgirls brought by their teacher. Mr. Price, Mr. Bliss, and Mr. Ridgewood encouraged the excursionists to descend with munificent smiles and waves. "By all means, stretch your legs, friends. An excellent lunch awaits when you return."

Hattie descended. At once, eager schoolgirls with pink cheeks all gathered about her. One touched her gown admiringly. Hattie had nearly forgotten that she wore it.

"Ooh, is this silk?"

"It is."

"It's such a beautiful color."

"But have you really traveled on this train all the way from Boston?"

"I have."

"Is it very fine within? The train, I mean?"

"It is, indeed." Hattie nodded but made no gesture to invite them upon it. Then she added, gazing around her, "This is far grander, though."

The girls looked at one another. Then they turned to glance at the forbidding mountain range behind them and laughed. "Pshaw—go on!"

When Hattie returned to the train, there was no sign of Louisa. Feeling anxious, she was about to go search for her when Alfred came through the car, calling, "Lunch. Lunch is being served!" The words were the same as always, but Hattie thought she detected a kind of panic in his voice, as if he too would flee their train if he could.

A bottleneck formed before the St. Cloud car; the excursionists seemed particularly eager for lunch. But when Hattie was finally able to enter, she saw that it was not lunch that drew the others to the car; it was the new edition of the *Trans-Continental* that had been placed on all the seats. Throughout the car, walls of open newspapers greeted her.

ACCIDENT ON THE RAILS

Early Monday morning, on the 30th of May, our gallant engine encountered an obstacle of a most peculiar nature: a rock of massive proportions tumbled down a hill on the northwest side of Promontory, Utah.

Gaining momentum as it fell, the rock landed upon our tracks some time before 2:00 a.m., derailing the front of the train. An expert team of engineers was on the scene immediately, and by sunrise, our Pullman Hotel Express was able to continue its historic excursion.

Alas, just as it is said the Lord giveth and the Lord taketh away, this wholly unforeseen and unpreventable act of God came with a cost: three souls whose names we hereby withhold out of respect for the families. We would do well at this sad time to recall that the price of progress was never free.

Hattie glanced about her as if she expected the other excursionists to share her amazement, but instead she saw noses glued to the newspapers in silence. She didn't hear a single objection, a single cry of "Liars!" The thought occurred to her that Mr. Crockett would have stood up to say it was all a pack of lies.

A sudden loud explosion of laughter came from the table behind her. It was Mr. Steele, who had read an amusing joke in the paper. Then he read it aloud:

When a boy falls out of the window, what does he fall against?

His will.

Mr. Steele laughed again and patted Mr. Byrne on the back. "Excellent, son. Excellent!"

But Mr. Byrne, who had been white earlier in the day, was now perfectly waxen.

"Oh, Odysseus!" Hattie called.

Odysseus approached with a fresh pot of coffee. Hattie drank it gratefully, holding the cup in both hands.

"I'm not very hungry, Odysseus. I'll just have the smoked salmon."

"Yes, miss. With a basket of bread?"

"All right. And some butter, if you would."

At the sound of Hattie's voice, Mr. Byrne winced. Whatever Mr. Price had said to him, Hattie thought it was not only about the attack or about Louisa but about her *and* Louisa.

After Odysseus had gone, Mr. Ridgewood entered the car, followed by his children. They moved toward the other side of the kitchen. Hattie saw Louisa enter directly behind them. Louisa had taken great pains with her attire. She wore a pristine hunter-green gown edged with ivory lace that made her peridot eyes even greener. Her hair was freshly brushed and pinned. She looked as if she were beginning a journey, not ending one.

"Your gown is so pretty, Miss Louisa," said Sheila, gently touching its sleeve.

"Thank you. It's new."

"I would love a dress just like that."

"I fear you would drown in it."

"Drown—" Sheila frowned. Then, catching Louisa's meaning, cried, "Why, I would need my own size, you old silly!"

"*You're* an old silly," Louisa replied, poking her gently. Sheila giggled. Frank then teased his sister but not harshly, and Louisa actually smiled before disappearing behind the kitchen. But Hattie somehow felt that the joke was on her.

39

HATTIE PUSHED HER FOOD AROUND ON THE plate, sipped her coffee, and tapped her foot. Finally, she rose decisively and went to stand by Mr. Ridgewood's booth.

"Louisa, may I have a word?" She proffered her hand, but Louisa did not take it. Instead, she glanced at Mr. Ridgewood as if seeking permission. The children made a grab for her.

"No, don't go, Miss Louisa!"

Hattie stood rigidly in place.

"I won't be a minute," Louisa said to the children. Then she rose reluctantly and glanced once more at Mr. Ridgewood, who nodded his assent.

In the aisle, Hattie made way for Louisa to go in front of her. Then she pushed her through the aisles with her fingertips and fairly dragged her over the gaps. When they finally reached the smoking car, Hattie turned to Louisa in a fury.

"Have you gone completely mad?"

Louisa looked down and said nothing.

Hattie pressed, "Why do you sit with Mr. Ridgewood and those despicable children? You can't tell me you don't despise them as I do."

"That's a strong word, *despise*. Anyway, I don't despise them. Haven't you noticed their improvement? I believe they grow sincerely attached to me."

Hattie reached up and actually grabbed Louisa's arm. "Come," she ordered, fairly pushing Louisa across the gap into the baggage car.

Louisa shook her bruised arm from Hattie's grasp.

"Louisa," Hattie breathed once they were in the baggage car. "What's going on? Why do you sit with the Ridgewoods as if you're still their nanny?"

"I *am* still their nanny."

"What? Why? I thought that was all over with."

"Mr. Ridgewood asked if I would remain, and I said yes."

"Why would you agree to remain with that man and his monstrous children? Has he offered you money? Has he—" Suddenly, Hattie realized it had been her own wishful thinking that made her conclude Mr. Ridgewood no longer cared to employ Louisa.

"Oh, Louisa, do you not perceive what's going on?"

Louisa smiled but not warmly. "Tell me," she said.

Hattie stared at her, although all she could see were Louisa's shining eyes. "I feel as if I'm going mad. How can I protect you if you put yourself in harm's way?"

"And you believe that's what I'm doing, placing myself in harm's way?"

Hattie answered Louisa's question with one of her own: "Have you read the paper?"

"Not as yet."

"Well, you should. It's all lies. Ones that shall possibly serve you well, however," she admitted.

"I never knew you to be particularly fastidious about the truth," Louisa replied.

Hattie's eyes blazed. "You must think me a monster to believe I condone this travesty."

"I think nothing of the sort."

"If I remain silent, it will only be to protect you."

"What does it say, the article?"

"Read it yourself. A rock fell upon the tracks, derailing the engine. There's no need for you to be selling yourself to Mr. Ridgewood. Their lie is your salvation."

Louisa put her face in her hands, and, at first, Hattie thought it was to cover a smile of disbelief. But Louisa had tears in her eyes.

"What did he say to you?"

Louisa closed her eyes. "He said, 'I must have you, Miss Finch.' Then he asked whether I was a good Christian, and he reminded me that good works lead to salvation. Oh, Hattie—he must *know*!"

"I doubt it very much," Hattie said. "What did you reply?"

"I didn't need convincing. I was frightened. And I felt—perhaps he was right, that the children *could* be my salvation."

"What nonsense." Hattie sighed. "But how can I argue with you, if you wish to remain blind?"

"Blind to *what*?" Louisa reached her hands up imploringly in the darkness.

When Hattie spoke again, her voice was filled with bitterness. "This is precisely what he did to Mrs. Ridgewood. He exploited her guilt and shame. He made her beholden to him, as he would now do with you. I do not doubt that people on this train know what you did. But I doubt he knows it, or he would have used it directly. He senses your remorse, that's all."

Louisa, worn down by Hattie's badgering, said, "You would risk my life upon that wager? All right, then. When we reach San Francisco, I'll give myself up."

"You don't mean that."

"I do. Only, could we *please* stop fighting about it?"

Hattie then did something she hadn't done since she was a very little girl: she burst into tears.

Louisa reached for Hattie, but Hattie shrugged her off. "Oh, leave me be! I swear, I feel like I'm on fire," she sobbed. "Touch me and I'll burn you!"

• • •

For the next hour, Hattie sat rigidly, her mind working through the possibilities. She felt as if she had entered a complex maze and could not find the exit. When they pulled into Soda Springs, she rose, unconsciously seeking to run from the conclusion she had drawn: that she and Louisa must part as soon as possible. If they parted now, she had a chance of comporting herself calmly before Mr. Durand.

But as Hattie imagined their parting, her face paled, perspiration beaded upon her neck, and the lump forming in her throat grew so big, she thought it would choke her.

Upon the platform at the depot in Soda Springs, a boy sat behind a rickety table upon which sat a neat display of blue bottles. They were filled with natural spring water. Hattie could hear the excursionists elbow each other for a place in line. She peered out through the window and saw Louisa get into line behind the others. Near the table stood a grizzled old miner, delighted to find himself among an unexpected throng of city people.

The day had now grown very warm, yet the old man seemed perfectly comfortable in his long wool shirt, dirty denim pants, and thick-soled boots. The old miner turned to the crowd of excursionists behind him, eager for conversation. "You'll find 'tis a singular place," he said, pointing to the land around the depot. "Dog on my skin if it ain't! Whar sweet and sour water comes oute'n the same hole—one bilin' hot, to look at it, but as cold as ice, the other looking warm and quiet but cold enough to freeze a feller to death!"

Louisa smiled at him, and he winked back at her, not rudely but in a fatherly sort of way. When it was her turn, she purchased two bottles of soda, thanked the boy, and returned to the train.

Hattie hastened to look away from the window, as if her eyes had not been fastened onto Louisa the entire time. She grabbed her magazine from her bag and pretended to read it, realizing too late that it was upside down.

"Here," Louisa said, proffering the bottle. She noticed the upside-down magazine but made no comment. "Why don't you open it? It will refresh you."

Hattie looked suspiciously at the blue bottle and then up at Louisa. But she was thirsty and went to pull out the cork. It was very tight. Louisa took it from her, saying, "Here, let me." Then she pointed the mouth of the bottle at Hattie and pulled the cork, and the water exploded, spraying Hattie in the face and soaking her blouse.

Hattie wiped the soda from herself with a frown just as Louisa began to giggle. "You said you were on fire, so there—I've quenched you."

"Indeed?" Hattie made a quick grab for the other bottle and pointed it at Louisa.

"No!" Louisa fended off the spray, but Hattie poured the remainder of the bottle over Louisa's head.

"Ooh, that's cold!"

The women began to laugh, and Hattie felt a welcome release of tension. What a fool she had been, to think she could ever willingly say goodbye!

Hattie wiped her face with her sleeve. Then she looked at Louisa gravely, water still dripping down her face. She placed a hand on her arm and whispered, "By all means, go with Mr. Ridgewood, if by doing so you're assured of saving yourself."

"Saving myself," echoed Louisa. She shrugged. "I'm not sure what that even means anymore."

40

Monday, May 30, Sacramento, 10:00 p.m.

LELAND WAS STILL LAUGHING AS THEY MADE their way home, his arm draped companionably about Madge's shoulders.

"Well, whaddaya know!" he kept saying.

His mother whispered to Mr. Durand, "The pressure has been too much for him."

But that's just it, he wanted to say: the pressure upon him had indeed been crushing, but he had placed it all upon himself, to impress Miss Eames. And maybe also to convince himself that he was destined for greatness. But now, by virtue of this catastrophic act of God, the artifice had collapsed. Literally! Miss Eames would have to take him for himself or not at all. Because there was nothing else.

"Perhaps we should call the doctor," Mrs. Durand added. "He's inhaled a great deal of smoke."

"*T'es sage,*" Mr. Durand replied. *You're wise.* He then sent a coded glance at his wife, which Leland caught as they passed beneath a gas lamp.

"No, I'm all right. There's no need. *Hic!*"

"Oh, son—"

The trouble was, Leland kept imagining Miss Eames standing before the ruined Mackenzie house, her expression sober. And him remarking,

"Well, here it is! Your new house!" He lashed himself with this image, but instead of pain, he felt only an unceasing tickle of hilarity.

When they reached Madge's house, Madge cast Leland a sorrowful glance.

"Good night, Mr. and Mrs. Durand. Good night, Leland." She curtsied. "I hope they can fix your house."

"Night, Madge. Thanks. Thanks a lot," Leland replied.

"Oh, Leland!" Impulsively, Madge turned back and threw her arms around his sooty neck.

He gently pulled away, embarrassed, and said, "See you tomorrow."

When the family was alone, Mrs. Durand said, "I'll tell Jane to draw a bath as soon as we get home."

Mr. Durand added, "I'll send a message to ze insurance man."

But Leland wasn't listening. By the time they approached their house, the hilarity had abated, replaced by an almost somber thoughtfulness.

His mother stepped past them and called, "Jane! Jane!"

Leland entered the dark kitchen and turned on the gaslights. He made himself a mug of hot cocoa and took the steps two at a time, spilling it on the way. As he waited for the bath to be ready, he drank the cocoa a little too quickly and burned his tongue.

"Leland, it's ready!" his mother finally called. He set the cocoa on his bedside table and, wearing only a towel, hurried toward the washroom at the end of the hall, where a steaming tub of water awaited him. He threw off the towel and stepped in with a sigh.

It was nearly scalding, but he liked it that way. He sank back into it and closed his eyes. When the water had cooled slightly, he held his breath and allowed his head to sink back beneath the water.

Just that afternoon, his father had mentioned something about luck. Leland had resented his father's words, for why should he need any special favor from the gods? Well, now he knew why. What hubris, to believe he was beyond the need of Fortune's favors! The gods had meted out their retribution with the promptness of a railroad timetable. And he had not even considered that Miss Eames might wish to voice an opinion about the home she would live in—to expect that she would simply fly like a bird into his gilded cage—well, the whole thing filled him with shame.

But the dream itself was sound, he believed. Better than sound—it was all a poor fellow had sometimes. Why, those men who had patted him condolingly had all lived on dreams when everything else had been destroyed. His own father had grown vegetables on a plot of dirt. And from those vegetables he'd bought a stand, and from the stand a store. From the store, Leland would create a business, far bigger than his father ever dared to dream. But he would do it step-by-step, with a little more humility and a little more consideration for others.

The bathwater was black when Leland stepped out of it and dried himself off with a towel. Leland ran to his room and changed into a fresh nightshirt. Then he stretched out comfortably on his bed. The linens were cool and crisp, and after drinking the last sip of his cocoa, he fell asleep like a besotted child.

41

Tuesday, May 31, Sierra Foothills, 3:00 p.m.

STILL GIGGLING, THEY WENT TO THE LADIES' dressing room, where they dried themselves off as best they could. When they returned to their seats, they found that Louisa's berth had been made up for the day. *How adept our train is,* Hattie thought, *at making things disappear!*

It was now nearly three in the *afternoon, and they were due in to Sacramento at six. The thought soon robbed them of their levity. Back in their seats, the girls stared out the window in stiff-backed silence.*

Hattie thought of changing her dress but realized there was no point. It was the best gown she owned. I mustn't forget my hat, she thought, and nearly burst into tears.

At Emigrant Gap, the train stopped so that the excursionists could admire the sweeping view. There were no crowds at all here, no musical bands, no eager schoolgirls. Yet few in the world could be immune to the grandeur beyond the train as it rounded the edges of a deep chasm and opened onto a mountainous forest.

"Would you like to step abroad with me?" Hattie asked Louisa.

Louisa said, "No, but you go. Enjoy the view. I must tend to the children."

The train had stopped at the summit of the gorge. Hattie descended and walked downhill, along the iron railing set at the edge of the cliff.

At one point, she leaned over and stared down in wonder at the sheer vastness. *It is an apt name,* she thought, *for land so formidable as to be nearly impassable by even the most determined pioneer.*

Hattie leaned even farther forward, until she had the illusion that she was alone on the planet. There were no people around her, no buildings, no trains. Only space as far as her eye could see. The space began to stretch her out, to pull her like a balloon. Time too began to lose its familiar contours of weeks, days, and hours. There was no time, no space. What was time or space if both were infinite?

Hattie continued slowly down the hill along the railing, unwilling to lose this strange, exalted feeling. She might have been an antelope or prairie dog, a creature with no sense of its own beginning or end.

Gazing out at the Gap, Hattie thought that all those innovations she so loved—the steam engine, Pullman's excellent new chassis design or ingenious folding berths, the Union Pacific Railroad, even their own great laws and democracy—were constructs dependent upon the sagacity and goodwill of a few good men. And what sagacity? What goodwill? On the Pullman Hotel Express she had seen only self-promotion and greed. Their train was not a paragon of civilization, despite what the editors of the *Trans-Continental* boasted. Alone, it was nothing but a heap of wood and iron. And in the service of these particular men, it was worse than mere inert matter.

Hattie lifted her elbow, and a pebble fell down into the abyss, making no sound. The fall of the pebble somehow reminded her that there could be no hope for her or Louisa in this world. Not separately and certainly not together. Could she renounce her dream of going to college and becoming an engineer, of having a hand in great new innovations, and still survive? How might she flee into this vast exquisite gap, as yet untainted by man? And even if she could, how might she get Louisa to follow her?

•   •   •

As the train left Emigrant Gap, Louisa thought Hattie seemed far away.

"You're thoughtful," she remarked.

Hattie nodded. "I'm thinking about whether one can or should act, and the limitations of doing so."

"With regard to what?" Louisa didn't know to what Hattie referred. She knew only that she herself had acted, truly acted for the first time in her life, and now a man was dead. Not a good man, not a man many would miss, but God had seen it. If He heard the fall of a sparrow, what must He think about the fall of Silas Crockett?

She had heard his skull crack, had felt it give way like a ripe melon, hard and then suddenly so soft, transformed with that single blow into something no longer human. There had been no struggle, not even surprise. Just a loud cry that seemed to taper off only after the man was already dead.

To act is not always a good thing, Louisa thought. *Even for the right reasons.* Yet she had meant to do it, she knew. Had it been *right*? Would she do it again, feeling as she did now?

A wry, hopeless smile came to her lips. She was no philosopher. She knew only her feelings, and they were mainly those of despair and entrapment, lightened here and there by a youthful will to live. But in the end, what difference did it make, these subtle nuances of her soul?

Suddenly, from nowhere, the children were before them. Sheila curtsied to Hattie, and Frank bowed. Sheila was carrying a white paper box.

"Would you like a sugarplum, Miss Louisa?" The girl offered up the box, her face aglow with the declining light. Then she added, "Or you, Miss Eames?" Her brother placed his palms beneath hers, wishing to offer it too. Standing there, their eager young faces tilted up at the women, their palms open with their offering, they looked like little angels.

"No, thank you," said Hattie, shocked at this change in the children.

"Oh, sugarplums! I would!" Louisa plucked a sugarplum from its paper nest and took a bite. Then she rolled her eyes and exclaimed, "Yum! Thank you."

The children giggled and ran off.

"Well, well," said Hattie. "Perhaps the little monsters do have souls after all."

"Hattie." Louisa pursed her lips.

The train chugged its way through piney Blue Canyon, then passed through a great gorge between whose massive stone walls the American River flowed. They began a rapid descent, and the excursionists fell silent, as if a mere breath might spell the difference between life and death. They rounded a bold bluff upon a ledge hardly wider than the train itself. The shrill screams of the locomotive produced distant echoes. The excursionists all leaned to the left as the train clung to the face of the precipice, with a thousand feet of crag above and two thousand feet below.

Finally, they arrived at Cape Horn, the most anticipated stop on the Central Pacific Line. The Pullman Hotel Express stopped upon a stunning cliff face, affording a grand vista and a view of the broad river one mile away.

But only one person descended the train; the rest had lost interest in the sights, however grand.

At first, Louisa watched with curiosity as Hattie walked toward the edge of the cliff. Watched her climb nimbly upon the lower bar of the double-barred guardrail and stand there, knees pressed against the upper bar, arms wide. Her eyes were closed, her face was pressed into the wind. Louisa rose from her seat when she saw that Hattie teetered, shifting her balance every second to keep herself from falling.

Then Louisa screamed. "Hattie!"

Hattie turned to see Louisa leaning out the window. The turning motion made her lose her balance, and for one moment she hovered between this world and another. But then she righted herself and fell to safety.

Mr. Price, hearing the commotion, reached Hattie when it was all over.

By this time, Louisa had limped her way to Hattie's side. "Oh, Hattie!" she moaned. "That was too *far!*"

Mr. Price took her roughly by the arm and said, "You're far too bold, Miss Eames. What were you thinking?"

"I wasn't thinking anything, sir. I just wanted to know what it felt like."

"What *what* felt like, Miss Eames?" he asked, no longer bothering to hide his disgust with her.

"Freedom," she said. "What freedom felt like. But don't misunderstand. I have no wish—but how that world beckoned me!" She glanced back almost longingly at the cliff.

"Come aboard now, Miss Eames." Mr. Price took her elbow in a show of chivalry. "We'll be in San Francisco in a few hours." Then he bent down and whispered to her, "Then you may jump off any cliff you like."

Once they had returned to their seats, Louisa whispered to Hattie, "Please. Don't do that again."

"Don't worry. There's no time for anything to be done again," she said bitterly.

Hattie sounded just like she had when she told Louisa that Leland had bought them a house. As if it were all somehow *Louisa's* fault. Louisa fought back silent tears.

"I'm sorry," Hattie said. "But tell me. What does one do with the *feelings?*" She fairly begged.

Louisa replied, "Only to know that it is your pain. You may give it to someone else, but you can't give it away."

Hattie turned, chastened. There seemed to be nothing more to say, and both women looked out the window. The sun was in decline now, casting a golden glow across the vast fields of grain and meadows and wild oats that waved up to the very rails. Blue lupine and bright-orange-and-gold poppies flashed by in turn.

Suddenly, Louisa stood up. "Look!" she cried.

Hattie looked: it was the grand black dome of California's state capitol, imposed against a flaming red sky. They had arrived in Sacramento.

42

Tuesday, May 31, Sacramento, 10:00 a.m.

"DID YOU MANAGE TO SLEEP?" MRS. DURAND ASKED.

"Like a log," Leland said, stretching his arms out and yawning loudly. "What's for breakfast? I'm starved."

Mrs. Durand looked at her son thoughtfully. "Lisa can make you some eggs."

"Could you tell her to throw in a slice of ham? And a biscuit? Two biscuits—if you would."

His mother rose from the table and moved off, but not without first glancing behind her.

When Leland's breakfast came, he downed it with relish, his mother filling the silence. "Your father has gone to speak to the insurance man. It seems something called a 'claim' must be filed."

Leland nodded, his mouth full. His mind was just then on the rooms he had rented for Miss Eames. He thought he would stop by and ask them to place some flowers in the foyer.

He soon finished breakfast and rose, feeling satisfied and brushing the crumbs from his lap. "That was excellent. You must thank Lisa for me. And Papa too for taking care of the insurance. Tell him I shall sign whatever is necessary. *A bientôt!*"

Leland took one last gulp of coffee and placed his hat upon his head, straightened his necktie, kissed his astonished mother on the cheek, and set off.

• • •

It was a fine spring morning. The trees were all in bloom now, and the streets were lined with the vibrant pinks and reds of hibiscus, dogwood, apple, and cherry trees. Many people were already about, and they waved to him with mournful faces, which, at first, he did not comprehend. *Oh yes. The fire.*

Leland soon arrived at the boardinghouse.

"Hallo, ladies!" he called at the door.

"Hallo! Is that you, Mr. Durand?"

"It is."

A housekeeper appeared, wiping her hands on an apron. She was a pretty brunette, hardly more than fifteen. She smiled at him, and Leland realized that no one had yet told her about the fire the night before.

"The rooms are all made up and ready. Would you like to see them?"

Leland nodded, and the young housemaid led him to a door at the end of the hallway. Opening it, she entered into a foyer where, upon a round oak table, stood a vase of cheerful yellow roses. Leland blushed, suddenly recalling that he had already made a request for flowers last week.

"Roses! How delightful!" he said.

The maid saw that he had forgotten all about them and smiled. "They're pretty," she agreed.

"Thank you. Thank you, I'm most obliged." Leland bowed and fairly raced away, still blushing and muttering something about the charming roses.

• • •

It was not yet noon, and having nothing else to do, Leland walked to the store. His father had not returned from the insurance man, but his shopgirl was there at the till, already selling chickens. A line had formed, and perspiration had beaded on the woman's forehead.

"*Bonjour,*" he said, then moved to the back of the shop, where he donned his apron. He then returned to the till and helped wrap chickens in newspaper until the crowd dissipated.

Mr. Durand Sr. arrived at noon and, seeing his son, asked, "Are you all right, *mon fils?*"

"Oh yes."

"I saw the insurance man. He said they would go by the house this afternoon."

Leland's face was blank, and his father closed the subject by remarking, "Zer are papers you'll need to sign."

"Mama told me already," Leland replied.

Mr. Durand Sr. was about to say something but thought better of it. He coughed and went to fetch his apron.

By four that afternoon, Leland could no longer concentrate. He kept handing customers the wrong items or giving them the wrong change.

Mr. Durand said, "Go on, son. Go home and see your mother." Leland nodded, took two hot chickens, wrapped them in paper, put them under one arm, and headed home. As he walked, the chickens warming the underside of his arm, his heart pounded. Once or twice, he even felt it skip a beat, and he marveled at how a body could remain ambulatory while the heart beat so irregularly.

At home, Leland set the chickens down in the kitchen. His hands trembled, but he endeavored to keep his nerves from his voice when he called, "I'm home, Mom!"

"You sound strange, Leland," his mother said at once, walking into the kitchen. "Are you well? You haven't caught cold, have you?"

"Oh, no. I'm well. A bit nervous, perhaps."

"Go rest awhile."

Leland raced up the stairs. He bathed, changed his clothing, and combed his hair with a neat part and a drop of Hovey's tonic.

When he descended, his mother said, "But don't you look handsome!"

"Thanks, Mom." He looked at his watch. It was now just a few minutes past five.

"Would you like to share a chicken with me?"

"Oh, no thanks. I'll accompany Miss Eames to her rooms. I suppose we'll dine there."

Mrs. Durand looked hurt. "What? And not bring her here to meet us?"

"Mother," Leland said gently, "recall that she'll have trunks and such. And she'll no doubt want a bath and a good rest. She's been on a train for more than a week! A luxury train, to be sure, but still."

"Oh yes. You're quite right." Hurt feelings averted, Mrs. Durand smiled at her son.

"I'll bring her round first thing in the morning."

"First thing?" Mrs. Durand asked. "No, you won't. Invite her for lunch so that I might have a chance to prepare. Will you show her—"

"The house? Certainly, if she wishes to see it. I suppose we'll need to make some decisions. But there's no great rush in that regard. The land isn't going anywhere—not like me!" He laughed. "*I* can't sit still! I think I'll walk. Don't wait up." Leland turned to go, then turned back with a brilliant smile. "Oh, Mom—you're a dear!"

Leland walked down Front Street to the far end. Then he crossed over to the other side and walked back, along the river, where he watched the steamboats coming in for the night. Every five minutes, he checked his watch, his hair, his collar, his breath, then back to the watch again: 5:20, 5:25, 5:30 . . .

Leland saw that a crowd had begun to form at the depot. Black-clad men and their ladies rushed past him, moving like scraps of iron ore toward a heavy magnet. Leland feared he might somehow miss the train's whistle, though one would have had to be entirely deaf to do so. He turned around and walked with the others toward the depot.

43

MUCH AS A MAN RIGHTS HIS MIND with his priest before his execution, Hattie and Louisa righted their minds before Sacramento. They spoke to one another in whispers, words meant only for each other. About the old Indian woman and memory and the enduring nature of love.

Hattie wished to accompany Louisa to San Francisco, but Louisa was having none of it.

"If you truly love me, you will descend. You will do what you had planned. Ensure for yourself at least a modicum of happiness."

"But I shan't be happy," Hattie said.

Louisa smiled. "Now you're sulking like a child. You *will* be happy. You'll go to college, and Mr. Pullman shall engage you to improve his . . ." She had forgotten what it was Hattie had spoken to Mr. Pullman about back in Chicago.

"Journal boxes," Hattie grumped. "Don't let Mr. Ridgewood bully you. Have you any money?"

"Money? Not much. Five dollars. No, wait—Didn't I spend one on the prairie dogs?"

"Four dollars! Your father sent you out into the world with such a sum?"

"He expected—"

"Oh, I know what he expected. But you must have more."

Hattie fished into her pocket for her father's billfold. She pulled out two ten-dollar bills. "Here. At least you may stay in your own hotel room, unmolested by anyone."

"I dislike taking this money from you, Hattie."

"It would be far worse for you to take it from anyone else." Then Hattie looked meaningfully at Louisa. "Promise me you shan't agree to suffer abuse."

"I promise," said Louisa mildly, tucking the money into her pocket.

The women were silent now, their fingers woven together. Suddenly, Hattie blurted, "Louisa, we haven't much time. Tell me what happened to you. During the war, I mean."

Louisa was silent for such a long time that Hattie thought she would not reply. Then she turned and looked at Hattie. Her face was that of a haunted child.

"I was at Manassas," she said. "Bull Run, some call it. The first one."

"At the battle?"

Louisa nodded. "It was in July of '61. A wealthy man named Pringle invited Papa to come out to his house. The old mansion had been converted to a hospital. My father and I went at once—he wished to comfort the wounded and dying."

"Why did he bring you, for goodness' sake? You could not have been more than—what, eight, nine?"

"I had just turned ten. He couldn't leave me alone. Evelyn, our servant, had fled by then."

"Oh, Louisa." Hattie thought of how she herself had been protected from the war. When Robert went off to fight with a heavy artillery regiment, he wrote home faithfully. Her father read his letters aloud at the dinner table, but he always skipped the parts describing the battles. After dinner, he locked the letters in his safe.

Louisa smiled strangely. "It took us all day to get there. We started at dawn. There was smoke everywhere from the burning bridges all along the railroad line. They'd been blown up. Others were still standing, barely, yet we crossed them."

"The bridges," Hattie murmured.

"And the trees had all been cut down . . ."

Louisa stared ahead of her, as if she were ten years old again, riding toward Manassas. "When we arrived on the hill overlooking the battlefield, people from Washington, dressed in their fine clothing, were picnicking and watching the battle through their field glasses. I heard a woman. She was on a blanket with her husband, looking through her glasses, and she exclaimed, 'Oh, splendid! Is that not first-rate?'"

Hattie grimaced.

"We stayed two nights at the hospital, at Mr. Pringle's. It was a stately old property, with many well-kept gardens. I wandered the rose garden while Papa tended to the wounded in the house. But boys were sprawled all across the lawns too. Moaning. Crying for their mothers. I approached one boy who had a canteen poised at his lips. I thought he needed help holding it. But when I got closer, I saw that he was dead. The smell of roses mixed with the smell of his blood . . ."

"No more. Louisa, no more," Hattie murmured.

Louisa was calm now, almost serene. "Would you like me to tell you the worst? The very worst thing?"

"If it helps you. Anything." Hattie grabbed Louisa's hand.

"As we headed home, we came upon a beautiful horse. He was pure white, and he still wore his saddle and bridle. He was calmly nibbling leaves from a tree, by himself. 'Oh, Papa!' I cried, delighted. 'Let us take him home!'

"My father descended the carriage and reached for it by the reins when we saw that its foreleg had been shot off at the knee joint and was pouring blood. It didn't have long to live . . ."

"Louisa, I'm sick—"

"That picture has been with me all these years. It has never dimmed, and it will never go away. I know that now."

Hattie murmured, "I could not have been as strong as you."

"You?" Louisa smiled at Hattie tenderly. Her green eyes were calm but infinitely sad. "You would have grabbed someone's rifle and entered the fray. I'm sure of it."

"Perhaps I could handle a battle," Hattie admitted. "But to love something so beautiful and good—and to lose it?" Hattie shook her head, for once unable to continue.

The train came to a stop just past the wharf; the sun sat on the horizon, obscured by low, dark clouds.

A large crowd awaited them. Hattie clung to Louisa's hand like a small child. She felt as if she were dying; she couldn't catch her breath.

"I can't do it."

"You can."

"At least allow me to accompany you to San Francisco. I can send a telegram to Mr. Durand. I can make something up. You know I can."

"No. *Please.* What's the point? You must go." There was an urgency to Louisa's voice that Hattie found strange. Tears, unchecked now, streamed down Hattie's face as she hefted her bag across her shoulder.

She leaned in for one last kiss and then leaped away with a groan. She stepped onto the platform.

A porter descended, carrying a small suitcase, and headed off, perhaps toward home. Apart from him, only Mr. Price, dressed in a very finely tailored suit, descended. He forced a smile and waved to the crowd.

No one else got on or off, and the train blew its whistle once more, which startled the mayor, who had already begun to speak words of welcome. He hastened to skip to the end of his speech, then waved frantically to the band. The children, lips poised on the mouthpieces of various instruments, began to play and sing when the train blew its whistle a second time and Mr. Price grinned grotesquely, tipped his hat, and made some comment that was meant to be amusing but that nobody heard. Then he fairly leaped back onto the train.

At the sight of Mr. Price, Hattie recalled her hat and raced back to retrieve it from under her seat. Louisa was turned away, and Hattie chose not to speak to her. They had said their goodbyes. She moved quickly, pinning her hat to her head as she descended the stairs. Then she looked about for her father. He should have been there by now.

A mail boy flew onto the platform, crying, "Telegram! Telegram for Miss Eames!"

Quickly, Hattie glanced at the crowd and then, seeing no one she knew, ripped open the telegram.

> Dearest Daughter,
>
> Do not descend in Sacramento. I repeat: do not descend. Continue on to San Francisco. I would have a word with you in private before you meet your betrothed. Then it shall be my pleasure to accompany you to Sacramento. It will be far more seemly that way. Mr. Durand has been apprised of our delay. As your mother has always reminded you, first impressions are important, and I would have Mr. Durand's first impression of you be that of a proper young lady on the arm of her loving papa. I hope this is but a small inconvenience to you.
>
> Your loving—

Hattie let out a cry of pure joy. Five more hours with her beloved— an eternity! She vaguely wondered what "word" her father could wish to have with her, but she determined not to waste another minute upon it.

When Hattie returned to her seat, she found Louisa curled into a ball.

"Louisa!" Hattie shook her. "I remain until San Francisco!"

Louisa looked up, no sign of happiness there. She asked slowly, almost drowsily, "You do? Why?"

Hattie tore off her hat and shook the telegram at her. "I've had a telegram from my father. He says he'll meet me there instead. He wants a word with me. Alone, I presume."

The train began to move. The crowd, feeling personally insulted at the brevity of the stop, grumbled as it began to disperse. Some even shouted angrily at the back of the train.

Meanwhile, Louisa stared out the window, and her eyes seemed to catch someone. She pointed. "Look over there." Hattie glanced out the window just as the train pulled out. She thought she saw a young man dashing to and fro, wildly waving his hat.

44

LELAND HAD PREPARED; HE HAD WAITED; HE had arrived early. Still, when the deafening blast came, he was so startled that he actually leaped off the ground in surprise and nearly sprained his ankle coming down upon it.

The train became visible, and Leland sprinted toward the depot one block away, where the Pullman Hotel Express, clanging and hissing steam, was just pulling in. Its gorgeous engine had bright-red wheels, a shiny blue cowcatcher, and bright brass fittings. A large crowd, lining both sides of the tracks, waved kerchiefs.

Just as Leland reached the platform, the crowd pressed toward the train, and he was caught among them, suddenly realizing that he did not know from which car Miss Eames would descend. The train was long, and he might be in the wrong place. He counted eight Pullman cars and found himself weaving back and forth among the packed bodies, hat in hand, calling, "Miss Eames! Miss Eames!"

Meanwhile, from the corner of his eye, Leland noticed Madge Perry. She was desperately trying to reach him through the crowd, waving a telegram in the air. Leland turned back around and continued searching for Miss Eames. The train had begun to move, and he ran after it, frantically waving his hat. Before long, it was a quarter of a mile down the track, and the deflated crowd grumblingly moved back, pushing Madge farther away. Leland put his hat back on his head and gathered his wits. There was no time to wonder why the train had not stopped as it was meant to, nor why Miss Eames had not descended. Whatever Madge had for him would have to wait. He needed to get to San Francisco—and quickly!

45

May 31, somewhere between Sacramento and San Jose, 7:00 p.m.

THEY BREATHED IN, BREATHED OUT. THEIR FINGERS were so tightly locked that Hattie's grew numb. "Poor Leland," she finally said. The train had pulled away, and the disappointed crowd was no longer visible. "I imagine he'll be frantic."

"Yes," Louisa agreed.

"But he'll go to San Francisco; indeed, he'll get there before we will, crossing by ferry," Hattie added.

Someone coughed. The two girls looked up to find Julia Hunnewell standing in the aisle beside them.

"Hello," said Louisa.

"May I have a word with you two?" Julia smiled wanly.

"Yes, of course." Hattie glanced at Louisa, who nodded.

"I'm afraid we'll miss the start of supper," Julia warned.

"I'm not hungry."

"Nor I," echoed Hattie.

"Come, then."

With both Hattie and Julia aiding Louisa, they crossed through the cars until they reached the baggage car. Once inside, Julia produced a candle and matches, and they were able to see one another as they spoke.

"Friends," she began breathlessly, "we are soon to part, and I didn't want to do so before saying that I shall miss you both greatly." She turned to Louisa and took her hands. "I'm so miserably sorry, Louisa, for everything you've had to suffer. When I saw you standing out there—God knows, but there were still Indians lurking about!—I simply couldn't believe my eyes. I could not be so brave, not in a million years."

Louisa quietly replied, "I was impulsive not brave."

"Perhaps they're the same thing in the end." After a thoughtful pause, Julia went on. "Their conspiracy of silence serves you—God pray it holds! But the terror of uncertainty must weigh heavily upon you."

"Less than you might imagine."

If Julia was surprised, she hid it well. She looked up into the darkness and said, "This journey has opened my eyes to a great many things. I love my father, but I know now that he's an unworldly man, caught up in his books and pet projects. He doesn't see the implications of his involvement in this—this farce. He's an arrogant man too, who cares more about my standing in society than the human cost of what they do."

Louisa heard the hard-won, painful certainty of Julia's words. But she also caught a note of finality in her tone. She asked, "Have you decided something, Julia?"

"Yes," she replied conclusively. "I'm not returning with him."

"Really?" Hattie asked. "What shall you do, then?"

"I have no idea." Julia laughed.

They embraced one another, and Julia wiped tears from her eyes. "Well," she asserted, "they won't get away with it, you know. The truth will come out."

Suddenly, Louisa inhaled sharply and stood up. "I must go check on the children."

•　•　•

Louisa's decision had been coming on so gradually that only then did it feel like one. One week earlier, nothing could have compelled her to take such action as she had now fully resolved upon. To run away, under no one's protection and with such little money to her name? It was madness. But then Louisa reminded herself that she could cook, sew, do laundry, and even teach art. She would find employment in the young, growing city of San Francisco.

Louisa envisioned the moment of her escape as if it were already happening: Mr. Ridgewood would have one of the porters take her trunk to the hotel. But while he instructed the porter, she would sneak away, farther and farther into the crowd, into the night!

The thought of leaving Mr. Ridgewood in the dark was a pleasurable one. But she would speak to the children. She wished to leave her mark upon them, to give them a taste of love, however small.

She found them fast asleep in their new stateroom in the Arlington car. Their arms were draped around each other over the blanket. She nudged them awake.

"What is it? Has something happened?" Sheila started up, frightened.

"Oh, no, nothing like that," Louisa whispered. "But there is something I must tell you before we arrive in San Francisco."

The children raised themselves onto their elbows and stared up at her, blinking in the dark.

"What is it, Miss Louisa?"

"Promise me something."

"We will!" said Frank eagerly.

"Promise me you'll be kind to one another and to others," Louisa said, her voice quavering. "As I am guided by God to love you."

"You *love* us?" Frank said incredulously. "Nobody *loves* us." His voice held no self-pity.

"Well, *I* do. Almost as much as I love the prairie dogs." She ruffled his hair.

Sheila, the more observant of the two, asked, "You sound like you're leaving us. You aren't, are you?"

"I'm afraid I must."

Louisa thought they would whine and protest, but they were eerily silent, almost as if they knew that their father was the reason.

"What will we *do*?" Sheila said, allowing herself a note of plaintiveness. Then she added, "Mommy was never happy."

Louisa paused. "I understand. I'm not happy now either; that's why I must go." Then she had a thought. What harm would it do to share it? "Perhaps, when you return to Boston, you might ask your papa to send you to boarding school. You shall—you shall be happier that way, I believe."

But Sheila was still wondering about Louisa. "Does Papa know you're leaving us?" she asked, a question soon echoed by Frank.

"No, darlings. And I don't want him to know. He would be very angry."

"We won't tell!" Sheila cried, happy to be in on Louisa's secret.

"We won't!" Frank agreed.

"I shall write to you often and think of you every day."

"Promise?"

"As God is my witness," Louisa promised. She kissed them. "Now go back to sleep."

•   •   •

Hattie had her eyes closed; Louisa thought she might be sleeping. This was fortunate, as Louisa had no idea how she would keep her decision a secret from Hattie. Hattie must never know of it—if she did, she would follow Louisa. She might even go so far as to leave Leland, ruining any hope of her own happiness. But how was she to keep this secret? She was no liar by nature; everything told in her face.

Except when I am drawing, she thought. Then nothing told. Nothing gave her away, because she wasn't there. She was elsewhere, utterly and completely.

Louisa took a long look at Hattie, still dozing beside her. She noticed the texture of her thick brown hair; her long, dark eyelashes; and the dewy lids, gently joined. She observed her full, soft mouth, utterly still and wordless. She gazed down at the tendon in her neck as her head fell to one side and the gentle lift and fall of her breast . . .

Then she picked up her sketchpad and began a new drawing. Night had descended completely now, and the gaslights were dim. Yet she continued to draw, removing different colors from her pencil case and brooding over an area toward the center of the page. She would draw until the very end.

Hattie woke with a start, as if sensing Louisa's energy beside her.

"What's that you draw so intently?" Hattie asked, trying to peer down at it. But Louisa concealed it from her with an elbow. Then she released her arm, because what was the point of keeping it a secret?

"It's you," she said.

46

BETWEEN SAN JOSE AND SAN FRANCISCO, THE train overheated half a dozen times. Excursionists began to disappear in twos and threes, like escaping prisoners, as Hattie thought they would. When Mr. Price got wind of it, he ordered the conductor to make no more stops until they reached the city, even at the risk of overheating. The great Pullman Hotel Express could not arrive with no one aboard!

The train approached the outskirts of San Francisco just before midnight. Louisa was finishing her portrait and had not so much as come up for air in about three hours.

Hattie was envious of Louisa's gift of oblivion. She pressed her forehead against the glass. Her breath fogged the window, and she kept wiping it away so that she could see what lay beyond the train. Some kind of paradise, it seemed: the engine's penetrating beam of light illuminated palm trees and masses of red-flowering bushes that grew all along the tracks. Here and there, Hattie saw trees from which hung yellow lemons the size of grapefruits.

So the apocryphal stories about California were true. It *was* a land of plenty, the likes of which frugal Easterners had never known. In the light beyond the tracks, Hattie saw more lemons, then oranges, then something else, quite red. She didn't think it was an apple. Could it possibly be that fruit she had only heard about but never tasted, the pomegranate?

The houses grew denser; the streets narrowed. They arrived at the depot, where dozens of Chinese, Irish, and Negro workers awaited the emigrant train going east. Their jobs building the railroad were over; time to find other work. As the train moved on without stopping, some of these weary workers looked up at it in surprise, and Hattie caught their curious faces. Their jobs had been arduous, dangerous, and poorly paid. Those standing there were the survivors. So this was the fruit of their labors, to leave the place they had created!

By special permission of the city of San Francisco, the Pullman Hotel Express traveled several hundred feet past the depot, down the horse-cart tracks to the Grand Hotel. Along the way, a number of buildings were brilliantly illuminated, and even at this hour, the sidewalks were thick with people waving handkerchiefs.

Finally, almost unbelievably, the train slowed to a stop. Before them stretched a massive crowd, kept back by a squad of police and thick, swaglike ropes that had been draped along iron poles from the hotel entrance to the train. Special gas lamps had been installed in the front of the hotel, the better to see the storied Pullman Hotel Express.

Mr. Price was the first to descend. He held aloft his bottle of Atlantic seawater with a dramatic flourish. "Lord, at last!" He smiled for the roaring crowd. "At last!"

Those excursionists who remained had long been packed and ready to disembark; they were not impressed by Mr. Price's display. When the doors finally opened, such was the outpouring of men and women that an onlooker might have thought a fire had broken out on board. They shoved and pushed their way through the narrow aisles and escaped onto the road, where porters strained to keep up with their frenzied demands for luggage.

Hattie reluctantly donned her hyacinth hat once more, took up her bag, and descended. She saw Mrs. Lovelace head away from the hotel with David. Hattie thought it odd that they were both carrying their own bags.

"Mrs. Lovelace, you forgot your plant!" she called.

Mrs. Lovelace turned around. "My plant? Oh, Miss Begonia." Mrs. Lovelace waved her arm dismissively. "I left it in Salt Lake, by the Tabernacle. It suddenly seemed quite idiotic to be dragging it about. Goodbye, my darlings! Good luck to you!"

"But, Mrs. Lovelace, where are you going?" Hattie cried. "The hotel is just *there*."

Mrs. Lovelace shrugged. "New York, of course. And the Metropolitan Opera. If they'll have me. But not on this godforsaken train!"

Mrs. Lovelace took her son by the hand and fairly pulled him along, ducking nimbly beneath the hotel's ropes to the freedom beyond.

A moment later, Hattie heard Mozart filling the night air.

Hattie turned to Alfred. "My trunk, please, Alfred. And I *shall* leave this time."

Louisa stood beside her but did not ask for her trunk. Both girls looked about them, Hattie expecting to see her father at any moment.

Dressed in the lavender-and-white-striped gown in which she had begun her journey, Louisa now imperceptibly retreated. She moved slowly, backing up behind the excursionists.

Alfred had just set Hattie's trunk down gently when he suddenly went rigid. He stared ahead and nudged her arm. The nudge was subtle; one might have taken it for an accidental bump in the crowded space. Yet Hattie felt its intentionality, enough to make her stop moving.

"Look," she whispered to Louisa, who was now several feet behind her. "I think that's *him*. That's Mr. Durand."

Louisa paused momentarily. Standing beneath a gas lamp before the Grand Hotel, a tall, handsome young man with light eyes and uncombed hair, neck craned and hat in hand, scanned the crowd. Although rooted to one spot, he gave the impression of being in perpetual motion: eyes, fingers, shoulders, all twitched nervously. Then he smiled and leaned over to speak to a rotund dignitary. The dignitary smiled back at him, his eyes never leaving the crowd of excursionists. This man went to check his pocket watch only to discover that he had none. He had given it to his daughter.

"Papa!" Hattie began to wave, but Alfred nudged her once more and glanced at her warningly. Not understanding, Hattie took a step toward the men, reaching unconsciously for Louisa's hand. At this movement, Leland spotted her, and their eyes met for a single electrifying moment.

Leland grinned, visibly relieved.

Hattie hesitated. It felt as if her muscles had locked, her heart had ceased beating. *I cannot go,* she thought. At that moment, Mr. Price and Mr. Bliss emerged from behind Mr. Durand and her father. To Hattie's left, two other men moved swiftly from the shadow of the street into the light of the gas lamps. One was tall and wore a gray uniform with the telltale gold badge of a police officer. Behind him, panting to keep up, was Mr. Byrne. He seemed to have strained an ankle in his haste to fetch the officer; his face was twisted in misery.

Hattie's eyes turned wildly to her father, who wore an eager, ingratiating smile. His arms were open, beckoning her forward with the promise of a loving embrace.

"My dear, dear Harriet!"

Unconsciously, Hattie took a step backward, where Julia stood. Mr. Hunnewell must have been retrieving their baggage.

"What's going on?" Julia asked, sensing Hattie's alarm. "What's the matter?"

Louisa, seeing the police officer standing at the ready next to Mr. Byrne, stopped moving. Alfred took a step forward and placed himself between the men and Louisa. He turned to the women as if he awaited a tip, buying them a moment's privacy. Hattie felt in her pocket for her dowry and whispered to Louisa, "Come here."

When Louisa hesitated, Hattie moved back toward her, Julia following. Louisa watched as Odysseus dragged her trunk toward the hotel.

"Leave it," Hattie said.

Louisa confessed, "I was going to."

Hattie caught her meaning and tilted her head. Then someone called, "Miss Eames!"

It was Mr. Durand, believing for a moment that perhaps Hattie had not in fact recognized him.

Hattie's father took Leland's cry as his cue to move and stepped forward.

"Louisa, do you trust me?" Hattie whispered.

"Yes, of course. But—"

"We must move quickly." Hattie removed her hat and handed it to Julia. Julia, realizing what Hattie wanted, quickly untied her own bonnet and donned Hattie's.

"Thank you, Julia. Now." Hattie turned to Louisa. "Lean on my shoulder. Let my leg be yours."

"But—"

"*Do it now.* Run!"

Louisa ran on only one leg, but she was suddenly flying, as if part of a swift mythical creature. A backward glance saw Mr. Ridgewood's grim mouth gape open like a fish out of water.

A few seconds later, she heard, "Lou-*eeza*!"

It sounded so much like Mrs. Ridgewood that Louisa shivered. But then Sheila repeated herself, and her meaning became clear.

"Run, Lou-*eeza*!"

Louisa and Hattie bolted down the cow path, and the men took off after them. But when they saw Julia in Hattie's hyacinth hat, they ran toward her, nearly tripping over several trunks that had, thanks to a clumsy young porter, been pushed directly into their path.

"But I merely wish to speak to you!" said Mr. Eames. He reached out to his daughter, only to realize with horror that the young woman in the hyacinth hat was no one he knew.

The men pursued flashes of the real Miss Eames as she and Louisa emerged and disappeared among the crowd, their shouts becoming at once louder and more hopeless.

"Run, Lou-eeza!"

But the two women had pushed their way through the crowd until they found a far different crowd at the depot, all elbowing one another to catch seats upon the train. The train going east.

47

SOMETHING HAD GONE WRONG. AFTER LOSING SIGHT of Miss Eames but finding that the men beside him pursued her, Leland joined the chase. Could it be that she had not recognized him? Could she have believed he was still in Sacramento? In any event, he couldn't very well stand there while the others were in hot pursuit of his bride. As he ran, Leland felt a growing apprehension that he was taking part in something he would look back upon with shame. It dawned on him that perhaps he chased someone who did not wish to be caught.

Leland leaped, a single, heroic leap, toward the woman in the hyacinth bonnet, whom for some reason the men all chased. But directly upon landing, his foot encountered an obstacle—a pale, trampled lady's bonnet. He tumbled forward and landed against the young woman in the hyacinth hat. She let out a great cry and fell backward into some abandoned luggage.

The young imposter's encounter with the luggage had the disadvantage of tripping Leland, who then fell directly on top of her. Her knitting, a green sweater, fell out of her bag and onto the dusty road.

"Oh, I'm so sorry! Allow me!" Leland cried. He scrambled to raise himself off her and retrieve the knitting. But instead of growing angry, the woman let out a beautiful laugh, revealing to Leland a most fetching gap-toothed smile.

"No, no, it's me. I've gotten entirely in your way."

In turn, Leland took the young woman's arm and helped her to her feet.

"Are you injured?" Leland asked, still aghast at what he'd done.

"Not at all."

"But I must atone somehow. I must. Miss—"

"Hunnewell. Julia Hunnewell. My father is just over there somewhere." She pointed vaguely to the baggage car.

Julia brushed herself off and, seeming to notice a stray thread upon Leland's handsome jacket, picked it off. Then their eyes met, and they regarded one another with dazed and curious looks.

•　•　•

Hattie and Louisa managed to board the train just as it blew its whistle and began to move. They kept on down the crowded aisles and through the seemingly endless cars until they found two empty seats. Here, every car was a smoking car: the air was thick with smoke that burned their eyes and made them cough. Hattie had thought the platforms upon the Pullman Hotel Express were smoky and unpleasant, but this was far worse.

Most of the seats were already taken up by weary families and exhausted-looking workers, many Chinese, already half-asleep, heads bowed from their shoulders as if they were used to sleeping in a chair with chaos swirling all around them. Hattie heard a babble of languages, several of which were entirely foreign to her. She herself was too winded to speak. So was Louisa, who looked close to fainting and who grimaced in pain, having run so long and hard upon her left leg.

Neither spoke a word until the train was far beyond the depot, beyond the reach of Leland Durand, Congressman Eames, Mr. Ridgewood, and the police officer.

After some time had passed, Louisa said, "Did you hear Sheila?"

"She called your name, I believe. She sounded quite like her mother."

"No." Louisa shook her head. "She called, 'Run, Louisa!'" She smiled. "But what was your father doing there? Why did he insist you meet him in San Francisco?"

"I suspect he meant to buy my silence before I met Mr. Durand."

"Oh? How did he plan to do that?"

But Hattie merely grasped Louisa's hand more tightly and looked out the window without answering. Eventually, Louisa would put it all together, but there was no need for her to do so now.

Once more, Hattie saw the palm trees and lemon trees and red-flowering bushes all illuminated briefly by the train's light before plunging back into the obscurity of night.

Louisa sighed and leaned her head against Hattie's shoulder, and Hattie felt her breathing slow; she dozed. But Hattie was wide-awake, her mind burning to make sense of it all.

She didn't know the details of her father's corruption, only that he was so. Their homes had been bought the same year that Crédit Mobilier was established. And just now, in his eyes, she had seen that same *fear*. He had known everything that Mr. Price, Mr. Bliss, and Mr. Hunnewell did: about the attack, Mr. Crockett's death, and her friendship with Louisa. Had known because he was one of them.

But none of those men was nearly as clever as they believed themselves to be. Someday, their schemes would be revealed for all the world to see. *But not by me,* she thought. *Not by me.*

Louisa woke up as the light of dawn penetrated her eyelids. "Where are we?" she asked, frowning at the bad taste in her mouth. She checked her breath and frowned again.

"The foothills of the Sierras," Hattie replied. She hadn't slept and had seen the snowcapped mountains come into view just as dawn broke.

"Where are we going?"

"I don't know," Hattie said matter-of-factly, as if going anywhere no longer much interested her. "I quite liked Salt Lake, apart from the Mormons."

Louisa shuddered. "Man-made nature. No, thank you."

"How about Wyoming?" Hattie suggested. "Remember Sherman? There was something special about that place, don't you think? I recall you wished you could stay to sketch the light over the mountains."

"Oh yes. I was greatly inspired. And by our ride on the cowcatcher." At the memory, Louisa glanced warmly at Hattie, who blushed to remember the moment she knew she was in love with Louisa.

Hattie said brightly, "We can vote there, you know. The population is so small that they're desperate for voters. I hear they even have some women judges. Imagine that! I could become a judge," she mused.

"That would suit you," Louisa replied with a small smile. "But I am saddened by the fact that you won't get to go to college and gain a degree."

Hattie was thoughtful, and Louisa feared she had wounded her by bringing up the topic of that long-held dream.

But Hattie surprised her. "I feared it myself. But you know, I've realized something on this excursion. Something you taught me."

"What is that?" Louisa asked, surprised that she should have taught Hattie anything.

"Knowledge is not wisdom. Not even close." Then Hattie, tears threatening to overwhelm her, looked out the window, indicating that she would speak no more upon that subject.

Another half an hour passed before Hattie spoke again. She said, "You know, the bison have dwindled, but there remain a great number of antelope and prairie dogs," she said. "I expect you may now have as many dogs as you like."

Louisa did not look reassured. "But, Harriet," she said, "have we any money? You know I have only four dollars. Plus twenty of yours."

Hattie pulled out her father's wallet and fanned a thick wad of twenty- and fifty-dollar bills. In among the green bills was Hattie's once-treasured bill of fare.

"Why do you have so much?" Louisa's eyes widened.

"My dirty railroad dowry."

"Your what?"

"My father's ill-gotten gains."

"What are those?"

"I'll explain another time."

"All right." Louisa yawned. Then she said, "I'm hungry."

"We must wait for the next big depot, I'm afraid." Hattie took the train's bill of fare from her father's wallet. She stuck her arm out the window, hesitating a moment, and said almost wistfully, "But those meals were so good. I shall really miss them. No more St. Cloud or St. Charles cars for us." Hattie opened her fingers and let the bill of fare blow away.

Louisa looked at her for a long moment. Then she grinned. "Thank God for that," she said.

Author's Note

THE PULLMAN HOTEL EXPRESS WAS A REAL train. It left Boston on May 23, 1870, headed for San Francisco, and returned to Boston one month later. For it, the Boston Board of Trade commissioned George Pullman to create the finest, most luxurious railroad cars ever made. All across the country, tens of thousands of people came out to cheer the extraordinary sight. By all accounts, the excursion was a great success, marking the beginning both of a luxury travel industry and of a truly transcontinental economy.

I was fortunate to ride this train in my imagination thanks to its onboard newspaper, the *Trans-Continental*, which published a total of twelve issues. Here, one reads about an opulence so state-of-the-art as to impress even the wealthiest Brahmin: a hairdresser's, a smoking car with plush seats, two saloon cars replete with Burdett organs (in the event anyone was moved to burst into song), and two sleeping cars with berths that ingeniously disappeared by day. Genteel porters, many of whom were former slaves, must have scurried back and forth like stagehands at a play: there was a great deal to do, but they were meant to be invisible. Their public speech was no doubt carefully crafted to match the affluent surroundings. Dining cars were decked with flowers, linen tablecloths, and crystal goblets. The cars featured etched mirrors, walnut-paneled marquetry, and an innovative system of gas lighting. Finally, to ease the excursionists' unspoken fears, champagne and wine were served with every meal.

In its physical traits, my train is a nearly exact replica of the original one, although, unfortunately, I gleaned this from descriptions and photographs alone. No original Pullman car from this era exists. Also factual is its timetable, which the *Trans-Continental* faithfully recorded. A delay west of Springfield, Massachusetts, really did occur due to overheated journal boxes. The train passed Niagara Falls before dawn on Tuesday and arrived in Chicago at midnight. On Saturday, May 27, a detour was made to Salt Lake so that excursionists could attend the theater and meet Brigham Young. And the train really did pull up in front of San Francisco's Grand Hotel at "seven minutes before midnight" on Tuesday, May 31.

Other accounts of railroad travel from the time inspired many additional scenes. Reading about a boy selling prairie dogs at a depot, I was moved to write the scene in which Louisa buys a crate of them. And several travel memoirs depict engines derailed by a wayward cow or ox. When I read an excerpt of W. F. Rae's *Westward By Rail*, in which he describes a passenger who endeavored to cut a steak from one such animal, it seemed just like something Silas Crockett would do.

The people in this novel are mainly fictional, although Mr. George Pullman puts in a cameo appearance as himself. Others, such as Hattie's father, Mr. Eames, were modeled on real people. Mr. Eames bears a great resemblance to Congressman Oakes Ames, down to his estate in Easton and his shovel manufactory. Julia's father, Mr. Hunnewell, is outwardly similar to railroad financier, philanthropist, and horticultural expert H. H. Hunnewell, founder of Wellesley, Massachusetts. However, both men's personalities are entirely my own invention.

Finally, passages pulled from *Crofutt's Guide* and Hattie's copy of *Scientific American* depict better than anything I could invent the optimistic yet somehow naive spirit of the times: mechanical inventions proliferated, and through the dark land of lurking beasts and savages, the light of Christian Civilization illuminated the Way.

The *Trans-Continental's* description of the "Thousand Mile Tree," a landmark measuring the distance west from Omaha, perfectly encapsulates this spirit:

> It stood a lonely sentinel, when all around was desolation: when the lurking savage and wild beast claimed supremacy, and each in turn reposed in the shade of its waving arms. How changed the scene! The ceaseless bustle of an active age, the hum of labor, the roar and rush of the passing locomotive, has usurped the old quiet, and henceforward the lone tree will be, not a guide to the gloomy past, but an index of the coming greatness of a regenerated country.

Of course, in hindsight we know what the railroad actually brought to the land, the buffalo, the Native American way of life, and soon, the Native Americans themselves: almost total annihilation. But the attitudes that allowed this destruction to occur did not originate with the railroad; they were a pervasive element of American culture at the time. The average Bostonian or New Yorker traveling the rails enjoyed shooting at buffalo for sport. And travel memoirs of the time depict both women and children teasing—often cruelly—the Native Americans they encountered along the way. Often, the memoirists meant merely to give a "flavor" of their travels, not to pass judgment. I hope *A Transcontinental Affair* conveys the "flavor" of this culture.

To be sure, the land was so vast, and the bounty so plentiful, that few fully understood how destructive the westward push would be. But in the early years of the transcontinental railroad, the line between resource management and pilfering, entrepreneur and common thief, often dissolved.

The incorporation of the Union Pacific Railroad is a good example. It came into being when President Abraham Lincoln signed the Pacific

Railroad Act of 1862. Lincoln was among the first politicians to recognize the importance of the railroads, both to the war effort and to the future prosperity of the country. He approved millions of dollars in subsidies to the Union Pacific Railroad and the Central Pacific to build the transcontinental railroad. But five years later, the men who had the vision to birth this unlikely enterprise—vice president Thomas Durant, Oliver and Oakes Eames, and other UPRR executives—secretly created a company to serve as the "independent" contractors for the building of the railway. They sold shares of this company, which they called Crédit Mobilier, to members of congress at a discount, in exchange for continued government support. Crédit Mobilier then charged Union Pacific inflated rates for services rendered, bills these same Union Pacific shareholders were only too happy to pay—to themselves.

When the Crédit Mobilier scandal broke in 1872, exposing the scheme, America saw some small measure of accountability. Oakes Ames was censured from congress along with another congressman. Outgoing vice president Schuyler Colfax, incoming vice president Henry Wilson, and future president James Garfield were also implicated. Alongside America's highest ideals, there seems to be an enduring Yankee tradition of "anything goes"—so long as one doesn't get caught.

•　　•　　•

Where did this story come from? I felt *A Transcontinental Affair*'s first spark of life several years before I began to write it. While clearing out my childhood home after my parents' deaths, I came across a volume called *Reports of Explorations and Surveys, to Ascertain the Most Practicable and Economical Route for a Railroad from the Mississippi River to the Pacific Ocean*. Opening this tome with its inauspicious title and flaking leather binding, I discovered a virgin American wilderness: dozens of watercolors and sketches depicted lakes, rivers, streams, mountains, undiscovered species of flora and fauna, and tribes of Native Americans upon whom no one had ever laid eyes before.

This volume turned out to be the third in a twelve-volume series published throughout the 1850s and then as a set in 1861. The volumes provide detailed accounts of four government expeditions, of which the middle route, along the 37th–39th parallels, was eventually chosen for the railroad. It's no exaggeration to say that these twelve volumes, with a thirteenth added later, comprise a national treasure, a veritable time capsule of America before the "Age of Progress."

Opening that volume for the first time, I was filled with both wonder and a sense of loss, feelings which grew into something like an obsession. Three years later, I knew I had the canvas upon which I would set my story. Hattie and Louisa arrived soon afterwards—to bear witness and, possibly, to provide an alternative narrative.

In May of 2017, my husband and I traveled by car along the original tracks, armed with the same edition of *Crofutt's Guide* that Hattie consults. We drove from Omaha to San Francisco, often detouring from the highway to find the original tracks and depots. It was valuable to be able to see the contours of the mountains surrounding us, the rivers traversing our paths, and the red sandstone formations of Wyoming, which remain as impressive today as when the Pullman Hotel Express excursionists first gawped at them.

But apart from the topography, little is left of the landscape depicted so faithfully in those original surveys. Little prairie remains; we saw none on our route. The Great Plains has dwindled to just over half its original size. We did see two buffalo: a mother nursing her bright-orange calf in a small fenced field. Antelope and prairie dogs still roam their old haunts; they will stare at you warily as you pass them by. The rest can be found only in the words and images that have preserved this extraordinary landscape for future generations.

It was only after I finished several drafts of *A Transcontinental Affair* that I noticed how the aggression these men enacted upon the American landscape had a counterpart in their aggression toward Hattie and Louisa. Like everything else, these young women are slated to become spoils of war. But this story, for all its horror (or perhaps because of it), allows my women a moment of transcendence. They are able to use their enterprising gifts to avoid victimhood. And to the extent that Hattie and Louisa have succeeded in this, I feel I've succeeded in writing the novel I wished to write.

Acknowledgments

THE EVENTS ON MY PULLMAN HOTEL EXPRESS all take place within a mere nine days. But the complexity of the story and the details of time and place made it just as challenging to write as my other novels.

I am indebted to my husband, Peter, who read both an early draft and a late one and made significant editorial suggestions. Peter also flew to Omaha with me and drove us along the old railroad tracks to San Francisco, enduring rough terrain, closed roads, and unexpected detours. Every writer should have such an editorially gifted and supportive partner.

Heartfelt thanks go to Lake Union senior editor Jodi Warshaw, who supported this novel when it was hardly more than a dream, albeit a vivid one. The entire Lake Union team needs a shout out for being such a great support to its writers and to this writer in particular.

This is the fourth novel developmental editor Jenna Land Free has edited for me. She seems to know my eccentric process even better than I do, and I can always trust her judgment and honesty.

Thanks go to Dr. Gloria Polizzotti Greis, who for decades has been my friend and living encyclopedia. No one else would ever give me such feedback as this: "The Ridgewood children wouldn't be pretending to be velociraptors because velociraptors weren't discovered until 1924." Thank you, Gloria, for catching some real bloopers.

Emma Patterson Martin, my literary agent at Brandt & Hochman, has been a pillar of support from the very beginning of my career. She negotiated the contract for *A Transcontinental Affair* in the final days of her pregnancy, making sure to resolve every imaginable detail before she went on leave. It was a close call.

I'd also like to thank all those friends and family members who either didn't hear from me for two years or heard far more than they wanted to about railroad trains. And finally, thanks go to my emotional support humans, fellow authors Thelma Adams, Joy Jordan-Lake, and Barbara Claypole-White. As they say, it takes a village.

The Union Pacific Railroad Museum in Omaha helped me get many of the mechanical details of this train and the railroad right. Thanks to curator Patricia LaBounty, who put me in touch with Dave Seidel, one of the museum's volunteers. Dave has a deep knowledge of nineteenth-century trains; in a matter of minutes, he was able to answer questions that would have taken me weeks to answer on my own.

The Central Pacific Railroad Photographic Museum has one of the most extensive online collections of railroad photographs in the country. Although I was able to view some original glass photographic plates, the museum's digital versions made it possible for me to zoom in to details the naked eye could otherwise miss: facial expressions, clothing, soil, pets, and even minute parts of the railroad tracks and construction. These are all now captured for eternity in photographs and stereoscopes by the extraordinary pioneer photographers A. J. Russell and Alfred A. Hart.

As always, the Massachusetts Historical Society produced a few startling treasures that had a great impact on this novel, most notably the Pullman Hotel Express's original bill of fare. The artifact was still tucked into its dainty gold-embossed envelope and was an instant hit with Hattie, who carries it everywhere and fantasizes about its tempting items.

Maps of this time period abound, but none came in quite so handy as David Keith's interactive Google map of the original transcontinental line, which can be found on the Central Pacific Railroad website. Keith managed to pin virtual yellow pushpins for every stop along the route. His map allowed me to see the topography and distances between stops, which was crucial in establishing the story's timeline. I studied this map for many hours.

Bruce C. Cooper, a central force behind the Central Pacific Railroad Photographic Museum, is also the author of *Riding the Transcontinental Rails*, an excellent collection of primary material that I studied over and over, each time finding new and inspiring details.

Finally, I wish to thank those memoirists who published their observations while traveling on the early trains. Some reports are filled with wonder and elation, others with fear and even disgust. And then there were outliers like Robert Louis Stevenson, who were courageous enough to condemn the injustices they witnessed—particularly against the Chinese railway workers and the Native Americans—at a time when it was more culturally acceptable to condone them. I could not have written this novel without the enduring testament of their own sharp eyes and brave hearts.

About the Author

Photo © 2019 Matt G. Norris

JODI DAYNARD IS THE AUTHOR OF THREE previous novels. When not writing, she is usually either swing dancing or playing jazz clarinet. She lives outside Boston with her husband and two springer spaniels, Rory and Bailey. To learn more about Jodi, go to www.jodidaynard.com.